S0-BZC-705

Jack's Favorite

ADVENTURES OF A COLONIAL SMUGGLER

Written by Alfred Picardi

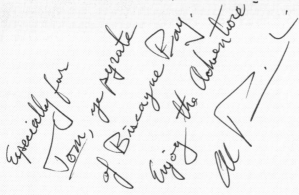

Especially for
Tom, ye pyrate
of Biscayne Bay.
Enjoy the Adventure ~
Al ~

Ye can buy this book on the internet at:
http://jacksfavorite.webs.com/

Copyright © 2010 Alfred Picardi
All rights reserved.

ISBN: 1452833184
ISBN-13: 9781452833187

Acknowledgements

First I'd like to thank my mother and father, Al and Mary, who read numerous drafts and gave enthusiastic support, and helped with the illustrations. My wife, Holly, gave her time, edits, advice and support, as did my sister Mary. My special thanks to Joan LaBlanc, Ed Beyersdorfer, Joyce Koch, and Pamela Leigh, who spent many hours giving me the best editing a humble pyrate could ever wish for; and thanks to Stephan Gorzula for the true tale of Angustine, the parrot who laughed at appropriate times, and my brother Tony for teaching Angustine some Shakespeare. Sailors and especially well-read friends Jeff Fones and Chuck Beck provided much needed editorial advice and support.

For my Parents

Table of Contents

Preface

In 1763 the instructions to Captain Walter Stirling of the Royal Navy frigate *Rainbow,* on station from Cape Henlopen to Cape Henry, were to guard the coast and secure trade against "pirates and others." The Royal Navy now had an open season on colonial merchantmen.

The first shots of the American Revolution were fired by the British Navy at colonial smugglers, long before the skirmishes at Lexington and Concord. Foment of the American Revolution is blamed by many on enforcement of the Navigation Acts after the French and Indian War in 1763. The unsung heroes of the birth of America as a nation are the daring colonial mariners who carried on the trade that enabled the colonies to prosper in spite of the Navigation Acts. The Navigation Acts were intended to establish a British monopoly over colonial products and shipping, and would have strangled the economies of the southern states.

The best records of these valiant little colonial smuggling vessels are the plans made of them at the Royal Navy dockyard in Deptford, England. Purchased or captured, the Royal Navy enthusiastically copied the colonial designs, more often than not changing them in ways that made them more acceptable to the Navy, but that spoiled their sailing performance. Said one British naval officer at the time, "We would never build schooners like the Americans, and if we did, we would never sail them like the Americans." There was more than a little derring-do involved in pushing a sailing ship to its limits, knowing that capsize or capture was the price of a mistake.

The colonial courts were reluctant to condemn smugglers, so in 1763 Parliament directed that smugglers be tried in Admiralty Courts, one of which was in Nova Scotia, the other in Jamaica. Colonial ships that were condemned for smuggling became prizes, with the value of the ship and cargo plus a fine to be forfeited by the owner – high stakes indeed for the smugglers. The prize money could be treble the value of the ship and cargo. This was divided equally between the governor of the colony where the seizure was made, the British Treasury, and the informant (spies, customs, or Navy). The British Navy and the customs service acted independently and often in competition for the prize money.

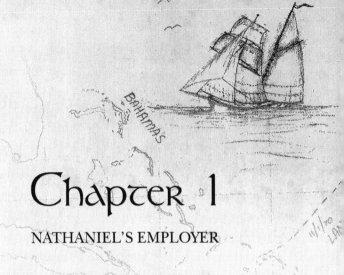

Chapter 1

NATHANIEL'S EMPLOYER

*1741 - War of Shipmaster Jenkin's Ear, on an Anchored Brig,
Coast of America*

"Hush, boy, or they'll slit our throats for sure!" These
words, like the hiss of a snake, shocked young Jonathan
Easton out of his daze. The captain put his forefinger
across Jonathan's mouth, beseeching silence. On
the other side of the barricaded greatcabin door, the
mutineer's guard slumped in his own vomit, an empty
bottle of rum in his hand. Jonathan's eyes darted
amongst the looming shadows of the greatcabin, his
haze of exhaustion cleared once more by mortal fear.

"Into the jollyboat with the chests now, quietly as
you can," whispered Captain William. The captain
stooped to pick up a heavy sea chest and trudged aft
to the transom windows. Jonathan pulled himself out
of his corner, donned his boots, and strained to pick
up one of the captain's small ironbound oak chests.
Turning his eyes from the horror of a mutineer and
the loyal bosun lying entangled in death on the
deck, he tried not to lose his balance as he struggled

through the pool of slimy blood. Cool night air hung about the transom windows, offering respite from the dank greatcabin. Captain William lowered the first sea chest by a short line into the ship's boat waiting below. Jonathan brought up the second chest and the captain eased it down into the boat. Easton dragged the third chest through the blood, and they lowered it onto the floorboards of the small boat, taking care for their lives to do it silently.

Turning back into the cabin, the captain impatiently waved to Jonathan to get into the jollyboat. As Jonathan climbed onto the greatcabin transom, the captain opened his parrot's cage and launched the bird out the window. Angustine, the bird was named, flew off toward the shore. Jonathan climbed out the stern window backwards and landed square in the middle of the boat as light as a cat, and with as little noise. The captain edged his legs over the transom, his booted heels dangling three feet above the middle seat of the jollyboat. *This will never do*, thought Jonathan. *If he doesn't capsize us when he drops into the boat, the noise will bring on the murdering mutineers.*

The captain twisted over onto his belly and slid down. Jonathan grabbed his boots and guided them to a balanced haven on the seat, and the captain dropped, grabbing the gunnels of the small boat for balance. Noise of the captain's thump into the boat was followed by the splash of waves the boat made as they slapped under the stern of the brig. Captain William and Jonathan Easton sat motionless, listening for the approach of doom on the deck overhead. A noise on deck rumbled towards them. They waited in silent terror, Captain William with his pistol at ready.

At length the rumble ended in the sound of a rum bottle bouncing into a scupper. Captain William grabbed the oars. Jonathan clasped onto a third oar to use as a rudder.

"Head for the inlet," whispered the captain. He leaned back on the oars as the boat slipped from under the moon shadow of the brig. The captain's face suddenly appeared in the pallid moonlight, startling Jonathan. Pain was cutting deep furrows in the captain's brow, but it was the fear in the captain's eyes that unnerved the lad. If the captain was afraid, this iron pillar of a man who had brought them through the raging hell of an ocean gale, there was not a moment to be lost!

"Pray, sir, give me the oars," whispered Easton as he reached for them. He knew he could row faster than the wounded captain. Jonathan rowed facing forwards from his seat in the stern. Only the top of the tree line on shore was visible in the gloom below the stars. He aimed for the notch in the dark wall of forest that must betray the inlet. With careful, silent oar strokes the jollyboat glided toward shore.

"They're gone!" shouted Deadlight, the ship's cabin boy nicknamed for the droop of his left eyelid, a wound inflicted by the lad's own mother.

"Give way, Jonathan, or we're dead!" wheezed Captain William. Jonathan Easton stood up and threw his whole weight on the oars. There was no need for silence now. Survival lay in getting out of musket range.

"Damn your eyes, boy, what is it?" boomed the drunken first mate of the brig. There were crashes and the whine of splintering wood as the greatcabin door was stove in. Stunned silence fell as the greatcabin was searched. Then the figure of the first mate stood in silhouette at the bulwark of the brig. "I'll send you to the Devil yet, Captain William!" the first mate screamed into the night sky. "That free booty's ours!"

Captain William's lurid grimace was punctuated by his eyes, defiantly flashing like slivers of ice in the moonlight. He pulled the pistol from the breast of his waistcoat and cocked it, holding it at ready, pointed at the stars. "'Twas never yours, and never will be, ye mutinous fools," snarled the captain. "You'd have prize money enough to buy every whore in Port Royal, if ye hadn't turned tail as soon as the Dons pointed their rapiers at ye! A fine crew of pups you be. And now you'll be helping yourselves to my own sea chests, eh? Devil take you!"

"Damn you to hell, Jonathan Easton!" came the shrill scream of Deadlight Helms; but he was instantly silenced with a slap from the furious first mate.

The curse of his young shipmate stung Jonathan Easton, and the captain sensed his strokes at the oars weaken. "Mind ye not the oaths of a villain, Jonathan," soothed the captain. "That boy Deadlight would just as soon watch the two of us lose our eyes to the knotted rope, aye, Jonathan, or slit our throats himself. The lad's a rogue. They'll try to murder us yet tonight! I'll wager he'll be to windward of that pack of dogs."

The first musket shot was wide. Captain William saw the smoke before he heard the crack. If only he'd brought a musket—but the mutineers had them all. He could only stare back at his would-be executioners as they squinted down the barrels of their pieces and fired. He set his jaw. Jonathan redoubled his labors at the oars. Sweat ran down his face and stung his eyes, yet though giddy with fear, he dared not leave off for a second. Then a lucky musket shot hit home. The starboard oar splintered and Jonathan fell forward onto the captain, both tumbling into the bottom of the boat, while buckets of water poured in over the side. Half swamped, the jollyboat spun off course, with the captain and Jonathan sprawled in a heap on the floorboards.

Mad cheering broke out on the brig. The mutineers fired several more rounds from the ratlines. A piece of the boat's gunnel exploded in splinters; another shot put a hole in her topsides.

"'Vast firing!" bellowed the first mate. "If we sink them, we'll lose those Spanish doubloons!"

"For the love of God, get up and row!" cried Captain William. Fear had made Jonathan lightheaded and awkward. He reached over the side for the oar he'd dropped in the water and nearly capsized the jollyboat again. Captain William dropped his pistol and doffed his cocked hat to bail water out of the ship's boat, keeping his eye on Jonathan. "Ship the oars, lad, and let's be off!" said the captain, emptying a hat full of bilge water into the sea.

"They're still alive!" roared the first mate on the brig. "Have at them, ye one-eyed sons of whores. Can none of ye aim a musket?"

Firing stopped as the captain and Jonathan glided out of musket range into the shadowy gloom of the inlet. Stars still shone in the western sky. The Eastern Hemisphere began to turn gray behind the brig. A receding wave hissed as the ship's boat ground ashore on the sand. Not one human footprint pockmarked

7

the smooth sand beach, where only crabs, seabirds, and an occasional deer had left their marks. The laughing calls of awakening seagulls played counterpoint to the alternating hiss and roil of the surf on the adjacent ocean beach. Several beach crabs lumbered sideways toward the jollyboat, their stalked eyes at attention. Jonathan could not move; his mind was frozen in the cold grip of fear.

"Come, lad, onto the beach with ye, and let's get these chests ashore, for there'll be more mischief afoot soon enough," cried the captain as he heaved himself over the side of the boat.

A geyser of sand exploded from the beach when the first round shot hit. A split-second afterward, the captain and Jonathan could hear and feel the bass boom of the brig's cannon thump their bellies.

"To starboard, ye blind rats!" spat the first mate. The undisciplined mutineers tumbled over themselves in their efforts to pry the heavy cannon the slightest bit sideways. The first mate squinted down the cannon barrel, aiming for where the captain and Jonathan would approach the ship's boat to drag the second chest up the beach. "Aye," he cried, and spun away from the back of the gun as he clapped the slow match down on the cannon's touchhole. The cannon roared out. Another round shot hit the beach and crashed through the undergrowth beyond, merely tearing a pathway through the tangled sea grape.

"Let those dogs fight over the last of it," huffed the captain when they reached the edge of the underbrush with the second sea chest. "They'll bicker and slow their chase. Aye, and perhaps a few of the rogues will kill each other."

"Captain, you'd leave a third of your fortune behind?" The captain hesitated and looked down the beach at the jollyboat and the remaining sea chest. A full third of his fortunes from years at sea lay there. He recalled the privation at sea and the many times he'd risked his own life in desperate sea battles with the Spaniards and French.

"Captain, look!" exclaimed Jonathan, pointing towards the brig. Captain William squinted into the pink dawn light and saw men plunging into the water beside the brig. The men who could swim were coming ashore! Could he and the boy drag three heavy chests into the swamp and still make their escape? A lip of the sun, in red and gold, began to shimmer out to sea on the eastern horizon.

"It's not for those dogs to have what isn't theirs by rights," said the captain. He set his jaw once more and started down the beach toward the ship's boat, young Jonathan at his heels. They were fifty paces from the beached boat when the round shot hit and the jollyboat exploded into a cloud of splinters. In that cloud of cedar and oak slivers, bilge water, and sand were thousands of glittering gold doubloons, at first flying towards heaven and then tumbling down and pattering onto the beach sand with the sound of hailstones.

"Aye, aye, lad, what's the use of a third part of one's fortune if you're dead?" The captain spun on his booted heel and limped back up the beach, his saber in its scabbard bouncing against his thigh. Young Jonathan followed, but took one more look towards the brig before diving into the underbrush. He saw the glimmer of steel blades in the mouths of the swimmers. Those who could not swim had lowered the other ship's boat.

Jonathan helped Captain William drag his chests through the sea grape at the top of the beach. They came out of a patch of thick brambles into the understory of a live-oak forest. Lichens, bromeliads, and gray Spanish moss festooned the twisted trunks of the stunted trees. Mist hung in the still air. They struggled on with the heavy chests, dragging them across the sand and dry leaves to a marsh. Jonathan shivered at the thought of seeing the flash of cutlasses behind them; he looked back to check if they were being pursued every time they stopped to catch their breath.

"Here it shall be," pronounced Captain William as he stood under a particularly large pine. He turned to Jonathan, drawing his cutlass from its scabbard and raising it over his head to swing it. Jonathan looked up and winced. Down it came, lopping off a pine limb, the sharp metal ringing. "Take this bough and brush away our tracks." Jonathan dreaded going back through the mist from whence they came, terrified he would meet up with the pursuing mutineers in the murky forest. The captain noted the boy's hesitation and said, "Take heart, lad; the sooner it's done, the sooner we can take our leave of that murderous crew forever." Captain William stood and memorized the scene in four directions of the compass, taking his bearings and committing the spot to memory. Then he dropped to his knees with a wince and began to scoop away the sandy soil with both hands.

Jonathan returned to the beach along the tracks they'd made in the sand. When he regained the edge of the sea grapes, he could hear the crew of the brig on the beach, laughing like excited children. He peeked through the broad leaves and saw a band of twenty men in soaked clothing, running to and fro, picking Spanish doubloons off the sand and stuffing them into their bulging pockets. Some of the men were already brawling. Others had stuck their cutlasses in the sand so they could collect the scattered doubloons with both hands. He saw his former friend Deadlight Helms amongst the mutineers, and he felt a pang of loss.

Jonathan bent down and walked backwards down the trail of footprints, brushing them into oblivion with a pine bough as he went. He'd made his way about a hundred yards from the beach when he saw the glint of steel between the twisted limbs of the live oaks. He ducked in back of a tree and listened. The noise of the fracas on the beach was faint. Hearing nothing nearby, he edged around the tree to have another look. A twig snapped on the other side of the tree. Jonathan spun around and found his nose within inches of the razor-sharp tip of the first mate's cutlass.

"There's a good lad, steady now," wheedled the first mate, "you just tell me where Captain William's got off to—that a boy, steady." As he spoke, the mate came closer and raised the blade of his cutlass higher. "Now, boy, tell me, don't be afraid of your old shipmate. Deadlight ain't afraid of me. He's your own true friend, and so is I. Talk to me, boy," said the mate in a tone meant to be soothing, but there was fire in his bloodshot eyes. The mate's cutlass swished through the air and cut a gash in Jonathan's cheek.

11

"By thunder, talk, boy! Where's that swab of a captain? Talk, or I'll stab ye through the vitals!"

Jonathan could not speak. The first mate drew back his cutlass to make good on his threat, screaming in fury. "Then damn your eyes, boy, and to the Devil with ye!"

There was a thud, and suddenly the mate dropped his cutlass and fell to his knees, his hairy face transfixed in a blind stare. Behind him stood Captain William, putting his saber back in his scabbard.

"Now, Jonathan, let us be gone!"

Angustine the parrot returned, and in young Easton's eyes rested like a guardian angel on the captain's broad shoulder, rolling with easy familiarity to the captain's stride. They slogged through the marsh, waist deep at times in muck and black water. When they finally came upon a road, they parted, for the mutineers would certainly make inquiries around the countryside about a man and a boy traveling together. Captain William went south. "To the Indies," he said. Jonathan Easton made his way north, secure in the knowledge that when he mastered navigation and seamanship, Captain William would make him a ship master.

Captain William said, before they parted, "See here, lad, if misfortune befalls me, I shall leave words for you where to find the rest of this hoard; it'll be your insurance against shipwreck, pirates, and privateers. Should you need it when I'm gone, I shall have left words on its whereabouts, and those words will set you on the lay line for it. Angustine will hold the key."

In the years that followed, Captain William made good on his promise to share the fortune they saved from the hands of the mutinous crew that dangerous morning. Over the next three decades, Jonathan Easton became Captain Easton and acquired two fleet and nimble Chesapeake schooners, *Jubilant* and *Berbice*. Jonathan Easton had learned seamanship and the art of navigation, as well as the Navigation Acts and the art of smuggling. In 1770 he found himself desperately in need of Captain William's hoard.

Gideon "Deadlight" Helms found that making a living by terrorizing victims and taking what he wanted from them suited his predilections. He preferred to sit and drink tea, thinking up schemes of robbery while avoiding physical labor or constructive occupations, and he would endure great hardship rather than work for his bread. He never forgot the gold that had almost been his by virtue of the mutiny, nor did he forget that Jonathan Easton had been instrumental in spoiling his access to that easy fortune.

Chapter 2

ANNE EASTON, THE CAPTAIN'S DAUGHTER

Harborton, on the Eastern Shore of Chesapeake Bay, 1752

"Mamma don't leave me!" Anne Easton clung to her mother's feverish hand. Tears of fear flowed down Anne's cheeks, "Don't die Mamma." A chill crawled up Captain Jonathan Easton's spine. He stood over the pair, feeling helpless and tired. The fever and flux was taking many; strong men and women brought down within three days. The physician had done his best with herbs and bleeding, but what good did they ever do? The tainted air of the flux hung about in the yellow light of the candles. A fire crackled in the bedroom fireplace but did not purify the deadly air. Captain Easton anxiously pulled at his graying beard, hot tears in his eyes.

Mrs. Easton looked at her child, "Mamma's right here darling, and if Mamma ever goes away, Daddy will be with you always." It was the last coherent thing she would say. She looked at her husband with pleading eyes. Captain Easton nodded; his stomach felt like lead. He would never leave their child to

15

someone else's care. Captain Easton was a large man with a big heart and rare loyalty. So it was promised, so it would be. He had a purse; he could stay ashore to raise eight-year-old Anne - for a while.

Father and daughter literally clung to each other for months after Mrs. Easton died, and found they could fill the emptiness with each other's company. Until now they had nearly been strangers. Captain Easton had been away at sea for long periods, which seemed like ages to the young Anne. Now for the first time she basked in this powerful stranger's full time and attention. As she and her father walked the dirt streets of Harborton after the funeral, she noted how the folk deferred to her father and showed respect. She had always been too buried in her mother's skirts to notice. Now her alert mind picked up the social nuances of station and standing and she understood her father was an important man to others. This was her father, so long absent before, now steadfast in his loyalty to her, kind and gentle. She began to worship him.

They lived in Harborton, located on the "Eastern Shore" of the Virginia colony, on the Chesapeake side of a peninsula between the Atlantic Ocean and Chesapeake Bay. On a deep natural harbor in Pungoteague Creek, the community boasted a shipbuilder, blacksmith, cabinetmaker, cooper, cobbler, candlemaker, several merchant enterprises and warehouses, and several large houses, among which was Captain Easton's. There were also several dozen shacks where the newly arrived and poor lived. Pigs and domestic geese roamed the dirt streets at will, feasting on the piles of kitchen garbage. Deep water extended right up to the shore at the town wharf, which was nothing more than a platform. Mornings in Harborton began with a raucous chorus of birdsong, pilfered by the mockingbirds, and then the steady tin clap of the blacksmith's hammer, and the drumming of mauls in the shipyard. The dirt roads were quickly churned into mud by hooves, oxcart, and carriage wheel when it rained.

In spite of Anne's frequent discipline problems at the Harborton dame school, she had learned to read and cipher quickly and well. Her parents had been proud of her for that. She had also beaten the tar out of most of the boys who offered to give her lip, and only her mother knew what to think of that. She was never scolded for defending her dignity, however unladylike and muddy it made her. Her mother knew the value of strength, and wished her daughter to learn the strength of knowledge. So Anne went to the widow's dame school, which was a rarity of higher learning in comparison to the situation in most of the colony.

At the end of one voyage Captain Easton brought home a huge Bible. Anne and her mother spent evenings reading from the tome by the wood fire that winter. For Anne, it contained a wondrous parade of characters to mimic and play. She began to make costumes out of scrap cloth to enhance her portrayals. Then one day Mrs. Easton drew a beard on Anne's face with charcoal for her private performance of King Herod. Anne looked at herself in a small mirror and a whole new world was opened up to her. Not only could she mimic and carry on like the characters she read about; she could look like them as well! Henceforth

Mrs. Easton was amazed at the alchemy her daughter performed on charcoal, walnuts, colored clays, flour paste, and a variety of other scrounged materials that held promise. She marveled at how Anne could make up her own childish face to look like beggar or king, princess, or scullion.

Captain William was a frequent visitor to the Easton household, like a great uncle he was always received with the warmest welcome. Captain William was both mentor to her father and tutor for Anne, as he frequently bore the precious printed word in fragrant leather bindings. Treasure troves of adventure! "We owe him everything," Anne's father explained, but only made reference to some deed in the past when Anne pressed him.

After the death of his wife, Captain Easton could not believe how fast Anne grew, as if she were a few inches taller every time he returned from Annapolis or Baltimore. How she begged to go on those excursions. There seemed to be nothing more for it at the school; after all, it was his own beloved wife who'd said, only days before the fever struck, "She's bored with the school I'm afraid, and I doubt that spinning and gossip will satisfy that mind of hers. What are we to do?"

Captain Easton always thought he would bring a son to sea with him, he'd never considered apprenticing a daughter to the sea. She was her mother's daughter, smart as fresh paint and strong willed; but there was another aspect to Anne that Captain Easton was quite unprepared for: she was a trickster. He learned this on a trip to see his merchant contacts in Annapolis. Captain Easton's purse was running low; it was time to go on shipboard again. What to do with the child? His mind troubled over this as he boarded the bay schooner in Harborton. Anne had made her customary petitions to accompany him, but he felt assured she was in good hands with a neighbor widow.

A young filthy boy about Anne's size, carrying a small bundle of clothes, brushed past Captain Easton just as the schooner cast off from the pier. The other boys aboard began a game of racing up the rigging, and the more adventurous slid down the backstays sailor fashion. The new boy began a tentative ascent into the rigging and was soon sliding down the backstay to land with a thump on the deck, and then up the rigging again like the others. The schooner captain was a white-headed tolerant man of many years, and even enjoyed watching the antics of the young boys, remembering his own abilities of an age ago.

Captain Easton barely noticed the antics in the rigging as he pondered what he would do with Anne. Would she even take to life in the greatcabin? It was not unprecedented that merchant captains take their wives and sometimes children on a voyage. Perhaps a large enough vessel would have an officer's cabin to spare, or some other sort of accommodation could be found in the more civilized portions of the ship. Unnoticed by Captain Easton, one of the boys had dropped out of the rigging climbing game and gone below with a bucket of water. Captain Easton came out of his doldrums with a start when he saw his beloved daughter standing right in front of him. "By God child, where did you come from?" he said. There she was in shirt and pantaloons.

"I've been here all the time, Daddy!" she said. Captain Easton was too flustered to make any sense of it. Well, the child was here now; perhaps he could show her a merchantman's quarters and appraise how she may take to the sea life. He lapsed again into a muse as he considered which of his business contacts in Annapolis he would see first. Probably Charles Caroll, he was doing quite well. When Captain Easton gazed again skyward, as sailors frequently do, his big heart nearly stopped. Up there standing on the foremast trestletrees was his beloved daughter.

"Child, come down!" He was instantly terrified, one of the few times in his life, and he made for the ratlines to help her down himself.

"Look, Daddy!" she called, and as Captain Easton's heart rose into his mouth, and he lost capacity for speech, she grabbed the backstay, sixty feet above the deck, swung her legs out and clamped them round the stay, and slid down with the greatest ease, pantaloons flailing in the breeze around her, to land soft as a cat on the deck. Smooth as any midshipman he'd ever seen. "Oh, Daddy, what fun!" she called as she raced for the ratlines for another ascent.

"Aye child, that'll be all for now!" said Captain Easton as he grabbed the charging youngster. "That'll do," he said with finality, and maintained his iron grip on her. His eyes cast about the quarterdeck as his mind cast about for moorings; what was he to do with this child? He'd never seen a female, girl or woman, climb about the rigging of a ship. Shouldn't his daughter be spinning and sewing? Would this adventurous spirit of hers spell trouble, and should he discourage it? How was she to find her station in life if she weren't trained in ladylike ways? Or should he give in to the pride swelling in his chest?   He saw the white-haired skipper give him a wink, a smile, and a nod. *A child to be proud of then; she'll find her station in life when the time comes.*

"How did you get aboard?" asked Captain Easton, his tone overcast with a coming squall.

"Why, I walked right past you, Daddy," replied Anne, who widened her enchanting eyes and put on a look of innocence, a maneuver that never failed to sway the Captain in her direction.

"You are never to travel about without my permission; this is intolerable." Captain Easton tried to summon up a storm, but it was useless. Anne was seeing right through his squall line, like her mother always did. He gathered himself once more to deliver an admonition, but gave it up. *The little vixen,* he thought, *I only hope her cleverness can carry her through what lies ahead.*

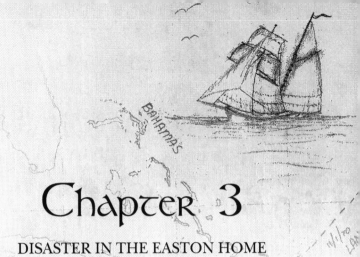

Chapter 3

DISASTER IN THE EASTON HOME

The Kitchen of the Easton Home, Harborton, 1762

"Oh, Papa, you've ruined everything!" Fourteen-year–old Anne shouted at her father, standing no more than two feet away. Her words were like a hammer blow to Captain Easton's chest. He was dumbfounded by her anger. Cherry juice, muddy feet, and an innocent enough draught of hard cider at Fowlkes Tavern with a likely young mariner in search of employment brought on this unforeseen disaster.

"What have I done, Lass?"

"Don't you see?"

He could see nothing in her disheveled appearance except for that which he dearly loved. Her mud-spattered ankles – how quickly she outgrew her frocks – and how strong she had grown. Her physical strength seemed to sprout right from her feet, toes splayed from her propensity to go barefoot. *Like the buttressed roots of a young oak,* thought Captain Easton. From her muddy feet to her cherry juice-stained face, there was not a feature he beheld that did not warm his heart with love, an aching love – for wasn't she the likeness of her mother – who had been taken from him so suddenly in her prime? He could do naught but everything possible for his dear daughter: but now he beheld her upturned face, tears washing streaks down her soiled face, and knew her distress was his fault. Captain Easton's big heart was once again on the verge of breaking. What had he done? Plenty – and nothing at all.

Captain Easton's transgression began when he'd arrived at the Easton home with Nathaniel Harte, a young mariner who just that day had entered into Captain Easton's employ. Anne, ignorant of their approach, sat at the kitchen table pitting cherries, a messy business, but one just as well done in the ragged old frock she'd soiled climbing the tree to get at the best of them. She smeared her face as she brushed her fair hair out of her eyes, and again as she wiped her brow, for it was a warm summer day.

Suddenly her father and a stranger stood at the kitchen door. Captain Easton expected Anne to rise and curtsey in her cute little way, but she remained frozen at the opposite side of the kitchen table. This immense transgression on Captain Easton's part can only be explained by his masculine incomprehension of feminine protocol – and that such now applied to his own dear child. It was simple for him. Here was his handsome new ship master and there was his cute little girl; they were in his house, and they should meet. That his new ship master and his child could have any communication beyond that of a grown man to child escaped Captain Easton entirely.

"Anne, this is Nathaniel Harte, my new captain for the *Berbice*. Nathaniel, my daughter, Anne."

Anne remained immobile and unresponsive, staring down at the table.

"Well, Lass, give us a curtsey now," commanded Captain Easton, raising his voice a little. Her face now as red as the cherry juice, Anne rose to comply, exposing her soiled frock and adding even more to her mortification. She could not even look at Nathaniel or her father; one glimpse as the two had appeared in the doorway had revealed Nathaniel was lean and young, sunbleached with eyes – aye, eyes that struck a chord in her very soul. And there she was, made to curtsey with smeared face and soiled frock. How could her father possibly work such a cruelty on her?

Later, when Nathaniel and her father had finished their business and Nathaniel had left the house, and when Anne was certain he was out of earshot, she charged at her father near the foot of the stairs, arresting him in the front hall.

"How could you, Papa? How could you do this to me?"

"Do what, Child?" He saw her bristle at the word child.

"You don't see? My feet are muddy…"

"But of course they are, Lass; you've been in the back yard picking cherries!"

"And I have cherry juice all over…"

"Aye, Lass, and pitting them's a messy business."

"How could you have been so mean to me?"

Still Captain Easton had no clue, for he bore no contempt for a carpenter covered head to foot with sawdust, or a teamster spattered to the knees with manure. He saw nothing unfit in his daughter's muddy feet or cherry-stained face.

"You have ruined my life!" The look Anne gave her father thunderstruck him as no man-made broadside of cannon could have. He beheld her eyes, tears mingled with red juice that dripped from her outward-thrust chin. His daughter was there, and yet she was not – not the daughter he knew. The unquestioned intimacy was there, but now he beheld a greater force – by god so like her mother he had to regain his balance by gripping the nearby banister as the thought struck him.

Each became aware of an unfathomable abyss opening between them, like ships at sea that had released their grappling hooks. Captain Easton first stared into this gulf with a feeling of terrible loss, while Anne beheld it with a feeling of wonderful potential. A tingling sensation made Captain Easton's hair stand up on his scalp, for now he beheld not his child-daughter's eyes, but those of her mother, through a glow that surrounded her face. Aye, it was as if the spirit of his dear wife he now beheld, but no, it was another. This spirit belonged both to his wife and himself. He felt the proximal vigor of new life and with it an inexplicable separation. No longer would he share every one of her secrets. Anne must have felt the chasm as well, terrible in it's loneliness, for she reached out and hugged her father, and then ran up to her room, sobbing into her apron.

Captain Easton stood at the foot of the stairway, staring at nothing, wondering at his unaccustomed flood of emotions, and finally it dawned on him, and lightened his heart, for this was no cause for mourning. His daughter was becoming a woman!

* * *

At breakfast, Captain Easton dearly hoped civil manners would return to the household. He noticed Anne had not washed her face since the previous day, but he chose to ignore this in hopes of establishing a voluntary peace without use of authority.

"I was having a draught at Israel Fowlkes Tavern, and mentioned to Israel how I weary of the long voyages, and fear for your education, Anne."

"Humph," Anne half-heartedly teased a piece of toast off the platter with her knife, seeming to be entranced with this exercise, and not a word that her father had spoken.

"I need a shipmaster to take shares in the *Berbice*, so I can stay at home more. Fowlkes says there are plenty of likely young men about…"

Anne gave her father's end of the table a contemptuous glance.

"But then I said to Israel, I need a fellow with a talent for getting the most out of a vessel. Many's the time *Berbice* has narrowly escaped with a full load of smuggled…ah, full load of cargo, from much larger vessels in the king's service, or pirates for that matter! It takes a shipmaster of special talents to make a profit in the business."

The toast Anne had been teasing off the platter finally dropped to the tablecloth. She listlessly poked it with her knife.

"A stranger walked in to the tavern, and Israel says, 'now there's a lad with a wizard's talent for sailing.' So I invited him for a draught. Turns out he was looking for a berth, and master suited him just fine, from the Indies trade he was. Has quite a reputation as a sailor and a rake...ah, anyway...humph. I really meant no harm in bringing him here to introduce my little girl. You're the only family I have dear one..."

Anne's fascination with the burnt bread slice continued unabated.

"And he'll be taking the *Berbice* south to the Indies this very afternoon."

Anne's knife clattered onto her china plate, breaking the silence from her end of the table. She was gone in an instant to the springhouse. While such lack of manners would have brought a reproach from her father in days past, he remained still. When he heard the well pump working, and the sounds of Anne washing herself, he allowed himself a chuckle.

* * *

Nathaniel Harte's new duties for getting *Berbice* ready for sea took him up and down the row of houses leading to the wharf at Harborton all day long. Preoccupied as he was, he took little notice of his environs, except to tip his cocked hat to passers-by as he lugged his personal gear and purchases on his many trips to the ship. Anne, unseen behind the row of houses, became furious every time he tipped his hat to one of the young ladies of Harborton.

Anne followed Harte's progress, from behind the houses, darting between them to peer around the corner of the next as Nathaniel made his way down the opposite side of the street. She noticed that several of Harborton's young women had found need to make several trips to the wharf and back on their own business, and Nathaniel dutifully made a leg and tipped his hat to each of them every time. Anne's fury at the brazenness of these harlots gave her courage to mount her own campaign. She ran the length of the street, passing Nathaniel by as she flew unseen in the back yards, skirts hiked to her knees, dodging clotheslines and manure piles near the stables. Once at the opposite end of the street from Nathaniel, she stepped out, careful to stay on the side of the street opposite Nathaniel. Her heart pounded as he neared, and she struggled to keep her eyes averted, stopping to gaze into a store window when she feared he'd noticed her gaze. Once he'd passed she ran to the opposite end of the street, to repeat the process again.

Out of the corner of his eye, Nathaniel had noticed a shadowy figure darting behind the houses as he made his way to and from the wharf. He thought on one occasion he recognized Captain Easton's daughter, that homely skinny girl; but today she was made up in a pretty frock and bonnet. When he saw her pass on the opposite side of the street for the third time he was sure of it.

"Why, Anne, good day to you!" Nathaniel called out. Anne could see her own face turn red in the window of the shop she'd turned to face, and was mortified to find she was staring at a display of perfumes, ribbons, and feminine finery. She could see Nathaniel's reflection in the window as he approached.

"It is you, isn't it, Anne?" She had to turn to acknowledge Nathaniel, yet she found she could not speak, nor could she think of a word to say even if the gift of speech had returned to her. "Well then, good to see you, Anne, I must be off," and he made a leg for her and tipped his hat, dropping one of his bundles in the process. Anne automatically stooped to pick it up for him, and without looking he stooped to pick it up as well. Their heads thudded together and they both fell on their bottoms in the street, all of Nathaniel's bundles now scattered about him.

"I say, are you hurt?" Nathaniel asked, giving his forehead a rub and smiling.

"I'm so sorry, I'm so sorry," Anne finally found her voice, her face an even darker shade of crimson, "I'm so sorry," she kept repeating.

"No matter, thank you,' said Nathaniel, beginning to laugh. Anne hastily piled his bundles back into his arms, making an unsteady stack of them. Nathaniel glanced at the window she'd been studying, and gave her a wink as he made off again for the wharf. Now and again he had to stop and turn a bit to peek around his load of packages. Anne's knees were too weak to move from the spot for some minutes, and she just stared dumbly at Nathaniel walking toward the *Berbice* at the wharf. As if he felt her eyes on his back, he turned as he reached the ship's side and gave her a nod before he climbed aboard. Now Anne realized she was the object of tittered laughter from some of the Harborton maids who had witnessed her accident with Nathaniel, and she hiked her skirts in a most unladylike manner and ran off in the opposite direction, towards home.

* * *

"Aren't you coming down to see *Berbice* off?" Captain Easton asked that afternoon.

"I really am too busy," Anne lied. The fact that she was in her best frock and bonnet had not escaped her father.

"I insist. That's an order young lady." It was the first time in her life he had called her a young lady. It seemed to Anne their walk lasted miles past the few houses and shops to the wharf where *Berbice* was ready to cast off. *Berbice's* new master, and his reputation, had made quite an impression in the small town, and there were more than the usual number of inhabitants milling about the wharf to see the ship off. Anne stopped at the edge of the crowd, and to her further mortification, as if no more could be endured that day, Captain Easton took her hand and lead her through the crowd. The tittering laughter started again, muffled but maliciously apparent to Anne, the intended victim.

"Rammed heads like a couple of goats and sat in the street staring at each other..."

"Like to have brained the poor sailor..."

"Hiked her skirts like the devil himself was chasing her home..."

"I saw her racing through the yards like a puppy..."

Then the worst of it all, "I think she's in love with the rake..."

The crowd parted in front of the commanding presence of Captain Easton, and they were now looking over the bulwarks of *Berbice* at the edge of the wharf. Nathaniel was on the quarterdeck giving orders to cast off mooring lines and hoist sails. Anne was grateful he was too busy to notice her; if he were even to say farewell her humiliation would be complete.

And then Nathaniel was standing on the wharf, shaking hands with her father as the *Berbice* drifted further away. Still unconcerned that his ship was drifting farther from the wharf, Nathaniel turned to Anne and handed her a hair ribbon, one from the shop window where they'd collided that afternoon. It was the ribbon she'd been pretending to examine as she watched his reflection in the window. He bowed and kissed her hand, and then made a great leap onto *Berbice's* side and waved. She waved back, ribbon trailing from her hand, as the *Berbice* drifted out the channel to the Chesapeake, and she was glad once more to feel her father's hand on her shoulder.

As fate would have it, Anne and Nathaniel crossed paths but a few times in the following years; Nathaniel on the *Berbice*, Anne at boarding schools. The two were sailing life's course on different seas, until they met again one day on a rutted woodland lane in the Virginia colony.

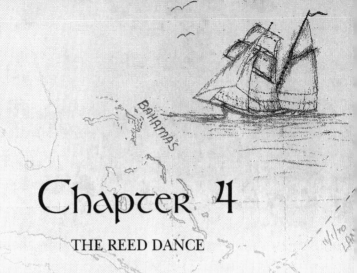

Chapter 4

THE REED DANCE

Barbados, August, 1770

"How do ye fancy *them*, Nathaniel?" roared Ordineaux, a drunken grin splitting his face from ear to ear as he slammed his leatherjack on the table and twisted around to leer at Nathaniel.

Nathaniel fancied them indeed, enough to readjust the swelling contents of his knee breaches again. Half naked men pounded clubs on hollow logs, filling the smoky bawdy house with counterpoint rhythm that seemed to thump inside Nathaniel's very chest. He stared at the mulatto girl's naked breasts that were tracing small circles each time she heaved her chest in perfect time with the beat of the drums. Nathaniel could almost feel the suppleness for her breasts in contrast to her lean and muscular body, and what it would feel like to squeeze both in his hands. He was mesmerized by the primal thrill of her constantly changing curves. Sweat broke out on his brow and he drained his tankard.

"Wench, two more!" There was no chance of being heard above the beating drums and raucous sailormen. Ordineaux held up his empty mug for the barmaid to see through the blue haze.

"Aye, aye, a lovely two indeed Ordineaux, har har!" Nathaniel shouted across the table.

"And these two ain't so bad either," quipped Ordineaux as the barmaid slammed two full mugs on their table, the beer slopping about. Ordineaux reached up and squeezed one of her breasts, so full they threatened to leap free of the drawstring of her bodice.

"Ain't you a fair coxcomb, with a pair o' goggle eyes like a dead fish? Ye gonna pay for these two?"

"And which two would ye be sellin' deary? Har har!"

"Two bigger cupfuls than ye be man enough to swallow, and I'm sure of it."

"Have a seat deary, and rest yer pretty bones, and we'll see what I can swallow right here!" Ordineaux circled an arm around the barmaid's waist and tugged her towards his lap.

"Stickin' up straight as it is, I'd hate to be breakin' yer wee little bone with me ass, love." The barmaid grabbed his crotch and tightened her grip. Ordineaux exploded with a surprised whoop. Whatever else came out of his suddenly agonized mouth was drowned out by the beating drums.

"Now where's me money?" she spat.

"Ah, ha ha, got the gentle touch, does she, Ordineaux?" Nathaniel pulled his purse from his waistcoat and shook out some silver. The barmaid had all the coins in her hand and was gone before he had a chance to count any out. Nothing came out of Ordineaux's gapping mouth as he leaned over, an inch above the rough-sawn planks of the table.

Nathaniel's eyes fastened once again on the honey colored skin of the dancer's naked back, watching her hips grind from side to side. He rearranged his painfully tight breaches once more.

The drum rhythm began to quicken, and the dancer's motions with it. She turned to face Nathaniel once more with breasts bounding up and down, her hips bucking back and forth in synchrony. Nathaniel felt the fever pounding in his forehead, and drained his mug with trembling hands. The drumbeat reached a frenzied crescendo and stopped suddenly. There was an awed silence, and then the smoky hubbub began again, as the trollops paired off with their sailor Jacks and agreed on price.

"We sail when the sea breeze fills in the morning," Nathaniel shouted at the back of Ordineaux's bowed head. *By the Powers, I hope I have enough money left for a taste o' that one!* He began to push his way toward the dancers, who were covering themselves with ragged shawls.

"Ye have put me in a fever," said Nathaniel to the girl he'd been watching. "I've seen a hundred virgins dance like that in front of a king in Africa. He picked another wife from the lot. They called it the Reed Dance." Thinking he'd ingratiated himself, he reached down and ran his hand down the muscular curves of her back.

"You're after a wife then?" She said sarcastically.

"Well, ah…well, ah," Nathaniel's sails were full aback, in irons he was.

She rolled her eyes and gave him an up and down look before she nodded toward the rickety stairs. They had to take their place in the line of inebriants already scaling the steps.

The room was barely big enough to surround the narrow bed, its only furnishing, besides two flickering candles in a rude wooden sconce on the wall. Nathaniel encircled her small frame and pulled her to him, until he could feel her breasts against his chest. His hands slid down her smooth skin and found her buttocks once more, this time squeezing them and exploring further. She gave a little gasp and fumbled with the buttons on the flap of his knee breaches. They fondled as they shed their clothes.

The door crashed open, just missing Nathaniel and the dancer as they stood in shocked silence beside the bed. The couple that staggered into the room was too much into their drunken rutting to notice them. Clothing flew through the air and fell to the plank floor. Nathaniel stepped forward and opened his mouth as if to speak but the dancer reached up and silenced him with her hand. The couple grunted on the bed, a red haired buxom lass and a blond boy of less than twenty years. They stared at the couple making the beast with two backs on the bed. The dancer grabbed Nathaniel's arm as he played with her, both regarding the couple making the trundle bed begin to bounce, the candle flames now flickering in the sconce on the flimsy wall. The red-haired lass gave a little exclamation with each of the blond boy's thrusts.

"Give a little leeway there, ye need not be a hog at the trough," said another inebriated young man who appeared in the doorway.

"Bugger off and pay for your own," answered the blond haired boy.

"I reckon ye owes me for a couple at least." The newcomer untied the manila line that held his breaches and climbed on the bed atop the buxom redhead and blond boy, "stand clear or be boarded!" With that the newcomer fell onto the couple and began humping.

The blond boy twisted around and Nathaniel could hear the wet splat of fist on cheek. In another split second Nathaniel saw the glint of steel in the dim light. The redhead let out a blood-chilling scream as Nathaniel leapt out the doorway, yanking the dancer with him, both of them stark naked. The redheaded woman continued to scream, pausing only to suck in more breath to scream again. Nathaniel saw one of the boys exit the room doubled over in pain. Yanking on his arm to urge him along faster, the dancer now pulled him away down the hallway, and soon enough Nathaniel saw why. A giant African man, the guardian of the place, charged up the stairs. In what seemed to be one blur of motion he threw both boys bodily down the hallway, beating them along the way with a short club. Splintering wood punctuated excited shouts and tortured howls. Two more young men ran out from the tiny rooms along the hallway and tried to restrain the African from behind, but he spun around and beat them to the ground with a savage whirlwind of kicks and blows. Grabbing them as if they were sacks of manure he then tossed them down the stairs atop their shipmates.

"He no stop when he like this, everybody get beat up," cried the dancer to Nathaniel, "we gotta run!" She ducked into a now vacant room and grabbed a wad of clothing, pushing a pair of breaches into Nathaniel's hands; then she led him at a run down the hall in the opposite direction. They came to a window at the end of the hall and the dancer turned around in terror. The huge African was thundering down the hallway towards them, smashing the walls with his club in blind fury. A woman appeared in the doorway of one of the rooms, only to be whacked in the face and drop from view as the furious African stormed by.

Nathaniel, still naked, leapt through the open window and skinned his knees on the gravelly alleyway. A wad of cloth – someone's pair of knee breaches, plopped on the gravel next to him. He heard the dancer laugh from the window, and looked up to see her put her arms around the huge African and disappear into the hallway. Suddenly out of breath, Nathaniel stared up at the vacant window. *She got my last shilling!*

"Buggers," he spat out loud in defeat, and turned to walk back to his schooner, the *Berbice*. In the street lay the blond boy, still naked and moaning, blood flowing over his hands. The rattle of the night watch and the sound of boots running on the cobblestones came from one end of the street, and Nathaniel took off, barefoot, in the other direction. Then he saw the group rushing towards the wharf – in redcoats and sailor's slops – the press gang or customs! Either would spell disaster for *Berbice*. He took off at a full run behind the next row of houses, and reached *Berbice* soaked in sweat, in spite of his lack of a shirt. Ordineaux saw him leap aboard and staggered aft to see what was up.

"Cast off," Nathaniel gulped in a breath, "customs… or the press gang," he wheezed, grabbing his knees and panting.

"Bloody hell!" spat Ordineaux as he charged down the deck, kicking sleepy crewmen, who instantly galvanized at the words, "press gang!" By the time he'd reached the bow lines the hubbub of the press gang could be heard right around the last row of buildings at the wharf.

"Pole her off, give me a hand," Nathaniel heaved a spar across the bulwark and began to push the *Berbice* away from the wharf. "Ordineaux, everyone aboard?"

"Wait!" the cry came as an answer to Nathaniel's question. Gunny and Jost were running towards *Berbice* from the opposite end of the wharf. Gunny missed a stride when he spied the press gang, and then he broke into a run in earnest, belying his greater years, and overtook Jost in his dash for the ship. The press gang broke into a run from the other direction when they saw *Berbice* pushing free of the wharf, and her stranded crewmen running to catch her. Jost stumbled and sprawled flat on his face, the wind knocked out of him. The press gang ignored him and ran to cut off Gunny before he could reach the wharf where *Berbice* now floated ten feet off. If the press caught Gunny, he knew he'd be hanged or worse for desertion from the navy. His heart was sinking, for there were two sailors with clubs in their hands drawing just as close to the wharf as he. Just a few paces more, it looked as if they would collide, and the two sailors raised their clubs to smash poor Gunny down. They cut him off, and turned at the edge of the wharf, clubs raised; but Gunny took a giant stride and dove at them, knocking them into the water. Typical British Tars, the press gang men did not know how to swim, and they bobbed and hollered at their companions for help as Gunny struck out for the *Berbice* with a thrashing stroke.

While the press gang crowded onto the wharf to rescue their foundering mates, Jost got his wind back. Crouching like a cheetah, he saw that the group was preoccupied with pulling their sodden mates from the harbor, and he bolted right towards them. A sailor was bent over, helping to pull a sputtering bosun from the foul water. Marking his last stride, Jost hurtled into the air and used the sailor's back like a springboard, diving head first into the stinking water a good five yards out from the wharf. That impact sent three of the press gang back into the water; unfortunately, the fourth was an officer with a pistol. Jost struck out for the *Berbice*, but he was not a very good swimmer, nor did he understand enough about the British navy and press gangs to have anywhere near Gunny's motivation.

The officer extended his arm and lowered his pistol to aim at Jost's head. Busy giving orders to loose sail, Nathaniel saw this from the corner of his eye and shouted to Jost. Hearing his captain yell, Jost stopped swimming, making matters worse. The officer cocked the lock on the pistol with a practiced thumb. Nathaniel looked about desperately for something to hurl at the officer, to throw off his aim. Jost saw Nathaniel pick up a rigging ax and draw it back to throw, and being as ignorant of his captain as he was of the navy, he ducked under water in fright. The ax flung from Nathaniel's powerful pitch just as the officer's pistol fired into the water over Jost's head. End over end the murderous ax wheeled through the darkness, unseen by the officer, Nathaniel watching in horror. To

Nathaniel, the ax seemed nearly suspended over the water, slowly wheeling its death blow. In a second that stretched to infinity, he regretted his impulsive action, and that his life would end in a hangman's noose. Aye he regretted the pleasure house, letting his men go there before sailing, and going there himself – all to end in his undoing.

"Bloody fucking Jonathan!" Lieutenant Lloyd screamed when the ax struck the piling next to his pistol arm. Now the commander of the *Inflexible* had yet another reason to hold the colonials in contempt.

"Jesus save me," muttered Nathaniel in relief. A deafening ringing started in his ears, and he did not hear the angry oaths hurled at the *Berbice* from the wharf. He saw but did not hear Jost get pulled out of the fetid water. He was deaf to his crew's taunting replies to the angry press gang. The ringing died down as *Berbice* began to gurgle through the harbor and out of danger.

"Frustrating evening, Nathaniel?" asked Ordineaux, "I see you've traded clothes." He shot Nathaniel a wry grin. A foul smell caught Nathaniel's attention, and he looked with disgust at his stolen breaches, ill-fittng and as rank as a billy goat.

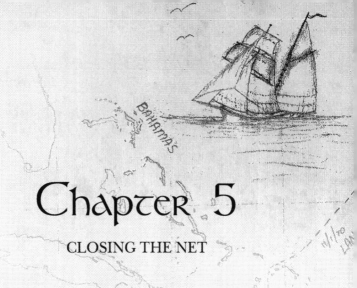

Chapter 5

CLOSING THE NET

*Atlantic Ocean, South of the Mouth of the Chesapeake Bay,
September 1, 1770.*

"Prime your gun! Run out your gun! Lay it true - a shot in their rigging will slow the Jonathans down." Prize money in the form of a colonial schooner lay ahead. A smuggler, no doubt, the American was slowly drawing away to windward of the frigate, ignoring the frigate's signal to heave to for inspection. "*Fire!*" The chase gun thundered as it sprang back on its breechings like a two-ton wild demon.

* * *

High above the ocean, a soaring gull looked down on the British frigate *Rainbow* and the puff of smoke drifting off to leeward. The frigate labored under a cloud of sail, white foam cresting at her bows. In front of the frigate, edging to windward, rolled an American schooner, small and fragile-looking. The gull saw a line of white rip toward the schooner on the background of deep blue, but the shot fell impotently into the sea. The schooner was out of range.

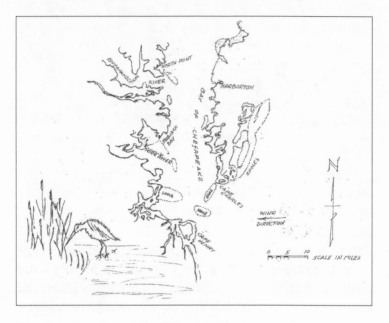

* * *

"Belay your gun, she's got the weather gauge of us," said *Rainbow's* lieutenant, in a more subdued tone. The chase was not over yet, for a well-planned trap lay ahead of the fleeing American.

On the deck of the American schooner *Berbice,* Captain Nathaniel Harte looked at the shortfall of the frigate's roundshot with relief. A bit more luck until nightfall and he could keep his ship, and the deserters in his crew would escape the hangman's noose.

* * *

In the Atlantic Ocean to the east, on the Royal Navy ten-gun brig *Inflexible,* the deep thud of cannon fire came from over the horizon. The decks and rigging sprang to life with sailors and officers. No doubt the frigate *Rainbow* was chasing a smuggler but losing the race. There was not a second to be lost in cutting off a smuggling Yankee pirate before he could reach the capes of Chesapeake Bay.

* * *

"Ahoy the deck!" shouted the lookout at the mainmast head of the schooner *Berbice*. "Brig, bears northeast, man-o'-war, ensign looks British!" Captain Nathaniel Harte bit his lip. He knew he had trouble again by the time they sighted Cape Charles. The British naval squadron was over the horizon to the south and east. They'd forced him to make for the Chesapeake in daylight. Now another British man-o'-war, probably a swift ten-gun brig, no less, was making all sail from the open sea, on a course to intercept *Berbice* before he could reach the entrance to the Chesapeake.

Captain Harte braced his lanky six-foot frame against the break of the quarterdeck. Crow's feet at the corners of his eyes testified to his years of squinting into sunshine reflecting off ocean water. His thinning hair was bleached in blond streaks from the relentless sun and tied with a black ribbon at the back of his neck, "clubbed" in the fashion of the common people who did not wear wigs. The muscles in his darkly suntanned, weathered face tensed once more as he scanned the eastern horizon. His beard stubble was three days old, marking the time *Berbice* had been fleeing the British warships, racing for freedom.

"Did you hear the *Gaspee* has been confiscating cargo without warrants in Rhode Island?" said Jack Ordineaux, Captain Harte's first mate. "They're even holding ships without evidence! Governor Wanton calls Lieutenant Dudington a bloody pirate. Dudington's had his men firing on market boats and shallops, and seizing everything down to rowboats. His shore parties are pilfering food and cattle."

"Lieutenant Dudington perpetrates his piracy under orders of His Majesty." Captain Harte's gaze was fastened on the square of Royal Navy sail now visible from the deck of *Berbice*. "We're the pirates here, Jack."

"He's after us—we're prize money for them!" Ordineaux said as he squared his stocky frame with the eastern horizon.

"We'll give the Navy a good run for their booty," said Captain Harte. "Fired on the market boats in Newport, say you?"

"Aye, Captain, fired shot at them, even a rowboat! He's more of a bastard than the Grand Turk himself. Dudington will be arrested if he dares go ashore," said Ordineaux.

"Doesn't do us much good out here, Mr. Ordineaux. If the Navy catches us, we're ruined, not to mention the poor lads forward. The Royal Navy can do with us as they please if they get us under their guns."

"If it's a brig, we've a chance to out sail them yet," said Ordineaux, his knuckles squeezing the hemp standing rigging as he squinted at the distant patch of sail.

On the foredeck of the *Berbice,* seaman Atticus Lewis, an Irish redemptioner, and some of his shipmates were taking a grim view of their chances.

"Didn't get myself free after seven stinking years of indenture just to be pressed into His Majesty's bloody Navy!" gritted Atticus through clenched teeth. He wore a rag tied around his head against the sun. His bronzed bare chest was well covered with a mat of hair, and his baggy linen trousers reached halfway from his knees to his feet.

"What means this thing, pressed?" said young Jost Weiser, a German Protestant Palatine recently transported through charity from England.

"Pressed you will be, Jost, if the British Navy catches us! You in da Navy den, mon—ha ha!" said Simon Livingston, a free black sailor from the Bahamas Islands. "Dey make free wit' da lash, and da pay no good."

"Little more than slavery, Jost, me lad," spat Atticus. "You're never let ashore for years on end, for fear you'll desert."

"But isn't being in the Navy just like being a sailor on *Berbice?*"

"Well, I'll be buggered," quipped Bosun Tiny. "If the lad's about to become a British tar, he'd best know the lay of it. Tell him, Gunny."

"A jack tar's life in His Majesty's Navy is worse than the clap," said Gunny, with a wink toward Simon, "and pressing Jack is illegal, lad; we got rights from Queen Anne's time. Navy's got no right to press us. Up in Halifax, Admiral Colvil's hanging deserters, giving out hundreds of lashes around the fleet for the others—torture to death, lad. The pay is less than half in any Yankee merchant ship."

"Aye, it's illegal, but that won't stop the captain of the brig over yonder," said Tiny, *Berbice's* huge bosun. Taking the roll of the ship as if on gimbals, Bosun Tiny stood stout as a capstan on the foredeck. His barrel chest was covered by a homespun shirt with baggy sleeves, innocent of buttons. His sun bleached hair was pulled back in a ponytail and tarred, sailor fashion. He looked at Gunny. "Tell the lad about how you got into His Majesty's Navy."

"I ran afoul of the armed sloop *Chaleur*," said Gunny, "under Lieutenant Tom Laugharne. The infernal swabs waited for unsuspecting merchantmen just off Sandy Hook and boarded us as we made the channel. They had us embayed by the time we smoked them. They took five of us Jacks, and it was hell on earth, with foul water and the cat-o'-nine-tails to whip a man within an inch of his life for daring to complain of it."

"But you're not in the Navy now," said Jost.

"Aye, aye, lad, feelings have been pretty high about the press gang. Laugharne made the mistake of going ashore in New York, with the Jacks he'd pressed at Sandy Hook in the boat with him. Next thing I knew, we were surrounded by an angry mob, shouting at Laugharne to give us back. Then a group of Yankees with clubs and belaying pins surrounded Laugharne and wouldn't let him or his men move. The mob kept yelling at us to run away! So I yelled back, 'Burn the boat, burn the boat!' By thunder, if that mob of Yankees didn't do just that! They ran down to the waterfront, grabbed the *Chaleur's* boat, and then paraded back to City Hall. Yankee Jacks by the hundred joined to carry *Chaleur's* boat like a feather on their shoulders, all the time Lieutenant Laugharne was fuming and sputtering, and his marines were loitering on the docks, afraid for their lives. They burned *Chaleur's* boat in front of the courthouse!"

"Where is your angry mob out here, mon?" countered Simon, his clear white eyes held open, making wide circles in his blue-black face, his eyebrows raised and his brow furrowed to punctuate his question. "Dey going to do just what dey wants with us here in dis boat *Berbice*. If we get caught, we be one sorry bunch of Jacks, mon. First ting dey do is look at the captain's list of sailors in dis boat. Ain't gonna be no rioting about *dis* bunch o' Jacks, mon. Ain't no riotin' mob in these Virginia woods. Ain't nobody gonna burn *dat* ship's boat. Some men gonna hang!"

"Are there criminals aboard?" said Jost.

"Aye, aye, lad, for the crime of taking leave of His Majesty's Navy without permission," said Tiny.

"The Navy will hang a man for jumping ship?"

"That or worse, lad. Ever heard of a Jack getting a hundred lashes 'round the fleet?"

"Nay," said Jost, the only landlubber aboard.

"If the Navy catches a deserter while the fleet's in, they have a special punishment to be seen by all the crews in all the ships. They give the fellow a hundred lashes on the ship he deserted from, and then they tie his arms to an oar laid across his shoulders and make him stand while they row him to another Navy ship. They give him another hundred lashes, and so on, around all the anchored vessels."

"How could anyone stand it?"

"The lads usually die."

"They'll hang Gunny, or lash him 'round the fleet?"

"That ain't all of it, Jost, me lad. Barbecue, on lookout up there at the mainmast head, is on the list of deserters, and so am I. The captain of the Royal Navy ship over yonder will have a list of deserters, you can lay to that."

"They'll hang you, Gunny, and Barbecue if they catch us? Press me into the Navy?" Jost hooked his thumbs in the drawstring of baggy cotton jean trousers that stopped a full eighteen inches above his bare feet, and cocked his head to one side. He found it hard to imagine that the English, who'd delivered him from poverty and persecution in Europe, would now possibly enslave him and hang some of his shipmates. His gaze went from Simon's nod to Tiny's sunburned face, which was furrowed with ill-disguised worry.

"Aye, lad, and they'll make sure you appreciate their fun with us," replied Tiny. "Our only chance, lad, is to outrun them, and if any skipper can conjure the Devil himself to help him do it, it'll be Captain Harte, for sure." Tiny looked down at the wooden deck and the pitch-filled seams dividing the bleached pine planks that followed the curve of *Berbice's* bulwarks. He remembered matching the ends of his bare toes to deck seams on the *Gaspee* and then looking up at the hanging body of a shipmate, kicking his life out at the end of a rope for the crime of trying to escape the brutal rule of Lieutenant Allen. It took the lad two hours to die. The crew was made to watch every minute of it.

"How did you get into the Navy, Tiny?" asked Jost.

Simon chuckled, "Don' matter how he got in, mon; it's how he got out!"

"I'll tell ye how we made sport of Lieutenant Thomas Allen when he had the *Gaspee,*" said Tiny. "May the powers forgive me; I signed on at Newport as bosun's mate for that devil. Allen was as free with the lash and the skin off Jack's back as ever I saw. He put into Casco Bay and saw Yankee ships running to and fro without a fare-thee-well to the customs house. So Lieutenant Allen seized three ships, but the customs collector refused to hold them. They hate each other, the customs and the navy, squabbling over the prize money. Meanwhile, the crew was deserting *Gaspee* like rats from a bilge awash. Some of the townsmen offered the hospitality of the place to any of Allen's crew who cared to take it, calling out to the *Gaspee* from the shore. Lads, mind ye, I was first for the cold swim."

"Tell him the rest, Tiny; tell him what happened to Lieutenant Allen," urged Gunny.

"The people on one of the ships Allen seized saw his crew deserting and made for it too, sailed right out from under Allen's nose. Allen couldn't go after the Yankee smuggler, since he didn't have enough crew left. We could hear him cursing us as he stamped on the deck of the *Gaspee.* 'Deserters—in the name of the King, you'll all hang!' he screamed at us. We hove-to in a tavern called the Indian Queen for a few drams of killdevil rum. Then Lieutenant Allen came ashore and pressed four Yankee Jacks into the navy right at the quayside."

"But he didn't get away with that either, did he, Tiny?" said Gunny.

"Nay, Allen's luck was hard that day. Those Jacks had wives and mothers in town. Sure enough, in no time the word was out and the townsfolk turned into an angry mob. They poured out of the Indian Queen like blood and thunder! Down to the quayside they swarmed, and hovered over Allen, with no mistaking they'd beat the tar and caulking out of him if he didn't give up the lads he pressed. Allen says, 'You're not within your rights; I'm an officer of the King.' Someone in the crowd yelled, 'We're free Englishmen, ain't we?' Everyone cried, 'Aye, aye!' Then the fellow shouted, 'We ain't at war now, are we?' Everyone yelled back, 'Nay!' Then the fellow screamed, 'You're nothing but a bloody *pirate*, Lieutenant!' Allen puffed himself up so his brass buttons almost burst off his coat, and spat, 'All right, take the whoresons.' The pressed men swarmed out of Allen's boat, free again!"

"That weren't the end of it, Tiny; the best part's next! Tell the lad," giggled Gunny.

"Aye, aye," Tiny grinned. "On his way back to the Falmouth customs house, Allen's oarsmen deserted! Left him alone with the empty boat to sputter and curse. He rowed his own gentleman's ass back to his ship, and a lubberly job at the oars, I say! Captain Allen went back to Halifax without seven of his best Jack tars, one of his midshipmen, and me, his bosun's mate, and never a prize to boot!"

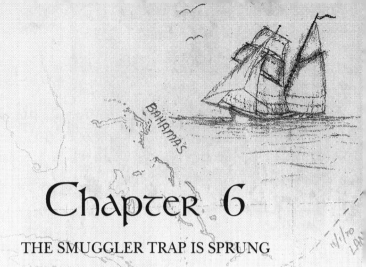

Chapter 6

THE SMUGGLER TRAP IS SPRUNG

Captain Harte saw his crew eyeing the brig, now it was known to be a British man-o'-war. He saw them look aft at him, every now and again. *Their lives depend on the outcome of this race, what terrible stakes!* First Mate Ordineaux was taking another bearing on the white patch of British sail, off on the northeastern horizon. His eyes met Captain Harte's, and with a nod they both went down into the greatcabin to have a look at the chart and a confidential parley on their predicament.

Jack Ordineaux was a head shorter than Captain Harte, and sported a tri-cornered hat when the breeze allowed it to stay put. Ordineaux was younger than Harte, high-spirited and given to athletic exhibitions such as standing on one hand on the head of a piling, if there were a sufficient number of young women about.

"Bearing's closing," said Ordineaux. That meant the brig was overtaking.

"She'll reach the cape before we do," said Harte, his forehead furrowed. He saw little hope in the situation. "Wind's from the east, and favors the brig with her spread of sail."

"Aye, Captain, we're close reaching, *Berbice's* favorite point of sail, but the brig will fetch the cape before us," said Ordineaux. "What do we do? We just squeezed past the British squadron, they must lie just over the horizon to the south. There's no escape in that direction."

"I'll wager that brig intends to cut us off before we can enter the Chesapeake. They know they'll lose us once we can fetch the creeks. We can go to weather—a damn sight better than that brig, if we can only make that play for us," said Harte, thinking, *if we gain the weather gauge once more, the brig cannot follow.*

"The brig's got the weather gauge now. Somehow we've got to get back upwind of them," Harte said as he leaned over the chart table. On it was a pen and ink chart of the mouth of the Chesapeake Bay.

Berbice mounted eight four-pound cannon and four swivels. The swivel was a sort of huge shotgun mounted on the bulwark. The cannon were sized according to the weight of their shot—that is, her cannon fired roundshot that weighed four pounds each. These were sufficient for self-defense in the seamier parts of the world, but no match for the armament and training of the British man-o'-war pursuing them. If they were pursued by a foreign power or pirates in some other part of the world, they'd put up a fight, but to challenge the Royal Navy was unthinkable. Harte looked at the chart as Ordineaux plotted the converging courses of the two ships nearing Cape Charles late that afternoon.

Captain Harte knew these waters like his own hand, and he had a reputation of repeated successes in eluding the British. Harte thought, *if we head downwind a bit toward Norfolk, we could prolong the chase. Perhaps in the evening the wind will die and give us a chance to slip away under cover of darkness.* He glanced at the chart again and grinned. Between Cape Charles and Cape Henry at the entrance to Chesapeake Bay was a line of shoals cut by two channels, one in the middle of the bay, and the other west towards Norfolk. But there was another possibility, risky and bold, but holding more promise for escape.

Captain Harte was aware more than any other that a great deal of his past success lay in luck. Considering the sea, the British Navy, unprincipled traders, privateers, pirates, and a thousand things that could go wrong on a sailing vessel, his strategies seldom came off as conceived. Unless he had to, Nathaniel wasn't about to say what he had in mind.

"All right, Mr. Ordineaux, I think I know what to do." His wry grin signaled the end of council and a return to the deck. "We'll fall off now, Mr. Ordineaux, but don't ease the sheets," said Harte.

The *Berbice* headed more to the west, toward Norfolk, and began to slow as her sails, sheeted in too tight for their best driving power, stalled. Atticus and Gunny rolled their eyes and gaped at the quarterdeck.

"What's this captain of yours got in mind, Tiny? Giving us over to His Majesty's Navy yonder? He's slowing us down in the middle of a chase, by the powers of Providence!"

"Aye, luff up a bit, lads. If you're real patient and attends your duty, you'll see some first-rate Yankee seamanship and His Majesty's Navy bobbing in our wake," assured Bosun Tiny, not quite so sure of this himself. The old man must have something up his sleeve—Tiny just didn't know what it was yet. It would be his own neck if Captain Harte didn't know his business. Among *Berbice's* small crew grouped on the foredeck, the elation of leaving the British squadron over the horizon only that morning was being dissolved in the stomach acid of foreboding.

Berbice, seventy-two feet long on the deck and twenty feet wide, drew about nine feet of water, depending on her load. She was a schooner, rigged fore and aft with gaff-headed sails on two masts that raked back to give the impression of speed and imminent flight. Augmenting this impression, she was painted yellow with black strakes accentuating her graceful sheer line. Because of her fore-and-aft rig, she needed relatively few crew to work her; there were six men before the mast, and usually two mates and the captain aboard. Her bows were flared, and there was no figurehead on her cutwater—expensive carvings were not for a smuggler. A gentle tumblehome was worked into her topsides aft, counterbalancing the flare of her bow.

Berbice was a fine example of the American shipbuilder's art. Of necessity, speed had been built into her for preservation of profits and liberty, for her profitable trade routes ran counter to the Navigation Acts. Her jibs stretched out along a bowsprit almost one-third of her total length. Her mainsail was so huge that the boom, which overhung the transom, was equipped with footropes to enable the crew to reach the aftermost end of the sail to furl it, since it hung well over the water. She crossed two yards on her foremast, on which a tremendous area of sail could be set for running before the wind; with studding sails set outboard of the regular yardarms, the sail area could be doubled. She had the sail area to drive her at speed in a light breeze, and more than enough sail to capsize her in unskilled hands.

Berbice had a quarterdeck with a greatcabin below it, normally inhabited by her mates and captain. The greatcabin had two portlights, or windows, per side, and there were two windows in the upper tuck of her transom. Harte and Ordineaux had to stoop below the massive deck beams in order to walk about in it. Forward of the quarterdeck, the guns shared the main deck with the galley stove, an open iron box with a pipe for a chimney. It was here all the shipboard meals were cooked over a wood or coal fire. The crew slept in a series of bunks in the forward end of the hold, where there was no headroom, packed in like books on library shelves.

* * *

On the ten-gun brig *Inflexible*, Lieutenant Winston Lloyd of His Majesty's Royal Navy was informed of what could be seen of the *Berbice's* change of course from the masthead, "Deck there, chase falling off three points."

Lieutenant Lloyd looked at the American schooner changing course as if to avoid interception and felt a triumph well up within him. "I can see their insolent faces now. Mr. Murty, we'll select some of her crew to fill out our complement and teach them the discipline of the Navy! Let us hope she's filled to the gunnels with French claret and Dutch dyewood!"

"Aye, aye, sir. You think she's a smuggler, then?" asked Mr. Murty, first lieutenant of the *Inflexible*.

"I'll search that schooner all day and the next if I have to, to find something to condemn them with, Mr. Murty, but I'll wager this Yankee's as foul of the law as we could ever wish," said Lieutenant Lloyd. "We'll put aboard a prize crew and sail her right out of the Chesapeake for the Admiralty Court in Halifax. I'll not be cheated in the provincial courts of these colonial pirates. Look how she sheers off toward Norfolk, as if she can still escape. Aye, Mr. Murty, there will be contraband aboard, for sure."

Lieutenant Lloyd went down into his cabin to look at the chart. If the wind held, he could be inside the capes and cut off the entrance to the Chesapeake before the American got there. He adjusted his powdered wig, lace neck cloth, and cockaded hat, looked with reassurance at the polished brass buttons on his uniform, and went back up on deck. With a self-assured grin, Lieutenant Lloyd looked at the crew on watch, lining the rails at the bow, eager for the triumph of the chase.

"Mr. Murty," said Lloyd to his first lieutenant, "we'll put out the stun'sls; it looks as if this American thinks he can fly on up the bay before us." The stun'sls were extra light-weather sails that hung from extensions on the yardarms, greatly increasing the sail area of the brig, and therefore her speed. "We shall reach the channel well before the Yankee, Mr. Murty; then we'll take her. Their only chance of escape will be to tack back out to sea, and *Rainbow* is there with the rest of the squadron, approaching from the south.

* * *

On the *Berbice*, Captain Harte wasn't satisfied with his speed either, so he said, "Mr. Ordineaux, sheet in the foresail, if you please." When the loose-footed foresail had been sweated in as tight as a board, Harte said, "All right, Mr. Ordineaux, ease the main until she backs, but not enough to luff her—we'd hate to put on a display of poor seamanship." Ordineaux was beside himself with apprehension but obliged. Captain Harte suppressed a wry grin; the ruse was working. As they wallowed south of Cape Charles, the Englishman had made all sail straight for the channel—that is, the only channel the Englishman was aware of. *Berbice* could claw up to windward of her now. As the brig passed the bow of the *Berbice*, many a heart aboard *Berbice* sank.

* * *

On the quarterdeck of the English brig, Lieutenant Lloyd said, "We've got him now, Mr. Murty. He can either tack back out to sea into our squadron or go aground on the shoals. He'll fall into our hands in either case." Lieutenant Lloyd considered his position: He was now approaching the channel in the middle of the entrance to the Chesapeake. With the wind still out of the east, this was the windward channel. "We'll heave to here on the windward side of the channel, Mr. Murty, if you please," said Lieutenant Lloyd. "If the Yankee makes for the downwind channel over by Norfolk, we can take up the chase again with the weather gauge once more in our favor."

"The Yankee will surely take the downwind channel, sir; it's his only clear choice," replied Mr. Murty.

Lieutenant Lloyd bellowed in a sea voice audible to all on the brig, "Take in the stun'sls, Mr. Murty, and clew up the course; heave to here on the windward side of the channel. It appears we have to wait for the hayseeds to catch up." There was a titter from the weather ratlines. "Take that man's name, Mr. Murty," said Lieutenant Lloyd, for humor was the exclusive prerogative of his quarterdeck. The upstart would be flogged. It had been three hours, and the brig had traversed fifteen miles since sighting the American.

* * *

"Give me a lay line for Cape Charles, Mr. Ordineaux," said Captain Harte, as he calculated the angle between the Cape and the easterly wind.

"Aye, aye, helm, nor-nor'east," said Ordineaux.

"Northeast then it is. Harden her up, Mr. Ordineaux, and let's start sailing like we mean it!" This last order eased the anxiety aboard, but it would be a hard chance to clear Cape Charles on the seaward side. Then the stakes got higher.

"Ahoy the deck!" the mainmast lookout on *Berbice* called. "Three sail to the southeast!" That would be the rest of the British squadron, springing the trap— or so they thought.

A great deal now rested on the tide flow, whether it would be slack, or flowing into or out of the bay. An outgoing tide would help them clear Cape Charles, but it would also help the *Inflexible* clear the shoals once the British realized *Berbice* didn't intend to make for either of the channels.

The easterly wind brought up the rich, clean smell of the sea. *Berbice* came out of her stall, and the bow wave began to boil once more. Harte listened as he drew a deep breath through his nostrils, savoring the tangy scent of the ocean.

* * *

"Deck there!" the call came from the masthead of the British brig lurking hove-to in the channel. "Chase now headed northeast."

"Bloody hell!" Lieutenant Lloyd spat his frustration. The prospect of sharing the prize money, because he was now in sight of the rest of the British blockade squadron, was bad enough. But now the crazy Yankee skipper seemed to be headed back out to sea. "Mr. Murty! Put her around east-southeast and get every stitch of fore and aft canvas on her! There's not a moment to lose!" bellowed Lieutenant Lloyd, more for the crew than for Murty, who fully grasped his changing fortunes in prize money. Lieutenant Lloyd now faced the dismal prospect that he might not even be the first to board the prize. The Yankee now had the weather gauge, the favored position for the race. The schooner could sail at a closer angle to the wind than the square-rigged *Inflexible*. Lieutenant Lloyd fumed, *What can I do? My orders are to seal off escape into the Bay's estuaries, which I have done. The squadron frigate* Rainbow *will now pick up the glory.* "We'll put about as soon as we have a lay line for the smuggler, Mr. Murty; we still have a chance of leading the pack into the kill," said Lieutenant Lloyd, then he spun on his heel. "Damn your eyes!" he bellowed at the bosun, "take that man's name and start the rest of these lazy sons-of-whores, or I'll take a belaying pin to them myself!" Lieutenant Lloyd turned back to his chosen confidant, Mr. Murty, and with an entirely pacified countenance said, "At least with our draft of fifteen feet of water aft, we shall lead the squadron for an inshore pursuit. This bloody Yankee is going to sail his ship up the lee shore, the ocean side of the cape, and right onto the beach if he's not lucky."

* * *

A close run onto a lee shore was what everyone, other than Captain Harte on the fleeing *Berbice,* was thinking as well. His fake move into the bay and then escape out to sea was now understood by all aboard, but the chance of weathering Cape Charles and clawing off a lee shore with the British squadron to weather seemed craziness atop folly. Was Captain Harte at his wit's end? Was there really nothing for it but a brutal future in His Majesty's Navy and the looped end of a rope for Barbecue, Gunny, and Tiny?

"Ahoy the deck!" the call came from *Berbice's* mainmast head. "Brig's made sail again."

"So the race is on again," said Captain Harte, "but we've gained some precious yardage to weather."

"Aye, Captain, every inch to weather will be precious indeed," said Ordineaux. He was sighting the cape every few minutes, keeping track of the bearing on this most crucial leg of their escape.

"We're wrecked for sure now," wailed Atticus. "The east wind will be blowing us to the lee of the cape. If divine providence sees us past the cape, then we'll be blown onto the ocean beach and drowned amongst the *Berbice's* splinters, with the waves crashing over our heads!"

"Belay that!" ordered Tiny. "We'll be clawing out to sea as much as we can. We've only to stay off the beach and in deep water. Aye, lads, and if we lose too much ground, we'll just tack and head east-southeast, back into deep water."

"And right into the guns of the bloody British squadron," moaned Atticus.

"That or be blown onto the beach and shipwrecked," agreed Gunny. "We'll lose way when we come around, and we're already a damn sight too close to Navy cannon for my fancy. Once we're in range, there'll be nothing for it but to lay-to and be boarded. That's when Tiny, Barbecue, and me will dangle from the end of a yardarm. God save us now!"

"Belay your whining," said Tiny. "Our liberty lies in weathering the cape by a good margin. We'll lay it for sure."

"Ask me, and I'd take my chances with a shipwreck on a lee shore sooner than with the British Navy," spat Atticus.

Every eye was on the set of *Berbice's* sails, and response was quick when Ordineaux wanted a sheet eased or sweated up. Tense men strained at the taut hemp lines. The adjustments he ordered were in inches, as Ordineaux used all his experience in sailing

Berbice to her limits. Captain Harte leaned against the taffrail, glancing at the ten-gun brig, then with approval at Ordineaux's sail adjustments. Harte also felt the gurgling of his stomach. *This will never do; a hungry crew cannot work as fast and effectively when I need them. A late dinner tonight— it is already just an hour before sunset.*

"Barbecue!" called Harte to the masthead, using the cook's nickname, referring to his reputed past in the Caribbean. "Down with ye and pass out some biscuit." This was the last of the biscuit Barbecue had made from the moldy wheat they had left over from the trip to the West Indies. "Simon," called Harte in his sea voice, "to the masthead with ye; I've need of a clear pair of eyes up there." Simon jumped to the weather ratlines as Barbecue slid down a backstay and landed with a dull, barefooted thud on the deck.

With *Berbice* setting every yard of canvas she could put up, she heeled ten degrees in the light breeze. The only noise to be heard was the roar of the bow wave, the sing of the foam past the lee side, and the flutter of taut sails in the breeze. As the tension rose, no one spoke. Every few minutes, another anxious sailor strode to the middle of the deck to line up *Berbice's* bowsprit with the cape. There were thoughtful brows on each seaman as he made the calculation of lost ground to leeway and the position of the cape. Could they clear the cape? The hard sea biscuit was absent-mindedly crunched in dry mouths. Anxious eyes traced the progress of the ten-gun brig across their track, for she was sure to wear around onto their own course as soon as she could lay it.

One of the last puffs of the afternoon breeze came, and *Berbice* leaned into it another five degrees. The flutter of the trailing edges of the sails quickened and increased in volume. "Let her come up in the puffs!" Ordineaux admonished the helmsmen, needlessly. The helmsmen had already eased pressure on the tiller in anticipation of *Berbice's* natural tendency to head more to windward as the breeze increased her "weather helm." They gained a few yards to weather as *Berbice* surged in the slightly stronger breeze.

"Don't let her luff!" encouraged Ordineaux as the puff blew itself out, but the helmsmen had already responded by easing *Berbice* back onto her course, keeping the sails filled perfectly all the while as the apparent wind changed. Ordineaux made the awful assessment, anticipated by some, "We must be getting set by the tide; she's making more leeway than usual. We'll not be weathering the cape on this tack!"

"By God, that's our bacon then," said Gunny. Knowing nods and whispers were passed among a solemn crew—a crew quickly growing morose. Captain Harte, always keenly aware of the moods of the men on which he depended, sensed the drop in spirits. All eyes were on the quarterdeck.

"That'll do just fine, Mr. Ordineaux," said Captain Harte in as loud a voice as he could calmly manage, as he swayed toward Ordineaux across the sloping quarterdeck. *The tension has risen too high. It's time to tell them what I'm up to.* In low tones Captain Harte revealed his strategy to Ordineaux, who slowly shook his head from side to side, then began to laugh in relief, his broad shoulders heaving with each guffaw.

The release of tension onboard began with the sound of Ordineaux's mischievous laughter.

"See there, mates, nothing to worry about," said Tiny.

"I'll lay the old man's got them buggered again," said Gunny, exchanging a knowing grin with Tiny.

Captain Harte approached the quarterdeck rail and faced his crew. "We're going up the bay," he announced," by way of Smith Inlet between Latimer shoals and the Cape, and we'll see His Majesty's brig run aground or wear away!"

The infection of Ordineaux's laughter spread into a wild, hysterical release. Atticus danced a jig and Barbecue sang, the entire crew joining in the chorus:

"The Royal Navy yonder, ain't gonna get me,

We're getting away with the set of the sea,

And yonder lieutenant, can cry in his gin,

Cause Captain Harte done buggered 'em again!

A hearty huzzah rose from the main deck, soon checked by the call of Simon on lookout above. "Ahoy da deck, brig, she's wearing 'round." All eyes now shifted aft to the British ten-gun brig as she ponderously turned full circle to come onto a parallel tack in pursuit of *Berbice*. Captain Harte noted with satisfaction that the British had gone a good deal to windward of the lay line before coming about, in their respect for the noted weatherly qualities of American schooners.

The resolution of all matters still lay with the caprice of the wind and tide. The breeze was dying rapidly as the sun sank lower. The breakers from the southeast ocean swell, rolling across Latimer shoal, were now audible above the flutter of the sails in

Berbice. From her deck, the breakers could be seen to rise above the other waves and then boil into foam, throwing white spray into the air above. Toward the sunset, the water was turning molten blue, red, and yellow. Seagulls wheeled over *Berbice,* seeming to call down their approval of her wind-borne nature. But the breeze was giving out. The set of the tide was pulling *Berbice* toward the shoal, and the falling wind was robbing her of progress toward the escape channel beyond.

* * *

The pursuing brig, in the broad water of the bay, still had the afternoon breeze and was closing the distance rapidly. Lieutenant Lloyd gazed at the closing distance with growing excitement. "Mr. Murty, ready the chase gun and prepare the boats. Parcel out their crews and weapons as well. If we can't bring that impertinent fool to heel by the time we get into his patch of foul wind, we'll launch the boats and board! The fool's run himself out of the breeze and can't tack back out to sea now. I believe we'll see a resolution to this smuggler's folly before sunset, Mr. Murty." *And no doubt floggings, if not a few hangings on the morrow,* he thought, in delicious anticipation.

* * *

"Let's get some water on these sails, Mr. Ordineaux," said Captain Harte, as he watched the breakers on Latimer shoal grow closer to *Berbice's* beam.

"All hands to wet the sails," bellowed Ordineaux. There was a sudden flurry of activity as buckets, and anything else that promised to hold water, appeared from below decks. They tied short hanks of line to the water vessels and plunged them into the sea, then took them aloft and splashed the water onto the sails. The fibers of the cloth sails tightened when wet, and *Berbice* wrung a little more headway from the dying breeze. They could see the geyser of the shot from the brig's chase gun before they heard the report. It was well short and wild.

"Mr. Ordineaux, start the lead line, if you please," said Captain Harte, looking not at the pursuing brig, but at the breaking waves on Latimer shoal. Their progress past the shoal was painfully slow, the tide pulling them toward the breakers. It was all the more nerve-wracking to know the brig still had the breeze.

A ball from the brig's chase gun landed only a hundred feet from *Berbice's* stern quarter. Captain Harte thought of the casks of illegal Dutch powder in the hold. A lucky round from the brig's gun and they'd be blown into matchsticks. He listened as Tiny swung the lead line in the bows of *Berbice* and called out the depth of water. "Two fathom!" They were cutting it mighty fine, only three feet of water below *Berbice's* keel. Everyone aboard could see the sand bottom through the clear water. Another ball of the brig's chase gun whistled overhead.

"We're under their bloody guns now," groaned Gunny. "We'd be splinters by now if they'd a real gunner aboard."

"Captain's gonna run for it!" squealed an excited Atticus.

"He'll put her on the beach!" Barbecue pointed forward, where the beach of Cape Charles was amazingly close at hand. It was astonishing to be so close to the beach sand and still afloat.

* * *

"He's driving into the shallows to lose us. Mr. Murty, lower the boats!" ordered Lieutenant Lloyd. With block and tackle the British sailors heaved the brig's two boats over the side, and the men, oars, and weapons dropped in. There was some confusion as the pressed men, who had never taken an oar before, tangled their oars and thrashed to no effect, save driving their officers into a shrieking fury. In a few minutes the oarsmen were sorted out and the boats got under way. The brig had made progress on the dying breeze and was now abeam of the westernmost end of Latimer shoal. The last shot of the chase gun was fired as the brig's boats put off toward the schooner.

* * *

"Ahoy da deck, brig's put over her boats!" Simon shouted from the masthead on *Berbice*. The crew anxiously looked at the British warship from *Berbice's* deck. A race between the becalmed *Berbice* and the brig's boats was no race at all.

The bulwarks either side of amidships exploded into a cloud of cedar splinters before anyone aboard *Berbice* heard the report. A cannon ball had blown through the ship from one bulwark across the deck to the other. The water butt disappeared into slivers, the remaining water making a fan pattern on the deck, reaching for the scuppers. The barefoot crew of *Berbice* felt as if the deck had been pounded by a huge sledgehammer. Simon at the mainmast head felt the mast shiver. *Berbice* was now no more than a hundred yards off the sandy beach of the cape, with Tiny swinging the lead and calling out his marks earnestly. The water actually grew deeper after *Berbice* cleared Latimer shoal. *Berbice* was now in a little-known channel that ran along the side of the cape. Here was a sheer drop-off just a few feet from the shoreline where the fast-flowing tide scoured a deep and narrow channel.

* * *

The British brig was also being set by the tide toward Latimer shoal, and being the less weatherly vessel, had come considerably closer to the shoal by the time the breeze expired. Lieutenant Lloyd paced the quarterdeck of the brig, once again beside himself with his misfortune. There was nothing for it: the anchor must be lowered away or his brig would be wrecked on the shoal, and the anchor had better find good holding ground straightaway! Lieutenant Lloyd's zest for pursuit had pushed him within a hundred yards of the breakers on the shoal. "Lower the anchor, Mr. Murty," ordered Lieutenant Lloyd, crestfallen. The brig slowly pointed her head into the oncoming tide and took the swell head-on, but the anchor dragged.

* * *

Tiny fancied he could drop the sounding lead on the beach of Cape Charles from the end of the bowsprit, they were so close. The channel was amazingly deeper, scoured by the tide ripping past the edge of the cape. *Berbice* moved sideways relative to the shoreline as she was taken up into the bay by the four-knot tide rip. Standing waves showed where the tidal current was swiftest; Captain Harte hoped *Berbice* would be drawn right among them. At one point, as the tide flow pulled *Berbice* in through the channel, her bowsprit actually overhung the sandy beach. Even so, the brig's boats were making steady progress toward them, carrying five times as many men as *Berbice*, all of them armed to the teeth.

"Mount the swivels, Mr. Ordineaux, and tell Gunny to load grapeshot." Captain Harte's frustration pushed him to make a show of violence.

Ordineaux's eyes grew wide; did Harte mean to fight? There was always talk of it. To resist a king's ship would make him and his men liable to charges of piracy. They would all be hung. Could the brig's boats be discouraged by a show of resistance? Probably not. They could sink them and hide, then hope to melt into the confusion of shipping in the Virginia colony, but this was not so easily done. These were desperate thoughts of desperate men, looking at their last day of liberty.

"Dare ye risk it, Captain?"

"Who among us isn't ruined if we're taken?"

"Ruined is one thing, hung for piracy is another."

"It's for the lads forward, just a show. I will do no murder today."

"Gunny, Captain says to load grapeshot," bellowed Ordineaux.

"Aye, aye, sir!" called Gunny to the quarterdeck. "If that ain't fair music to me ears!" said Gunny to his astonished shipmates. Gunny's weathered countenance cracked into a grin as he pranced down to the shot locker. He'd been pressed into the king's service and then jumped ship in Baltimore. His knowledge gained in gunnery was a valuable skill.

* * *

Lieutenant Lloyd felt the abrupt stop of the ten-gun brig's rise to an oncoming swell as the heel of her rudderpost pounded into the sand bottom. The jolt was felt from the deck to the masthead as the keel hit bottom. The masthead lookout nearly lost his grip and fell. Lieutenant Lloyd turned purple. At that moment the roar of the breakers on the nearby shoal seemed deafening. The anchor was dragging! Pulled up on each swell, the anchor was slowly plowing a furrow through the sand bottom.

"Mr. Murty!" screamed Lieutenant Lloyd. "Recall the boats, not a moment to lose!" Saving the ship was now paramount. He'd be court-martialed if he grounded her here, so far out of the navigation channel. The recall signal was run up the flag halyard and a rapid series of three guns was fired, also a recall signal. The officers in the brig's boats looked back in disbelief. The recall guns were repeated again; the boatmen could see their comrades waving frantically from the rigging of the brig.

So the boats put around and returned to the brig to begin a nightlong ordeal of towing the brig, against the tide, into deeper water. They were assisted by a gentle breeze from the southwest in the early morning hours, along with the change of tide.

Lieutenant Lloyd was not to be so easily done out of prize money. Before retiring to the fleet, he put a midshipman off in the *Inflexible's* longboat with as many seamen as he could spare, to root out the smuggler if possible and inform the customs house in Accomack with all dispatch. They could still lay claim to at least a share of the prize money. The British sailors would have to make their way overland to the inland town of Accomack.

The customs office was one end of a storehouse, and here all ocean-going shipmasters were to report to bond their cargoes and pay the customs duty. The jurisdiction of the Accomack customs house spread over fifty miles north and south, including the oceanside ports of Metompkin, Assawoman, and Chincoteague, and the Chesapeake rivers from Cherrystone Inlet near Cape Charles to Onancock Creek.

Inflexible's open boat made for Pungoteague Creek, to be picked up by the *Inflexible* after Lieutenant Lloyd reported to the squadron. In the meantime, perhaps the midshipman could discover the smugglers and lay claim to the prize for *Inflexible*.

Chapter 7

SAFETY

The same southwest breeze that allowed *Inflexible* to avoid shipwreck on Latimer Shoals made up a little earlier where the *Berbice* lay close in to shore, nearly invisible in the darkness against the trees. Without as much as a lit tobacco pipe, the *Berbice* glided northwards into the Chesapeake. The set of the tide and the southwest breeze put them abreast Hungar's Creek in a little over two hours. Captain Harte thought it prudent to put into the creek and drop anchor for the coming day. The entrance was guarded by a sandbar that stretched to the southwest, but if one knew the channel, there was a good twenty feet of water in the creek right up to the shoreline, one reason the aging widower Custis had located his plantation there.

After seeing the anchor set and checking again that they would not be grounded if the wind changed, Captain Harte took his leave of the deck and retired to his quarters in the greatcabin. It seemed to him that the creek had shoaled remarkably since the plantation had civilized the shoreline. Years of cultivating sot weed in the Mould of the virgin forest, now gone forever, had reduced the topsoil, and now the ochre clay loam peaked through, and to Nathaniel's practiced eye, the crops were getting thinner.

Jack Ordineaux stepped in and took his customary seat at the greatcabin table. A candle lamp swung from a deck beam over the middle of the table, the deck beams overhead casting deep shadows. Harte surveyed the placid scene of the anchorage through the transom windows by moonlight. Ordineaux handed Captain Harte a pewter tankard of ale. "I expect you'll appreciate this now."

Harte clawed at his face as if to clear cobwebs, took a deep breath, and gathered himself. "Indeed, Jack, I almost lost the ship, three good men, and all my own fortune today," said Harte, as he took a deep swig of the warm ale. "The brig must have grounded on the shoal. They'll be having a devil of a time of it tonight."

Jack Ordineaux brightened and raised his tankard. "Aye, to the Royal Navy and the shoals—may they always find each other!" The two men laughed and drank, too exhausted from their thirty-six-hour run for liberty to be sleepy.

Barbecue pounded on the companionway door with his horny bare foot, his hands full. "Here be your victuals," he said. Ordineaux eagerly opened the door to reveal Barbecue with a dented pewter tray stacked full of roasted oysters in one hand and a steaming pail in the other. The oysters had been roasted on the coals in *Berbice's* iron deck box that served as galley. Out of the steaming pail, the red legs and claws of two blue crabs the size of dinner plates pointed stiffly at the deck head.

"Atticus and the others went over to the shallows in the ship's boat with some torches and got these, soon as we anchored," explained Barbecue. After an open-water voyage, the bounty of the Chesapeake was always a welcome feast.

"Heavenly!" exclaimed Harte in delight. Initiative was never crushed on his ship. "My compliments!"

"The crew's having the same," offered Barbecue, as he made for the companionway door. He always had to get in the last word, even if it was with the captain. This had been the cause of his frequent floggings during his short tenure in the Royal Navy, a tenure that ended with a long swim to an American vessel one night in the Caribbean.

Ordineaux and Harte sat at the table, where lay their wooden trenchers that served as plates, and produced their knives. Barbecue had brought in the *Berbice's* flatware, a pair of two-pronged forks with bone handles. With the aid of these instruments, Ordineaux and Harte set to their feast of fresh shellfish. Ordineaux, a newcomer to the Chesapeake from New York, took a crab from the bucket, placed it right side up on his trencher, and was about to smash the top carapace with the butt of his knife when Harte, looking on with growing anxiety, bade him stop.

"That'll wind up in a hellish mess," said Harte, referring to the crab's imminent demolition at the point of Ordineaux's knife. "The cabin will stink for weeks. Let me show you the way Mama Oakes did it," referring to the huge black African woman who figured so prominently in Harte's earlier life on the plantation, "clean and simple." Harte reached for his crustacean, let it drain out into the bucket, and laid it on the table upside down. He took his razor-sharp knife and sliced the bottom off the shell. Then he took hold of one of the crab's two rear fin-shaped legs and carefully pulled it loose, along with a huge chunk of attached meat. With a wink at Ordineaux, he took a bite and rolled back his eyes.

Ordineaux grinned. "Beats hell out of picking through meat and smashed guts," he said, and proceeded with the same ventral entry dissection. Barbecue made timely appearances with more tankards of ale; the mound of opened oyster shells grew until the pewter tray was empty and the crab shells lay hollowed. Ordineaux then proposed one more toast, "To the generous Captain Easton, and how glad we are we got his *Berbice* home again, not to mention saving our own share of the fortunes lying safely in her hold."

Harte raised his tankard, strangely full once more— he'd lost count of Barbecue's comings and goings— and drained it. "Aye, aye, one more profitable voyage without being caught, and I'll be owner of me own schooner."

"Aye, best of luck then, Providence and profits in our favor!" Ordineaux staggered off to his cabin, along the companionway forward of the greatcabin. The cabin opposite Ordineaux's had been empty since the West Indies—the second mate had died of the bloody flux on the return trip.

Bosun Tiny was on anchor watch, they were within miles of home, and the ship was safely at anchor. Harte lifted himself stiffly and stumbled to his cot, where he fell into a very deep sleep.

* * *

Meanwhile, to the west, on the bay, *Inflexible's* boat carrying the midshipman and six British tars had just tacked. It was time to put the boat ashore for the evening. The midshipman considered the wind and the boat's progress, trying to decide whether to beat up into Hungar's Creek or to make an easy run for it into Cherrystone Creek. He decided on the easy run to Cherrystone, where they beached the boat. The midshipman was a bit at a loss as to what was to be done and stayed next to the beached boat, the symbol of his authority. The sailors went off after clams in the sand shallows, oysters and mussels in the marsh grass, and driftwood with which to build a fire and roast the lot.

"As fine a mussel as ever I seen on the coast of Brittany," commented one of the sailors, a former English Channel smuggler, to the midshipman. "Too bad we ain't got some French claret to go with it." The midshipman missed the quip, while the sailors exchanged mocking grins. There was plenty of French claret in the colony, and truth be known, more of it nearer to the speaker than he could have imagined. If the wind held fair, in one more day they would reach Harborton on Pungoteague Creek, the nearest landing to the customs house in Accomack.

* * *

Captain Harte opened his eyes with a start. Barbecue stood in front of him with a steaming earthenware mug of tea, having just kicked open the door of the greatcabin. Harte stared up at the deck beams overhead and realized he was in his cot in the greatcabin of the *Berbice*, soaked in cold sweat. Someone had laid a blanket over him in the night.

Barbecue cleared his throat. "Morning, sir; watch changing, you asked to be woke up." Harte took the tea mug from Barbecue and nodded his thanks. It was full of East India tea smuggled in *Berbice* from the forbidden Dutch islands of the Caribbean. Nathaniel propped himself up on one elbow and looked out the transom windows at Hungar's creek.

In the distance and out of view, a ship's boat came about and tacked back northeast, the determined midshipman of the *Inflexible* in the stern sheets gripping her short tiller.

A double-ended shallop with two leg-of-mutton sails set wing and wing was sailing down Hungar's Creek toward the bay. *The wind must be out of the east again,* thought Harte. *Berbice* had swung on her anchor until her stern pointed down the river to the bay. The waters of Hungar's Creek were murky brown with topsoil, runoff of a recent rainstorm from the newly plowed and naked plantation fields.

The shallop reminded Harte of his boyhood on the Rappahannock River, racing two-masted craft against the young gentlemen. That was where Harte had learned to squeeze every last ounce of speed from a sailboat. The Stolmoore boys of Sybarite Hall and other local young gentlemen never tired of wagering on their sailing races; they seemed to have limitless supplies of coin for wagering. As Captain Harte watched the two-sailed shallop run before the wind down Hungar's Creek, an unpleasant memory crowded in on him; he recalled the violent ravings of Landon Stolmoore that prefaced his expulsion from the idyllic Sybarite Hall. This was succeeded by a more pleasant thought of the Dutch smuggler that picked him up as he drifted, aimless and abandoned, down the Rappahannock River. Nathaniel's local knowledge and pilotage of the creeks won him his first berth as an apprentice seaman on that Dutchman.

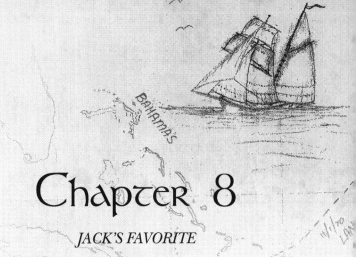

Chapter 8

JACK'S FAVORITE

Rappahannock River, Virginia Colony, 1740's

Nathaniel Harte was born out of wedlock to Sarah Harte, one of Landon Stolmoore's indentured servants. Nathaniel's mother had been brought to the colony in the bondage of indentured servitude, as were well over sixty percent of white immigrants to America before the revolution. Sarah Harte died at the age of sixteen bringing Nathaniel into the world, and as the wagging tongues would have it, much to the relief of Landon Stolmoore. Landon Stolmoore's moralizing was nevertheless gratuitously inflicted henceforth with renewed vigor and without discretion. The vicious gossip allowed that this moralizing was a result of the workings of a dark secret on his conscience. Landon Stolmoore saw that the boy, called Harte after his indentured mother, was cared for, at a distance. Nathaniel Harte was brought up as the ward of the plantation's overseer, a German redemptioner named Johannes Woolf.

Nathaniel Harte was never for want; on the other hand, through childhood he never knew the truth of his origins and never held the same social status as the plantation's young gentlemen, John and Wormeley Stolmoore, the legitimate spawn of Landon Stolmoore, master of Sybarite Hall.

Almost all the Virginia planter gentry were related to one another through decades of intermarriage of the dominant families. Throughout Nathaniel's childhood there were plenty of young Stolmoore cousins, nephews, and in-laws about the plantation for playmates, as they followed their parents on visits from neighboring estates. Marriage in Landon's social class was much a business deal, for combining and solidifying wealthy estates. It would have been unthinkable for Landon to marry out of his exalted social level of the gentry, especially to the poor (landless!) indentured Sarah Harte. Landon did receive a land grant for bringing Sarah and several dozen other miserable wretches across the Atlantic; he sold the others around the local villages at a tidy profit.

Nathaniel Harte's clothing was less abundant and a good deal plainer than the raiment of the young gentlemen, which was imported through the tobacco factors in London. Nevertheless, on orders from Landon Stolmoore himself, the young Nathaniel Harte attended the tutored lessons in Latin, Greek, and mathematics at Sybarite Hall with the young gentlemen. A dueling master tutored young Nathaniel in fencing and the gentlemanly sport of epee. One never knew when a Virginia gentleman would be called upon to defend his honor in a duel. Nathaniel took to the use of epee and saber with the same innate talent that he showed sailing *Jack's Favorite*. Nathaniel was even allowed the privilege of attending the lessons of the English dancing master, who instructed the young gentlemen and visiting young ladies in the minuet and the country dances, such as the reel and the jig.

* * *

"I scorn the base courting of popularity," Landon Stolmoore asserted to his son, Wormeley Stolmoore, in the preamble to one of his many long-winded lectures, "and if this evil wagering you do has purpose to gain popularity with the other young gentlemen, then that is a better reason still thou best leave it off. There is no profit in wanton amusements and idleness. Thou must lecture thy young gentlemen friends against these evils."

Wormeley Stolmoore looked on at his father in disbelief. *Lecture the other young gentlemen he was accustomed to wager with? After settling accounts all round, perchance?*

"I provide the lesser men around me, those of meaner condition, with the benefits of my reasoning," Landon droned on, gazing up at the lofty ceiling as if to track his discourse on lofty thought, "reasoning that has been the product of my own superior education. To provide the lesser men with the benefits of one's superior mind is one's duty to the community. This is not all, Wormeley; you must be constantly vigilant against character flaws in others around you, and provide the lesser men with your advice on how they should improve themselves." Landon's own attendance to this particular aspect of his self-assigned duties did not endear him to his neighbors.

Landon took in his son from the corner of his eye, for the preamble was over and the theme of this discourse was about to be delivered. "Guard thee against such frivolous pastimes as wagering on the ponies." Here Landon squared his cleft chin and fixed young Wormeley in his imperious gaze. Wormeley felt as if he had been skewered and stapled to the floor by an iron Roman lance. "There will be an end to this gaming and wagering; henceforth you will attend to your lessons and have no more of the trifling habits of the other young gentlemen. Those who partake in these base pleasures are undermining our aristocracy. The pony races and the card gaming are beneath your station in life; thou wilt henceforth partake of these wanton amusements no more." Landon's voice was rising in pitch as he became inflamed. "Another wager against your fortune and I shall have you answer to the whip, young man!"

With the promise of corporal punishment, often meted out to the young gentlemen of Sybarite Hall, Wormeley visibly shuddered. Seeing the impact of his words, Landon sought to soften the blow. "Although an occasional cockfight can do a man of superior breeding no lasting harm." At this Wormeley visibly brightened, for he had six shillings on a particularly beautiful red rooster to be put in the pit that very night. Landon continued his monologue, "It will likewise fall to your shoulders to provide the community with the reason and guidance of your superior, inherited intellect."

* * *

The race started in Carter's Creek by the mooring buoy. Wormeley tacked his shallop and headed straight for a broadside collision with Nathaniel's boat. Nathaniel put his tiller up, luffing his two-masted rig a bit as he missed the rudderpost of Wormeley's boat by inches. Wormeley tried to come back up into the wind again to head Nathaniel off, but Nathaniel had the wind in his sails, and Wormeley had stalled out in his maneuvering. *Jack's Favorite* was now hard on the breeze. Nathaniel sat on the gunnel and leaned out to weather. Wormeley tacked inshore, keeping close on a rhumb line to the plantation wharf, the agreed finish of the race. Nathaniel looked at the tide, racing out past the mooring buoy at the mouth of Carter's Creek, and decided to make one long tack into the Rappahannock, and as soon as he had a lay line, one long tack back to the wharf downstream. *I'll have to allow for the set of the tide on the tack into the wharf,* he thought. Nathaniel knew the tide and the wind would be stronger toward the middle of the river— besides, he'd lose time while in the stays with too many tacks. Wormeley was furious: His attempts to ram or overturn Nathaniel's boat had failed, and now there was nothing for it but to finish the race and probably lose the wager.

Nathaniel saw a strong gust of wind coming, shown by darkening wavelets across the water, and braced himself to ease his mainsheet to avoid capsizing. As the gust came on, Nathaniel eased the sheet ever so slightly, keeping the lee gunnel of *Jack's Favorite* just about an inch above the waves. The same gust reached Wormeley, straining with all his might to keep the lee rail of his own boat above the water and to keep his sails filled to the maximum at the same time. He didn't see the gust of wind coming; it struck him unawares. As he desperately tried to untangle the mainsheet, the lee gunnel went under and his shallop shipped green water.

"Bail, you bloody little fool!" Wormeley shouted at his brother John, who had cast off the jibsheet entirely and was hanging onto the weather gunnel of the *Sultan* with white knuckles. Wormeley struggled to haul the sheets back in and steady the boat as his brother set about bailing with a large scoop carved from a single piece of pine.

Jack's Favorite had been a badly neglected cast-off ship's boat when Nathaniel found it drifting into Carter's Creek the previous year. Nathaniel became a virtual apprentice to a local boat builder until the nineteen-foot shallop had been put to rights. Henceforth, Nathaniel kept *Jack's Favorite* in Bristol condition with all his spare energy, always stopping by the plantation wharf to see if there was any leftover line or pitch or maybe even the bottoms of some paint. *Jack's Favorite* was an open lap strake double shallop—that is, double-ended, with a sweetly curved sheer line. The foremast was stepped in the eyes of the boat, and the longer mainmast slightly forward of amidships. The two sails were club-headed, with the mizzen loose-footed and overlapping the boomed main. She was trimmed in black with yellow sides, the lower strake chocolate. Her masts were yellow, the top of the foremast black, while her mainsail boom was tarred.

On seeing the launch of *Jack's Favorite*, the young Stolmoore gentlemen begged Landon for a shallop of their own. Of course the Stolmoore boy's shallop was a couple of feet longer than *Jack's Favorite.* The *Sultan* was built by a local shipwright, who dressed her out as a proper gimcrack for young gentlemen. *Sultan* had a transom stern with carvings and a cuddy forward. The Stolmoore shallop boasted three sails: main, mizzen, and jib. John Stolmoore never seemed to set *Sultan's* jib correctly. Wormeley always assumed the role of captain, being the eldest son.

Nathaniel especially loved the secret wagering on the shallop races, now that Wormeley was forbidden to wager on more public events. Landon would have been infuriated had he known of these regattas, and further inflamed to learn that Nathaniel Harte always won the prize money in his old cast-off ship's boat. The Stolmoore boys were poor sailors, always too full of nervous excitement to take the time to comprehend the flow of the tide or the changing caprice of the wind. These things of nature were too slow or subtle to attract the interest of the young gentlemen, and passed them by. To Nathaniel Harte, the wavelets on the water, the tilt of an anchored buoy, the feel of a slight breeze on one side of his face or the other, were a basic language that told him how to handle his beloved shallop. His comprehension of these was the foundation upon which he won a sizeable bag of the young gentlemen's coin.

Alas, the friendship of the young gentlemen, though craved by Nathaniel, did him no good. The mischievous Wormely Stolmoore paid disrespect to the hallowed grave of the revered King Stolmoore, at which opportunity Landon levied the blame on Nathaniel. Landon Stolmoore disowned him in order to terrorize his legitimate progeny into moral behavior. In any case, Nathaniel's presence was becoming increasingly embarrassing for Landon, as he fancied Nathaniel began to bear his own looks. The young gentlemen were admonished to henceforth guard against pollution of their behavior by association with those of lower bloodline. Nathaniel set out in self-imposed exile, but not before the two young gentlemen had stolen his wager winnings.

* * *

Captain Harte broke out of his reflections on the past. Over the horizon across the Chesapeake lay the Rappahannock River, Carter's Creek, and Sybarite Hall. Fifteen years of seafaring had seemed to put a whole world between the greatcabin of the *Berbice* and the musky boxwoods of Sybarite Hall. With a snort of disgust he flushed the young gentlemen from his mind and turned his thoughts back to *Berbice*. Having just escaped from the pursuing *Inflexible* and lying now at anchor, there was much to be done before the ship was safe from seizure.

The ship seemed strangely quiet after the constant commotion of the long sea voyage. Bosun Tiny was allowing the crew to take advantage of the opportunity for a much-needed rest, no doubt. Harte sipped at the tea Barbecue had brought him and wondered if the British would recognize *Berbice* if they saw her again. He took comfort in the fact that there were literally hundreds of schooners like the *Berbice* plying these waters, and as soon as her illegal cargo was unloaded, the British would have no more claims against him or his ship. What he needed to do now was to arrange for wagons and oxcarts to be ready when *Berbice* made her nighttime move. The sooner rid of the contraband, the sooner *Berbice* would be safe from the navy and customs. Barbecue reappeared to collect his precious tea mug, the pride of *Berbice's* collection of odd pieces of mostly chipped and cracked earthenware.

Harte gathered himself on deck in the reassuring sunshine and said to Ordineaux, "I'll make arrangements for unloading now in Harborton. I'll ride there while you bring the ship around to the creek at midnight a day hence.

Ashore and on his way to the plantation's barn, Captain Harte walked past the headstone of the late John Custis and paused to read it. If the epitaph bore any truth in it, old John was having the time of his life since his wife's demise and his own removal to the Eastern Shore, for it was freshly carved in stone:

"Aged 71 years, and yet lived but seven years,
Which was the space of time he kept
A bachelor's home at Arlington
On the Eastern Shore of Virginia."

As Captain Harte read the newly carved stone with such a blatant message, he took it as a personal warning, and with furrowed brow reviewed his thoughts on marriage. He had recently been preoccupied with the matter of taking a mate, for the range of highest as well as base cravings haunted the mind of this healthy, athletic young man. The corners of his mouth drew down, and his teeth worked on the inside of his lip. The social pressures to marry were great, even for men whose calling was the sea. But then there was the Fiddler's Green, the waterfront haunts of sailormen and loose women. They seemed separate and irreconcilable to Nathaniel, who felt a surprisingly strong lust arise and looked forward to his first opportunity to satisfy this craving on the journey north, a journey that would take him to the wooded lane south of Harborton.

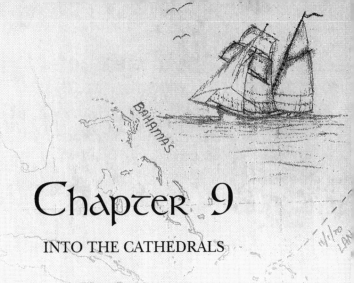

Chapter 9

INTO THE CATHEDRALS

That Same Day

Captain Harte borrowed a fine black Narragansett mare at the Custis plantation stables. He cut a dashing figure in his shore side dark blue jacket, plain linen neck cloth, white skin-tight knee breeches with silver buttons, and his only pair of precious silk stockings.

"Mind, there's been talk of highwaymen on the road north," the plantation overseer said, "Take this with ye," handing Nathaniel a pistol, powder horn and a sack of lead ball.

The loaner flintlock was stuffed into one of the special long, inside pockets of Nathaniel's waistcoat. He'd been known to stuff as many as four charged pistols in that coat on shore side visits in certain ports of the Caribbean, South America, and Africa. But he was home now, and felt secure, so he didn't come ashore armed. He rode north from the Custis plantation at an easy canter.

While ships had been built from the abundant wood on the eastern shore of Virginia for a hundred years, it was still a land of virgin forest. Nestled in the forest were clearings for small farms. There were settlements where commerce took place at the good natural anchorages that abounded along the numerous deep creeks. These creeks together had hundreds of miles of shoreline.

On this clear autumn day, the haze and humidity of summer had gone, yet it was pleasantly warm. Captain Harte was enjoying the ride. In the distance now he could hear a rubbery "*honk*," repeated and growing louder, now joined by others, dozens, hundreds, growing louder. He looked up into the northern sky and saw the chevron formations of Canada geese, line after raucous line of them, thousands filling the sky for a time in a vast aerial invasion, raining down cacophony. Captain Harte felt a sense of powerlessness in the face of the waves of airborne creatures, bent on their irresistible journey. He could only watch in awe as the living sound beat down around him from the sky, like hail from a squall line. As with a squall line, they soon faded off into the distance.

He rode into an oak forest along carriage tracks that entered an archway of green leaves, the entrance into the shadowy interior. The hand of man had not yet borne an ax to these woods. In the virgin oak grove, the trees stood over a hundred and fifty feet high, with trunks eight feet in diameter. The massive trunks towered fifty feet before branching. There was little under story, so one could see quite a distance through the columns of the grove. With an almost solid canopy of leaves above, sunlight came through the openings in shafts, illuminating the surroundings in soft, filtered light. The whole gave Captain Harte the impression he was in a giant cathedral, the massive oaks holding up the roof. Fifty feet above Captain Harte, a bald eagle dropped from its perch and glided silently down in front of him. It flew on down the road at eye level, directly in front of Harte, and disappeared among the trees. This was a very good sign indeed; Nathaniel felt the sighting of a bird of prey was his lucky sign.

Near noon, Captain Harte came to a crossroads: to the west lay the settlement on the Chesapeake; to the east, an ill-defined track led to the marshes of the coast, where hidden inlets harbored pirates and shipwreck robbers. Spanish ponies that swam ashore from wrecked galleons foraged on the barrier islands across the lonesome wilderness of the marshes. Hanging from a modest one-story weatherboard building at the crossroads, a crudely painted wooden sign proclaimed, "King's Head Ordinary: Food for the Hungry, Lodging for the Weary, and Goode Keeping for Horses."

Nathaniel ventured in to find a group of locals seated along the benches of a rough-hewn table. They were well in to their cups, as a noggin was passed along the table and a drinking song roared,

"Oh, we can make liquor to sweeten our lips,
Of pumpkins, of parsnips, of walnut tree chips."

Nathaniel was offered the noggin and gulped perhaps a bit more than he should have.

"Been traveling?" asked a burly planter, noticing the short beard on Nathaniel's face.

"Aye, to the Indies and back."

"Have another quaff then." Nathaniel was only too eager to oblige. "Barkeep, another noggin for our seafarin' friend!"

95

"Nathaniel Harte, shipmaster, at your service sir." Introductions were made all around, the group being the local yeomen. Urgent to accomplish his mission, Nathaniel asked the innkeeper for some bread and a bottle of brew.

"Persimmon beer's all we got, by the half-jug."

"I'll take it then," replied Nathaniel. The innkeeper ambled off in no great hurry to fetch the brew. A place was made at the head of the table and Nathaniel took the seat that was urged upon him. There was nothing else to do until the innkeeper reappeared.

The burly planter moseyed over to the hearth, where he took the smoking tongs and selected a conveniently sized ember. At the table, the clay pipes appeared and the tongs were passed around. Soon a blue haze of sot weed smoke filled the room. The conversation turned to taxes. Behind Nathaniel's back, the innkeeper hesitated in the shadows.

"Tell us, Captain, what has been done about this cursed Townsend Act?"

"Nay, I've been to sea these months, but I know the Baltimore merchants have resolved against importation of British goods," said Captain Harte, "Of your Burgesses I know not."

"Well, let us bring you up to the date, good Captain," said the burly planter, red-faced with drink. "George Mason drew up resolves against the Townsend Acts, and they were adopted by the Burgesses. The resolves say only Virginians can levy taxes on Virginians, which seems a natural and scientific principle to me own uneducated mind. We've not been swilled with bumbo at the courthouse on election day to send our men to Parliament. Our man goes to Williamsburg.

Burgesses is our government, and we've got rights, same as any Englishmen."

"Right you are, sir," Harte heartily agreed, perhaps too heartily, but the innkeeper had reappeared with his jug of persimmon brew.

"Rights o' man!" roared everyone at the table. The innkeeper narrowed his eyes and returned to the shadows.

"Nay, Captain, you ain't heard the lot of it yet!" It was an incautious and familiar group of strangers, loosened with drink, united by these new ideas— feelings that they had rights, though they weren't quite sure what they were.

But the innkeeper's eyes narrowed each time the conversation took a more flagrant and dangerous turn. *This talk is sedition—treason! The drunken fools should be hanged,* he thought.

"A group from the Burgesses met at the Raleigh Tavern in Williamsburg and resolved to prohibit all imports of dutiable British goods," said the red-faced planter.

"What of it, then?" said Harte, his interest now piqued.

"What of it, says ye? The group's from the Burgesses itself. Governor's struck blue, I'd say! Which you ain't got no British goods aboard your schooner, now do ye, Captain? Would be a raw time to show up with them; feelings are high."

This was good news for business, and Harte's caution flew out the window. "I daresay I do not, and never will, deal in dutiable British goods," spat Captain Harte, and he laughed and raised the noggin. The table joined in the merriment, while the innkeeper slapped the jug of brew in front of Nathaniel and accepted his money. Nathaniel excused himself and remounted for the last of the ride to Harborton.

Several hours later, the innkeeper stole out of the building and set out on horseback, bearing intelligence of a Captain Harte and his smuggling schooner. He dreamed of the prize money to be had by informing on the smuggler. Nathaniel rode on towards the wooded lane south of Harborton.

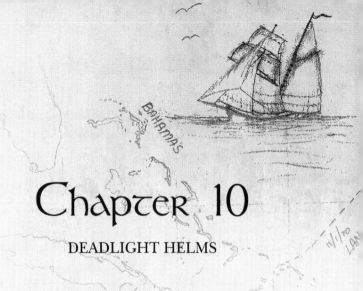

Chapter 10

DEADLIGHT HELMS

Eastern Shore of the Virginia Colony, a Wooded Lane South of Harborton, September, 1770

Anne Easton, as some townswomen now whispered a "stale old maid" of over twenty years, sat sidesaddle on her mare as she toured the empty woodland road south of town. It had been nearly two months since her father had set out on another trading voyage in his topsail schooner. The *Jubilant* was laden with bread, flour, salted pork, and beef: the local goods that were so much craved in the French, Spanish and Dutch islands of the Caribbean. However illegal it was to trade with these foreigners without transshipping the goods through English ports first, smuggling was nevertheless profitable and her father prospered. In any case, it was until recently considered a gentleman's sport. Smuggled French wine was available from any shop along the Chesapeake, yet most ship captains who did bother with the customs house, registered "in ballast"—that is, no cargo to declare, just rocks in the hold for stability.

Any day now her father was expected to return to the Tidewater. Anne had set out on her daily route to exercise her mare. The boughs of oaks and hackberries arched over the rutted lane. Goldfinches flitted in and out of the shadows, and the mockingbirds sang various verses to the consistent refrain of the redwing blackbirds in a nearby marsh. Anne reined in her mount to avoid a limb that had recently been felled acroos the rutted lane.

"Good God!"

Deadlight Helms appeared silently in Anne's path, his left eyelid drooping lifelessly, the rest of his visage animated in an ingratiating grin. A younger man joined him. Greasy scarves were tied about their heads. Anne noted the pistols stuck in their waistbands, and she assured herself that she had loaded the pistols in her saddlebags. Hearing a rustle of shrubbery in back of her, she turned to see a potbellied rogue with unruly white hair thrusting from the sides of his otherwise bald head. He stepped into the rutted lane, blocking the direction from which she had come. His teeth were few and tobacco-stained. The baggy sleeves of all three men's filthy shirts lacked the ruffles of the upper class; their pantaloons ended in raggedness halfway between knee and foot.

"Begging your pardon, Miss Easton, it were never our intention to startle ye. Gideon Helms, at yer service. Ye may call me Deadlight, Milady." Deadlight Helms showed a leg as if he were a gentleman.

"How do you know my name?"

"Shipmate of yer father is I."

"I've never seen you in Harborton before," Anne's eyes narrowed.

"Which yer father and I have been cast off as late. I knew him as a bright young lad, and was in yer father's service this last trip of the *Jubilant*, Milady."

"Where are my father and the *Jubilant*? Has *Jubilant* arrived back in Virginia?"

"Aye, Milady, the *Jubilant* ain't here, nary is your father." Deadlight Helms put on an apologetic look.

"What are you doing here?" asked Anne, her surprise giving way to alarm. *The Jubilant and my father should be here!*

"Ill fortune—that's the long and short of it," replied Helms in a wheedling tone. "Ill fortune and bad luck's the thing, which is why your father has sent us to find you. What a stroke of divine Providence you just happened to be riding towards us on this here lane, giving Godspeed to our long, hard, and troublesome journey on his behalf." Deadlight Helms and his accomplices had in fact lain in ambush and had picked their spot with due care.

"There ain't a moment to be lost, do ye see?" continued Helms in an urgent tone. "Why, even now your father's on a lee shore, and begged us find you at all cost! Which we've had a miserable hard journey at his behest, but lost not a minute. So here ye is, pretty as a painting, comfortable as a sow in mud, and unawares of the danger and anguish your dear father suffers! It pains me sore to bring ye such news!"

"Gideon Helms, tell me directly! What's become of my father? Where is he and what danger is he in?" cried Anne, reining in her suddenly agitated horse, as Deadlight Helms and the others crowded nearer.

"Aye, aye, you'll have it directly from me then, without pretenses, but wouldn't ye care to dismount from that there fine horse so as to hear my tale with greater ease?" Helms asked, as sweetly as he could muster.

"Do you play with me, Deadlight Helms?" cried Anne.

"Avast, not I!" declared Helms. Anne stared from one to the other of his cohorts. She did not recognize these hairy, dirty fellows, for they were certainly not from her father's crew.

"Why, see here, it's like this: your father's run afoul of the Royal Navy."

"Oh my God, have they taken the *Jubilant?*" cried Anne, her voice rising in alarm. It was becoming more common for a smuggler to be caught, and Admiralty Courts now tried the cases, instead of the sympathetic colonial courts.

"Aye, aye," said Helms, "*Jubilant* lies condemned now, with tide watchers aboard, and there's a heavy fine been levied on your dear father by the Admiralty. It's the debtor's prison in Jamaica for him." Helms shook his head in mock dismay. The other dirty fellows mimicked him, rolling their heads from side to side. They looked down at the ground and then shot furtive glances at Anne when they thought they were unseen. Deadlight Helms urged her curiosity to fever pitch; he wanted her to throw caution to the winds and give him what he so craved.

"Debtor's prison! My God! What has happened to my father's funds? He always kept sufficient specie with his agent in Jamaica!" Her caution had flown; Deadlight knew he would find Captain William's hoard at last!

"Aye, aye, and ain't that at the heart of it, my pretty one!" The black spirit of Deadlight Helms soared— he was so close! "It's just so, milady, your father's trusted Jamaican agent, this here Captain William, ain't nowhere to be found; the specie box is gone from his moorings in Kingston. When the Admiralty Court took the *Jubilant,* and your father sent for his money to pay the heavy fine their lordships levied on him, there was nothing to be found of old Captain William." Helms left out the fact that he had raced the fat and lazy British constable to the house of Captain William. Helms and his waterfront scum then ransacked the house, meaning to collect the specie box for their selves. When they could not find it, they beat the old buccaneer until he could be revived no more, demanding to know where the specie was kept. They left Captain William for dead among the ruins of his furnishings.

"Captain William gone, and the specie as well?" cried Anne, incredulous. *This is impossible! Not my father's trusted mentor, Captain William,* she thought. Anne cherished the worldly old sailor's tutelage, reveling in his tales of the buccaneering days and the books he gave her to read. The trusted mentor and lifelong friend of her father would not have absconded with the specie! Anne became guarded.

"Are you sure that Captain William has left Jamaica without word of where he can be found?" asked Anne in a skeptical tone.

"Aye, aye, that's the lay of it, and hard luck it is for your father. I only hope he escapes the jail fever until we can rescue him," said Helms. There were pious looks and heads wagging in mock dismay all round her.

"The jail fever—Jamaica—oh, no!" Anne began to sink into panic. "How do you propose to rescue my father?" asked Anne.

"Aye, aye, strike me blue if ye haven't cut to the quick of it again," said Helms. "We must rescue him, but there's naught I can do for your dear father without your help. Think on it, now! We simple sailors have done our part, and by the grace of Provenance have found ye. Now it's up to you to honor your father's request." Once again Helms bowed his greasy scarf-covered head and looked up at Anne, his one eye wide in his best innocent look, the other eye inert.

"What request is that, Deadlight Helms?"

"Your dear father only needs a recollection from ye, and that will set him free, and that's the lay of it."

"What is this recollection, Helms? You play with me again," said Anne, impatience rising as her caution waned.

"He's told us what he needs to know to pay his fine and escape that hellhole jail!" cried Helms. "Ye see, he's asked us to find out from you where Captain William hides his specie box!" Anne's heart sank in her breast. "Your father says to me, trusted Deadlight Helms—" Helms stole a sidelong glance through his half-shut eye at her, "trusted Deadlight Helms, my dear daughter was thick as fleas with this here Captain William; why, if anyone may know where that scoundrel has hid the specie box, it would be her! 'Thick as fleas,' he said! So your father sent me and me mates to find ye, so we can go back and fetch the specie box, pay the Admiralty fine, and get your suffering father out of that fever-den. If it weren't for that villain Captain William, your father'd be right here now to embrace ye."

"How dare you call old Captain William a villain? I'll have none of it!" cried Anne, confused. In truth she'd never heard of such a specie box either from William or her father. She knew Captain William kept a sizable hoard somewhere safe for her father, for just such an eventuality as this, his ship condemned for smuggling. She also knew in her heart that Captain William was no villain. The conviction that this story of Helms' was all a lie began to take hold. "I believe none of this, Mister Helms!"

Fury born of frustration ignited within Helms, and an involuntary roll of his eye betrayed his rising anger. Helms capped his rage and gulped, then in his most honeyed voice entreated Anne once more, "Begging your pardon, my lady, I'll slit me own throat if I've given ye offense. I meant no harm. A simple seaman I am, with simple words, and if I see the old buccaneer take off with the specie box, I just figured him a rogue."

After this speech, Helms once again swayed his head from side to side and looked up at Anne from under a respectfully lowered brow, the picture of innocence. "But don't ye see? This here Captain William has got your father's gold and specie hid somewhere. Captain William ain't nowhere to be found, and your father needs that fortune to pay off the Admiralty and get out of that there hellhole of a prison." Helms watched carefully as Anne flinched when she heard his last words.

"It weren't nowhere in the captain's house," offered the dirty old fellow next to Helms, showing the palms of his hands, with his shoulders raised in an expression of guileless exasperation.

"Silence fore and aft!" Helms roared suddenly at the witless rogue, his fury bubbling to the surface once more at the fellow's blunder. Deadlight took another step towards Anne's horse.

"You'll get nothing from me, Mister Helms. I'm sorry for your wasted journey, but I shall go to my father's aid myself," declared Anne, bridling her horse. She meant to leave.

"Stand fast and belay there!" ordered Helms as he grabbed the reins of Anne's horse. The rogue behind Anne fingered the handle of a cat-o'-nine-tails he had stuck in his belt. Helms grabbed the bodice of Anne's dress and dragged her off the horse, ripping it open in the process. Anne stumbled to her knees, cold panic and fear gripping her.

"You'll be telling us what we need to know," growled Helms, grabbing one of Anne's wrists as she struggled to get back on her feet.

"I swear I can tell you nothing! I never heard of such a specie box, or where it was kept!" cried Anne.

"Avast your lies!" Helms twisted Anne's wrist and dragged her up, face to face. His breath stank of stale rum and corruption; his face bristled with a week's worth of beard. "Make it easy on yourself and tell where that specie box is." Helms's other hand roughly squeezed one of her breasts that had broken free of her torn bodice. He chuckled at her helplessness.

"Let me go, you dog!" Anne kicked at Helms' knee. With cold fear numbing all her senses, she could hardly feel if her foot connected.

Helms lost his grip on her wrist, and she turned to run. Her escape by the road was blocked fore and aft by the other two rogues, so she took off straight into the woods. The bottom of her dress tore on the blackberry brambles as she crashed through them, and the thorns made deep scratches on her legs.

"Give chase to port and starboard!" ordered Helms in his quarterdeck voice.

Deadlight Helms pursued in the swath Anne had made through the blackberry brambles. Anne made a desperate run, and fueled by her fear, she outdistanced her pursuers in moments that seemed like hours. Her breath burned in her throat and she felt giddy and weak-kneed. She hiked up her dress with both hands as she ran. The sight of the flash of her white thighs through the underbrush spurred her pursuers on, but their sea legs were unused to sprints, and their shouts at last came from a safer distance away. Anne rounded a massive oak and leaned against the far side of it, panting for breath. She felt as if she could not suck enough air down her burning throat. There was no time to rest. The foul oaths of her pursuers drew nearer.

Anne lunged from the protection of the massive tree and ran down a streambed, crouching low behind the bushes along the banks. She ran back towards the road and her horse. Her boot slipped on a root in the streambed, and she tumbled headlong into the shallow water. On her hands and knees she froze, listening for her pursuers. A hundred feet away in the dense woods, Deadlight Helms froze and listened too, for he thought he'd heard a splash. He held his finger to his mouth and glared at the nearest rogue, who caught the meaning of his action and silenced his fellow.

All four now hung in silence, pursuer and pursued, Anne taking her breath in gulps. She heard the crackle of dried twigs snap under the boots of the sailors as they made their way cautiously toward the creek bed. She shot up and ran once more, stumbling over the tree roots and twisting her ankle. Had it not been for her boots, she would have surely broken it. She got up once more and ran on, heedless now of the noise she made. She ran back towards the road and the safety of her horse. Once she got on her mount, no one on foot could catch her.

She slipped on the mud where the road crossed the small stream and went down again on all fours in the ruts. Struggling back onto her feet, she could see her horse in the road a mere fifty feet away. There was a crash of sea boots into the creek bed behind her, and a bloody oath. Anne dashed the last fifty feet to reach her horse. She bounded to leap onto the saddle. With only one more yard to go, an iron grip fastened onto the collar of her dress. She lost her balance and stumbled backwards.

"Belay there!" ordered Deadlight. Her head pulled backwards, Anne stared up at Deadlight's hairy face. There was a smug grin on his full lips.

"Belay there, or I'll snap yer bloody arm!" growled Deadlight as Anne struggled in his grip.

"Let me go!" She tried to twist around out of his grip, but he quickly grabbed a wrist, twisting her arm painfully behind her until she cried out in pain. She was exhausted. Cold fear grew once more in her stomach as he marched her back into the woods. Every time she gave resistance, Helms twisted her arm up behind her back, causing her to yelp with pain.

"Let me go, I know nothing of Captain William's specie box," Anne cried repeatedly, but her cries served only to convince the rogues she was hiding something they could beat out of her.

"This way, lads," Helms called. "Fasten her there," he pointed to a small tree with a low crotch. One of the rogues took off the length of rope that served as his belt and grabbed Anne's free hand, tying the rope around her wrist. Helms pushed her other wrist around the other side of the tree, passed the rope over the crotch, and tied her other wrist. They backed off then to appreciate their work and catch their breath.

"Now, I guess you'll remember where the old villain's specie box is," growled Helms.

Anne twisted around to face him and spat, "Untie me, or my father will take his revenge."

"Your father's in Jamaica, rotting in a debtor's prison. He's no threat to us. I mean to know where that specie box is hid," answered Helms.

"I know nothing of Captain William's specie box."

"We'll see if the cat can't get it out of ye, then," said Helms. The young rogue with the cat-o'-nine-tails took it out of its leather pouch and swung it, hissing, in the air a few times. He grinned broadly, looking forward to inflicting pain.

"Strip her," ordered Helms. The toothless rogue moved in on Anne and she turned towards the tree again.

"Oh no! I tell you, I know nothing," cried Anne. She yelped as the toothless pirate roughly grabbed the collar of her dress from behind and yanked her garments down to her waist. Anne pressed her naked breasts to the tree. The pirate stepped up and reached around to squeeze her breasts. Anne pressed herself into the rough tree bark.

"They'll be time aplenty for that," growled Helms. "Gag her." The toothless rogue took the greasy rag from his head and tried to stuff the rag in her mouth; but Anne bit his hand and drew blood. She spat the foul rag out.

"Aye, aye, we'll be teaching you some discipline," hissed the toothless pirate. He took a handful of Anne's dark blond hair and yanked her head back, and as Anne's head reeled he made fast the gag.

"Stand off now," ordered Helms, "and we'll soon hear the tale of sweet William's specie box, I trust." Turning to the other rogue he said, "Lay it on her."

Anne twisted once again to look at her tormentors, and saw the young rogue with the cat move up and lift his arm. She hugged the tree bark once again and steeled herself for the blow; but nothing could have prepared her. The sting of the first blow took a moment to fully inflame her naked back. She screamed through the gag and pulled with all her might against the knots holding her wrists. She gasped for air and stiffened against the tree as the second blow of the cat landed. Red welts were now rising on her soft skin. Tears streamed from her eyes. She choked when the third lash of the cat landed on her back with a wet slap. Blood now began to drip from the angriest welts.

"No!" Anne screamed through the gag as she twisted once more to face her tormentors.

"Avast there," ordered Helms. The cat-o'-nine-tails hung limp in the callused hands of the pirate. Helms walked towards Anne and she pressed her nakedness once more into the tree bark. "And now let's hear all about sweet William's specie box," cooed Helms in mock gentleness as he untied her gag. Anne gasped for breath.

"For God's sake, I know nothing of it!" pleaded Anne, panting and sweating from the pain.

"Well then, more's the pity," said Helms, fury rising in his cold blue eyes again. He held his hand out. "Give me the cat."

"Oh no!" Anne screamed and she turned and pressed herself into the rough bark of the tree once more. Helms laid on several blows with the cat, back and forth in quick succession.

Anne gasped with pain, choking and unable even to scream. Blood began to trace down the white curves of her back. She finally fainted and sagged against the tree, hanging by her bound wrists.

"Belay all, ya swabs!" hissed the toothless pirate. "Someone's coming!"

Deadlight Helms ducked his head when he saw the horseman through the brambles. "Now mind ye, don't get too hasty to do him in, he may not have heard anything. So do nothing until I give the order."

* * *

Nathaniel heard a feminine scream from the direction of the wooded lane up ahead. There could

111

be nothing but trouble from the tone of it! Digging his heels into his mare's ribs he urged her into a full gallop across an intervening field, dreading the scene he must come upon, and steeled for action. He slowed to a canter as he entered the woods, so as not to overshoot whatever trouble was brewing.

* * *

"Stand and deliver!" ordered Deadlight Helms, leveling a pistol at Harte's head. Two figures suddenly strode into the lane. Nathaniel's mare reared up on her hind legs as he pulled her up short with the reins. Captain Harte instinctively looked sideways and checked the path behind through the corner of his eye, struggling meanwhile to control his prancing mare. He saw a bald pate surrounded by a shock of white hair, and then the potbellied rogue stumbled into the lane, armed with a pistol. Three pistols to his one—he was checked. Had this been the Caribbean, or Tunis, he'd never have let himself be caught out. But this was home, the place he thought of as safe, his refuge. Anger began to stir within him, anger at the invasion of his last retreat.

"I'd as soon blow your head off as look at you, so we'll be taking your saddlebag and what valuables you be carrying."

"You bloody bastards," murmured Harte. His hand began a slow ascent towards his pistol pocket. There were no more words to Harte, but the sound of three pistols being cocked arrested his reach.

"So you jolly rogues are done with me, is it?" A woman's voice came from behind the two rogues in front of Harte. Anne had come round a bend in the trail and was walking towards them, leading her horse, her hands behind her back holding the reins.

"Anne?" cried Nathaniel. She looked like Captain Easton's daughter, but it had been years since he'd last seen her. She looked at him briefly and shook her head, as if to silence him.

Nathaniel was shocked by her condition. Her dress was torn to shreds up to her knees; there were patches of mud at her knees where she must have fallen. Her torn and hastily tied bodice displayed, more than covered, her breasts. She was now a young woman, so much different from when he'd last seen her. She had a slim but womanly physique, no longer the gangly fourteen-year-old he remembered. Aye, her tall forehead and high narrow cheekbones set off large, enchanting eyes; but she was more suntanned than any proper lady Harte had ever seen. The way she held her arms behind her accentuated her womanly figure, and a look of helplessness, as if she were bound. Ugly red welts reached up from her back across her shoulders. Her hair lay in tangles, wet with sweat, and there were streaks of tears on her cheeks.

"Well now, what have we here? Knows the gentleman, does you? Cast yourself loose and come to play with us again?" mocked Deadlight. "Let's have a go, then." He half turned from Harte to Anne. "You'll have a chance to pleasure all of us, Doxie," he scowled.

"Don't you be cutting me out then, mates," said the potbellied rogue behind Harte. "Let's do him in now and have some fun with the girl, proper-like."

"Stand fast and keep your gun on his lordship," ordered Helms. "Now let's get off of the path so as not to be disturbed with our games, Doxie." Anne took a step back as Deadlight approached her. The top lacing of her bodice chose this time to come undone a little more—or had she shrugged it loose? However docile she was playing it, Nathaniel could see a lethal fire in her eyes. The younger rogue could not abide her lewd spectacle and his thirst for rape. He walked sideways towards Anne, keeping his pistol leveled at Harte, but his eyes on Anne's breasts.

"You'll not be getting away again," said the young rogue. "Me mates may as well use you and take our time, seeing as how there be few people ever on this road. Then it's to be the end of you." He leered at her breasts, which were nearly completely exposed. Five paces from her he looked down and lowered his pistol into his belt so he could rip the rest of her dress off.

"Stand fast, ye dog!" The young rogue found himself looking down the half-inch-diameter barrel of Anne's pistol. He froze.

Deadlight Helms scoffed and leveled his pistol at Anne from the other side. Anne whipped her other arm up, her trembling hand aiming a second pistol between Deadlight's eyes.

"Dare thou test my mettle?" gritted Anne through teeth clenched in pain. "You'd not be the first pirates I've sent to the Devil."

Deadlight slowly backed away behind the old toothless rogue. "Now look at this, mates," he snickered, "a doxie holding a man's weapon!"

"It looks to me as if a woman equally armed has you taken full aback," spat Anne.

"Aye, aye, look's like she's got our young mate pissing his pants!" sneered Deadlight. "The look of a doxie with a pistol has got him dismasted. Ha! Shoot her, ye son of a whore!" The young rogue slowly drew his pistol out of his waistband, his breath short and his hand trembling. Deadlight crept behind the potbellied rogue, putting the old man between himself and Anne's pistol. "Shoot the witch!" hissed Deadlight. The toothless old man took his pistol aim off Nathaniel and turned toward Anne, aiming his pistol at arm's length. The weapon trembled at the end of his outstretched arm.

Now! Captain Harte whipped his own pistol out of his waistcoat, aiming it at Deadlight as the pirate spun around. Nathaniel's weapon misfired. Deadlight fired his pistol as Nathaniel lunged out of his saddle. The two men crashed to the ground, Nathaniel using the butt of his pistol like a club, Deadlight drawing his dagger. Nathaniel's horse reared above the struggle. Four more rapid shots roared out. The struggling men paid no heed. Deadlight regained his feet and slashed Nathaniel's cheek to the bone. Nathaniel staggered backwards as Deadlight slashed again and again at Nathaniel's belly. Nathaniel stuck his misfired pistol in his waistband and crouched, his hands open and his arms held wide, dodging the deadly blade and looking for his chance. But he backed into a tree and Deadlight lunged for the kill. Harte grabbed Deadlight's wrist and spun towards the tree, and Deadlight's dagger stuck deep in the bark. Harte grabbed for his pistol butt and brought it down on the side of Deadlight's head. Deadlight staggered backwards, cast a glance to where his comrades had been, spun on his heels, and ran off.

The woods fell silent as a tomb. Harte's cheek seared and blood streamed down the front of his shirt. He regained the rutted lane on wobbly legs, and witnessed Anne standing where he'd last seen her, a smoking pistol in each of her hands, arms lowered, staring into space and sobbing. The two pirates were on the ground on their backs, glassy eyes staring unblinking at the sky, ripped cloth and red gore in the middle of their chests.

"Are you unharmed, Anne?" She seemed not to hear him. He strode up to her, holding the gash on his face to stem the blood flow. "Anne . . . Anne, are ye hurt?" He walked right in front of her and reached out, putting a bloody hand gently on her cheek. Her eyes focused once more at his touch.

"The bloody dogs are dead, Anne; the other's run off. Are ye hurt?"

She rallied, "Do you see any bullet holes in me?" Nathaniel blushed. She was barely covered. "I've been lashed with a cat-o'-nine-tails."

"Good God!"

"They were going to kill me."

"Bloody Hell!"

"My father's in prison, or so that pirate, Deadlight Helms said. *Jubilant*'s been condemned in Jamaica for smuggling."

Nathaniel opened his mouth as if to speak, but uttered nothing. *Jubilant* was *Berbice*'s sister ship, both belonging to Captain Easton. Nathaniel commanded *Berbice* in the employ of Captain Easton, taking larger and larger shares in the cargoes in each as he could afford them. Now they could both be ruined. It was he who now stared off into the woods, seeing naught, dumbstruck by his own misfortune.

"Captain Harte, have ye been struck on the head?"

"Stabbed in the vitals!"

"How so? We must dress the wound."

"Nay, a figure of speech; my only cut is on my face."

"I shall sew it up. In a fortnight it shall be good as new."

"Are ye a surgeon, then?"

"Sewed up many a jack tar when I sailed with my father—oh God! Could it be true? *Jubilant* condemned?"

"We were chased by the Navy at Cape Charles."

"Then they do begin to enforce the Navigation Acts."

"It is so."

"They said my father is in jail."

"I must pay his fine; he's my cherished benefactor and employer. I shall bribe whom I must to get him free. The Jamaica jail is an unhealthy place."

"I shall be part of any rescue, Captain. It's my own dear father we speak of."

"But this will be a wicked business—bribery and the seamier parts of Kingston before it's ended."

"We must away, then! Not a moment to lose!"

"But, Anne, there could be foul play, as you've very well seen today, perpetrated on yourself. I trust you want to know little more of these things. A lucky shot!" He glanced at the bodies of the pirates.

"Aye, aye, Captain, but two, as you say, lucky shots. I marvel that you think there was no skill involved!"

"It is no endeavor for a young woman, however skilled a marksman," Captain Harte maintained.

"There's a little metal lever on that thing that will fire a pistol shot, Captain; you don't have to use it as a club," Anne laughed, pointing at Harte's dangling pistol with the smoking one in her left hand. "It really is more convenient." With that quip she overflowed into hysterical laughter, nearly shrieking at times, as the horror of the preceding moments echoed in the empty forest air.

"I fear you make jest of me. Who taught you to fire a pistol?"

"My father gave me a quick lesson as we drew away from the Barbary Coast; the rest I learned in the rigging that day."

"My compliments to your father on a timely lesson, and to you, Anne, for a timely deliverance. These pirates were going to shoot me."

"Anne Easton at your service, Captain." She imitated the typical male introduction and made a leg. Nathaniel's wobbly legs nearly failed him as he looked down the front of her dress.

"Captain Nathaniel Harte, at your service, milady," said Harte, his voice cracking while he bowed. "I thank you for delivering me." He took off his blue jacket and placed it over her shoulders, and was again shocked to see the angry red welts and droplets of blood on her back.

"Think nothing of it, Captain, but I pray we be gone from this awful place. Shall we ride on and get you sewn up? You'll have a scar to match my father's." She attempted to button Nathaniel's jacket to cover her nakedness, her hands trembling and fumbling.

"Aye, we must see to your injuries first, milady: Ye must be in terrible pain."

She answered with a nod and when she blinked, another set of tears rolled down her cheeks. "Let us be gone, Captain."

"With pleasure, milady." Harte's estimation of the capabilities of womankind had just undergone a shocking revision. He respected the boldness and bravery of his fellow men, with whom a mutual respect and companionship was shared. Now he was confronted with a woman who commanded the same sort of respect. They mounted their horses and rode toward Harborton in silence.

At length Nathaniel said, "I think it unwise to report this to the sheriff, should he discover any hint of smuggling, he'll be after some prize money. We still need to unload *Berbice.*"

"Where do you discharge your cargo?"

"Harborton. I was on my way to make the arrangements."

"Then we'll be off to Jamaica?"

"It's my duty to Captain Easton, if the story that Deadlight Helms tells is true. I know only that *Jubilant* was bound for Jamaica. If you are determined, I cannot deny his daughter passage. I can promise dealing with the customs, and the Admiralty will be a rum business. We must keep a watch out for Deadlight Helms, though I think he has no wish to confront the law."

"They keep sending us convicts from England; some of them are the meanest sort of villain," Anne shuddered. "Transportation, they call it, as if the colonies were the end of the world, and not decent society."

"What did you do when you weren't sailing the seas with your father?" said Nathaniel, to shift Anne's thinking away from her ordeal at the hands of the pirates.

"My father wanted me educated, so I got what education is allowed women on shore—not much, I may add—and my father tutored me aboard ship. As you know, mother died when I was young. My father had interesting friends in many ports, and it was always a treat to learn from them what I could."

A treat for them as well, thought Nathaniel.

"Then there was an unfortunate incident in Algiers," said Anne. "I daresay the Sultan's men wanted to abduct me to sell as a Christian slave for someone's harem. When we again reached the colonies, my father enrolled me in a subscription school for the finishing education of young ladies in Baltimore. Ha! Some idea of finishing education, it was a needle and spinning shop in disguise as education and refinement. There was no Latin or Greek, only spinning and needlework, the proper pastime of illiterate and proper young ladies. Poise and appearance, this was all that our headmistress thought went into the making of a woman. She had us sit for a couple of hours a day strapped to a board to make our backs flat. She made us wear sheet-metal or wooden stays to make our waists slim. And as for books, the only thing that ignorant wretch did with them was to put them on our heads and make us walk around like African stevedores, to train us in poise."

Nathaniel chuckled, so Anne decided to tell him the rest of it. "I had a falling out with the witch when she rapped my knuckles cruelly while at the spinning wheel. 'This is the *proper* start,' says she, and she tied the most lubberly granny knot I've ever been embarrassed to see. To which I replied that her knot work wouldn't be worth a fart in a gale of wind."

Nathaniel let out an uncontrollable peal of laughter, for he'd heard the oath many a time aboard ship, but never from lips as genteel and delicate as Anne's. The contrast between the grizzled old sailors and the lovely creature that had just uttered such an oath tickled Nathaniel no end.

"So how did the matron of the laboring children take your oath?" asked Nathaniel.

"I was delivered forthwith back to my father's house—not without a whipping first, of course," said Anne. "He sent me to another boarding school, saying he could not raise me as a wild thing on the sea. I do so long to go to sea again! I shall never forgive him for sending me away. I fear we have grown apart because of it; I do not fit into the mold of what he wanted a daughter to be. I could never bring myself to become a powder puff."

The sun was setting when Anne and Nathaniel approached Harborton, and Anne led the way to a house overlooking the round, deep cove from which the town got its name. It was a house befitting a prosperous mariner, as was Captain Easton, until late. The house was white clapboard of two stories, with a high-pitched roof and gables on the second story. Every window was equipped with shutters on iron hinges, painted a charcoal gray. On the very top was a widow's walk, surrounded by a white turned-post fence. In the Eastern Shore fashion, the house was only one room wide, so the breezes of summer could flow through unimpeded. There was a brick landing in front of the house entrance and great hall, located in the center section. The great hall extended right through the center section, with vaulted ceiling and staircase, and there was another set of doors which opened via another brick landing to the back of the house, where the outbuildings were located.

The dependencies included the kitchen, smokehouse, a cold storage house for foodstuffs sunk deep into the cool earth, a well house, stables with tack room and stable servants' quarters, a workshop, and tool shed. A formal garden occupied the middle of the square formed by the dependencies. A kitchen vegetable and herb garden of large proportions lay in back. There was another entrance to the house near the kitchen, which led to an antechamber used to warm and stage meals, next to the dining room.

The stable boy took their horses, eyes wide as saucers when he viewed the condition of his mistress. Anne directed Nathaniel down the brick walkway to the well house where he could clean himself up in privacy. Ellie, the Easton's diminutive teenage house servant, appeared and Anne gave her a heartfelt hug.

"My God, what has happened to thee, mistress?"

"Pirates on the road, Ellie; pray fetch me wash water, a poultice and some rum."

Ellie caught her breath and curtsied again before she rushed out, reappearing in moments with hot, moist towels and a collection of herbs to tend to Anne's wounds, and bottles of rum and limejuice. The two women retired to the upper floors, Anne taking along the bottle of rum to deaden the pain. Nathaniel stationed himself in the well house and began to wash. He heard yelps of pain from an open upstairs window as Ellie cleaned and poulticed the welts Anne had suffered from the wicked cat-o'-nine-tails.

At length Ellie reappeared at the well house, where she stood and looked Nathaniel up and down. She then asked for his soiled clothes. He was immensely grateful to have his best shore side rig put in for repairs, and told Ellie. "But what am I to wear in the meantime?" he asked. Ellie produced what must have been one of Captain Easton's rigs, and Nathaniel tried them on. The knee breeches had quite a bit more paunch and were too short, but they'd do while his own were laid up for overhaul.

Nathaniel emerged from the well house without his boots, which were being cleaned by a stable boy. This fact was immediately noted by Barnardo, the chief gander and leader of the Easton household's flock of domestic geese. Barnardo and his flock roamed the house grounds and the streets nearby at will, terrorizing with their raucous alarm any late-night strollers that passed the house. As Nathaniel padded on bare feet toward the outhouse, Barnardo made his charge, wings flapping, neck extended, bill gnashing in menace and the most threatening squawking. It was a close race, with Nathaniel barely gaining the door ahead of Barnardo. Captain Harte heaved a sigh and sat to the necessary, only to see Barnardo 's head appear under the door and begin to peck at his bare feet. Barnardo had poor Nathaniel fairly dancing at his seat until the all-observant Ellie chased the beast off with a birch-splint broom, effecting Captain Harte's second rescue at the hands of the fairer sex that day.

Anne appeared again as Nathaniel strode into the central hall of the Easton house. She stifled a giggle at his appearance. "Please forgive Barnardo; he feels he's watchman while my father is away—when father is here as well, for that matter. We may have to put a goose yoke on him," she said. "You must accept the hospitality of my father's house, and my deepest thanks for your heroic rescue today." She put one finger to her lips and wagged the other at Harte as he began to protest this last statement. He nodded dumbly at Anne.

Ellie appeared with a tray on which were a needle and silk thread, two glasses containing a precious teaspoon of limejuice and rind, and a squat blue bottle of rum.

"Captain, please," said Anne as she poured one of the glasses full of rum and handed it to Nathaniel.

"With pleasure, thank you," said Nathaniel, and he took a swallow with relish.

"Now sit, Captain. We have to sew you up. Perhaps you should have a bit more killdevil first?"

"Aye, aye, Mistress, another spot of rum, if you please. I shall have a scar to match the Old Man— er, Captain Easton's, begging your pardon, but mine shall be on the left cheek, and his is on the right."

"Hold steady, Captain; you mustn't speak. Have another swallow of rum; I am ready with the needle."

"In case I shall be sewn up and stiffened beyond speech, I must give my thanks to Ellie for delivering me from the vicious bill of Barnardo."

Ellie curtsied, her cheeks reddened, and the diminutive fourteen-year-old Scotch-Irish girl rushed from the room.

"She really is quite a help to us. She runs the household quite efficiently. Father bought her indenture one day when a Bristol brig came to Harborton. The poor girl and the other unfortunates were paraded through Harborton in chains to the auction. My father's heart broke; he claimed she looked like my mother when she was young, so he paid off her passage.

"Ouch!"

"Be still! There, that's the last of it. In a week or so you can pluck the stitches back out."

Ellie reappeared, and after a second of shock at seeing the black threads crisscrossing Nathaniel's cheek she declared, "Marlinspike work, milady!"

"Thank you, Ellie; it is the badge of a hero. The Captain was wounded in my rescue."

Reinforced with her rum and lime, and soothed with Ellie's poultices, Anne repaired to the kitchen outbuilding. On return she declared, "I've directed the cook to bring us supper directly. It will be such a treat for you after your long sea voyage: roasted oysters and blue crabs!"

"Aye, aye, a welcome novelty." Even if Nathaniel had eaten the same for the last six months, he would have said this, for he was foremost a Virginia gentleman.

A spoon bread pudding made from cornmeal and dried huckleberries, close as raisins in a plum pudding, came as the first course. Then they dined on the bounty of the Chesapeake, followed by a rectangular "trap" pie, without an upper crust—apple, of course. They washed it down with good quantities of Madeira, a specialty import of Easton's smuggling schooners. "Captain, this has been one of the most horrifying, trying, exhausting days of my life, and I wish to beg your leave until the morrow," said Anne.

"Aye, aye, your father would be proud of the account you've made of yourself today. We were in greater hazard than I realized. I shall be about his deliverance as soon as we can get *Berbice* back out to sea."

"I assure you, Nathaniel, I shall be part of that deliverance." She curtsied and strode off to the staircase in the great hall. Nathaniel's cheeks burned at hearing her call him by his first name. The butterflies came back to his stomach, and he gripped the arms of the chair.

As she passed the spirits cabinet, Anne took out another bottle. It was going to take more than Ellie's poultice to reach a comforting sleep this night! As she undressed in her bedroom, she looked at the welts on her shoulders in the mirror and shuddered in renewed horror. Exhausted by the violence and emotion of the day, Anne was soon asleep. She did not hear the night watch, a young man and a gentleman of a more sober age, carrying lantern and rattle. They walked past the darkened Easton household and cried out, "Midnight, and the clouds are clearing."

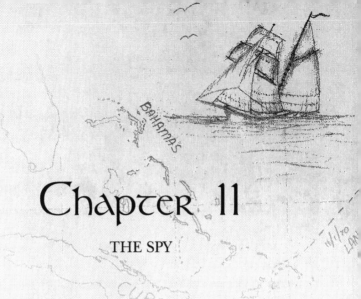

Chapter 11

THE SPY

Nathaniel sought accommodation in a tavern by the town dock. He walked in the door, and as his eyes grew accustomed to the dim candlelight, he observed the interior consisted of one large room, with a lean-to shed attached as an afterthought, where the family bed lay on the sanded floor. In the middle of the room were two long puncheon tables. Benches without backs sat at the tables, as well as several very well-worn Windsor chairs, which found their level by virtue of pressing their uneven legs into the dirt floor to a greater or lesser extent. One sole customer sat with his back to Harte at one of the tables. Harte took his seat at the other. Along one wall was the bar, behind which the rum kegs and beer were kept, and it was evident that meetings and spirits were the main entertainments. The place fairly swarmed with children who, from their uniform reddish hair, appeared to be the progeny of their prolific mother, a red-haired woman not yet twenty-two, who sat on a three-legged stool near the hearth, engaged in sewing. The fireplace and hearth occupied one entire wall. A black smoke stain ran up the wall above the fireplace and onto the ceiling of rough-hewn beams and shake shingles.

The innkeeper stood up from a table to greet Harte. He was a short, portly fellow with a bald head rimmed by white hair that thrust out above his ears like a fallen halo. "Good evening to you, sir, and what be your pleasure? We've an assortment of the finest fruit brandy and killdevil rum. Would your fancy go to a rum punch? We've the fresh limes and sugar. Or will ye have some metheglin or hot mulled ale? Do ye fancy a flip?"

"A flip, good sir," answered Captain Harte. Flip fitted his fancy, since a chill was on the evening air, and the novelty of the country brews had in no way worn off. The proprietor set about preparing this drink, first thrusting a poker into the embers of the fire, and then drawing off a generous half-tankard of pumpkin beer. Into the wooden tankard he added a dram of rum. This rum, Harte could tell from the trademark burned into the cask, had arrived in the colony from Puerto Rico, in spite of the Navigation Acts. The potbellied innkeeper removed the top of a large earthenware jar of brown sugar, and before thrusting his hand into the stuff, looked over his shoulder at Harte and asked, "Would sweet or sour be your fancy, sir?"

"Mild sweet, if you please," replied Harte, at which the innkeeper thrust his hand into the crock, letting a certain amount of the brown sugar sift back through his fingers. The sugar that remained in his hand, he tossed into the tankard. He then licked his fingers. With a flourish, he delivered the tankard to the table Harte occupied, and then retrieved the red-hot poker from the embers. The tankard danced on the tabletop when the red-hot point was thrust into the brew; an aromatic steam rose from it and mixed with the haze of tobacco and wood smoke in the room. A sip of the stuff and Harte sighed, relaxing his saddle-sore haunches, trying but failing to find a comfortable position on the wooden seat of the chair. He cast his eye over to the gentleman seated at the other table, who had shifted his own position to face Harte across the gap. The man's garb was plain, all severe black and white—not even a gray tone broke the somber vestment of this gentleman.

"I've not seen thee before, and I expect you're a traveler," stated the preacher in a proprietary tone. "Where dost thou worship? To what church dost thou belong?" It was a leading question, innocent enough on the face of it, which Harte decided to parry.

"On the sea generally, is where I worship," replied Captain Harte, dreading the equivalent of a religious press-gang that was surely to come next.

"Ah, a sailorman! I should have known it from your immodest dress. Tell me, sir, is it true the tales I sometimes hear of what an ungodly lot sailors are? Surely not you, of course, sir," said the preacher, in a condescending manner, believing only that he had correctly baited and was now reeling in the fish. He planned to exhort Captain Harte on his sinful nature and press him to contribute to his own private charity. But with religious freedom in the colony, Captain Harte was feeling this fellow impertinent, as well as feeling his own saddle sores, possibly one confused with, or aggravating, the other.

"I consider myself closer to God than most, sir," answered Harte, an enthusiast of the Enlightened Age of Reason, "for I am nearly always in the awesome grasp of the wave, wind, and tide and must follow God's natural laws under pain of death! It is an unceasing and close relationship I have with creation, natural laws, and the Creator. The natural laws can be understood by any intelligent man. Have ye heard of Sir Isaac Newton? I thought not. Anyway, the Creator has set the universe in motion according to natural laws, and if we but understand these, there are no limits to the improvements and progress that can be made! Take ship design, for instance . . . ." Captain Harte stopped, for he could see the preacher's eyes had glazed over.

"But a consecrated house of the Lord is the only proper place of worship, as you must surely know. Ye sailor lot should spend your time ashore seeking forgiveness, and less in fornication," said the preacher through a counterfeit smile, ignoring Harte's remarks, for it was his habit not to listen to argument. The preacher's tactic was to embarrass and humiliate with whatever may lie latent in the conscience of his fish, and to set his hook in some raw flesh of remorse.

Captain Harte ignored the direct insult, and having no soft flesh of troubling conscience into which the preacher's hook could be set, said in reply, "I spend the majority of my days under the clear blue or the raging torrent, with naught between me and the power of nature. There's no better place for worship. I don't mean for the limit of an appointed hour or so, on the Sabbath, sir, like some landsmen. No, sir, I mean watch on watch, every day. Nature's my church. Why would I need to cower under some roof made by the imperfect hand of man?" *Especially your roof, you sanctimonious whoreson*, thought Nathaniel.

"But only in church can be found the divine presence, pure and uncorrupted," contended the preacher.

"I've certainly a feeling of uncorrupted divine presence when I view an unbroken sky above my naked head and the clear deep blue below my keel off-soundings, yeah, or under the celestial sparkle of the navigation stars on a clear night. There's no purer element than the sea, off-soundings, sir— the corruption begins only as ye draw near the settlements!"

"You speak only of the savage wastes; there is naught for man's soul in such deserts. I have the joy of knowing God." The preacher beamed his fabricated smile.

"Savage nature may be, at times, sir, but not waste! Doesn't your dismissal of the finest work of the Creator as so much waste, strike you as ingratitude of the meanest sort? Now as to your second point, we all have our aptitudes, Preacher," said Captain Harte, "and yours is perhaps to know the Creator at a pretty fair offing from his works—in the lee, I'd say, of the settlements, under the roof of a church. But my predilections are those of a sailor, abiding mainly in the watery parts of the world, being surrounded by nature itself, which I take to be the Creator's masterpiece – aye perhaps all of nature is the Creator himself!"

"Ah, a pantheist! Like Spinosa, the excommunicated Jew. God is a fatherly diety, Sir, not this corruption that surrounds us!"

Harte continued on his lay line to windward, "There's a freedom of spirit afloat, sir, a lightness of mind and a joy in the small and simple workings of the ship. The sea is ruled by the natural law of the Creator, which has its own logic and order. There be none of the artifices of human meanness prevailing on the water, sir . . ." at that point Harte hesitated and added, "with the exceptions of pirates and the Navigation Acts."

A sly smile spread across the preacher's face when he heard those last two words. Then he continued, "The Bible sayeth nothing of freedom, sir, of spirit or otherwise, but only of your obligation to enslave yourself to the will of God."

And you are an aspiring slave master, thought Captain Harte. Harte said aloud, in a more controlled vein, "Give me the simple beauty of the wind and the wave for my place of worship."

"Only divine Providence maketh the heavens move and the winds blow, dear sir, and you are powerless," said the preacher, the condescending grin now pasted on his face. "But to get back to my point, it seems you have strayed from the righteous path with these Cartesian rationalist delusions of science and reason. Heresy! You verge on atheism! Divine presence must be sought only on consecrated ground, at very least on every Sabbath. You must be converted, or ye have no hope of salvation. You will tremble before the awesome power. You must be converted by an emotional experience; it is a pity you seek not your salvation."

"Salvation from whom? The Royal Navy perchance?"

"Through the guidance of the men of the cloth. Surely you cannot give credence to your pathetic insights while suffering in the corrupt world?"

"I hold with Anne Hutchinson. I can experience the wisdom of my God as well as you."

"Another excommunicated heretic!"

"As for your emotional experiences and salvation," maintained Harte, "there's naught can compare with a landfall at the end of a dangerous and trying voyage: rock and headland, mountains that burst from spray and spume and disappear in a cloud mist that drifts about the forest and the island parrots. How about the egret glowing brilliantly against the marsh grass in the sunset hours when the water turns all manner of diverse colors in infinite pattern? That's divine work to be appreciated by us mortals, and as consecrated as I need. Aye, sir, if you've ever witnessed it from a wooden deck, you're sure to see awesome power in the wrath of a squall line, which hath settled many a sailor's account. Sailor Jack decides to haul in his canvas or not, according to his understanding of the natural laws of the squall line. If he's fool enough to fly all his canvas, he may drown for it, but that ain't the hand of God, sir, it's wind on canvas and an overpowered hull."

"I am saved, Captain, and fear not the wind, but you stand on the edge of eternal flames! Ye must be saved, sir, ye must seek salvation!"

"I do indeed feel saved, after the emotional experience of three days in a full gale. Your church is a timorous haven of safety, sir! I meet my God full and by." With that, Captain Harte slammed his empty tankard on the table.

The preacher stared dumbly from his seat across the gulf between the tables. He was impressed by the heartfelt and impassioned speech of Captain Harte, and a bit envious, for Harte's speech reminded him of the oratory of the more accomplished preachers he tried to emulate. As for the content, Harte may as soon have been explaining spherical trigonometry to the man. As the moment of envy passed, the preacher rose abruptly from his rude peg-legged bench and regained his condescending attitude.

"Heretical doctrines of the excommunicated! I can see bringing the word to drunken and fornicating sailormen will take extreme efforts and patience. Good evening." With that insult, the preacher turned and tramped out the door of the tavern. Harte snorted, for the insult of the narrow-shouldered zealot wasn't worth a challenge.

The preacher trotted from the ordinary to the stable. "Find my horse!" he hissed to the stable boy. He was soon off to the royal customs house at Accomack with due haste. As Nathaniel's luck would have it, the preacher was one of the many colonials paid by the royal customs service to spy on the smuggling activities of their countrymen. The preacher only hoped the ship had not yet been unloaded, and he could get there in time to be the first informant. Aye, and reap a share of the prize money!

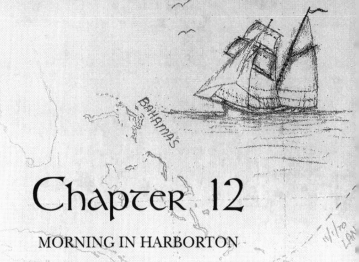

Chapter 12

MORNING IN HARBORTON

Master Shipwright Mathias Davis was always awake before sunrise. This morning the quiet restfulness of twilight had not yet given way to the boisterousness that sunrise brought to Chesapeake country. The night's insect symphony had stood down, and the daily cacophony of birds, beasts, and men had not yet filled the silence. He stood and drew a chest full of air through his nose, savoring the smells. He took another stroke on the timber at his feet with his broadax. The nutty smell of newly hewn oak was his favorite. It mingled with the aromatic freshness of the sawn cedar planks stacked several yards upwind. As he sighted down a white-oak apron timber, he could see in the background the glassy calm waters of Harborton. Between him and the water lay the timber sleepers on which newly built ships slid into the deep waters of Harborton Cove.

Down by the water's edge was a strip of light yellow sandy beach. The water of the cove, a gray sheet, outlined deep green reflections of the overhanging pines that lined the opposite shore. Dewdrops on the timber sleepers and tufts of grass along the path to the water sparkled in the first direct rays of sunlight, bejeweling the path. Mathias straightened from his work to stretch. Above the scent of the fresh timber, hanging in the air with the cool mist and water vapor, was the mixed aroma of living soil and pine. His broadax rang again in the morning stillness as it bit into the virgin white-oak timber. A blue heron took flight, squawking a raucous protest to this sharp imposition of industry into the primeval calm of the dawn. Mathias straightened again to watch the huge bird glide past the pines overhanging the water. He saw the heron's mirrored reflection flying upside-down directly beneath, cutting through the deep green reflections of trees on the water.

Mathias picked up his next tick mark and began to work the broadax toward it to hew out a graceful curve. This timber would define the saucy bow of another "Virginia-built flyer," as the British naval officers called the small schooners. The broadax rang out as he found his rhythm and became absorbed in the graceful curve taking shape at his feet. Captain Easton's new schooner began to take shape.

* * *

Fowlkes Tavern rested along the road two leagues from Harborton, near the cypress swamp ford. The tavern was a roughhewn two-story post-and-beam structure painted ocher on the outside, with brown shutters. A local institution, it was over a hundred years old. Travelers could find food and drink there, news was eagerly exchanged, and the benches of the front porch or dimly lit tables inside hosted transactions of the local businesses of farming, fishing, and boat carpentry.

The tavern was a place to buy seed or sell produce, a place where loads of merchandise could be organized into a cargo for Baltimore, Annapolis, Norfolk, or the West Indies. Here extra hands could be found either for the plough, before the mast, or the quarterdeck. Privateering, of course, topped all, both in adventure and profit, but this required a war and an expensive bond from the government equal to the cost of the vessel. The last privateering had ended with the Treaty of Paris in 1763. Nowadays there was much enthusiasm for the lucrative business of smuggling, a massive black market undertaken under the noses of the commissioners of His Majesty's customs and the newly-vigilant Royal Navy.

At Fowlkes Tavern, one could make arrangements to discreetly and quite profitably dispose of a cargo from the French or the Dutch West Indies, far away from the customs house in Accomack. There were few colonial skippers who didn't have some contraband stuffed behind the heaviest casks in the hold of their ships. The small shallow-draft colonial schooners and sloops could enter any one of hundreds of creeks that lined the Chesapeake, and discharge cargo tens of miles from the nearest customs house.

Israel Fowlkes, proprietor, was a lusty individual who enjoyed life—that is, everything sensual in life. His triple chins bounced as he smiled and nodded at the barmaids. If there were women, drink, or food at hand, he was game, and an experienced connoisseur of all three. The swell of his brocade vest tended to be speckled with bits and drops of the day's menu. His obvious enjoyment of his surroundings, especially the consumables in them, gave him a personal magnetism. It was difficult to dislike a man who was always so much in heaven. As Nathaniel Harte entered, he nodded to Israel Fowlkes, who answered with a hearty greeting and proffered a tankard.

"Sit, Captain Harte; it's been three months and more. Settle thee with some hard cider and tell me of your adventures."

"Aye, aye, Israel, my adventures of this last voyage are not over! Everything hangs by a thread. We were chased into the bay by a naval brig with the frigate *Rainbow* and her squadron behind her, and escaped by luck. The *Berbice* stands off and on as we speak and still holds her cargo, a ripe prize for the Navy, informants, and the customs. It's to you I look, good friend, for a successful conclusion."

"Quaff thy drink and speak of your needs in low tones, my friend. There has been more than one curious rogue about, and I fear they spy for the royal customs."

"And what be the look of these knaves?"

"Indeed, a self-styled preacher, too interested in what ships are just come in, and if they be off-loaded as yet."

"Dressed in plain black and white?"

"Aye, aye; ye've clapped eye on the creature?"

"Spun philosophy with the same, for which he did me the compliment of naming me *Fornicator marinus*."

"*Hor hor*! Barmaid, more cider! Will ye step to, lass?"

"How long past did the holy man pass through?"

"Late last night; he could be in Accomack customs house as we speak."

"Strike me blue! There be another?"

"That Tory of the King's Head Ordinary, now that you raise the question, came through last evening."

"He's a Tory?"

"Aye, aye, Nathaniel, did ye mind the name of his tavern?"

"Damn me, if I've split my garboard on him!"

"Did ye mention thy business?"

"Aye, aye, that and a few precious words for the Navigation Acts!"

"Then I expect he vies to be first to the customs house."

"Damn and blast!"

"There be another."

"It could be no worse!"

"Aye, aye, Nathaniel, a strange one with a drooping eyelid."

"Blood and thunder!"

"Ye know that one, too?"

"He offered to send me to the Devil with a pistol pointed at my head, and I daresay he's done Captain Easton's daughter far worse."

"I knew he'd the foul scent of a vagabond! Said he was an honest seaman, of course, merely inquiring as to the sailings to the south this next week."

"Is the hellhound still about?"

"Nay, I doubt it; asked about where the *Glad Tidings*, at anchor in Harborton, was bound."

"Where is *Glad Tidings* bound?"

"Jamaica."

"Devil take me, what ill luck!"

"By the powers, Nathaniel! What sort of mischief confounds ye?"

"There'll be time enough hence to spin that yarn, Israel, but for now, there's not a moment to lose! I require a great many oxcarts and wagons tonight in Harborton. Make arrangements for the barns and storehouses. And the merchants, whosoever can proffer specie; I am in great need of it. Captain Easton is in jail in Jamaica."

"Didn't old Captain William keep a hoard for just such an occasion?"

"If the dog with the drooping eye can be believed, Captain William is dead."

"By that scoundrel's hand, I'll wager."

"Aye, aye, but he bothered Captain Easton's daughter for the hoard's whereabouts, so there's still a chance to find it first and bail Captain Easton out."

"By thunder!" Israel slapped his meaty hand on the oak table. "There ain't a moment to lose! That vagabond with the drooping eye is bound for Jamaica!"

"Let us unload *Berbice* this very night, and I shall be off! There's a chance we can out sail them." Nathaniel drained his mug and stood to go.

* * *

The midshipman of the *Inflexible* was at this very moment galloping towards the customs house in Accomack. As the horse was driven mercilessly onwards, its rider dreamed of the betrayal of smugglers in the moonlight—and prize money!

* * *

Captain Harte left Fowlkes Tavern and rode his horse back to Harborton. With foreboding, he approached the sheriff's office. What if the rogues Anne had dispatched were from the community, well known and possibly liked, and only secretly thieves? Would he and Anne be questioned when the murders were discovered? What if he and Anne were accused of murder? *Duels are tolerated, the death of two highway robbers at the hands of a sea captain should not be too suspicious.* It depended on the reception of his word on the events. He could well hang if things went badly. Of course, it would be unthinkable to involve Anne; he was committed to that. She would be hanged for sure, rape or no. The stocks, the pillory, and the whipping post were in sight in front of the meetinghouse as Captain Harte approached. The grim sight made him giddy.

In front of the jail, Captain Harte saw an oxcart out the back of which protruded four human feet. A group of people stood around the morbid scene, in the midst of them the constable. The constable was a huge man, both in girth and height, these being his principal and popularly recognized qualifications for the job. He did a great service of rounding up rowdy drunks and seasoning them in the stocks until fit for society once more. He was a little out of his depth when it came to the finer points of jurisprudence and investigation.

Captain Harte secured his horse a few fathoms down the street and edged closer to the group on foot. *Could these be the bodies of the men Anne shot?*

"That's the one, sir, sure as I'm looking at him, what robbed me on the 'Nancock road, and his bloody friend to boot!"

Robbed? Thought Captain Harte when he overheard this, *Could it be them?* A general agreement murmured through the crowd; apparently amongst them were some past victims of these thieves. There were nods and affirmations, all of which the constable took in as sworn testimony. Captain Harte looked on noncommittally, and stole a glance at the faces of the dead men in the dung cart. He recognized the red stains in the middle of their chests, the stubbly beards; they even died with snarls engraved on their faces. Someone had relieved them of their pistols, cloaks, and shoes, but not their socks. Random toes protruded from their stockings.

"Then who killed them?" inquired the constable. He pointed to each of the persons testifying against the deceased. "You kill them?" he asked in staccato fire. There were negative mumbles and shaking heads all around.

"Maybe they killed each other," volunteered a twiggy adolescent, whose arms and legs exceeded the length of his homespun shirtsleeves and trousers by a good foot.

"Maybe so," conceded the constable. If his constituency was in general agreement that these were the very highwaymen that had been plaguing travelers between Onancock and the Custis plantation, then he was satisfied and pleased that his domain was once more in order. In his simple mind he reasoned, *Why wouldn't desperate men shoot each other?*

"Let's go to the sheriff then, you who've been wronged by these fellows, and have done with it," proclaimed the constable. *Identify the rogues for the sheriff and that will be the end of it.* The constable was well pleased. So was Captain Harte, as he stole away, as if from a passing curiosity, using all his control to keep his pace to an unconcerned amble.

Captain Harte dropped into the general store at the wharf and lounged while his raging pulse slowed and his temples stopped throbbing. Harte grinned with fascination to see some of his own smuggled goods for sale on the shelves, and caught his breath at the prices asked. He picked up a long, thin bottle of milky Bristol glass labeled Bloom of Circassia, and read that it would "bring a rosy hue to the cheeks that would not be rubbed off with a handkerchief." There was Eau de Fluers de Venice, Venetian Bloom Water. Harte raised the small tinted bottle and read, "Without dispute the most excellent cosmetic or beauty wash ever discovered." Harte browsed on, amazed at the bombastic verbiage. He chose an elegant-looking jar, Lady Molyneux's Italian Paste, "guaranteed to make the roughest skin like velvet and a preventive to sunburn." Nathaniel thought this could be construed as an insult, and the lady of his current fantasy was not to be trifled with; besides, she seemed indifferent to the maintenance of her complexion. Most ladies he knew—indeed, even small girls—went out-of-doors equipped with a mask to protect their faces from the sun, and of course gloves well past the elbows, and a bonnet. Nathaniel continued to graze among the scented waters, "for preserving the bloom of youth." He settled on some and brought them to the shopkeeper.

"I pray, how much for this one?" asked Harte.

"In pay, pay as money, hard money, or credit?" asked the shopkeeper. "I'll not give credit to a seafarer. Have you grain, pork, or beef? It is two shilling six in pay, at twice the government rate."

"Nay, I have no provisions for pay," said Harte.

"Pay as money then, one shilling and six. Have you *rials* or pieces of eight?" asked the shopkeeper. Harte shook his head.

"In hard money then, one shilling," said the shopkeeper.

"Eight pence," countered Harte, "or I'm off to Baltimore, where the luxuries ain't so dear."

The shopkeeper rubbed his chin at the expected counter, giving adequate time to make it seem he'd given thorough consideration. "I can give it over to ye at ten pence, and it is wonderful gent a perfume to be had at such a price. You should try it on spoiled meat—it'll make it savory for the table. Have ye interest in silk and ribbons for the lady, as well?"

"Ten pence then, English coin, which has been neither sweated nor pinched," said Harte with a wry grin. He bade the shopkeeper good day and headed back to his horse. He couldn't help but grin as he passed the dung cart pirates, remembering their threat, "I'd just as soon blow your head off as look at you."

"It's to the Devil with you, foul bastards," Captain Harte muttered as he strode past and gave a mock bow. A large collection of flies had gathered to suck the juices from their wounds, lips, and eyes.

Now that he considered Anne safe, Nathaniel's attention focused on the unloading of *Berbice* and the start of yet another voyage. Ordineaux would bring *Berbice* into Harborton this very night, and a small regiment of oxcarts and stevedores would be mobilized in the moonlight to unload and quickly disperse the cargo. There was much to do.

* * *

In his mansion in Onancock, the sheriff snorted his displeasure and shuffled once again through the papers lying on a massive oak desk. He looked up at his clerk and snorted again. "Preposterous!" he said, waving a filthy parchment scrawled with large irregular letters in the air. "Does that simpleton of a constable think I can report this to the governor? I'd be the laughingstock of the colonies! The one stood with a hole in his heart, took aim and shot the other expertly in the same manner? Is that the conclusion of my gigantic simpleton of a constable? This exceeds in absurdity his report that Hosea Thompson 'woke up dead' one morning last year. Woke up dead! Damn and blast!" His eruption quelled momentarily and he asked his clerk, "At least we're reasonably sure these two rogues were robbing travelers on the road to the Custis plantation?"

"Yes, Your Honor, we've testimony of the victims," said the clerk.

"These rogues could have come to their just end in a thousand ways," said the sheriff. "What bothers me is that most likely they were done in by someone the likes of themselves, and we'll be hearing from those fellows in turn. Write my report to say we suspect they were murdered by some of their partners in crime. We have eyewitnesses who identified the bodies as the rogues who were robbing travelers along the road south. Say no more; write it thus."

* * *

Inflexible's Midshipman Adams was riding his mount to a lather but could not reach the Accomack customs house soon enough. There was prize money to be had! The collector at Accomack received one hundred forty-two pounds nineteen from the Crown that year, his portion of the duties collected, and little enough for a collector of customs of the time. Captain Stirling of the *Rainbow* received twenty-five pounds per annum for his constant sea duty, and Lieutenant Lloyd received nine pounds per annum from the Royal Navy. Skilled labor in the colony could command fourteen pounds per annum. The midshipmen and crew of *Inflexible* received wages of nineteen shillings a month. Prize money was the dream of every officer and tar in the British Navy, for it was the only way to amass any small fortune.

"Midshipman Adams, sir!" the young man burst into the ten-by-ten office space of the Accomack customs house, located at the end of a warehouse. "I am here to make complaint and supply information on a smuggler!"

"Whereabouts, lad?" Isaac Smith, the collector, sat up to attention at the prospect of prize money.

"Last seen headed north on this side of the bay, sir, a yellow and black schooner," replied the breathless midshipman.

"My lad, there are over one hundred schooners sailing out of my district, and fully half or more are painted yellow and black. I'm afraid you'll have to do better," said the collector. The midshipman's heart sank; he'd not considered the smuggler could be lost to them. The collector pondered the limited alternatives open to the smuggler: There were only two bayside ports available to land a seagoing cargo, smuggled or not. Excitement sprouted in his venal boots.

"How did ye come to this place?" inquired the collector.

"Overnighted in Cherrystone, then sailed straight for the Pungoteague," replied the innocent young man.

"And of course the smuggler was not to be seen in Cherrystone?" asked the collector, faking boredom and disdain for the midshipman's information.

"No, sir," said the distraught midshipman, his dreams of prize money and wealth in the process of being dashed on the rocks.

"Not much we can do, I guess; I'm sorry your efforts have come to naught," commiserated the collector. "If it's any consolation, two others were here just this morning, all in a lather to report on a certain sea captain, but did not know where his vessel was, or even what kind of vessel he commands. Of course, if this Captain Harte walks into this office, I shall give his papers and his vessel extra scrutiny, and perhaps something may be in it for the informants. You can hope for the same—that is, if I happen across any yellow and black schooners in this landlocked place." The collector tittered and turned his back on the midshipman. The midshipman returned to his mount and led the exhausted animal away on foot. The collector immediately scribbled out a legal form. After an anxiously measured period of time the collector set off to see the constable, to serve him with a Writ of Assistance.

* * *

An hour or so passed as the depressed midshipman led his mount toward Harborton, where his men dallied on the waterfront. The young man's spirits began to rise again, and with the optimism and energy of youth he determined to gather his men and check the waterfront in Harborton; after all, there was little else to do until they were to be collected by *Inflexible*. He cantered into Harborton and directly to the pier where his men had gathered as ordered—all but one of them.

"Where's Wilson?" demanded the midshipman of the cox'n.

"Took to his heels as soon as we come ashore and your back was turned, sir," answered the cox'n.

"We'll put out the word and he'll hang for it," threatened the midshipman, for indeed if the deserter were caught he would hang. The midshipman tried to look dangerous to the grown men of twice his strength under his command.

"Beggin' your pardon, sir," said the cox'n, shifting his raw muscle uneasily from foot to foot. "There's to be a landing tonight, sir, smuggled goods to be sure."

The midshipman gave up his affected attitude of deadly authority and lapsed into a more characteristic boyish enthusiasm. "Tonight, is it?" he said. "Then we're bound for prize money if we play it right, men! Let us make an obvious departure, and a cloaked return!"

With that, the little band shoved the ship's boat into the water and gave way down the creek with a will, the midshipman standing in the stern sheets with overflowing excitement. The men at the oars burst into a randy shanty that would have put each in the stocks or worse if uttered within earshot of the civilized citizenry. Near the mouth of the Pungoteague they pulled into a tiny creek that snaked into the marshes and waited impatiently for sundown. As they lay about the open boat the sailors smoked long-stemmed pipes filled with tobacco acquired while in Harborton. The smoke kept most of the mosquitoes at bay. Such were the luxuries of this special service!

Chapter 13

A PETTY TYRANT BROUGHT LOW

The night after chasing *Berbice*, the British ten-gun brig *Inflexible* had worked off the shoal at the mouth of the Chesapeake and returned to the squadron. On return, Lieutenant Lloyd's presence was requested via signal flags aboard Squadron Commander Captain Walter Stirling's frigate *Rainbow*. "Repair aboard flag at once!" the signal flags demanded, once decoded by the midshipmen aboard *Inflexible*. The midshipmen exchanged cautious looks. The "at once" had ominous import, under the circumstances.

When he arrived in the greatcabin of the flagship to see his lordship the commander, Lieutenant Lloyd was not asked to sit down. He stood uncomfortably before the seated Captain Stirling, who was reading through some papers, seemingly oblivious to Lloyd's presence. Lieutenant Lloyd's gruff demeanor began to fall away with the minutes. Captain Stirling was a demigod, and here Lieutenant Lloyd was an underling, not the supreme lord he played on *Inflexible*. He began to feel like a schoolboy brought up to the headmaster for punishment. Indeed, this feeling was never far below the surface in Lieutenant Lloyd, but as he exercised his little autocracy aboard the *Inflexible*, it was easily ignored.

Captain Stirling, fully aware of Lieutenant Lloyd's presence, chose to ignore the subordinate and continued to pursue a letter from John Williams, inspector general of the royal customs service. The letter contained intelligence on the smuggling trade along the Rappahannock River:

American Customs Commissioners, Virginia

Honourable Sirs,

May it please you, I beg to put before you the Facts pertaining to recent Accusations made against this person by the Honourable Inspector General of the American Customs, regarding a Bribe of twenty pounds to release the schooner Berbice in April, 1769, and also allowing the schooner Jubilant to unload without proper papers. Upon my Sacred Honour, I wish to assure Your Excellencies that these accusations are inaccurate, and must stem from a lack of Understanding on the part of the Inspector General as to the details of these transactions, due to the brevity of his visit, which I cannot fault, since the Honourable Inspector General endeavours to carry out the King's business with the utmost efficiency.

By your leave, allow me to provide the Facts in these matters as follows: Jubilant was at the time bound by proper Bond to produce said papers within a limited time, and, as your Most Obedient and Humble Servant, I was loath to impede the Flow of Commerce over such a Trifle.

Regarding the matter of the Berbice and what the Honourable Inspector General has seen fit to characterize as a Bribe, let it be known by these Presents that according to the Prerogatives held by virtue of my Office as Royal Customs Collector, I had already determined to release the Berbice prior to said Bribe being proffered, which I Refused. Besides which it was only twelve pounds. As to the matter of the lack of a cash box in the Collector's Office, may it please you to know I carry out transactions at mine own House. The amount due the Crown has been fully detailed and Balance Due is in my custody, to the complete Satisfaction of the Honourable Inspector General.

I am most respectfully
Gentlemen
Your Honours' most Obedient and most Humble Servant

Captain Stirling leafed through more pages sent from the Royal Customs Inspector's report, his eyebrows rising another inch with every page.

> ...as elsewhere in the Chesapeake, ships enter from Rotterdam, Harve de Grace, St. Ubes, Leghorn, Lisbon, Oporto, Madeira, and from many Foreign and British West Indies islands: ships, brigs, snows, schooners, and sloops, this diverse Commerce being Uniform only as to arrival in this port in ballast...

"In ballast, my ass," grumbled Captain Stirling, slapping the letter down on his desk. He shot an irritated glance at the waiting lieutenant.

Lloyd's uniform was impeccable, as was the grooming of his orange-red hair and fingernails. He would no sooner have exhibited himself in shabby uniform than he would have mutilated his own flesh. The longer Lieutenant Lloyd stood before the captain, the more his self-confidence melted away, until he was soon fidgeting and shifting from foot to foot. Captain Stirling sensed the change in Lloyd's demeanor from captain to schoolboy.

"Lieutenant Lloyd, if I may have your written report—that is, if we're not keeping you from pursuing prize money?" said Captain Stirling at long last.

"No, sir; I will submit it directly, sir," said Lloyd.

"And I'm sure this report will include a tale of exemplary British seamanship?" asked the commander sarcastically. "Let me be more direct," he said after a pause in which Lieutenant Lloyd managed only a few gurgles. "Is the *Inflexible* damaged?"

"N-no, sir," answered Lieutenant Lloyd, thinking, *After all, pumping the bilges a bit more often doesn't mean real damage.* He stung from the sarcasm, something

154

he relished giving out himself. Winding up on the humiliating receiving end was his biggest nightmare.

"It may not bother the colonials to wreck their ships on these shores, but let's mind to our charts, shall we, Mr. Lloyd? Have you ever heard of a sounding lead, Mr. Lloyd? You do understand that breakers mean shallow water; *don't you*?" This last phase was a controlled shout. "Wreck a king's ship in fair weather and in broad daylight, and I shall have you court-martialed, do you understand? I am so embarrassed by your poor seamanship, I refuse to write a report on it to my superiors, for fear it may reflect negatively on my command. Put on a poor show like that again, sir, and I shall report you, *out of the service*! Well? What say you?"

"Y-yes, sir."

"If you've nothing more important to do, Mr. Lloyd, I'll be sending my orders to the *Inflexible* directly. You shall be soon enjoying the climate of Jamaica." That the commander had dropped his rank from his title when addressing him, stung Lieutenant Lloyd. He lived for his rank, and advancing it. He relished the power it gave him over others. He never let the lower strata forget where they stood in relationship to himself. The world for Lieutenant Lloyd was clearly divided between those who had power over him, and those over whom he had power—functionally, those he had to please at all costs, no matter what he thought of them, and those he could make miserable for his own entertainment. He usually wallowed in self-importance.

A very humiliated Lieutenant Lloyd left the greatcabin and returned to the *Inflexible*, ever more determined to get his revenge on the colonials for this episode. If he ever sighted that yellow and black schooner again, well! Meanwhile, the living was going to be hard for those out of favor aboard *Inflexible*.

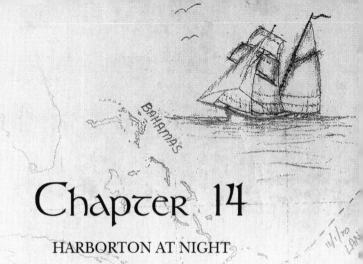

Chapter 14

HARBORTON AT NIGHT

"Ellie, I cannot decide what to bring! My seagoing clothes for sure, but what if I must go before the Admiralty Court or the governor—what then?"

"Then bring everything! And put it all in that big trunk, Anne, my dear."

"There would never be enough room in the *Berbice*, Ellie! I must decide."

"What about starting with the wee things, say your toilet and makeup box?"

"I was thinking of leaving it behind. If I should appear before a judge or the governor, I shall want to cut as innocent a figure as possible. They have painted ladies enough in Jamaica, so I hear."

Thus the evening prior to *Berbice's* departure was spent by Anne and the house servant Ellie: packing, unpacking, and packing again. Who could foretell the situations for which she must prepare? Indeed, in the end all was for naught; what Anne least expected to be of use saved the day, again and again.

"Aren't you frightened of the long voyage at sea, Anne?"

"After my mother died, I took many voyages with my father. It was wonderful. The liberty one feels gliding across the vast sparkling sea! No old women gossiping about one's every move and word. Then there were the new places to see at the end of the voyage. Ellie, how I loved that life!"

"Why don't you sail with your father now?"

"He put me ashore to attend a boarding school so I could find a husband and have babies." Anne made a spitting sound. "I'd sooner put myself in jail."

Ellie wondered that anyone could prefer a roving life on the perilous sea to the safety and comfort of the house in which they stood. But her mistress was a special sort of woman, educated in letters, for one thing. Anne had organized a small troupe to put on bits of Shakespeare at Fowlkes Tavern. That got the Harborton gossip tongues wagging, allowing that an education was not becoming for a young woman of Anne's station in life. Perhaps this was the motivation for her mistress' wanderlust.

Just after dark, Anne had got it down to what she hoped would be an acceptably small luggage consisting of but three trunks. Ellie was dispatched to fetch the stable boy to help load the luggage into the chaise. She pranced down the staircase into the great hall, turned, and padded out the back door towards the stable. As she cleared the door, she was grabbed from behind, a callused hand over her mouth, and her arm was twisted up behind her back. She tried to scream, but the hand muffled her attempt, and then the pain of her twisted arm took her breath away. She gulped in a silent scream and groped helplessly with her free hand.

"Where's the mistress? Quick now, or I'll run ye through, lass!" hissed her assailant.

Ellie shook her head, but the man twisted her arm higher behind her back until she danced a gruesome jig on her tiptoes.

"A sound and I'll carve out your vitals, now show me to her, quiet like." He turned to push her back toward the door, and she felt the hot stab of a dagger tip pierce the soft flesh of her back.

Then a cacophony from the gates of Hades blasted in from behind Ellie's captor. Barnardo and a half dozen other geese were right at her attacker's heels, pecking, beating their wings, and raising raucous alarm.

He let Ellie go to face the surprise fury, and Ellie whipped round inside the back door and slammed it. She fumbled with the bolt, and her attacker pushed the door part way open from the outside. She threw her body against it to shut it again, but her hands were trembling so she could not grasp the bolt. The door smashed open and sent Ellie sprawling onto the floor of the great hall. She screamed and looked up at a man in the shadow of the threshold, with a rag-bound head and a drooping eyelid, menace and death in his other bloodshot eye.

"Murder! Help! Murder!" she screamed.

In the bedchamber above, Anne's scalp tingled in cold fear. She had not reloaded her pistols! She ran into her father's bedchamber and grabbed a saber from over the fireplace, and then took the stairs two at a time. When she saw the drooping eyelid in the shadows of the back door, she was overcome with rage and made a wild charge at the hated man, holding her saber in front like the cavalry. Her slipper skidded on the Oriental rug and she sprawled headlong in the hallway, the sword at Deadlight's feet. He moved forward and dropped his boot on the blade, fastening it to the floor, and chuckled at her defeat.

Ellie wrestled a musket from the wall rack in the hall. She nearly dropped it when she pulled it away and bore the full weight of it. She crouched and rested the muzzle on one thigh, while with both of her delicate hands she cocked the lock, as she'd seen the militia do on parade days. Deadlight Helms looked up when he heard the familiar click to find Ellie holding the cocked piece by her hip; she couldn't lift it to her shoulder. Ellie squeezed the trigger, the pan fizzled, and the weapon roared out, filling the hall with the acrid smell of burned gunpowder. Anne felt the wind of the shot pass close over her head. Ellie screamed at the deafening roar and kick of the musket and dropped it at her feet. She covered her face with her hands, only her wide eyes visible.

"Did I kill him?"

"No, Ellie." There was neither man nor goose on the back-door stoop. Deadlight Helms had disappeared. Anne sat up on the floor and looked round at Ellie. "I've never seen that last part in the parade ground drill, Ellie; you must instruct the sergeant about it! All arms to drop, is it?" They chuckled at her joke, but their elation was mostly from victory.

Ellie picked up the musket, which was fully as long as she was tall, and said with newfound fascination, "Show me how it is loaded." Hence both pistols and the musket were reloaded, Anne instructing while Ellie took to the lesson with enthusiasm. Here was power over evil even she could wield!

With Ellie standing guard at the bottom of the ladder, Anne ascended into the attic, to search out a chest not opened since her father dragged it up there at the end of the French and Indian war in sixty-three. She lifted the oak lid, and a faint smell of the sea, tobacco, and sweat permeated the air. She took out a handkerchief and held it to her face, and as she recognized the odors, the tears came. She stuffed the handkerchief in her bodice and rummaged through the chest. She found a tomahawk, a bayonet, another set of pistols, and a ditty bag with her father's slops, the clothes he wore aboard the privateer. She gathered up the bayonet, pistols, and ditty bag. Returning down the ladder by candlelight, she gave the pistols to Ellie to load.

Back in her own bedchamber, she flung open the three chests so carefully packed an hour before and began tossing out the contents, fixing on an item now and then and carefully placing these necessities in the ditty bag. Now it was time to go aboard the *Berbice*.

"What does Deadlight want of you, Anne?"

"He's after a hoard he thinks Captain William kept for my father."

"Is there such a hoard?"

"I don't know for sure."

"Your father has been good to me, Anne; I shall do all I can to help. What shall I do now?"

"Stay with the house and run things as before, for with luck we shall all return, and soon. For now, Ellie, can you guard my back? I'll wager Deadlight Helms lurks somewhere out there."

* * *

"Aye, aye, Anne; I'm with you!" In a moment, Ellie presented herself in the hall with the musket, not the smaller pistols; and she had figured out how to affix the bayonet. Musket and bayonet now towered above the skinny girl.

"Isn't it too big for you, Ellie?"

"Aye! But you should've seen his eyes when he saw this pointing his way!"

"And the bayonet?"

"He shall not get close enough to stab me again, as I live!"

So the two set out in the darkness, Indian-style, scampering from bush to bush, to the landing where Berbice was due. Ellie took the rear guard, struggling with the heavy musket, the bayonet pointed at the stars. They crept from hedge to hedge, taking a roundabout way to the landing, as the direct road was beginning to bustle with oxcarts and men preparing to unload the Berbice. The men carried lanterns and hallooed to each other in passing. Anne did not want her name to be spoken out loud or to be seen on the road, for she was sure the miscreant with the drooping eyelid lurked somewhere.

Making for the harbor, they crept behind a tree for a view of the threshold to the dock. Near the foot of the dock was a lean-to, a lantern hung on its opposite side lighting up the dock. Anne rose to walk to the dock, but Ellie suddenly grabbed her and pulled her back behind the tree.

"Ellie!"

"*Shush*! It's him."

Deadlight was there, hiding in the shadows behind the lean-to near the foot of the dock and peeking around the corner every time he heard a new voice. He'd come prepared: slung round his neck by a lanyard were two pistols; a saber glinted in the moonlight, ready in his hand.

"What will you do now?"

"I have an idea, but we must hurry! Back to the house; let us run!"

* * *

Anne, her wind gone from the run back to the house, climbed back into the attic and threw open her father's old sea chest. There they were! His old sailor slops, and not too awfully large for her!

"Ellie, we must hurry!"

Petite Ellie slouched against the front door in the great hall, the musket leaning up against the corner. Red-faced and panting from the exertion of toting the musket to and from the harbor, she rolled her eyes up toward the voice calling from the attic and rallied, "Coming!"

Anne suddenly peeked over the banister, face flushed with excitement. "Bring needle, wax, and thread!"

In a moment, while Ellie was still trying to get her woefully strained muscles to move, Anne popped over the banister again. "And some tar from the tool shed!"

They set to work on turning Anne into a credible-looking sailor Jack, complete with tarred ponytail.

* * *

Berbice made way into the mouth of Pungoteague Creek in the dark of early evening, sailing up the creek from the Chesapeake. The ship made a quiet gurgle as she glided through the dark. This night there was little moon, but the crisp, clear sky was aglow with stars, clearly visible from one horizon to the other. A gentle, warm breeze from the southwest carried a faint scent of mimosa, bayberry, and pine. Phosphorescent comb jellyfish exploded in orange fireballs in *Berbice's* wake, and microscopic diatoms made yellow-orange fire out of the foam made by her bow wave and the eddies of her keel.

Berbice's faint moon-shadow passed over a raccoon by the edge of the marsh grass on the shore. The raccoon, masked as if for a costume ball, looked towards *Berbice,* and not at what she was doing with her paws. She felt along the edge of an oyster shell until she found the hinge, set her thumbs into it, and pulled the shells apart with apparent lack of effort. Still looking in *Berbice's* direction, she pulled the oyster from the shell and washed it in the creek water. Only then did she partake of the shellfish, her uncomprehending gaze still fixed on the silent motion of the ship.

A blue heron stood atop a fallen cedar branch at the water's edge. The weathered limb shone bone-white in the faint moonlight. As *Berbice* approached, the heron jumped aloft and squawked as if it were being strangled, ripping the evening stillness asunder.

On the lee shore, a vixen sniffed the air in a newly harvested cornfield. She watched the *Berbice* glide by on the last whispers of the evening breeze. With her nose held high in the air, she drew in the exotic scents of *Berbice's* cargo of pepper, ginger, gunpowder, nutmeg, cinnamon, saffron, and cloves. Only the vixen noticed *Inflexible's* boat put out of the marshes in pursuit, with oars muffled.

Ordineaux brought *Berbice* into the Harborton cove, and a swarm of lighters came alongside and attached themselves to the moving ship. Israel Fowlkes was one of the first aboard, approaching in a small rowboat. Ordineaux stood bemused as heavyset Israel was pushed from below, pulled from above, and finally rolled over *Berbice's* bulwark. "Everything is at ready aboard ship," said Ordineaux.

"Everything is ready ashore," gasped Israel, short of breath from his exertions hoisting himself over the side of the ship. Dispatch in off-loading the cargo was now everything. It appeared as if a candlelight parade had begun from the *Berbice* at the waterfront up into Harborton itself, with stragglers roving out into the countryside. The sails on *Berbice* were triced up, drawn up to their gaffs like curtains instead of being lowered, since this was faster. Even before *Berbice* made fast to the town pier, bales and sacks were being loaded into the lighters. Israel checked his lists with the lighter captains and dispatched them.

Once *Berbice* was made fast to the town pier, two continuous lines of men rolled casks and carried wooden boxes to the waiting oxcarts. Captain Harte kept the shore side operations organized and moving, ready to relieve anyone who so much as slowed in their relay race with time. It would never do to be here when dawn broke! He walked off the dock and up the road a couple hundred feet to help untangle a knot of oxcarts and swearing yeomen.

The oxcarts rumbled off to their prearranged barns and cellars, the warehouses of smuggling infrastructure. Some of these barns were over a hundred years old, having been used for smuggling since the first of the British Navigation Acts were passed in 1673. Most of the cargo would be shipped on to Norfolk, Annapolis, and Baltimore in smaller, inconspicuous shallops and fishing boats, not the kind of boats in which one would expect to find casks of Dutch gunpowder from Curacao or sacks of sugar from Guadeloupe! *Berbice's* cargo included French wines, brandy, and molasses; satins and silk; a variety of manufactured goods from Germany, France, and Holland; tea shipped via the West Indies; salt; limes; and a collection of spices.

Three generations of men and boys toiled to unload *Berbice* in the darkness. It was business as usual, but business at considerable risk. There was a feeling of brotherhood and community among the men and boys who toiled that night, and a little triumph of defiance against their common oppressor, the British Parliament. Some of them had joined the local Sons of Liberty during the Stamp Act crisis; some had even been in Annapolis and helped tear down the Stamp Act Commissioner's house, board by board, the night of the riot.

* * *

Around a giant oak that stood a hundred feet off the road, unseen eyes observed the oxcarts moving in the night. It was almost too good to be true: The midshipman had been right!

* * *

Ordineaux searched around in the hold with a manifest in his hand, directing men to unload this cask or that chest, while Israel Fowlkes sat on the ladder that led from the main deck up to the quarterdeck. Captain Harte noted with satisfaction from the dock that somehow Ordineaux had obtained wood at the Custis plantation to repair the shot holes in *Berbice's* bulwarks. *Berbice* was most vulnerable now, tied to the end of a dock, divulging her smuggled cargo.

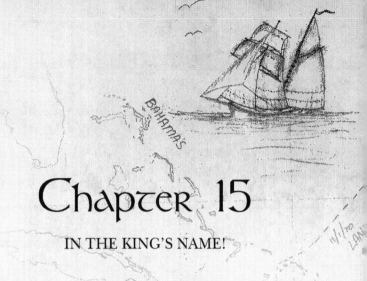

Chapter 15

IN THE KING'S NAME!

"Stand fast! In the King's name!" The order was bellowed from the shore by *Inflexible's* cox'n. Two shots rang out as punctuation to the order. "Stand fast, damn you!" squealed the midshipman, as he raced out onto the pier with his armed sailors. Instantly Harborton became littered with abandoned oxcarts. Trapped by the midshipman and his crew, those caught on the pier dove into the black water and swam for it, their swimming strokes lighting up the phosphorescence in the water. Israel Fowlkes was unceremoniously dumped over the side of the *Berbice* into a small boat. Ordineaux cast off the stern line and called to let fall the main and mizzen. Bosun Tiny cut the bow line and hauled up the jib.

Captain Harte ran towards the *Berbice* behind the trees. *Blast! We've been found out! The Navy's on the town pier!* Harte dashed into the water and began to swim. *Inflexible's* midshipman was strutting down the pier, now deserted except for the five sailors under his command.

Isaac Smith of the royal customs service arrived by carriage, the driver thrashing at the idled oxen blocking the road. The constable, who rode outside next to the driver, climbed stiff-legged from the high seat, while Customs Collector Isaac Smith emerged from the padded carriage. "That will do, Mr. Midshipman," called Isaac Smith as he reached the threshold of the dock. "I will take charge of the prize now."

"The prize is ours, sir!" contended the midshipman. His men filed up behind him at attention; it was their rightful prize money, too.

"You have no jurisdiction ashore, or even near it! You've no legal claim to this prize; but I thank you for identifying the vessel for me, young man," said the customs collector, his cold manner giving away his smug triumph.

"The prize belongs to *Inflexible!*" shouted the midshipman, turning red with anger. The collector was stealing a fortune in prize money from under his very nose.

The dock lines having been cast off as soon as the *Inflexible's* men had appeared; *Berbice* now drifted ten feet off the pier. By the time Collector Isaac Smith paraded down to the end of the town pier, *Berbice* had dropped her main and mizzen from their tricing lines and was slowly wheeling on her backed jib.

Collector Smith glared at Ordineaux across a dozen feet of water. "I demand you belay and let me and the constable board! I am seizing this vessel in the king's name!" As he spoke, oxcarts still laden with merchandise were quietly disappearing from the streets of Harborton.

"What in ever for, governor? We've just put in for instructions; we've nothing to unload here," said Ordineaux.

"Where are your papers? Where did you clear? Where did you come from? I demand to come aboard this instant!" Collector Smith screamed.

"We're in ballast, Collector, and you have no right without a warrant," shouted Ordineaux across the growing gulf of water.

Captain Harte slithered over the opposite bulwark and flopped onto the deck in a pool of water. The *Berbice* continued to drift away from the pier. The situation was fast getting out of his control, for the customs service had no boats in which to pursue *Berbice*. The midshipman had remained in the middle of the pier, red-faced and mute in rage, backed by his men, all glaring, not at *Berbice*, but at Collector Isaac Smith. The collector wheeled on them and screamed, "Board that vessel at once! Level your weapons on that man!" The Royal Navy men stood stock-still.

Collector Smith, now in the grip of his own rage, screamed at the midshipman, "I demand you have your men level their weapons and fire on that man! You must seize that vessel!"

"You've no officer's commission, sir! And you do not give orders to the Royal Navy, sir!" spat the midshipman. He and his men stood frozen in place, the butts of their muskets placed firmly on the deck of the pier.

"You little prig!" Collector Smith shouted in the face of the midshipman. "I'll have you before the Admiralty Court!"

"Not bloody likely," answered the midshipman, emboldened by his outrage.

"You useless little fool!" raged the collector.

"I demand satisfaction, sir!" answered the midshipman.

"Piss on you!" countered the collector, and he turned to storm back down the pier.

The midshipman pulled his pistol from his belt and leveled it at the collector's back. There was murder in his blind fury. "Mr. Collector, sir! Stand your ground and face me! I demand satisfaction!"

Age, tempered with more reason, intervened at the last moment. An iron grip clasped the midshipman's wrist and raised the weapon up. "We've buggered him enough for one night without putting a pistol ball up his arse as well, sir," said the cox'n with a friendly wink. Had it been Lieutenant Lloyd, the cox'n would have hanged for touching an officer, but then the cox'n wouldn't have thought of interfering with Lloyd's self-inflicted demise, either. The cox'n had the young midshipman down as a better sort of young gentleman.

The defeated collector stomped back up the town dock, to find his way blocked by the massive body of a wandering ox. "Out of the way!" He kicked at the huge dumb beast and was answered with a volcanic fart.

While the Royal Navy was thus engaged, Israel Fowlkes rowed over to *Inflexible's* longboat, which was drawn up on the beach some distance from the dock. Israel frantically looked the boat over, poking the wooden planks with the tip of his sheath knife. Near the stem he found what he was looking for, a soft spot in the hood-end of a plank, below the waterline. He dug through the rotted wood, making sure he made no obvious hole that would be seen. He probed until he'd made a slit clean through the plank, just enough so the leak would go unnoticed for a precious few minutes. With luck, someone would put his foot on the plank and break it free, sinking the boat. For good measure, he wedged his knife in next to the boat's stem and loosened the hood ends of the adjoining planks.

* * *

Anne and Ellie had bolted both doors and windows against another appearance of Deadlight Helms. Ellie was just finishing tarring the braid she'd made in Anne's hair, now cut to proper seaman's length, when someone came pounding on the front door.

"Anne, open up. Hurry!"

"Who's there?" Anne demanded from a second-story window.

"It is I, Israel! Anne, there is not a moment to lose! The customs collector raided us, and the *Berbice* has made sail!"

"The Devil take me, it can't be!" wailed Anne.

"Quick now, we must ride to the sandbar on the point! Mind, bring thou a lantern!"

Anne donned her father's privateering slops she and Ellie had sewn together to fit her smaller frame. His old cocked hat completed the outfit. She grabbed the ditty bag and ran to the stable. It appeared as if a young sailor on horseback had joined Israel.

"Where's Anne?" Israel asked the young sailor.

"Right here, Israel," Anne answered.

"I'll be buggered, I'd have taken ye for a Jack tar! But why do you masquerade so?"

"There's a man with a drooping eyelid; he is trying to kidnap me," Anne started to explain. They started off at an easy trot through the streets of Harborton.

"Aye, aye, I've heard the yarn from Captain Harte. So that's the lay of it! My dear, you cut as handsome a sailor Jack as ever was, fear not on that account. We must be off to the sandbar on the point before *Berbice* fetches it. The *Inflexible's* boat will not be far behind. They had a disagreement with the royal customs over seizure of the *Berbice* tonight. I've no doubt they lust for their prize money yet."

Deadlight Helms ducked into the bushes when he heard the riders approach. He saw the corpulent innkeeper and a young sailor ride by. When he was sure they were far enough away, he stepped back into the street and headed back to Captain Easton's house, to keep a lookout for his daughter.

Anne and Israel took off at a gallop outside of town, bound for a narrow neck of land that extended into Pungoteague Creek, the last dry land before hundreds of acres of impassable salt marsh that bordered the creek and the Chesapeake. When they reached the point, they were relieved to see *Berbice* still upstream of them, ghosting down the channel. Israel lit the lantern and raised and dipped it in the private signal.

"Lantern off the port bow!"

"Aye, aye, the private signal, Captain."

"Lower the jollyboat, keep way on. *Inflexible's* longboat shall not be far behind."

"Aye, aye, Captain. Unfasten the falls, port and starboard, Atticus! Man the starboard falls . . . together, now . . . handsomely . . . now together, belay! Atticus, let her transom down—let her go! Port side, bring her painter forward."

"You and Tiny into the jollyboat, Mr. Ordineaux. Mind, this may be foul play; bring Atticus, he's a good marksman. See Tiny brings his cutlass. Hurry! We'll take some way off the ship so you can catch up with us again. Godspeed, man!"

Tiny, Atticus, and Ordineaux dropped into the jollyboat. "Cast off the painter."

"Row, boys! Captain thinks the Royal Navy will be after us soon," urged Ordineaux.

"Aye, and if it ain't the Devil himself, sir! The Navy just cleared the point upstream—four banked oars, and I can see the bone in her teeth."

"Then row like Beelzebub himself is in yonder boat, by damn!"

On the shore, Israel Fowlkes saw *Inflexible's* longboat round the point upstream as well, and he put out his lantern. *Berbice's* jollyboat approached the sandbar that extended from the point into the creek. "Wade out on the bar and meet them; they'll not want to tarry long."

"Goodbye, Israel; thank you for bringing word."

"Aye, aye, it's the started planks in yonder longboat ye'll be thanking me for soon enough!" Israel chuckled to himself.

"Ahoy the boat!" bellowed Israel.

"Aye, aye," shouted Ordineaux. He then whispered to Tiny and Atticus, "Don't stop your stroke until I give the word. It'll be hard enough catching up with the ship if Harte don't slow her down some more!" When they were in no more than a foot of water Ordineaux ordered, "Into the boat with you, Sir! Hand him over boys—hey! Mind the trim, ye lubbers! Capsize us now and the Navy will have us for sure. Now give way! Pull, damn ye! Don't ye see the hounds of hell right aft? Pull together!"

"They're bailing her out!"

Ordineaux twisted round to look at *Inflexible's* longboat. Sure enough, he saw phosphorescent slashes as buckets of water were tossed over the pursuing longboat's side.

"Blow me down! She must leak like a sieve. Well, ain't that lucky! Pull, boys: They gain on us! Together now—again, together now, backs into it! That's it, ye sons o' whores—ah, beggin' your pardon, Sir! Guess I ain't used to having the genteel aboard, sorry."

To this Anne answered, "They gain on us! Think ye Beelzebub would hang as many of your whore mongering mates as fast as yonder midshipman will? Pull, damn ye . . . together . . . again . . . put your backs to it, lads! You'll get a lashing round the fleet if you dare lose this race! Put your bloody backs to it while there's still flesh on them! Pull together, damn ye! Pull—again, boys!" Anne thus assumed the roll of cox'n, to the astonishment of all aboard. They pulled with a will, for what she said was true.

Tiny's gaze fell aft as he recovered his oars. *Inflexible's* boat was narrowing their lead. The short stubby jollyboat was no match for the longboat. Even with two of the crew desperately bailing her out instead of rowing, the longboat was gaining.

Captain Harte made close inspection of his jollyboat's progress and the approaching longboat. "Start hauling in the mainsheet, Gunny; we need to get some way on her." The gurgle at *Berbice's* bow picked up in meter. "Toss them a line and haul them up to the main chains," Nathaniel ordered.

Atticus in the jollyboat caught the line thrown from *Berbice* and tied it to the stem head. The men aboard *Berbice* hauled the jollyboat the last few feet to the ship, alongside the platform that held the mainmast shrouds away from the hull.

"Heave-to, in the name of the King!" *Inflexible's* long boat was coming up fast. "Heave-to and be boarded!"

No one on *Berbice* acknowledged the midshipman's high-pitched command.

"Very well, we shall get their attention. Smithers, fire your musket over their heads, but not too far over." Smithers dropped his bailing bucket and fired his musket into the air above *Berbice*. No one on *Berbice* even looked around; however, the mainsheet was trimmed for better speed.

"Keep rowing, lads; we shall board them in any case. Ready with the boat hook." The midshipman screamed at *Berbice*, "Avast there! I order you one last time, heave-to in the name of the king, or there shall be consequences!"

"If that little bugger gets aboard us, there'll be consequences indeed," grumbled Tiny, now at the *Berbice's* tiller.

"They're gaining way on us, sir," said Smithers.

"I can see that. Very well, Smithers, shoot the helmsman." Bosun Tiny's broad back made a large target from such a short distance. The longboat was no more than a hundred feet from *Berbice's* transom. Smithers gingerly picked his way to the bow of the longboat, mindful that an unbalanced move would capsize the narrow boat. Once astride the forward most thwart, he carefully stood, then brought a fresh musket up to his shoulder. He aimed right between Tiny's shoulder blades. The shot would shatter his backbone and rip through his heart, dropping him stone-dead at the tiller. That would get the Jonathan's attention! A pressed man at the pair of oars aft of Smithers missed his oar stroke recovery. He was exhausted from the long chase; the midshipman had been relentless with the pace. As he brought his oars forward to take another stroke, he did not raise one of them high enough to clear the water; it dug in and suddenly tipped the longboat. Smithers, tottering, planted his foot heavily on the planking near the stem at the front of the longboat. The hood ends of the planks Israel had loosened with his knife let go, and a torrent of water poured into the longboat. Smithers' musket went off at the sky as he stumbled, his foot stuck in the loose planks.

"Christ, sir, we're sinking!"

"Bloody hell, row for the shore!"

Berbice glided out to Pungoteague Creek, with her jollyboat in tow. *Inflexible's* men were able to swim their swamped craft to the shore; those who could not swim helplessly clung to the boat's gunnels. With the dawn they swam the longboat back upstream to Harborton, to the amusement of a small crowd that gathered at the waterfront to view the spectacle. Shipwright Mathias was only too happy to make repairs to the longboat's planking, at thrice his customary rate.

* * *

"We missed you at the dock; I feared you were lost to us," said Captain Harte to Anne.

"Deadlight Helms was lurking in the shadows; I could not get near. He was armed to the teeth."

"The brazen pirate!"

"At least we know he's not on his way to Jamaica."

"Aye, he could make trouble for us yet. Israel said he was asking where *Glad Tidings* is bound. He may ship out in her for Jamaica. It is amazing your father would ever have trusted him."

"I don't believe a word of his story."

"Yet he knew that Captain William maintained an account for your father. Tiny will show you your quarters; I regret the *Berbice* is cramped. You shall have the greatcabin."

"I am in your debt, Captain."

"It is an honor."

* * *

Deadlight Helms made his way back to Captain Easton's house in the dark, and settled behind a hedge where he could see both the door and the bedroom windows. Ellie and the stable boy had bolted the doors and closed the shutters on the ground-floor windows. Ellie stood in a shadow in her room in the third-floor attic and observed Deadlight take up his vigil behind the hedge. As the hours wore on, his presence vexed Ellie no end, so she decided to fire a shot across his bow.

Ellie took the bayonet off the musket, lest it gleam in the moonlight and alarm her quarry, and rested the muzzle on the windowsill. With only half of the weapon to lift, she could sight down the barrel and make a bead on Deadlight's hat. She allowed herself a mischievous chuckle. She withdrew and sat on her bed with the weapon in her lap, for she could not hold the heavy thing and cock it at the same time. With the weapon now cocked, she approached the window once more and rested the muzzle on the sill.

It should be said in Ellie's favor, that even as she played thus with her place on the gallows as a murderess, Isaac Newton's theories of gravitation were unknown to her. She did not know that a bullet falls just as fast whether propelled from the muzzle of a gun or simply dropped from one's hand. She really did aim *above* Deadlight's hat, a little. There was no murder in her heart, nor the vision of a head exploded in gore as she squeezed the musket's trigger.

Chapter 16

THE OLD MAN'S DAUGHTER ABOARD

"We're buggered now; I hardly got through unloading the first tier," said Ordineaux to Captain Harte when Anne went below. The *Berbice* was snoring along to the north-northeast under a clear starlit sky. The Milky Way stretched across the black sky from horizon to horizon, and Orion proudly displayed his belt above. The sails made black voids in the sky, outlined by the billions of stars. A gentle breeze fluttered the leech of the foretopsail.

"Mr. Ordineaux, I've no experience with your royal customs service in New York; but I can assure you we're in no difficulty in the Chesapeake," said Captain Harte.

"If I were on my way to New England, I'd put in at Rhode Island, where one can get what one needs from the collector without inconvenient reference to the actual ship, last port o' call, landing place, or cargo," quipped Ordineaux. Ordineaux hailed lately from New York. The Chesapeake was new to him.

Captain Harte grinned, "Mr. Ordineaux, we have our choice, there being two royal customs collector's districts off our bows: first is the Patuxent, which spans about seventy miles from the Patuxent River to Baltimore on the Patapsco River of the western shore, and the Big and Little Choptank Rivers with the town of Oxford on the eastern shore. The Patuxent collector runs the district through deputies, one each on the Choptank and the Patuxent, but since he affords them only eighteen or twenty pounds per annum, there's little enough effort made, and the masters of ships report what they wish, inbound and outbound."

"But what of the customs house in Baltimore? Surely the collector has a deputy there, thriving with trade as it is," said Ordineaux.

"The customs house for Baltimore, and the rest of the district, for that matter, is in Annapolis on the Severn River," said Harte.

"There's much seagoing traffic in Annapolis?" asked an increasingly incredulous Ordineaux.

"Not as much as Baltimore, but it's a pleasant place to abide, and the society life of the capital can be enjoyed by statesmen and servants of the Crown alike on the Severn's bucolic shores." Harte found it hard to suppress a laugh, but he held himself in check; the best was yet to come, and it was fun to scandalize Ordineaux.

"Our other choice is the Chester River," said Captain Harte. "The collector keeps his office in Chestertown—we used to call it New Town. Of course no one bothers to warp and scull twenty-six miles up the winding river to New Town, when just about anywhere else below the customs house will do for landing dutiable goods before getting there."

"But couldn't there be trouble like we had in Accomack from the collector in Chestertown?" asked Ordineaux. Looking into musket barrels once a week was enough for him.

"Not if he values his business interests, which are well tied up in his joint ownership of a West Indies trading brig which he owns with the local merchants. We'd not see trouble from that quarter," said Harte.

"This is astounding," said Ordineaux.

"If Grenville persists in his efforts to change a system of such long usage and to squeeze us for duties, there'll be deep trouble. It's bad business enough they send these venal fools of the royal customs service amongst us—I'd prefer they lounge about in England and collect their pay as before—but to charge them with collecting revenues and destroying the trade! We tore down the house of Zacharia Hood, the Stamp Act collector, board by board, mind you, the first day he got to Annapolis, and that day he got back out of Annapolis! We have to worry about a raise in the cost of bribery, which ain't likely, since undue greed on the part of any one collector will just drive the trade to another district."

"Then what of last night in Harborton?" contended Ordineaux.

"Perhaps a temporary infestation of honesty in the royal customs service," laughed Harte. "I suspect that young midshipman had something to do with it, though it's puzzling, since the Navy and the customs service hate each other so. We have more to fear from the Navy, since they're desperately after prize money, and *they* have boats."

"What now, then?"

"I shall take *Berbice* up the Patapsco River to Baltimore to sell her cargo; there are ready markets, and we can get along without an agent. Oxford is too close to *Inflexible's* enterprising midshipman. You shall purchase a bond from the customs collector in Annapolis. False papers can be had at a reasonable rate of bribery, since his deputy will issue them—he is dissatisfied with his allowance in that post, and appreciates what the trade can bring him personally. He cares not to look at vessel or cargo. Have him forge a false bond for us to land in Jamaica—barrel staves and the usual."

"The market's far better in Puerto Rico or the French Islands."

"Aye, aye, we shall see what happens after we get the Old Man out of prison!" Captain Harte looked over his shoulder to see if Anne were about, for he did not want her to hear him call her father the Old Man, the mariner's slang for captain.

"Ah! Miss Easton, still in sailor's slops, I see."

"The most comfortable way to get about a ship, Captain; do you object?"

"'It is not mine to approve or disapprove."

"Very well then, Captain; if you please, I would like to purchase another set of slops from the ship's store, for washing day."

After a bit of dumbfounded silence, Ordineaux and Harte responded in chorus, "Aye, aye!" After all, she was the Old Man's daughter, and this was his ship.

"Tiny, fetch the slop chest; we shall make issues."

Tiny brought up the slop chest, and Anne proceeded to dig through the short pantaloons and shirts, holding likely specimens up to herself for size.

"Charts her own course, that one," Atticus poked Gunny in the ribs approvingly. "Aye, hear she's squeezed more saltwater out of her stockings than many a Jack has clapped eye on."

"Went to sea with the Old Man, did she?"

"Aye, when he lost her mother. The Old Man couldn't bear to leave her ashore. They say the likeness is uncanny. She took to the sea like a seal. The Old Man even taught her to navigate!"

Anne finished her selection from the slop chest and went below.

"Ha! She'll be in the foretop next!" quipped Barbecue.

"Care to wager on it?"

"Ladies of the finer class! They can act as outrageous as they please; they don't have to answer for it like the common folk," grumbled Barbecue.

"Belay that; she's just a girl. Ain't no harm in the Old Man's daughter playing Jack tar," said Tiny, carrying the slop chest in his huge arms. "Especially since I hear she can hand, reef, and steer as well as any of ye."

"Care to wager on that?"

"Aye, aye, Barbecue, ye sour old Jack tar. I say within the week she's in the foretop taking in the view."

"Ten pence then, and none of yer tricks, Tiny."

* * *

Berbice was off Annapolis in the middle of the next morning, hove-to with her lug mizzen set and

185

her jib backed against the mizzen shrouds to hold her motionless. Ordineaux was to be sent off for the customs house in Annapolis in *Berbice's* jollyboat. He hung onto the main chains while Atticus stepped the short mast. Captain Harte gave his final instructions to Ordineaux, "Head west when you clear Horn Point; you're bound to see the Statehouse by then. The customs house is abeam the city dock. Benedict Calvert is collector. His nickname be Swingate—give him my regards if you see him, which ain't likely. He operates by deputy, and that miserable fellow should be found in the customs house, or more likely the Gentlemen's House of Entertainments, a pie-shaped building on the hill by the Capital. If ye have time, do see if a Christian price can be argued for a new mainsheet block. There be a chandler in town, but it's run by a pirate—name of the place escapes me."

"Aye, aye, Captain. Cast off, Atticus!" The jollyboat paid off on a broad reach into the Severn River. A sporting morning breeze of fifteen knots had made up from the south. Ordineaux sat on the weather rail and enjoyed a rollicking sail, black-headed laughing gulls wheeling overhead and giving raucous voice to the joy of the moment. To make this trip overland from Baltimore would have been tortuous and slow, over rutted and bumpy dirt tracks, in a cloud of dust, seated on wooden planks without backrests, in a carriage without springs.

* * *

"Always a pleasure to do business with Captain Harte," said the deputy collector. Ordineaux had to canvas every tavern in the town to find him, raising him finally as the deputy was taking his morning dram and smoke in the taproom of Thomas Hyde's "house of entertainment," as predicted by Captain Harte. A bribe of another dram and pipe was required to extricate the jovial fellow. The fur edging on his tricornered hat, the lace at his collar and wrists, and the silver buckles on his shoes indicated to Ordineaux that this deputy collector was living well beyond his eighteen pounds per annum. The mate of the *Berbice* wondered if the set rate of bribes had gone up.

They broke out upon the doorstep of Hyde's establishment, and the deputy collector declared, "Why, strike me blue! Where are those useless brigands? You there, Sean, get that other knave and fetch my sedan chair."

Ordineaux gawked at the chair, made of inlaid mahogany, fringed with lace curtains, sporting silk brocade seat cushions, borne by Sean and another unhappy Irish indentured servant. They set the chair down on its short legs in front of the deputy collector and Ordineaux. The deputy collector made a posture to a passing young woman, knee raised and toe-tip touching the ground; tricornered hat raised above his head, as if he were on a stage, and then seated himself in the sedan chair.

"Sean, let us be off to the customs house." Ordineaux strode along abeam the sedan chair, embarrassed to be part of such a scene, stumbling on the cobblestones and dodging the occasional pile of horse manure.

The redemptioner carrying the rear end of the sedan chair was not afforded a view of such obstacles, and slipping on a rather large pile, said to his counterpart forward, "Hey, mind the shit piles, Sean, will ya!"

"Of course I don't live down there by the customs house," the deputy collector assured Ordineaux as they descended the hill toward the water. "It's only decent to live up top." Indeed Ordineaux noted the garbage and stink grew stronger as they proceeded downhill, the accumulation having washed to the lower end of the street during the last rain, hence the higher real estate values near the top of the hill. The waterfront was the final resting place for all the accumulated offal that the wandering pigs and ducks didn't consume.

At the newly built customs house, the deputy collector duly signed the bond, and Ordineaux passed him the Spanish dollars, which he pocketed. The false bond would be an insurance policy of sorts against being boarded by the Navy. Costing but a pittance compared to a real bond, it nevertheless would put a naval officer at bay, for it looked real enough, and how could it be checked for authenticity on the high seas?

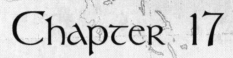

Chapter 17

FIDDLER'S GREEN AND THE LIVING TABLEAU

Berbice was warped into one of the outer city docks with a line passed over in the ship's boat. It was illegal to tie a ship to the Baltimore City dock unless it was there to load tobacco, for any other vessels could interfere with this most lucrative commerce, so *Berbice* had to make due with the outer dock.

Anne sallied forth to find herself some apparel more ladylike than sailor slops. Bosun Tiny oversaw the unburdening of the *Berbice*. He ticked off the casks and barrels, boxes and hogsheads on *Berbice's* cocket, stuffing the iron specie box or taking letters of credit for tobacco in exchange. Captain Harte went ashore to bargain, dicker, and deal with the local merchants, more than once feigning to depart and visit a competitor to get his price.

Baltimore absorbed the prized European and West Indian luxury goods from *Berbice's* hold like a sponge. Oxcarts lumbered down to the dock empty and away again laden with untaxed merchandise that had never seen the ports of England or paid duty and transshipment dues. Some merchants from the far-western lands of the Shenandoah Valley thought they'd had quite a windfall on finding the *Berbice*. When the first Conestoga wagon lumbered back towards the land of apple orchards, its owners went off in search of another of the venerable vehicles, anxious that they not lose the opportunity to avail themselves of the treasures in *Berbice's* hold that could be had at such a bargain.

The crew worked into the night, for there was no time to lose. A man could die of the jail fever in Jamaica within a week, of the bloody flux within three days. Captain Harte and the crew were all fond of the kind-hearted Captain Easton, and they worked with a will, for the rescue could not start until *Berbice* was laden again.

At ten o'clock the *Berbice's* hold was empty. Tiny dismissed the crew, who wandered off to the grog shops and whorehouses close to the waterfront. Captain Harte watched the young men amble off for a night's entertainment and realized all he wanted to do was sleep. Was his age creeping up on him? He climbed down the companionway ladder and took the mate's bunk in a small cabin off the companionway. The Old Man's daughter, Anne, was fast asleep in Harte's greatcabin.

The second day in Baltimore started before sunrise for Captain Harte. Barbecue knocked on the mate's cabin door with a mug of India tea in his hand.

"Mind ye, don't wake the lady." Anne had quickly become an important personage among the crew. The greatcabin was the fitting place for her. If the mate's bunk had been only an inch longer, Nathaniel would have shared the crew's enthusiasm for the arrangement.

Captain Nathaniel Harte traded their tobacco credits for barrels of salted meat, bread, and grain, commodities in great demand in the West Indies. Because of the lack of coin, tobacco was used as currency, locally and in trade abroad. While *Berbice* was being loaded, Harte ventured off into the burgeoning ramshackle town. It had none of the newfound opulence of the shipyards and grog shops on Fells Point. Pigs, ducks, and geese wandered about the dirt streets, picking at the piles of kitchen garbage dumped there and wallowing in the puddles of wash water and sewage. Young boys in one-piece suits with ruffled collars gamboled about, whipping tops or rolling hoops down the street with the aid of a stick.

Captain Harte wandered the streets, looking into the windows of the wooden clapboard shops. He had to walk clear around a wallowing swine and her suckling pigs blocking his path. Everywhere the carpenter's saws and hammers were busy; new buildings were being thrown up in a frenzy fueled by the prosperity of overseas trade. Besides the native colonials, the streets were populated with French, Germans, English, and Dutch. Deep brown suntans indicated who the sailors most recently from the West Indies were.

A gentleman in satins, embroidered silk and grizzle wig was borne past Captain Harte in a sedan chair. The four slaves carrying the poles of the chair huffed and gleamed with sweat. Captain Harte read the social status of the individuals in the throng by the cloth of their garments. Plantation owners, gentlemen of business, and their ladies wore silk, satins, and brocades. Stoic dark blue or green jackets and light-colored knee-breeches were for the ship masters, rough-looking homespuns and vests for the farmers, leather aprons for the craftsmen, plain homespun or cotton for the sailors, and outrageous French concoctions for the tarts.

In some districts the shops had no windows, but were merely open narrow cells six feet wide, bound by rickety walls and a roof of scraps. In back of his wares in this cube sat the shop owner, often with a scale and a few spare sacks.

* * *

At length Captain Harte grew tired and picked his way back to the docks along the unpaved streets strewn with dung piles and black rivulets of sewage. Duty done, his mind fell to grog shops and whorehouses. He'd been promising himself a trip to the Fiddler's Green since before *Berbice* ran *Inflexible's* blockade at the mouth of the Chesapeake. It was time to look up Maggie!

Nathaniel made his way to Gay Street and climbed the familiar row house steps. A strange feeling of embarrassment overtook Nathaniel, lest Anne should see him enter such a place. He looked up and down the street to assure himself she was not around, and then confidently rapped the shiny new brass doorknocker.

"Captain Harte to see Maggie." He strode forward but the door remained cracked open, the chain still on. "What is this? Where's my Maggie?"

"There ain't no Maggie what lives here," claimed her mother's familiar voice.

Nathaniel placed himself square before the crack in the door. "Bess, you know me! Let me in to see Maggie."

"She ain't in house."

"Then I shall wait."

"She ain't taking visitors."

"She'll be happy enough to see her Nathaniel, fresh back from the sea, with a present!"

"It wouldn't be gold, from the likes of ye, be off!"

"Nay, but some of the finest French scent."

The old hag took the chain off the door, snatched the vial from Nathaniel, and sniffed it.

"Waters, ye fool, they be waters only. Get off with ye; my Nell has important visitors." She thrust the vial of scent back at Nathaniel.

"But what of the five pounds I gave her for safekeeping? Am I not to see her again?" *Or my five pounds?*

"Not until the Devil takes ye both!" The door slammed in Nathaniel's face. He pushed it open again before the old hag had got it chained, and caught a glimpse of Maggie, running up the stairs clad only in a shift. Two greatcoats strewn carelessly across the parlor chaise brought him aback. One was gold brocaded silk, the other a Navy officer's. Maggie had gentleman visitors from the highest ranks. Nathaniel knew in an instant why she was no longer interested in the tawdry favors of a country sailor. The old hag suddenly appeared from behind the door with a switch broom, wielding it like a club and meaning to brain Nathaniel. "Out with ye, swab!" Nathaniel backed down the steps into Gay Street, stinging with a sense of betrayal. He stood in the street, staring at the door, dumbfounded and more than a little heartbroken.

An old bearded sailor ambling by took in the familiar scene and slapped Nathaniel on the back. "Aye, aye, laddie, any port in a storm! There's better pickin's ta leeward."

Nathaniel shook himself and strode down Gay Street, determined as ever to have a romp in Fiddler's Green. A block away he slipped into an establishment that must have been approved by the Royal Navy, for they proudly displayed a ceramic cat in the window.

Inside, the red velvet on the walls contrasted with the white petticoats of the young tart that greeted him. He was led to the drawing room, where several Royal Navy officers and a few colonial merchant captains sat around tables, leisurely smoking long clay pipes and sipping French brandy.

At the sight of the uniforms, Nathaniel felt a knot form in his stomach. Only hours before he had been chased and fired on by the Royal Navy. His own Maggie was consorting with an officer. He could not stomach Royal Navy officers now. He made his excuses to the befuddled petticoated tart and reeled back into the street, determined to avoid the Navy cathouses henceforth. *So this is it,* he thought to himself. *Perhaps I am no longer an Englishman, if I must avoid the Englishman's Navy.*

Nathaniel made his way down Gay Street with a weather eye out lest the Old Man's daughter should see him there. It would be strange enough for Anne to wander into such an area, but irrational unease chased him up the street. He looked into the windows of the various establishments of gentlemen's pleasures, searching for one that did not display the telltale ceramic cat. A small and narrow, but clean clapboard row house seemed to be the right kind of establishment. There were no Navy uniforms or ceramic cat to be seen in the window, and the matron beckoned him from the stoop with her ample bosom overflowing her bodice. He trotted up the steps, looking to the street once more to assure himself Anne had not seen him, and doffed his tricorn hat as he entered.

Once seated with rum and limejuice in hand, he pondered why he felt embarrassed that Anne, the Old Man's daughter, should see him in such a place. After all, this was his traditional shore side entertainment, once business was done. All thought of Anne Easton vanished when a buxom young blonde sat herself brazenly in his lap.

"Join us for blind man's bluff, sweetie? If you catch one of us, you get to peel a bit of me dress off!" she whispered in his ear, "ten pence." He handed over a generous amount of coin.

"To be sure!"

At that very moment another customer walked into the room and glanced at the two with a lurid grin. Nathaniel coughed and stood in embarrassment, and the young blonde giggled and put her hand over her mouth in a show of sham mortification and disappeared up the stairs.

"Aye, ye have to make fast to the blond one or she'll cast ye adrift before you get your hawser wet. Mind ye, there's no cat in the window, some of the lasses may be poxed. Have a glass with me; ye look like an honest seafaring man." At that, the fellow slapped the table in friendly invitation.

"Master Nathaniel Harte, sir, at your service." Nathaniel gave a mock bow and seated himself at the young man's table.

"Call me Joshua Humphries, sir, apprentice shipwright. Enjoying the sport of Baltimore before returning to my duties in the shipyard."

"You've been here before, sir?"

"Aye aye, last night, and the blond one served me the same. It is a common enough trick with the doxies in Philadelphia."

Nathaniel felt a little embarrassed at his own naiveté, in comparison to the worldliness of this young apprentice from the city.

"A nasty cut on your cheek, sir!"

"Aye, aye, been to the sail maker for it."

"Ha ha! A toast to the artisans of the canvas, then!"

Nathaniel blushed when reminded of the needlework he wore on his cheek, Anne's work.

"Do you countenance more sport this night, Captain?"

"Aye, aye, the need rises!" They laughed and drained their glasses.

"Have ye ever seen a living tableau, Captain?"

"You mean a ribald painting?" These Nathaniel had seen in plenty at the various houses of gentlemen's entertainment.

"Aye, aye, but of living creatures, to be sure! A novelty lately imported from the London sporting clubs, so I hear."

"Nay, this thing I have never clapped eye on!"

"Let us be off, then, for the showing is on the hour."

The two sallied off, following the brick sidewalk to a new and ornate brick building. Nathaniel noted with dismay the ceramic cat displayed in the window by the front steps.

The matron behind a gargantuan doorman demanded a large fraction of a Spanish dollar each. Nathaniel reached into his pocket and came up empty. He'd been pick-pocketed by the blond! His last recourse was a Spanish dollar sewn into his waistcoat. In the excited expectation of this new erotic experience, he blew caution to the winds and tore it free. The matron took it with no indication she expected to give him change.

"Humm," murmured Nathaniel, "my change if you please, madam."

"Very well; you provincials are so threadbare," she snickered. "Allow me to advise you, your enjoyment here will be in proportion to your generosity."

Nathaniel reddened at the insult but held his anger in check. The naval uniforms he could see in the parlor were giving him discomfort, as well.

"In here," said the eager Joshua, leading Nathaniel by the hand past the condescending madam of the house. They entered a room filled with wooden chairs in rows, in front of which was a richly embroidered silk curtain that blocked the front of the room from view. Joshua excitedly pushed through the milling gentlemen to claim the last two seats at the end of the front row for himself and Nathaniel. Nathaniel sat down, crossed his legs, and nervously wiggled his foot, taking in the sumptuous and ribald tapestries that hung on the red velvet walls.

Presently Madam appeared in the doorway. "Gentlemen, please take your seats; you will have an experience beyond your imaginations. Our living tableau is about to begin." A young boy and Madam turned the oil lamps down, whereupon the room was plunged into darkness. Nathaniel heard rustling and a giggle from behind the curtain. He felt a knot of excitement form in the pit of his stomach. There was a swish as the curtain was pulled aside, and the oil lamps were turned up again.

On the platform were four young women and two men, dressed in casual attire. They held each other in several attitudes of embrace, all facing the audience, including the women. The oil lamps were turned down and the curtain pulled. With rising apprehension, Nathaniel thought he'd been robbed again. He gave Joshua a nudge and looked at him with eyebrows raised in an unspoken question, *Is that it?*

Joshua grinned and raised his index finger in another silent signal, *Wait and see.*

The oil lamps were turned up and the curtain pulled open to reveal the couples had changed partners—but the embrace! The couples were frozen in passionate embraces, arms entwined in the act of unbuttoning and pulling garments off each other. The breasts of the women were exposed and cupped in the hands of their partners. Nathaniel's eyes fastened on the couple in front of him, where the man stood behind his partner with his arms around her shoulders, his hands under each of her breasts, lifting and squeezing them so the nipples jutted forward in display. At some unknown signal and by some devilish device the dresses and undergarments of the women were shucked off instantly. The shock of suddenly naked flesh aroused the most jaded old sailors in the audience. The actors froze once more and the oil lamps were dimmed.

There was a low mumble in the audience, as whispers of amazement and approbation were exchanged. Nathaniel let out a sigh and nodded to young Joshua. Supposing that this was all he was going to get from his investment, Nathaniel made to get up and leave, but was stayed by Joshua's hand. The oil lamps were turned up once more and the curtain drawn.

At first Nathaniel could not make out what he saw on the low platform. Then with a shock he realized in front of him lay a tangle of naked arms and legs. His breath caught as he discerned two men and four ladies entangled in various postures of sex acts. Nathaniel flushed with feverish lust. The oil lamps were again turned down and the curtain drawn closed.

"Thrashing good show!" The gentleman's friend silenced him with an elbow into his ribs. Someone tittered in nervous amusement.

This time the curtain opened first, before the oil lamps were turned up. An anticipatory "ah" rose from the room. Everyone leaned forward in the chairs, straining to see the next spectacle through the dark. At length the oil lamps came up to reveal a young woman with an hourglass narrow waist and full breasts and hips, naked except for a tiara, sitting in a velvet chair. She sat with her left arm covering her breasts, her hand cupping her right breast. Her right hand covered her pubic area, buried between her closed thighs. Her eyes were downcast in a look of provocative modesty. The sputtering oil lamp played gold and amber shadows on her naked belly.

There were noises of appreciation from the gentlemen.

She slowly assumed a position that gave Nathaniel a fever–his ears were hot and his temples pounded. The oil lamps went down.

"Ah!" The oil lamps were turned up again. The stage was empty. After a moment of stunned silence, the gentleman sports began to rise stiffly from their seats.

"I say, how much for that one?" the gentleman implored Madam.

"She is very special—a contessa, your lordship! She rarely takes visitors."

His lordship and the Madam were walking out of the room into the great hall.

"I must have that one!"

"I trust you are planning to be quite generous with us, your lordship? Possibly, if the contessa is favorably disposed, I could arrange a rendezvous."

"Quite so, quite! But hurry!" The gray-haired lord was led up the stairs by Madam.

Nathaniel noticed his own hands were trembling. "Would monsieur care for a drink?" A young girl had appeared, holding a tray of glasses filled with rum punch. She was dressed in underclothes only, with a bodice that squeezed her breasts over the top until the pink areoles of her nipples showed.

"Aye, aye!" Nathaniel and Joshua were then relieved of another sizable fraction of a dollar for the drinks. Nathaniel emptied half of his in a gulp and felt the pleasant burn of the rum as it wetted his dry palate. The men milled about the great hall and adjoining parlor, lighting pipes and drinking highly expensive rum punch proffered up by scantily clad young girls. A stream of young women so dressed filtered into the milling men and struck up conversations with their only-too-eager guests. Liaisons were made, and a trickle of couples mounted the stairs to the upper chambers.

"This ain't for us, mate. It'll cost ye more than the bitter end of your Spanish dollar."

"Aye, time to cast off for a humbler port."

"You find none of my girls attractive?" pouted Madam.

"Which could be had for thirteen pence?"

"You ignorant Jonathan, you can't even buy a rum punch in here for that! Sean, did they pay their bill?"

"Yes, madam."

"Then you may go, if you please."

"With pleasure, madam."

Nathaniel spied the sneer of a Navy lieutenant who overheard Madam's insults. It was high time to go.

"Maybe you should check the purses of the country bumpkins before you let them in, madam." Nathaniel spun back about and faced the sneering officer, his passionate lust now turning into passionate anger. Madam retreated into the parlor, for she knew the lieutenant's game.

"Perhaps a true gentleman, sir, would keep his sneering insults to himself!"

"Ah! What have we here? Jonathan speaks of a gentleman's manners! And I suppose I am to treat you, sir, as a gentleman, albeit a penniless one?"

"My name is Nathaniel, and I'd advise you to use it with respect."

"Nathaniel, Jonathan, the same—ignorant provincials!   If you know nothing of gentlemanly sport, sir, and if you don't have the money, perhaps you shouldn't sport with the gentlemen, heh?"   A few of the lieutenant's fellow officers began to gather behind him, tittering at each new insult.   Several Yankee sailors and landsmen joined the group, glowering at the insolent naval officers.

"I can best the likes of you at any gentleman's sport."

"Ah!   A challenge!   Why not take wagers?   What shall it be then, Jonathan, er, Nathaniel?   Swords? Pistols?   How about swords, so I can give you a scar to match on your other cheek?"

"I'll wager I take that insolent grin off your face, and a brass button or two."

"The buttons, sir, are gold."

"Say you; they have the tarnish of brass.   Perhaps they're just filthy."

"You go too far!"

"I'll take the wager; half a pound says the lieutenant draws first blood," one of the Navy officers said.

The setup was progressing nicely.   The officers had run this game many a time in many a port, and had supreme confidence in the swordsmanship of their lieutenant.   They also looked forward to emptying the pockets of the locals with outlandish bets.

"I'll see my half pound on Nathaniel," blurted a drunken landsman, more used to betting on horses; he liked the look of Nathaniel's calves.

"Anyone else? You, sir, very well, half a pound again. Yes, and you, very well! The money shall be held by Madam with half as prize for the winner." Soon the officers had gathered up a small fortune in bets. "To the courtyard!"

"Nathaniel, are you sure? Perhaps we should just make our apologies and leave."

"Here sir!" The lieutenant took a pair of sabers from a wall mount and handed one to Nathaniel.

"I prefer the rapier, if the gentleman knows how to use one? Much lighter, and much faster." Nathaniel took down a pair of light Spanish rapiers and handed one to the lieutenant, hilt first. The lieutenant paused, dumbfounded. His fellow officers raised their eyebrows. Perhaps they had made a rash choice. They had assumed the wound on Nathaniel's cheek was the mark of a loser, and easy money.

In the courtyard the men took places around the brick wall, leaving the center open for the two duelists.

"You here, and you there. When Madam drops her handkerchief, you may begin—right. First blood, then!"

The lieutenant was used to knocking the sword out of the bumpkin's hand at the first parry. Sometimes there would be fights over so much money lost so easily. He and his fellows could handle that. But this bumpkin looked as if he knew what he was about. Could they be trained in such gentlemanly sports in this backward place? He assured himself no such training would be available and confidently stood forward, *en guarde.*

Nathaniel extended his right arm and held the rapier's tip up, putting his left arm behind. He made a three-point stance and tested his balance, swaying about and rising up on tiptoe, as he had been taught by the dueling master at Sybarite Hall. Next he assessed the balance of the blade, making a few practice parries and lunges. He was mindful to keep his lunges short while in the eyes of his adversary. Struck with an idea, he made another practice lunge and feigned to stumble.

The lieutenant took heart at this, and glances were exchanged among the officers. Another easy victory was about to be had, and enough money for as much whoring as they pleased!

Madam dropped her handkerchief and retreated into the house. The lieutenant made a swipe and a lunge, which Nathaniel easily parried. Nathaniel made a lunge, and the lieutenant made a swipe at his cheek. Nathaniel spun around like a ballet dancer and whacked the lieutenant's backside with his rapier. The colonials roared in laughter. More bets were placed; Madam was summoned to hold the growing purse. The lieutenant's face flushed with rage.

"I told you I'd take that insolent grin off your face," reminded Nathaniel.

The humiliated lieutenant fell into an uncontrolled ferocity, lunging repeatedly at Nathaniel in an effort to kill, not merely draw blood. Nathaniel expertly parried and danced around the raging lieutenant, clearly the master of the engagement.

"There goes me half pound. I thought your lieutenant was handy with a saber?"

"Aye, with a saber the lieutenant's a lion. He ain't got the polish for the epee."

Madam did not like to see the colonial getting the best of the engagement. This foretold the loss of her take of the prize money. Moreover, in the long term, a profitable sideline of baiting and then betting on gullible country gents was going awry. "Tell them to stop!" she ordered.

Just then Nathaniel swatted the lieutenant's backside again as the lieutenant lunged past, and the onlookers roared with laughter. The duel had become a comic scene. No one paid Madam the least bit of attention. The betting was now shifting heavily in Nathaniel's favor.

"Stop this instant! I shall summon the constable! This is my house! I shall not have it disgraced by ruffians!"

With the lieutenant recovering from his latest lunge at the opposite side of the courtyard, Nathaniel put down his guard and made a leg to Madam. "At your service, madam. I shall desist."

The colonials in the crowded courtyard roared with laughter once more. The lieutenant charged toward Nathaniel's turned back, swiping port and starboard in preparation for a deadly lunge.

"Nathaniel, look out!" shouted young Joshua.

Nathaniel spun on his heel and with a lightning flick of his rapier knocked the lieutenant's weapon out of his hands and over the courtyard wall. The colonials applauded and shouted, declaring Nathaniel the winner. Some looked to Madam for distribution of the purse, but she had disappeared, and Joshua as well. The lieutenant came on like a bull with his fists, disregarding the fact that Nathaniel was still armed. Nathaniel tossed down his rapier and assumed a posture to meet the lieutenant's charge. Several colonials ran forward to block the lieutenant, followed by naval officers. The courtyard soon devolved into a general brawl. Nathaniel was knocked down under the two brawny colonials who blocked the lieutenant's charge. With a struggle, he pulled free and hopped over the brick courtyard wall. The roar of the free-for-all within continued. He spied the lieutenant's rapier on the ground and picked it up. Picking his way over chamber pot waste tossed from the windows above, he made for Madam's front door.

"Good evening, sir, I am here to return Madam's rapier and claim my prize money."

"Madam is engaged."

"I will take my purse then, without further ado."

"Wait here."

In a few moments the doorman reappeared.

"Madam has been robbed; there is no purse. Madam has instructed me to say you are not welcome here, sir, and she will summon the constable if you do not leave at once."

So that was it, no prize money. "What a convenient robbery for Madam," scowled Nathaniel. He turned on his heel and descended the brick steps to the street. With a look to port and then to starboard, his mind whirling with anger and disappointment, he took the starboard tack towards the harbor and his berth onboard *Berbice*. He possessed no more pocket money. As the rush of nerves from the duel wore off, he felt more and more physically drained.

"*Pissst!*" The summons came from the shadows of an alley as Nathaniel strode by.

"What is it?" Nathaniel was in no mood for another encounter. On the other hand, he thought, he could be robbed of nothing but his well-worn clothing.

"It is I, Joshua!"

"Devil take you! I wondered where you went."

Young Joshua appeared from out of the shadows. "I kept an eye on Madam. She does not play a fair game."

"She claims the purse was stolen—how convenient!" spat Nathaniel.

"Aye, aye, Captain, stolen it was. In the press of the crowd watching the brawl, I was able to relieve her of it and escape the house!"

"Strike me blue! Is that the purse?"

"Aye, and a fat one, since Madam did not have a chance to extract the house's due."

"*Ha*! We shall share it out!"

"That is too kind of you, sir; I cannot. But do ye countenance more drink and sport? It is your night! I shall be glad to partake in merriment to celebrate this unexpected victory."

"Aye, a rum and lime would do quite nicely to steady my course." Nathaniel noticed his hand was again trembling.

"I know just the place."

To Nathaniel's surprise, there was no ceramic cat in the window. The Blue Bell Inn was small but well kept. A fire served to take the chill off the night air. Nathaniel was relieved this was not a bawdyhouse. He'd had enough hard knocks for one night.

"Two cups and a bottle of rum, sir, if you please."

"Aye, aye."

"I often come here to rest my spirits before I return to Philadelphia," said Joshua.

"You take the long voyage on horseback?"

"Aye, the coaches are insufferable. I do not relish being stuffed between my fellows like a sack of flour, sitting on a wood bench for hours without the least opportunity to move the slightest bit, and listening to some oaf snore like a saw pit."

"The greatcabin has its advantages."

"It'll be a cold bed for either of us tonight."

"You long for a wife?"

"Aye, I wish for the companionship. A comely face to look upon, a friendly greeting, and familiar conversation. These I crave. I weary of the trick and swindle, a bounce in a strange bed and then it's, "Off with ye, sir; others await your place in the saddle!"

"Not to mention the pox."

"Aye, I had to take the mercury cure once. An experience I care not to repeat."

"I must say the fire of lust has gone out of me this night. That lieutenant was earnestly trying to kill me. I am spent."

"I'm exhausted as well, the strain of adventure! On my usual visit I take in two or three houses of entertainment. But by the end of the night, when the lust is satisfied, it's the hearth I crave."

"I crave a companion as well, but I see no landsman's life for me, and aren't all ladies land lovers? Would I not make a widow of any wife the day after the wedding, when I board ship again? When I was disowned, the sea was my salvation, and I have grown to love it. To wed and give up my roving, or to wed and make a widow, or to pine in solitude: It is a puzzle." With these words, Nathaniel, exhausted and sated with rum, began to nod off.

"Up with the two of us, then! Captain, you have a greatcabin to find, and I have a cold bed awaiting."

Nathaniel roused himself and stood. "Good evening to you, sir. I must say, it was a splendid adventure. I shall never forget the living tableau!"

"And I shall never forget the look on that smug naval officer's face when you flogged his ass with your rapier!"

"Aye, that was almost worth the prize purse in itself!" *But perhaps not so special,* thought Nathaniel, reflecting as he picked his way over puddles and piles of offal in the street on his way back to the *Berbice.* He had bested young gentlemen at their own game before. It was how he made a living, running the blockade of the Royal Navy's young gentlemen.

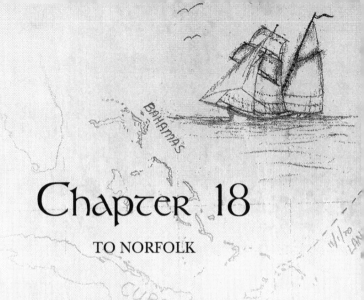

Chapter 18

TO NORFOLK

Berbice made sail as the breeze rose from the northeast the following morning. Captain Harte was happy to be gone; his adventure of the previous night aside, he didn't care much for the stench of cities. The mixture of horse, pig, cattle, and human waste draining into the harbor was disgustingly fetid brew. The offal of the city was dumped in the marshlands along the north side of the harbor. Night soil, fish, and kitchen waste rotted there in steaming heaps of microbial bounty. The citizens couldn't stand the stink when the wind blew it over the city; most suspected the stench had some connection to the yellow fever epidemics that plagued Baltimore. But year after year, decade after decade, the stinking waste was piled in the marsh.

Out of the stench and the muddy brown waters of the Patapsco River, *Berbice* sailed. She passed Fells Point, where sharp-ended ships were being built, their frames resembling the ribs of giant sea creatures. Gliding past the schooners delivering virgin timber, she sailed past the color change where the waters of the Chesapeake and the Patapsco met, as clear as if it were painted. Flotsam danced on the drift line: dead fish rejected from fishing boats, old shoes, broken casks, half-rotted spars, and planks from crumbling piers. Captain Harte felt an indefinable feeling of release as they escaped the sick brown upper Patapsco and entered the fresh, clear Chesapeake. *Berbice* cleared Rock Point Shoal at the mouth of the river and headed southeast.

Another drift line on the edge of the channel off Sandy Point was festooned with barrel staves and rotted planks. Staying well to port, Harte used it as a reliable channel marker. He sent Simon Livingston aloft to search for *Berbice's* jollyboat when they opened Whitehall Bay on the starboard beam. A short club-head gaff caught his eye, and Harte put his glass on the craft. After the chocolate-colored masthead confirmed *Berbice's* jollyboat, Harte ordered Jost, at the helm, to bear down on it. The jollyboat soon hove up under *Berbice's* lee, and in one smooth motion Ordineaux tossed her painter aboard *Berbice*, then scrambled up the mainchains. Captain Harte chuckled to himself at the finesse of the maneuver; way never came off the schooner, and the jollyboat soon bobbed and surged at the end of her painter in the wake.

"Did ye come off with a mainsheet block?' asked Captain Harte as Ordineaux collected himself on the deck.

"Nay, sir, for the chandler is indeed a freebooter, that's sure."

"Aye, Jack, that is why we call the place 'the baubles shop'. Perhaps we'll find a swap chest in Norfolk."

said Harte, forgetting the rusty mainsheet block, its ring worn thin on the iron horse.

Off Eastern Bay they passed a variety of sail, from shallops with one or two leg-of-mutton sails to ship-rigged cargo carriers, bound to Baltimore or the open sea. When they could see the cliffs of Calvert at midday, the northeast breeze died out and backed west. They made enough leeway toward Tilghman Island to require a tack, so they put *Berbice* about and sailed toward the Patuxent River mouth, a nice long tack, making good way again as the breeze freshened. Harte figured he'd gained enough ground to weather, and fell off again below yellow-ocher cliffs at the north side of the Patuxent. Towering over them a hundred feet, the cliffs turned gold in the afternoon light. From the deck, men looked up into the forest of eight-foot-diameter virgin oaks that capped the cliffs with black columns and a roof of green. The upper leaves sparkled over the forest gloom, and the fresh scent of moist leaf mold was in the air.

As they passed Point Lookout, where the Potomac meets the Chesapeake, they came upon a school of feeding bluefish. At first they saw only a cloud of seagulls wheeling in mad frenzy. Closer, they could observed the water beneath the gulls roiling and splashing, then exploding from below as a school of silver baitfish sailed into the air to escape the bluefish. Here and there a five-foot-long bluefish would burst from the water, in an arc before plunging back into the roiling water.

After they had passed through the acres of this primal fury, they could still see bluefish burst from their wake, while the fleeing baitfish ripped through the surface in silver sprays. At last only the seagulls were visible, wheeling, diving, and screaming over the slaughter. Ordineaux and Nathaniel leaned against the quarterdeck rail, regarding the violence behind them.

"The amazing cruelty of Nature," commented Ordineaux.

"How can a bluefish be cruel, Jack, they just eat, as they must," replied Nathaniel.

"If I were a baitfish, I'd regard them as malevolent, aye, the meanest sort of fish."

"God's manifestation of the rancorous for our edification? But surely, Jack, you can see that your view lies entirely in whether ye be baitfish or bluefish?"

"A smuggler's lot Nathaniel, but I do I feel like a baitfish these days."

* * *

The first gray of dawn had not yet lit the sky when *Berbice* put into Norfolk to load barrel staves and hoops for her cargo, and fresh water. This was not just any fresh water Captain Harte sought, but the black water of the Dismal Swamp. Colored like tea with the leaf tannins of the swamp, it would not go foul on an extended voyage, as other fresh water would. Captain Harte stowed all the water butts he could below decks, and then took on more and bade Bosun Tiny lash them securely on deck.

Berbice's small "greatcabin" was now crowded with barrels of water and beer, sacks of foodstuffs, and the odd bale of cured tobacco leaf. Waxed sausages and cheeses hung from the deck beams and in the greatcabin windows. Barrel staves and hoops protruded from every available crevice. The ship was down on her marks, but she sailed well in a breeze when loaded, and a breeze was what they would likely encounter in the Atlantic in September. Anxious to visit Fiddler's Green before their ocean voyage, her crew asked Captain Harte for leave to go ashore.

"Mind ye are back aboard before dark," warned Harte. "The press gangs have been known to be about this city." Unmindful of Captain Harte's warning, Jost Weiser headed to a grog shop at the city dock on the far side of the wharves.

* * *

An hour later, Lieutenant Winston Lloyd of the *Inflexible* and thirty of his men tied the ship's armed tender to the end of the Norfolk City Dock. "Aim the swivels down the pier," he ordered before they left the boat. His men were armed with oak belaying pins, for they were on a mission of no mercy. "Let us find a grog shop to whet our resolve," cried Lloyd, and they set off in a group, the bosun bringing up the rear to make sure there were no stragglers, soon they burst through the louvered door of a likely tavern that displayed a tiny anchor and rum barrel hanging over the door from an iron bracket. "Rum! Bring us rum and be quick about it! Bring rum all around, ye hear me?" Lieutenant Lloyd charged across the room to the innkeeper and stood over him, two inches from the old fellow's nose. "Rum all around, I say, Jonathan, or me and me lads might get angry!"

The innkeeper had been through this scene with the Royal Navy before. "I'll see your gold first; then they'll be rum aplenty," he stuttered. The old fellow's hands began to tremble. *Inflexible's* bosun was already passing out tankards of rum from behind the bar.

"Gold you'll have, swab." With that, Lieutenant Lloyd slapped a Spanish doubloon on the barrel that served as the innkeeper's writing desk. It would hardly pay for half the rum, but the innkeeper had noticed the belaying pins stuck into the belts of the Jack tars, and knew they were bent on violence. He prayed his daughter and wife would stay upstairs.

As *Inflexible's* crew grew louder and began to make bolder inroads on the rum, several of the larger fellows began to jostle each other, and soon a wrestling match began. The innkeeper used this as his chance to slip out of the room unnoticed. He climbed the back stairs as fast as his tired bones could take him.

"It's the press gang again, isn't it?" said the innkeeper's wife. Their daughter cowered in the shadows behind her. They could hear shouts and curses, the pounding on the floor, and the smashing of chairs.

Lieutenant Lloyd stood on a table and thundered above the melee. "All right, me hearties, out with ye now, and we'll take in another grog shop or two before we get down to business!" He drained the tankard he had kept as his own, tossed it on the floor, and staggered toward the entrance to the inn. The bosun cuffed and kicked the drunken sailors toward the door and up the street. They followed the lieutenant to yet another grog shop, where they chased the patrons out and made free with the rum, with little payment for it.

At last Lloyd assessed there was enough belligerence in the rum-fired crew to undertake what they were about.

* * *

Jost Wieser emerged from a whorehouse where he had spent his last copper. He gained the street with an unsteady gait and staggered in the direction of *Berbice's* berth at the wharves.

"Got a pipe for a plug of sot weed, mate?" The friendly question came from an alleyway Jost staggered past. He hesitated and turned toward the speaker, only to be confronted by five of *Inflexible's* burly seamen. The speaker punched Jost a hammer blow to the stomach, and as he doubled over, cracked him under the jawbone, sending young Jost into black unconsciousness, then they bound his hands and slapped his face until he awakened.

"On your feet, you son of a whore!" One of the crew kicked Jost in the ribs where he lay. Jost struggled to regain his feet, and was dragged through the streets like an animal, tied by a short tether held by the *Inflexible's* bosun.

"Ye cannot take him, he's my husband!" The cry came from a window on the second floor of a rooming house.

"Shut your gob, ya filthy whore!" Even in the street below, Jost could hear the slap of a hand connect with her soft face. Into the street tumbled her husband, a youth who now had a wickedly swelling eye. The little band of bruised young men, bound by their wrists and tethered around their necks, grew to ten in number as the *Inflexible's* crew rampaged down the street toward the wharf. They were herded in the center of the street, the press gang raiding the rooming houses and taverns on either side.

Alarmed by the noise, the night watch ran to the street and halted when they saw the tumult, then turned tail and ran to the mayor's house, screaming as they went, "Riot by man-o'-war's men! Press gang!" By the time they reached Mayor Paul Loyall's house, the night watchmen were leading a small mob of angry citizens. When he was awakened by the noise, Paul Loyall put his head out his bedroom window. After hearing the watchmen's warnings, he ripped off his nightshirt and cap, and quickly pulled on knee breeches and shirt. He was on his front stoop by the time the crowd arrived.

"Where are they?" he cried to the watchmen.

"Headed to the wharf, sir!"

"Do they have any of our sons with them?"

"Aye, aye, sir, to be pressed into the navy!"

"Let us be after them and put an end to this outrage!" It was Loyall himself who now led the mob of angry citizens to the wharf, calling out at each house for assistance in putting down the rioting press gang. The ranks of angry citizens grew all the way to the wharf; they numbered over one hundred when they halted beneath a huge oak tree at the top of the wharf. Just coming down the street, the lieutenant and his press gang confronted the citizens barring his access to the wharf.

"Out of our way, you miserable sons of whores! Stand clear, or we'll split your heads open!"

Paul Loyall calmly strode out between the citizens and the press gang, and said quite loudly, but in measured tones, "What's the meaning of this disturbance of the peace?"

"Who the bugger-all are you? Out of my way, or I'll knock the fucking tar out of your fucking seams!" bellowed Lloyd. He drew his cutlass and pointed it at Paul Loyall.

"I am the mayor, sir. You shall return those pressed men to their proper homes, sir, and get your drunken brigands out of our town and back to your ship at once!"

"The bloody fucking mayor, are you? Well I'm the bloody fucking captain of a royal fucking ship of war, and I intend to take these fucking little lubbers for my fucking crew!" Although he had difficulty maintaining his balance—he nearly stumbled on the cobblestones as he approached Loyall, he waved his cutlass toward the knot of miserable pressed men and then pointed it once more at Loyall's chest.

"I assure you, sir," said Loyall, not moving an inch to back away from the threatening cutlass, "the city magistrates will have you up on charges this very morning if you do not give up those illegally pressed men and return to your ship, *this instant*!" He delivered these last words through clenched teeth.

"Damn you, and your buggering magistrates, to the Devil!" thundered Lloyd, "You'll not be giving orders to the Royal Navy. Clear out of our way, or I'll run you through!"

"Spoken like a true pirate." Loyall and the citizens at his back still did not back off.

"Inflexibles! Out of the buggering boat and clear these assholes off the dock!" shouted Lloyd to the armed guard in *Inflexible's* tender, which was tied broadside to the end of the wharf. The redcoat marines sprang onto the dock and charged toward Lloyd's rescue. Paul Loyall and the citizens refused to budge. Lloyd and his crew ran through a gap in the crowd to join the marines, leaving the pressed men on the other side of the angry mob.

"Back to the boat," shouted Lloyd. When they reached the *Inflexible's* tender, they found the mob had followed them down the pier. He wheeled around and pointed his cutlass once more at Loyall's chest. "Stand off, you son of a whore!"

"I'm afraid I shall have to arrest you and your men for disturbing the peace of our town; come along, then." Paul Loyall spoke these words loud enough for everyone to hear.

"Not bloody fucking likely." Lloyd turned to the lads manning the swivel guns, which were aimed into the crowd. "Fire the swivels!"

The lads looked at him in disbelief.

"Fire the bloody fucking swivel guns, you whoreson bastards. *Fire!*"

No one moved. The slow match burned in the hands of the gunners, but they dared not mow down a hundred innocent Englishmen and women.

"Fire, or I'll take the lash to your backsides!"

No one moved. No one spoke. Except for the sputtering slow match, the crowd was silent. The gunners stood wide-eyed and frozen.

"There, lads." Paul Loyall strode toward *Inflexible's* tender. "If you do not cherish a trip to the gallows, put the slow match down, and let that raving lunatic take the consequences of his own immoderate actions."

The lads at the guns put their slow matches back in the sand pail.

"You fucking little cowards!" With this last insult to his own men, Lloyd commandeered a longboat and ordered the bosun and his coxswain to row him back to the *Inflexible*.

"Captain, you cannot go. By authority of the magistrates of Norfolk, you and your men are under arrest!" Loyall said as he strode to the edge of the wharf.

"You and your fucking magistrates, go bugger off!" With that, Lloyd turned his back on the mayor, the citizenry, and the rest of his crew still ashore.

Paul Loyall now turned to the crowd of citizens at the end of the wharf. "Who among you has been harmed by one of these men?"

"That one came to our room and knocked my husband down," said the young wife, her cheek was swollen and turning black and blue.

Loyall turned to the constable. "Arrest him. Madam, who was the one who struck you?"

"It was Lieutenant Lloyd who hit me."

"Aye," Loyall said with disgust, "and who else among ye has a complaint to make before the magistrates?"

In all, ten of the most brutal of *Inflexible's* press gang were arrested. The lads in the tender were allowed to return to the *Inflexible*.

* * *

221

When Captain Harte came on deck the next morning, evening dewdrops still clung to the fibers of the hemp standing rigging.

Tiny approached the captain and put a knuckle to his brow, Navy-fashion. Harte knew this meant bad news of some kind, pertaining to the crew.

"Jost Wieser didn't come back aboard. Sent Atticus to check the likely bawdyhouses; but he ain't there."

"Damn and blast!"

"Aye, looks like Jost has lost his taste for hazarding the Royal Navy."

Anne came up the companionway from the greatcabin; she was dressed in feminine finery she'd purchased in Baltimore, a full-length frock and matching sunbonnet.

"Morning, ma'am."

"Good morning, Captain, and to you, Mr. Ordineaux. Bad news?"

"We're short a seaman. Jost did not return last night."

"Oh my! You were shorthanded before!"

"Aye, we'll have to make due; we cannot afford to wait and find crew. The weather could turn foul this time of year. We'd best make our easting as soon as we can."

"I shall lend a hand as required, Captain. You can rely on me."

"With thanks, milady, but I don't see what you could—"

"Sir, I can hand, reef, and steer as well as any seaman aboard!"

Harte grinned. Maybe she could—after all, she was the Old Man's daughter. "You may yet have a chance, milady."

"Why not give me a watch?"

"Aye, no need of that yet. Mr. Ordineaux will take starboard, and Tiny shall have the larboard watch. You may take your ease, milady. If it comes on to blow, well, then we may need your able hands."

"Aye, aye, Captain," said Anne, for she would not defy the authority of the captain. He would have enough on his hands, in her assessment. She made herself available to help when the time came.

A gathering morning breeze was making from the northwest, pressing *Berbice* against the pier. Stun'sl spars, boathooks, and oars were used to keep her off as several of the crew hauled her stern-first to the end of the pier with dock lines. When they reached the end of the pier, the crew scampered back aboard over the bow, since the ship had her momentum and continued out into the fairway. One last dock line was kept fast to the stern quarter. Bosun Tiny and several others began to haul on this with all their combined strength, orchestrated by Barbecue, the ship's chantyman. He sang in basso, with a slow, rolling rhythm:

> "A long time and a very long time,
> Give me way, hey and away ho!
> A long, long time, and a very long time,
> A long time ago.
> There was tinkers and tailors and sailors and all,
> Give me way, hey, and away, ho!"

Berbice's crewmen sang the chorus as they hauled together on the dock line. The ship began to turn slowly around. Another three heaves and her bows crossed through the eye of the wind. No more need of the shanty now.

"Get your dock line back, Tiny," ordered Captain Harte. "Set the main and mizzen. You, foredeck, raise the jib and set the Yankee flying!"

Dewdrops fell on the deck as the main and mizzen sails dropped from their tricing lines. Bosun Tiny waved at a man on the pier to slip the loop off the piling. The dock line was pulled back aboard as *Berbice* gathered way out into the Elizabeth River. Several other sailing vessels were making for the open sea, cream-colored sails standing out in graceful curves against the blue-green water. Cumulus clouds made puffs of white cotton against the clear sky. The orange rim of the sun broke out on the eastern horizon and cast the cloud bottoms in blue-grey shadow.

"Pilot schooner ahead," said Ordineaux as Captain Harte came on deck.

The captain took in the sleek lines and high, unstayed rig of the schooner with admiration. "Helm, see if you can drive to windward of them." Always pitting his vessel against anything else under sail was habit, an American habit. Though *Berbice* was the larger vessel and faster by virtue of her waterline length, he didn't hold much hope for overtaking the lithe pilot schooner to windward.

Virginia pilot schooners were the naval architect's experimental racing machine. In this class of small vessel, usually less than fifty feet long on the deck, the next theory of fast sailing ship design was tried full scale. The crews on each of the ships, *Berbice* and the pilot schooner, looked admiringly across the rushing water at the other sails, dancing now over the rollers coming into the Chesapeake from the open sea. As the breeze freshened, the bow waves curled up foam that streaked hissing down the side.

At length the crew of the pilot schooner waved goodbye. The little schooner dropped her main and jib, to spend the day on her loose-footed foresail tacking to and fro until an incoming ocean-going ship required delivery of her pilot. Several aboard the pilot schooner longed for the adventure that lay ahead for those on the other ship.

A thin sailor dressed in slops climbed up *Berbice's* weather ratlines to the foretop and sat on the trestletrees, legs dangling in the breeze, an arm casually around the mast, as she enjoyed the view.

"There you go, mate; now you owe me ten pence," said Tiny to Barbecue. "The Old Man's daughter herself is up yonder in the trestletrees, just like I said."

"This ain't but one of your tricks, Tiny. You asked her to go up there. Probably shivering like a leaf with fright. You should be ashamed of yourself, putting the Old Man's daughter in peril like that!"

"It be no trick of mine, Barbecue, but I will confess I sailed with the Old Man when she was a gangly slip of a girl. She was all over the ship, stem to stern, bilge to trestletrees, and truth be known, that be her favorite spot to watch a sunset."

"I'll be buggered."

"Now, I did collect her from the foretop once— had to peel her off the stays like a frightened kitten. We was off the coast of Barbary, and the pirates made after us from Algiers. Captain Easton raked them stem to stern with grapeshot, and slaughtered a good many of the rag-headed villains. Then we fired our last rounds at the xebec's waterline. Those who were still alive, boarded us like hounds from hell. Their ship was sinking as she lay alongside us."

"Anne was aboard? Barricaded in the greatcabin, of course! Or did ye put her below the waterline?"

"That was the thing of it! We didn't know where she was when the fight ended. The last of them hellhounds fell from our own rigging, and when we looked up, there was Anne in the trestletrees, and a puff of black powder smoke to leeward of her."

"Who did for the pirate?"

"Anne did! The Old Man had taught her to shoot a pistol just that morning. Aye, she's deadly with a pistol, and did for that pirate, but not before he cut her cruel in the leg."

"By the powers, sent a Barbary pirate to the Devil, did she?" Barbecue looked with new respect at Anne, sitting in the trestletrees, clothed in sailor's slops.

"Aye, she did. If ye bet on her, best remember she's a special one. Ye can forget the ten pence."

Chapter 19

THE ROGUE

Deadlight Helms swam the swamped old wreck of a ship's boat to midchannel. There was a chill in the pre-dawn air, and he actually felt warmer under the water. The rotted boat he clung to had little buoyancy, but floated at the surface of the water, which served his purpose well.

Glad Tidings rode at anchor in Harborton while the fall harvest of wheat and hard rye bread was stowed in her hold, bound for Jamaica. Under the Navigation Acts, grain could only be exported to an English possession. The price in this captive market was depressed, causing farmers in Fowlkes Tavern to grumble over the price, as well as the Navigation Acts. The Accomack customs collector had been given a fiery sendoff from *Glad Tidings*, but there was no violence, this time.

"Anchor hauled up short, sir."

The captain of *Glad Tidings* squinted at a piece of yarn in the shrouds. When the telltale indicated the ship had swung so that the wind came over her right side, he took a deep breath and bellowed, "Haul up and cat the anchor, lively now! Let fall the mizzen!"

"Aye, aye, mizzen tricing lines free." The mizzen sail fell from the gaff overhead.

"Sheet home on the starboard tack."

"Aye, aye."

The handy schooner began to gather way.

"Let fall the mainsail."

"Aye, aye, mainsail sets."

"Hoist the staysail."

"Aye, aye, staysail sheeted home."

There was a flurry of activity aboard. The staysail obscured visibility forward as it unfolded and fluttered in the breeze from the bow of *Glad Tidings*. The schooner gathered speed as she gurgled down the creek on a fair wind.

Suddenly the smooth motion of the schooner was broken.

"Christ, what was that? Are we aground?"

"Can't be, we're midchannel!"

"Look forward!"

"A boat—we've run her down!"

"By damn, pick up her crew!"

"Are others with ye?"

"Devil take you, ran me down! No others than me, by the powers! You've sunk my boat, ye villains!" As if to punctuate this exclamation, the bow of the rotted ship's boat rose above the ripples behind *Glad Tidings* and then rolled over and was seen no more. The captain was dumbfounded that such a rotted thing could float.

"Are ye hurt?" Blood was streaming down from the man's ear.

"Aye, aye, nearly took me ear off in the bobstay!"

"I find that unlikely."

"It is true! Now see here, I demand to be put ashore, and to see the constable to make good on my losses! Oh! Me purse! I've lost me purse! I must find it!" At that, the man with the drooping eyelid made to jump back over the stern rail, but he was restrained by the mate.

"There'll be no finding it now."

"It's to the constable, then! Put me ashore, ye blackguards!"

"Very well, Bosun, put her head to wind." The captain reluctantly acquiesced.

"But wait, sir; there may be another way, if you're willing to make good on the damages ye've caused me."

"Say it."

"Where would ye be bound, Captain?"

"Jamaica."

"By the powers! And I just on my way to book passage. But ye see, sir, with the loss of me purse, I cannot pay for it. Unless you were to provide passage in this here *Glad Tidings*, by way of making amends."

"I saw no purse, sir. Am I to take you at your word?"

"Aye, to the constable then, and be quick about it!"

"Nay, ye shall have passage."

"And as to the rest of me purse?"

"Passage only."

"And the food due a landed gentleman such as myself, being put to such hardship and loss by your lack of seamanship."

The captain bridled at this. "Mind your tongue, sir! Ye be no landed gentleman! You've the mouth of a common Jack tar. And its officer's food ye'll have, is it? Why didn't ye call out before ye were run down? Or get out of the way?"

"Do not use me cruel, Captain. My misfortune at your hands burns the hotter. Besides which, I was looking the other way."

"In a tiny ship's boat, ye saw not my masts towering above?"

"Oh my ear, I'm grievous hurt, sir! You use me cruel."

"Very well then. Bosun, a poultice and bandage for his ear. You, sir, shall have your passage to Jamaica—before the mast."

Deadlight made a grimace to register his unhappiness with his accomodations, but accepted the deal, being inwardly thrilled to have gotten free passage so easily. When at last he was poulticed and bandaged and had a few swallows of rum in his belly, he felt quite well. Better, in fact, than he had felt since Ellie shot his earlobe off.

* * *

Berbice cleared the Chesapeake through the middle bay channel. With the wind now on her stern quarter, she made good time with her fore and aft sails, but she could do better. It was time to set her square sails to traverse the open ocean.

"Let's get the topsail and course on her," said Harte to Bosun Tiny.

"Aye, aye."

Tiny mobilized the young men of the crew, who raced up the ratlines to the topsail yard to toss off the gaskets, while others raised the course to the yardarm. *Berbice* now spread a proper amount of sail for good speed, yet not too much to be dangerous. Her several sails allowed her skipper to adjust their driving power to match the wind conditions. Sail could be reduced or added as the wind grew stronger or abated.

Berbice, a finely tuned, living machine, was now roaring through the deepening blue of the Atlantic at seven knots. Her hull made one long wave that reached from the foam and spray at her bow to just below her quarter windows. In the forward end of the ship, her bow wave sounded like a waterfall. On occasion, when her forward rush annihilated a wave, the spray would leap over the bows and spatter the deck. In the after end, the flutter of the edges of the sails and the creaking of straining hemp line and wooden spars made background music, timed to the roll of the southerly swell, when *Berbice* sailed out of sight of land. The whole world was now the ocean she swam in, rolling in long hills of deep blue that came ever from the south. Under Tiny's watchful eye the helmsman kept time with the swell, hauling the tiller to windward to meet the rise of each, then easing it back to keep the ship on a straight track.

"Tiny, you shall have the port watch, Mr. Ordineaux shall have starboard," said Harte. Tiny grinned; this meant he'd be off watch in half a glass, and on duty again in the last half of the night. He enjoyed being covered by a blanket of stars on a clear night, and the anticipation of the gray dawn, waiting for the orange sun to emerge from the Atlantic.

Tiny was a stocky man with a deeply pockmarked face and broad neck to match his shoulders. He wore his brown hair in a tarred ponytail, sailor-fashion. His massive hands could turn out the finest splice or sail repair, and while they were too big for the fiddle, he played the Celtic drum with a passion. Tiny was the link between officer and crew before the mast, and he exercised his authority with a quiet assurance none of the young men ever questioned. He was neither jealous nor threatened by the young men aspiring to be mates, for he was a young man at heart and hated responsibility, a reason he steadfastly refused to become a mate.

The wind died during the night, and by morning they were becalmed, yet an alarming big swell still swept up from the south. *Berbice* rolled in it; Tiny had his watch trice up the sails to keep them from flogging. At nine o'clock a light breeze made up from the west, and all aboard were grateful when the sails filled again and steadied the rolling. By nine-thirty the breeze was from the southwest, and the tops of cumulus clouds rose above the horizon to the southeast. The swell was increasing, up to ten feet by Anne's reckoning, but it was strange that there was little wind to power it. The wind changes were coming counterclockwise, an ominous sign.

Atticus was spending his off-watch leaning on the weather bulwark gazing at the waves. The tops of each moving hill were higher than *Berbice's* sides, and sloped gradually to crests a hundred feet apart. The ship would linger between the waves, where all that could be seen from the deck was blue water in any direction, charging from the south and rolling away to the north. She would then slowly rise on the swell to the top, where the whole horizon was visible. Some of the deep blue rollers were topped with white breaking crests.

Tiny approached, using the rolling gait sailors used to balance on a heaving deck. "You think this is rough now? Just wait," he advised Atticus, in one of his rare loquacious moods. "This is easy as pissing abed."

"Think we're in for a blow?" said Atticus, privately appreciating Tiny's gratuitous vulgarity.

"Wind's been backing all morning," Without further comment he rolled off to help Barbecue secure the firebox.

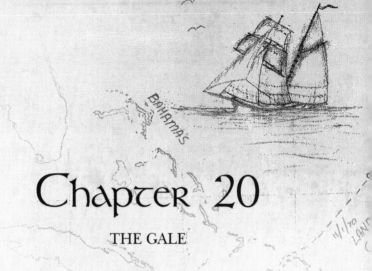

Chapter 20

THE GALE

By ten o'clock the sea had risen, and ominous whitecaps came more frequently.

"Have the watch drop the course, furl the topsail, and take in the flying jib," ordered Captain Harte.

"Aye, aye, all hands to shorten sail!"

Nathaniel Harte felt as if he had lead in his belly each time he appraised the sky. When the clouds started to appear in windrows spiraling to the horizon, he called all hands, and preparations began in earnest.

"Tiny, we need to snug her down. Mr. Ordineaux, keep her going as fast as she'll go; we need every sea mile we can get."

"Aye, aye."

Berbice would have to claw offshore as far and as fast as possible. If she were blown back to shore in the coming maelstrom, it would be certain death for all.

Captain Harte, Ordineaux, and Tiny now wore looks of sober concern that spurred the crew to doubled efforts, as they could see something bad was in the works. Everything that could be gotten below decks was stowed and lashed down. Tiny got some oiled canvas out of the bosun's locker and directed a party to put in the wooden hatch boards, and then cover the hatches with the oiled canvas, secured with wooden wedges. Gunny directed another party to rig lifelines from the forward part of the vessel to the taffrail. Everyone glanced anxiously to the southeast as they worked. To the unknowing eye, it was still a pleasant day with plenty of sunshine and a fair breeze.

Anne, dressed again in a full-length frock, had been sitting in a folding canvas chair lashed to the quarterdeck. As the breeze freshened and the ship began to heel, she unlashed the chair and went below. In a few minutes she reappeared, wearing a slicker over her sailor's slops.

"Of all the things ye must not forget," Captain Easton had often told her, "remember always to bring a good slicker to sea. It will keep ye warm, especially if you put it on before you get soaked." She took a station on the windward side of the quarterdeck and clung to the taffrail.

"You must go below!" said Captain Harte when he came up to the quarterdeck. "You'll be soaked in the coming gale, and you may be in danger."

"But you may need another hand, Captain Harte. I can see the coming gale; I've weathered them with my father on the quarterdeck. I'm not some landlubber who's going to ride out a gale cowering below, retching into a bucket." She saw something she had said weighed in with the captain, for he soon acquiesced to her defiance.

"Aye aye," said Nathaniel Harte, turning before she could see his sudden break into a broad grin. *No landlubber, she says! Aye, my own self-pitying words on women confounded! Is the lass more sailor than landlubber?*

The cloud cover was closing in, and while it was only ten o'clock in the morning, the day was growing dark, with an eerie green light in the southeast. Suddenly the wind died. Now over fifteen feet high, the rollers had an odd, glossy smooth surface. Below decks Captain Harte anxiously calculated *Berbice's* distance offshore, and then plotted their dead-reckoning track, noting the time and position with a pencil mark on the chart. The ship surged with each rise and fall of the rollers, and Harte had to clamp himself onto the chart table with elbows and stomach in order to work.

A light breeze began again from the southeast. With it came an oppressive humidity and the faintly sweet smell of an electric storm. By this time *Berbice* was sailing east, close-hauled under her fore-and-aft lowers.

"Wish we had time to strike the topsail yards, or at least send down the sails," commented Harte. "Put double gaskets on them; perhaps they won't blow out."

"Aye, aye. They may be off her, directly," answered Ordineaux, as he assessed the awesome scale of the approaching storm. The eerie green light was all around them now, and in the southeast, a curtain of black with lightning flashes within. Low rumbles came from the same direction. A sudden gust of wind heeled *Berbice* over until the spray swam past her side at the level of the gunwale. Green water tumbled over the rail onto the leeward deck.

"Time to get the sail off her, Mr. Ordineaux," said Captain Harte, holding onto the taffrail. The deck was sloped at a twenty-degree angle, and dipped more as the ship rolled on the seas. She surged as the rollers, now the size of hills, lifted her up for a view of the horizon and then dropped her in the trough, where those aboard could see only moving walls of clear water towering above all around. The Yankee and staysail were hauled down to the bowsprit, and the crew edged out on footropes, leaning against the bowsprit to gather in the sails. With every third wave they were plunged into the sea, holding on for life itself. It was impossible to work without one hand holding onto the bowsprit rigging.

"Unhank them both and pass them in," directed Tiny. The struggling seamen at length wrestled the precious sails off the bowsprit to be stowed below. Moving inboard to the lug-footed foresail, they unlaced the bonnet and double-reefed the sail, reducing the sail's area to the minimum. The mainsail was lowered and lashed tightly between boom and gaff. The breeze was all the while strengthening, and whitecaps appeared once again, cascading down the moving hills of water. When the wind reached a sustained thirty knots, streaks of foam blew across the waves parallel to the wind. The wind began to howl in the rigging, first only in gusts, and then continuously. Lines slapped against the spars in a discordant cacophony, some slowly, others quickly, dozens at a time, ceaselessly. This cacophony increased its nervous counterpoint as the howl of the wind rose.

In the southeast a tabletop of black cloud appeared, low on the horizon, sounding like a distant artillery battle. The low rumble of thunder cut through the whistle of the wind in the rigging. At the foremast a halyard came loose and stretched out straight from the masthead, snapping like a whip. The wind had built to forty-five knots. Spray shot up along the windward side of *Berbice* and ripped across the deck. The wild slapping of lines on the spars became lost beneath the shriek and howl of the rigging, but the endless dull thudding of the halyards could be felt. Below the approaching tabletop of cloud was a black wall, in which lightning bolts flashed. The rumble of thunder was more regular and louder, as if they were racing toward the destructive fury of the artillery battle. Rail down, *Berbice* ploughed through the sea with only her small triple-reefed foresail set.

Anne and Ordineaux clung to the weather rail of the quarterdeck. "Waterspouts!" she shouted into his ear, and pointed to three funnels dropping from the tabletop edge of the squall line. The seas were now the height of two-story buildings. Tiny and Gunny were stationed at the tiller, which Simon held to the weather rail with a preventer tackle. The men at the tiller gripped the deck with their bare feet, hardly noticing their numbness.

The power of the gathering storm awed the crew. Whitecaps, blown off the tops of the seas, tumbled downwind. Ordineaux could not tell if the stinging drops that whipped his face were salt spray or rain. When *Berbice* reached the top of each wave, she rolled her lee rail under, and the water on the deck cascaded off through the scuppers as she righted in the troughs.

The heaviest rain was in the squall line approaching as a gray wall. At it's base the surface of the sea was blasted into the air. With a constant series of thunderclaps the eerie green light was behind and above them now, as they approached darkness before noon.

Captain Harte, Ordineaux, Simon, and Anne fastened themselves to the weather rail of the quarterdeck with short loops; the men at the tiller had lifelines around their waists. A lifeline had been rigged fore and aft to enable them to traverse the sloping deck. As the wall of wind and water drew close, everyone was filled with wonder, soon replaced by terror, and a sense of helplessness.

Right above them a bolt of lightning ripped across the sky with a deafening explosion. The first gust knocked *Berbice* was down on her beam-ends like a toy. In a sickeningly violent roll she went down until her masts were nearly parallel with the water; the tip of the main yard actually went under. Those on the quarterdeck hung from their lifelines on the high side. With the violent roll, another thunderclap exploded right aboard, but this time it was the triple-reefed foresail that had torn loose at the sheet cringle. With no sheet to hold it, the sail boomed with the sound of cannon fire, within moments it had flogged itself into shreds and was gone, disappearing into gray spume to leeward. Without a foresail, *Berbice* surged into the wind. The rainsquall bore down in an opaque wall. The roar of rain hitting water was like the clapping of a hundred thousand hands.

"By God, don't let her come about!" screamed Captain Harte at the helmsmen. They saw his mouth move but heard nothing over the deafening noise. Even so, like good sailors they tried to haul the tiller up to windward to prevent *Berbice* from crossing into the eye of the wind and coming about on the other tack. But they could not fight the momentum of the ship and the force of the gale. As the ship came around, the gale caught her on the other side, she rolled violently down and payed off on the other tack, one that headed her toward the mainland, and certain death for all.

The windage of the square yards held Berbice on a downwind course, raging through the sea, out of control. The rudder was useless against the force of the hurricane. She charged towards death on the deserted ocean beaches. Harte knew he had to act fast to save the ship.

"Have Tiny put the drogue over by the port cathead," he screamed into Ordineaux's ear. "Rig a spring line under the bobstay to the starboard cathead. When she comes into the wind, cut the spring and let her ride by the starboard cathead. Let's hope to God it drags our head to wind again."

The heavy canvas drogue and attached line weighed over a hundred pounds. Simon, Tiny, and Atticus scrambled to the bow on a wildly pitching deck. They clung to the lifeline with one hand when their feet were washed out from beneath them, the other hand clutching the drogue.

"The spring line has to pass under the bobstay!" Tiny shouted in Atticus's ear.

Tiny straddled the bowsprit and began to edge out, while Atticus fed out the spring line. Nearly invisible only ten feet away, Atticus saw the bowsprit plunge into a wave and Tiny disappear below the water.

As the ship rose, Simon saw Tiny clinging to the bowsprit with arms and legs, but the spring line was not in his hands! Simon knew there were seconds before the bowsprit would plunge into the next wave. Spring line in hand, bent over so as not to be blown off by the howling wind, Simon scrambled out on all fours onto the bowsprit and grabbed Tiny's oilskin at the neck with one hand, and with the other hand threw the spring line below the bowsprit. The spring line whipped under the bobstay and slapped Tiny a wicked blow in the face as it came up the other side, but he grabbed it. Simon was not so lucky on the return. *Berbice* made a dizzying fall down the back of a wave, and Simon lost footing and fell into the sea, hands flailing for a grip on something solid.

Tiny and Atticus cast the drogue into the sea. The line whipped over the bulwark as if attached to a harpooned whale. When the line snapped taut on the half hitches holding it to the cathead, the water in the rope sprayed forth as if wrung by a giant hand. But it held! *Berbice* pointed into the roaring wind. As she swung into the eye of the wind, Tiny cut the spring line with a hatchet, and with Gunny and Barbecue holding the tiller hard over, *Berbice* payed off on the other tack. The small ship lurched and wrenched as if trying to escape the grip of the enormous wind, then slowly backed down to leeward.

The lifeline around Simon's waist came up taut as *Berbice* rolled and flung Simon into the side of the ship. Simon clawed at the smooth planks, desperately trying to climb up the side. The ship moved past and began to drag him by his lifeline. He now fought to push off the side of the ship as it rolled down. He swallowed water, fought for breath, and tried to keep off the ship while being dragged. Lifeline or no, it was the end; he couldn't breathe. Groping for the lifeline, he tried to haul himself up on it to get a breath. His lungs felt as though they would burst. He flailed in the foam and spray, tied to the side of the surging ship. Coughing and gasping, struggling for breath, he couldn't believe his life could end so suddenly. He vomited seawater, gasped for air in the foaming sea, and slammed against the side of *Berbice*.

Two heads appeared above him. One hand found something and grabbed, and then Simon was hauled over the bulwarks, only to be left to vomit and gasp on the deck. The ship was in mortal peril—a sail must be set to claw off the lee shore or they would wreck before the storm blew out. There was no time to tend to this half-drowned seaman.

Tiny, Gunny, and Atticus wrestled with the flailing lines and canvas of a storm sail, in a desperate effort to rig it. Tiny and Gunny had to wrestle the still-folded sail with the weight of their bodies to keep it from becoming instantly airborne. There was so much windage on the halyard itself, it nearly dragged Atticus overboard. The sheet had to be hauled in while the sail wildly snapped back and forth. No one dared approach the wildly thrashing sail, for the iron cringle sewn into its corner could easily break an arm or skull. Nerves were as taut as the canvas as the small crew struggled to haul the sheet until the sail stopped booming and flailing in the moaning wind. Then they prayed the sail would not give way at some seam or cringle and again flail. If it did, it would rend itself to bits, leaving *Berbice* to surge once more toward the lee shore and certain destruction.

When the trisail set, Tiny cut away the drogue, for there was no hope of getting it back aboard. *Berbice* surged once more out to sea. Tiny and Ordineaux loaded Simon's limp but breathing body into the companionway and shuttered it as seawater cascaded down the steps.

Just as Tiny and Ordineaux reached the ladder to the quarterdeck, a massive rogue wave swept over the *Berbice*. Atticus was washed off his feet and smashed into the ship's boat. It shattered into splinters that washed over to the lee bulwarks as the ship struggled to free herself from under the weight of water on the deck. Atticus' hand groped above the water in the lee scuppers. When Ordineaux and Tiny reached Atticus, they found he could not get back on his feet. They struggled to carry him to the fo'csle hatch, hanging on for themselves and hanging onto crippled Atticus as boarding seas repeatedly knocked them off their feet.

It began as a cruel slapping noise, a few stray edges of the mizzen topsail reporting louder and louder as more sailcloth broke free of the gaskets. Then the yard started to shake as the wind, a solid force, ripped at the sailcloth. There was nothing the crew of *Berbice* could do but watch as the sail broke free. Then it became a menace, dragging *Berbice* down to her beam-ends, until her masts were nearly parallel with the sea. They were lost now in the charging gray spume that covered the sea surface. Her lee rail was buried in green water, the deck canted at such an angle it was impossible to stand and difficult to hang on with both hands. *Berbice* was being dragged on a wild ride across the sea, out of control. Shipwreck was at hand; at very least, the flailing yard and tremendous drag of the shredded topsail would bring down the mizzenmast.

"Cut it away," Captain Harte shouted into Tiny's ear. Tiny climbed forward, holding onto the weather bulwark; hand over hand, his feet sliding out from under him on the wildly canting deck. When he reached the ax stowed on the bulwark below the mizzenmast's pinrail, he used his tremendous strength to hold on with one hand while he swung at the mizzen topmast backstay with the ax. It only took one stroke of the ax. The backstay parted with a wicked snap, and would have beheaded Tiny on its way up if he had not ducked. As loud as the crackling of thunder all around them, the mizzen topmast snapped, and the short mast, yard, and rags of sail flew off into the gray maelstrom to leeward. *Berbice* righted enough so that Tiny and Gunny could labor about the deck and chop away the rest of the mizzen topmast rigging. *Berbice* was again free.

Six more hours into the gale, the rusted mainsheet block broke free of the horse. *Berbice's* huge main boom caught Captain Harte in the head from behind, and he sprawled senseless on the deck. The gaff and boom swung viciously with the roll of the ship, until they settled into the torrent of water passing by the lee side of *Berbice*. Tiny and Anne wrestled the limp Captain Harte down the companionway and laid him out in the wildly pitching greatcabin.

"He's still alive!"

"A good crack on the skull for him; expect he'll have an aching head for awhile. We should get back on deck."

The cannon crack of the storm trysail blowing out turned Anne's attention to the deck. Tiny dodged the flailing sheet, which held nothing but the pitiful rags of what had been the storm trysail. Anne went forward to help Tiny roust out another sail to use as a storm trysail. Hand over hand on the jack line; Anne pulled herself across the wildly canting deck, trying to hang on when green water swept the deck. As she clamped onto the new sail to help drag it over to the ringbolt, Tiny screamed in her ear, "Go up to the quarterdeck—it's too dangerous down here!" As if to punctuate his order, a wave swept the deck, knocking them both off their feet. Still hanging onto the jack line, they struggled to regain their footing.

"I got duty!" screamed Anne into Tiny's ear.

This raged against all of Tiny's big brotherly protectiveness, but they had only eight souls aboard to save *Berbice* from destruction on the shore to leeward, and four were already down below, groaning from cracked bones and bruises. So Tiny didn't repeat his order; but he double-checked every knot Anne tied, as if she had suddenly become incompetent. This cost him a painful crack in the ribs from the flogging trysail clew when he went forward to inspect Anne's job at securing the tack of the sail to the ringbolt by the foremast. Afternoon gloom turned to pitch darkness, and *Berbice* continued her desperate claw off the lee shore.

The storm trysail held, and the wind abated in the early hours. The seas still ran mountainous in size, but the tops no longer came crashing across *Berbice's* deck. To the south, the stars began to twinkle, outlining the black forms of scud clouds racing to the north. Dawn on the Atlantic is always moving, especially to someone who has survived a hard chance in a gale.

"How beautiful it is!" said Anne as she took her turn at the tiller. The gray was giving way to hues of pink.

"Aye, and it's wonderful to be afloat still," answered Tiny. In the relative calm, he and Barbecue were able to get some rest.

"Barbecue, let's see what the pumps tell us."

The news was not good. The men pumped the bilges for an hour, but in another half hour there was more water, too much water.

"Short-handed and leaking, a bad lot. We'll be manning the pumps until we can careen."

Numbed with fatigue, Tiny sat and stared at the sunrise. The only two seamen who could navigate *Berbice* to a safe harbor were below, one unconscious, the other unable to rise from his berth. Tiny was lost on this expanse of heaving blue. His mind froze.

"How many knots do you think we were making the last two hours, Tiny?" Anne asked.

"Oh ma'am, about ten knots while the wind was highest; been falling off steady for the last hour, put us at about four knots and a bit right now."

She frowned as she thought out the speed, time, and distance problem of the last hour. "Take the helm, if you please, Barbecue, I shall have to advance our dead-reckoning track." Barbecue took the tiller and gave Tiny a questioning look. As she descended the companionway, she popped her head up. "What course were you steering in the night?"

"Same as now ma'am, east by southeast."

"Aye," she answered and disappeared down the companionway.

Barbecue gave Tiny a wink and asked, "Reckon she can navigate?"

"Wouldn't doubt the Old Man taught her how. Why, yes," Tiny's mind awoke again, "I recall the Old Man showing her how to shoot the sun with his octant."

Anne reappeared. "We shall need to heave the log; could you fetch it, please?"

"Yes ma'am." Tiny roused himself. Barbecue gave him another wink.

"Let's get some sail on her after we heave the log."

"Aye, aye, ma'am!" *Berbice* had a new navigator, the Old Man's daughter.

The log was a triangle of wood attached to a reel of light line. Tiny took the reel in one hand and tossed the wooden triangle into the sea aft of *Berbice*. Anne upended a small hourglass at the precise moment the log hit the water. Tiny stood poised to grab the line and stop it when the hourglass ran out. "Ready? Now!" Tiny grabbed the logline and counted the knots that had unreeled.

"Four and a half knots."

"Let us make sail; there's not a moment to lose! I'll take the helm."

Anne took *Berbice's* tiller and stood behind the compass box, glancing from the compass to the approaching seas and then to Tiny and Barbecue as they made sail. When they had hoisted and trimmed the lower fore and aft sails, the spray once again hissed along her sides. When they heaved the log again, they were delighted to find she was making seven knots. But the pumps had to be manned on the hour. It was exhausting work, with no end in sight.

"Must have worked some of her caulking lose in the gale."

"Aye, shall we farther it?" Farthering a canvas patch over the area from the outside could slow the leak.

"Don't know where she's split. Besides, the canvas would slow us down."

"Aye, it's to the pumps again for us, then."

As the wind moderated to a breeze, *Berbice* slowed.

"Time to get the main topsail on her, don't you think ma'am?"

"Yes, Tiny, if you please."

In a few moments Tiny and Barbecue returned to the quarterdeck. "Main topmast's cracked. She won't hold sail."

"I guess we'll have to jury rig something." Anne didn't know what or how, but she'd heard her father say that in a similar situation.

Tiny's face brightened, "Aye, aye, ma'am." He knew how to do it.

In four hours *Berbice* sported a new topmast, crafted by Tiny from one of her spare topsail yards.

As the ship worked to the east, Anne advanced the dead-reckoning track on the chart every two hours. Simon was the first of the injured to reappear. His ribs pained him; but he could do duty at the helm.

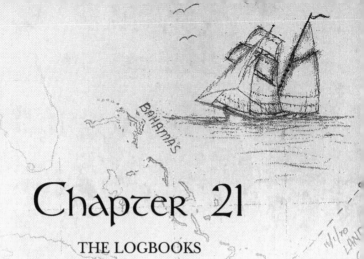

Chapter 21

THE LOGBOOKS

Berbice, October 14, 1770

The following entries are made by myself, Anne Easton, acting navigator. We have an old octant aboard, but our precious reduction tables were soaked in the tumult of the gale. I shall be hard put to reduce sights, except for the noon latitude, and I trust not my estimations to reduce the noon sight. I am continuing our dead-reckoning track, and believe that to be the most accurate, although it could be off by several leagues.

D.R. position 72°36' by 36°58', light wind NNE.

Weathered a bit of a blow heading out of Norfolk for off-soundings. Clawed off under triple-reefed foresail until it blew out. Cap't. Harte had a drogue rigged to a bridle to haul the ship's head around, or we should all have perished on a lee shore that night. First storm trysail blew out also. Currently making five and a half knots in a light breeze south by southeast. Hoping to pick up the Trades in the next few days.

Captain Harte has been struck on the head and cannot stand by himself. His head pains him sorely, and he complains his vision is blurred. Most worrisome is that he cannot keep victuals down, not even sea biscuit. I have dosed him with laudanum and he sleeps fitfully. Should this come to no good and he withers, let it be known by these presents that he was injured doing his duty, and were it not for his efforts, the ship would surely have been lost with all hands. He was struck by the main boom when the rusty ring on the mainsheet block parted. I for one am sure the rusty ring was not suffered to remain until it broke through his negligence. The sea always has a way of seeking the weakest parts of a vessel and reminding the mariner of these inadequacies at the most inopportune moments, as when the gale is raging. I shall act as navigator until he recovers enough to resume duty. In the meantime, Bosun Tiny does double duty in command, along with Gunny and Barbecue, who alone with myself came through the gale uninjured.

Atticus has a sore ribcage and a swollen hand that speaks of cracked bones. Ordineaux could finally make his way up the companionway to sit in the fresh air today, this third day after the gale. Simon does light duty, and can take his trick at the helm.

The ship leaks badly, and all who can, do their duty at the pumps, including myself. It is an exhausting hourly chore. We cannot find the leak, and can only guess it is the garboard strake.

Everything below is wet. The deck looks like laundry day, with all the clothes and linen hanging about to dry. A few of us have saltwater boils, but the dry weather and our precious lime juice should soon take care of them.

After weathering such a maelstrom, something more wonderful than simple relief settles upon one's soul. I have renewed confidence in meeting the challenges of rescuing my father. What could pose more of a challenge than awful nature itself? What circumstance could stand in my way more deadly or powerful than the ocean gale?

Captain's Logbook, Berbice, entry by Anne Easton, October 19, 1770.

D.R. position 69°42' by 33°28', light wind ENE.

Another day of easting and we shall point Berbice's bowsprit to Jamaica! Tiny has made Herculean efforts to come at the garboard strake from the bilge, moving cargo around and even out of the hold. Let it be known by these presents that he has done commendable duty, and his efforts at caulking from inside have slowed the leak. Although none of us expect this repair would last the trial of a gale, it has relieved us of some of the most burdensome duty of pumping. Now we man the pumps only every two hours.

Captain Nathaniel Harte can now sit up in his cot without retching. Barbecue has made a lobscouse that he has kept down this hour. While he is awake, we entertain each other with tales of our travels at sea, and I find him quite amusing, with a light spirit in spite of his grievous hurt. I can only hope he finds my company a comfort. I feel guilty that he has been so hurt in the rescue of my own dear father. I would gladly take his place in the sickbed, were it in my power to make that sacrifice.

Captain's Logbook, Berbice, entry by Anne Easton, October 21, 1770

D.R. position 68°02' by 30°12', the Trades!

We have picked up the trade winds, and are boiling along on a beam reach making seven and eight knots. Glorious weather and fine sailing! We shall try to make landfall at Turks and Caicos and use the Caicos Passage past Great Iguana. I worry that our dead reckoning is imprecise and that we shall miss landfall, or fall in with the shoals at night. I find myself constantly peering ahead, trying to see breakers before we ground, to avert disaster. I have run through my dead-reckoning calculations thrice. I sit in the foretop dressed in sailor's slops at sunset and search the horizon for telltale cloud tops or breakers on the reefs. My anxiety grows by the hour! The safety of the ship and all aboard her is in my hands. This is a worrisome duty; I know now why Bosun Tiny shuns it!

Personal Logbook, Anne Easton, October 22, 1770

I have begun my own log, as I find it inopportune to express my personal thoughts in the captain's very own log! Nathaniel has been able to come out on deck, and I believe the fresh salt air has done him wonders. I removed the stitches put in his cheek, the last evidence of our encounter with Deadlight Helms. I shaved him with a bucket of brine and a well-stropped blade for the first time since the gale, and note his comely features. My heart flutters at times when I'm near him. I held his dear face in my hands and only wished I could heal his hurt with a kiss, and oh, I wish I had the courage to do so! But how would he receive such a bold maneuver? I find he is a man of the world and, I suspect, not the chaste virgin I am!

P. S. Chaste virgin—ha! I find myself dreaming of his protecting arms encircling me and his showering me with kisses. And more! Chaste virgin, indeed! My thoughts can wander to sensualities I'm sure would make my dear captain blush.

Mr. Ordineaux says Captain Harte had a heroic encounter with a Royal Navy officer in Baltimore, but he declines to give me any details. I shall have to bring it up with Captain Harte when I gain his trust. A duel! He is so modest, to keep such a thing to himself. I shall savor all the details.

Personal Logbook, Nathaniel Harte, October 22:
    I have begun a personal logbook, as I find it inopportune to express myself in *Berbice*'s log. My vision remains blurred but improves by the day. This entry shall be short, as close work with pen brings on nausea. Have informed Mr. Ordineaux in no uncertain terms that my exploits ashore are not to be repeated. The Old Man's daughter asks embarrassing questions. And what a delight she has turned out to be! I expected a spoiled and childish creature, demanding comforts we cannot supply aboard ship. Perhaps the thunderclap of the main boom has loosened my prejudice and cleared my heart, though my vision remains blurred. I think now that Anne is as able a seaman as any aboard. Let it be known by these presents, if by none other, that Anne has taken over navigation of the ship and is quite assiduous in her duties. I can find no fault in her reckoning (which I have checked in her absence) and agree that the D.R. track is probably better than our best guess at local apparent noon. Hats off to the Old Man for raising such a daughter! She is no powder puff, and can discourse on the Sons of Liberty and Rights of Man. Her stories of travels with the Old Man at sea are truly

entertaining. I had no idea she sent a pirate to the Devil off Algiers. Yet she is a sweet and light-hearted girl, a joy to have aboard, besides the navigation.

Anne's Personal Logbook, October 25

I find Nathaniel enjoys my company, and we sit for hours in the canvas deck chairs (Gunny has sewn up another) and converse. He has read the great books! I delight to find he has a gentleman's education and can discourse on natural law and philosophy. Not since my last visit with old Captain William have I been able to discuss the brotherhood of mankind and the natural laws of freedom and equality.

Upon hearing Nathaniel's agreement on the natural laws supporting one's right to the personal freedoms of life and liberty, I gained the courage to broach a subject that has been most troublesome to me. Should I feel guilt at taking the lives of those pirates who accosted me in the woods with Deadlight Helms? Was it within my rights to send them to the Devil, or am I a foul murderess? I asked Nathaniel his opinion, as I cannot live with this feeling that I should have remorse. He replied that it is within the natural rights of man, as he sees it, that one should defend one's personal liberties, and if he who would tread on them pushes the contest to a mortal combat, so be it. "You are justified," he said. I am easier now that I know Nathaniel does not consider me a murderous villain!

Captain's Logbook, Berbice, entry by Anne E. October 28, 1770

D.R. position 69°35' by 24°42', Fresh trade wind, beam reach with lowers, eight knots by the log.

I have asked Tiny to post watch all night, as I fear our dead reckoning may be off. I could never forgive myself if we were to wreck on the Caicos banks! They are but low islands and can only be discerned by their overhead clouds at a distance. Perhaps I should have shaped course for a landfall easier to make out at night! I am every hour haunted by uneasy feelings that my navigation has us bound for disaster!

Anne's personal logbook, October 29, 1770

I continue to feel guilt, as if I should be walking in the shadows of the gallows, for the murder of the two accomplices of Deadlight Helms. Yet they said they intended to kill me! Why should I feel remorse for the lives of those who would have taken that which I hold dearest, my own life and liberty? Nathaniel says I should view the matter thus: that I have a right under the natural laws to my own life and liberty, and anyone who threatens either, does so only at their own mortal hazard. I find comfort in his viewpoint!

This is much the same viewpoint as my father's, and I shall try to take their well-meaning counsel to heart. After Algiers I was shaken with horror, and then came these feelings of guilt over what I had done to the pirate who climbed the rigging after me. My father said of the matter that when a man becomes a pirate, he signs his own death sentence, and it is an unwholesome burden on the rest of us to carry out that sentence, but an obligation of civilized men, nevertheless. We sent over a hundred pirates to the Devil off Algiers that day, and he says he only feels the better for it. I pray the same lightness of attitude may someday release me from my feelings of guilt and shame. Such a silly woman—the victim of such offenses, and yet I feel at fault! Shouldn't the guilt and shame be on the heads of those pirates, as they roast in Hell?

Anne's Personal Logbook, November 1, 1770

Nathaniel has resumed his duties of command; but has asked me to continue with my navigation, as he is still prone to headaches and has trouble with his vision when figuring or plotting the course. We made landfall at Caicos in daylight, thanks be, and now head down the Windward Passage between Hispaniola and Cuba.

The wind remains fair, and we fly along at nine knots on a beam reach. The sunlight dances gold on the water this afternoon. Ever since Caicos, the gannets and boobies have flown about the ship on their graceful wings, performing aerial ballet for our enjoyment. What must they think of the huge white wings of *Berbice*? I so much enjoy my place in the deck chair on the quarterdeck, the sea foaming and hissing by the lee side. I do not stay under a parasol (there is none on board), so I have a tan unbecoming a proper lady. I don't care! But I do love the sailing so much. There is no other mode of travel—no, there is no other occupation—so satisfying and peaceful as these days in the trade winds. Nathaniel has said he enjoys the sailing for sailing's sake, as well. We seem to be two souls alike, he and I, never more happy than wandering the ocean billows. I fear Ellie and her land-loving kindred shall never understand.

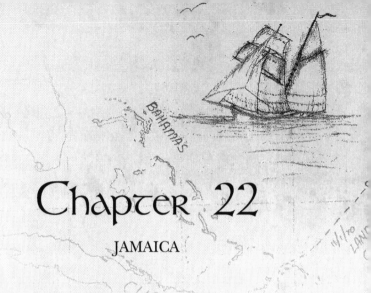

Chapter 22

JAMAICA

Captain Harte, Ordineaux, Tiny, and Anne held a council in the greatcabin. "I do not think it prudent to land in Kingston," said the captain.

"Aye, we dare not allow the Royal Navy to inspect our crew list for deserters!" said Ordineaux.

"We could run afoul of that ten-gun brig."

"Not so much chance of that, if the Navy keeps her on station off the Virginia capes."

"Aye, perhaps, but she could be sent to Jamaica or Halifax at any time."

"We should see what foul play has put the Old Man—er, begging your pardon, ma'am—Captain Easton, in jail, without raising suspicion."

"We need to careen to get at that leak," said Ordineaux. *Berbice* continued to leak badly, and the physical strain of manning the pumps with a shorthanded crew was telling.

"I want to see my father at the first possible moment! We must get him out of that fever den before he succumbs!"

"We could put into Port Antonio."

"Too far over the Blue Mountains to Kingston. We must get into Kingston quickly."

"Aye, laddy, and out again as quick, I expect."

"Aye, here's what we'll do," said Harte. "We put in to Morant Bay and careen; Ordineaux will be in command there. Anne and I will get some local mounts and ride into Kingston. I'll make soundings there and see how foul the bottom of this thing is."

"We can re-caulk in one tide, if the leak is within reach."

"If her garboards are sprung, it's the pumps for us until we get Captain Easton out of prison, agreed?"

"Aye, aye."

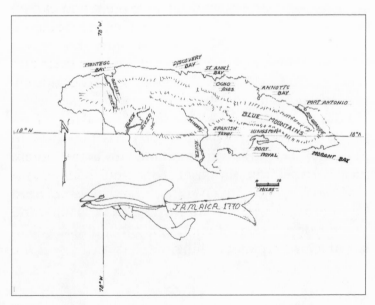

* * *

"Land ho!" Simon called from the maintop. The first sight of Jamaica was a castle of towering cumulus clouds on the horizon, where a dark blue mass rose to meet the clouds. As *Berbice* neared, the height of the Blue Mountains seemed to increase, and greens of the forest canopy began to appear. As she skirted the eastern end of the island, they watched dark gray-green shadows of clouds create a moving patchwork on the verdant hills.

Anne clung to the rail when they opened Morant Bay on the south side of the island. The steep hills that dropped to the calm bay waters were covered in palm trees that swayed in the breeze. She breathed in the musty smell of moist soil and wet vegetation. Tiny heaved the lead as *Berbice* made way towards a rim of white sand, a promising place to ground and careen her on the falling tide. They could see the ripples in the sand bottom of the bay, as if they were gliding over the desert in the ship, with nothing between them and the sand but a sort of translucent air. "Two fathom, one fathom four."

"Round up, Atticus," said Captain Harte. "Tiny, drop anchor when she backs."

As *Berbice* turned up into the wind, the breeze caught her square topsails and backed them against the foremast, rapidly slowing the ship's forward motion. Tiny cut the anchor free as soon as she made no more forward progress. They were within sixty feet of the shore, and could hear wavelets rustling on the ivory beach sand.

"Perhaps you can warp her in from here, Mr. Ordineaux; leave the anchor where it is and use it to pull yourselves off again."

"Aye, aye, Captain, a capital spot! Would make a fine shipway for the inclined, *hor hor*!" Captain Harte missed the quip, as his mind was already on the problem of finding some local horses for the trip to Kingston.

"Lower the boat, Tiny; you shall row Miss Easton and me ashore."

Anne appeared on deck in a dress. Strapped to her thigh out of sight was her dueling pistol and a dagger. Her second suit of Baltimore finery, an ankle-length dress that billowed out at the waist, was carefully tucked in a large canvas sea bag.

"Ma'am, I am going ashore to find mounts and traveling directions overland to Kingston. Do you care to come ashore?"

"At your earliest convenience, Captain!"

"We shall buy you a parasol straightaway," said Nathaniel as they climbed down into the boat. "All the proper ladies sport them in the tropics."

Captain Harte noted the steep drop-off between *Berbice* and the shore, where the water turned from turquoise abruptly to white, almost blinding in the bright sunlight. The jollyboat ground onto the beach. Tiny jumped over the side and dragged the boat another few feet up the beach. Anne disembarked without so much as a wet ankle.

Tiny took his leave and shoved off to *Berbice*, while Anne and Nathaniel walked up the squeaking sand to find some habitation. They walked in the shade of the palm trees that lined the upper beach, forming the fringe of the steep, forested hills. In a quarter hour they came upon a thatched camp inhabited by impoverished blacks dressed in shredded rags or less. Several of them ran when they saw the whites approach.

"Runaway slaves, no doubt," said Nathaniel in a low voice.

A goat was tethered near a group of tiny thatch huts so low one could not even stand upright in them. They blended with the vegetation and were nearly invisible from the bay. Two roosters vied for midday crowing dominance.

As they approached the group of huts, a young man strode forth to meet them.

"You come to take us, Massa?"

Nathaniel noted the young man held a machete behind his back, and his compatriots, armed in a similar fashion, glowered from behind the palm trees.

"No, we come from the boat," Nathaniel motioned toward *Berbice*.

"We all sure see dat!"

Nathaniel realized his answer did not allay any fears, for the ship could well be a slaver. He continued, "We need horses to ride to Kingston; can you help us?" It was plain that this impoverished group could not afford horse feed, much less an entire animal. The young man turned to a large man behind a towering bay tree nearby. The man stepped into the open and approached, putting his machete between his breeches and the rope that served as a belt.

"Captain Matumbwe, sah," he bowed from the waist.

"Nathaniel Harte, sir," he made a leg. "I escort Miss Easton, the daughter of the owner of yonder ship." Anne curtsied.

265

"We come only to find mounts to make our way to Kingston."

"Why you not sail da boat 'round?" asked Matumbwe.

"Some, ah, problems with the governor." At this, Matumbwe's skeptical frown broke into a broad grin. Two rows of perfect white teeth constrasted with his blue-black face.

"Ha ha ha! You got da problem with da gov'nor? Ha ha! Maybe take his ladyfriend? Ha ha ha, come have some of da hospitality wit us. We got da gov'nor problem too—see? He think he own my lady friend—and me too! Ha ha ha! Come hab da hospitality." He motioned them to follow towards the huts. They sat on a palm log facing the bay, while Matumbwe took the throne, a stump facing the forest.

"I nebber turn my back to da woods. Get shot like dat!"

A shockingly beautiful African woman appeared with an offering of coconuts. Matumbwe thanked her and mumbled something in her ear, upon which she disappeared behind the huts once more. Matumbwe drew his machete and deftly opened the coconuts, turning each into a drinking bowl.

"I know da man from da ship, he thirsty one."

"Aye, Captain Matumbwe, thankee."

The African woman reappeared with an offering of jerked goat meat on a banana leaf. Harte graciously accepted and found the strip of dried meat a challenge to his mandibles. More of the group of escapees began to filter back from the forest.

"Now we get down to da business, but we got no horse. Can show you how to find da horse, but you got to go yourself. And you don't say notting about Matumbwe, 'cause he be gone anyways to join the maroons, ha ha ha!"

"We have no interest in returning you back to your masters, sir. It is against the natural laws for one man of reason to enslave another." Anne looked at Nathaniel in sudden admiration.

"I don' know da natural law, but da Massa get his hands on anyone here, and it go mighty poorly for him. How much you pay for to find da horses? We a mighty needy group."

"Can your men help us careen yonder ship?"

"Don't know notting about da careen, sir, but we got plenty strong men!"

"A shirt or pantaloons for every man that aids us in careening the ship."

"How about da shot, powder, and da musket?"

"We have only two muskets, and we need them," Nathaniel lied. He dared not supply arms to such a desperate group.

"Dat's fine, we got plenty musket hid somewhere anyhow. How about da shot and da powder?"

"We are a merchant vessel, not a man-o'-war; we carry no great store of weapons, shot, or powder—except, of course, for the cannons."

"Da cannon too heavy, never make it up da mountain."

"Sailors slops for the lot of you, then."

Matumbwe grinned, "An' for dat, I throw in da women folk, too." Anne sucked in her breath in horror.

"He means to work on the ship, my dear; isn't that right, Captain Matumbwe?" Nathaniel gave him a wink.

"Dat's de sum total. Ha ha ha! And dat's dat!"

Nathaniel stood and shook Matumbwe's massive hand. His worries about how his injured crew could careen and re-float *Berbice* in time for any possible trouble were relieved. As he turned to walk back down the beach, he noticed two men had been standing behind him at three paces, in case negotiations did not go well, he surmised.

* * *

"Mr. Ordineaux, look at that! They've got the captain and Anne!"

Captain Harte and Anne were marching down the beach toward *Berbice*, at the head of a column of Africans, men first, women trailing behind. Next to the captain strode the massive Matumbwe, a bandoleer holding a pistol and powder horn slung across his chest.

"Fetch Gunny and have him load grapeshot, on the double!"

Behind the ship's bulwarks, the deadly grapeshot was rammed home over measures of gunpowder. The crew waited helplessly to see how the scene on the beach would unfold. Tiny and Atticus were in the palm trees, rigging block and tackle to pull *Berbice* over by the mastheads when the tide went out. They stood warily behind trees and watched the procession stop on the beach.

Captain Harte bellowed at the ship, "Send the jollyboat ashore; we've got help!"

A huzzah sounded from *Berbice*. Ordineaux and Gunny hopped into the jollyboat. Atticus was about to join in the merriment, but Tiny's iron grip stopped him dead.

"We best wait and see how this plays out," he said, and he motioned for Atticus to fetch the pistol and musket they'd brought ashore.

Within a few minutes it was clear Ordineaux had organized the small band into work parties; the help was welcome indeed. A procession of African women carried the ship's cargo on their heads to safe hiding up the beach, while the men aboard ship unloaded the hold and used the boats to bring the cargo to the water's edge.

"Mr. Ordineaux, a word, if you please."

"Aye, aye, Captain."

"We struck a bargain from desperation on both sides. He wanted weapons; I have promised slops for all. Mind you keep a guard with all of our muskets, and have the men carry pistols. A man must always be watching for mischief from the quarterdeck, never two paces from the swivels. And mind to keep a slow match lit."

"Aye, aye."

"Anne and I will go to the nearest plantation and get mounts to proceed to Kingston. Captain Matumbwe will be our guide. I don't think any mischief will befall you while he is with us. Get the ship careened and afloat again as quickly as possible."

"Aye, aye."

* * *

At dawn the following morning, the party of three—Anne and Captains Matumbwe and Harte—set off into the forest. They followed a footpath up a streambed, and in an hour were treated to a view of the bay below. With *Berbice* too close to the beach to be seen from that vantage point, Captain Harte breathed a little easier.

The Scottish overseer of the first plantation they came upon flatly refused to lend them mounts, on the grounds that their story was suspicious. "I can see losing one horse, but nay two." Luckily, Matumbwe had agreed to guide them to the next plantation. Avoiding the roads, they trekked through the forest over footpaths that scaled hills and traversed streambeds. Fortunately, the overseer of the next plantation was happy to assist them, and agreed to pick up his mounts in Kingston at an appointed stable in a week or so. He even insisted Nathaniel and Anne accept his hospitality that evening, and so they passed the night in the lavish style of the planter.

* * *

Matumbwe returned to his camp on the beach via his network of secret footpaths. He heard thunder as he approached the crest of the hill overlooking the beach. Listening, he felt a chill pass through him as he realized the noise came from down on the beach: horsemen! He ran down the footpath in the darkness, thorny vines ripping his legs and arms as he crashed through the undergrowth. His throat ached and his breath came in gulps, and yet he ran on. He charged down the slope to the palms fringing the beach and stumbled headlong into some low mangroves. A horseman charged by with a cutlass in one hand and a man's head in the other. The horseman reined in and turned to make another pass at the scattering slaves on the beach. As he went by, he tossed the head like so much garbage into the bushes where Matumbwe crouched.

Matumbwe ran down behind the fringe of palms and beheld a scene of mad slaughter: horsemen circling a group of slaves, brutally cutting down those who fled and randomly firing pistols into the huddled, pleading group. Some of the horsemen carried torches in one hand and a cutlass in the other. The beach was strewn with brown bodies, blood pouring into the white sand in the moonlight.

At length the orgy of slaughter ended, and the survivors were chained together by the neck and made to march down the beach. As they passed, Matumbwe did not see his wife among them. He ran onto the beach and looked at the faces of the fallen women, frozen in death agony. His head pounded in fear every time he came upon another and turned it over to see if it was his loved one. Where *Berbice* had been anchored, he saw only a patch of sail out on the bay. The huge man sat on the sand and cried, tearing at his hair in a frenzy of grief.

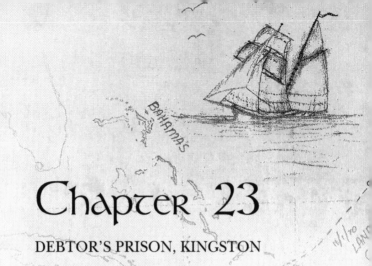

Chapter 23

DEBTOR'S PRISON, KINGSTON

When the two hot and weary travelers arrived, Anne had to make several applications before she found suitable lodging. Her only reference was her father in debtor's prison, which caused them to be turned down at the first boarding house. In contrast, Captain Harte found lodgings aplenty for seafaring men of all social castes. Before they parted, they agreed to seek out Captain Easton immediately on the morrow.

* * *

Anne shivered in dread as she approached the walls of the debtor's prison. They were cracked, and covered in green and black patches of mildew and algae. Captain Harte pounded the heavy knocker on the massive iron-strapped oak door. A window in it opened, the stubbled face of a guard appearing.

"Don't open until ten." This statement revealed the guard had but two opposing teeth left in a mouth foul with decay.

"Half a Spanish dollar says you open now, good sir; show us to our friend."

The bolt on the door was drawn. "We would like to visit the good Captain Easton," said Anne.

"If he were much good he wouldn't be here, now would he?"

"Hold your tongue, you miserable wretch! Defile a better man than yourself again, and I shall have satisfaction."

"Nay, good sir, I only thought it were to you he owed money," the jailor groveled. "Better victuals for your friend can be had at a mere sixpence a day. Another sixpence and some straw with fewer beetles could be found. A laundress can be had for tuppence a week," and so the jailor outlined the cost of each item that would make the miserable place a bit less hellish.

"Is it really you, Anne, my dear?" The voice was weak; the good Captain Easton barely recognizable with his scraggly beard and sallow complexion. Visible through his tattered clothes, insect bites covered his arms and legs, and he stank. Flies buzzed around the mephitis of the chamber pot. Anne was reduced to uncontrollable sobs to see her father in such a condition, and looking far older than his years.

Captain Harte carried on, "What happened, sir?"

"We were on our way to St. Eustatius. A Navy frigate ran us down off Anguilla. They tried me in Admiralty Court, and of course, they were anxious that their fellow officers get their prize money. I felt like a baitfish in a school of sharks."

"You had no lawyer?"

"*Ha*! And what good is an Admiralty lawyer residing in the Navy's home base? I wouldn't be surprised if he sees his share of the prize money! They have fined me treble the value of *Jubilant* and her goods, upon auction of the same, as an example to other rebellious Jonathans."

"My God!"

"Aye, *Jubilant* and cargo are up for auction, tied to the wharf at Kingston."

"And what of the crew?"

"Those who weren't pressed into the Navy have disappeared into the waterfront of Kingston, I expect."

"Can ye not post bond and get out of here?"

"Aye, lad, now there's the rub. The specie box on *Jubilant* disappeared, seems like, during the chase by the Navy frigate. I suspect Gideon Helms had something to do with that."

"You mean the one they call Deadlight, with the drooping eyelid?"

"Aye, that be the one. Would that I had never clapped eye on the brute, or took any pity on him. He was a mutineer these many years ago. I should have listened to Captain William and never trusted Deadlight's woeful story."

"What of Captain William? Can he not make bail?" Anne spoke while tears ran down her cheeks.

"More's the mystery, for he did not respond to my most urgent messages. I feared the worst for him. Way back in the War of Jenkin's Ear, we took Captain William's fortune off his privateer to save it from a mutiny. Deadlight was one of the mutineers, and has informed me Captain William is nowhere to be found! He still has a sizable fortune left, I believe.

The mystery of it is, he said he would leave words if he were gone. Aye, that's just the way he's always said it, a queer bit of phrase, but always the same. He was always fond of playing the riddle games with me when I was his cabin boy. Said he would 'leave words' where the remaining fortune is, if ever I should be in need of it. I daresay I could use some now!"

"We shall make some arrangements with the jailor and seek out Captain William directly, sir!"

"I am most grateful, young man."

Anne embraced her father, breaking down once more into tears.

"One last thing, my daughter: How did you know I split on these rocks?"

"Deadlight Helms told me."

"Aye?"

"A story I shall relate later, father; we'd best be off to find Captain William's gold!"

* * *

They found it easily enough, a two-story half-timber townhouse. The sign nailed to the front door announced, "Property in Probate." The door was open. A clerk of the colonial government sat at a desk in the middle of the room.

"Auction at midday on the Sabbath; you may look around for what may be of interest to you."

"Dear sir, we came looking for Captain William!"

"Then I am sorry to inform you . . . how do I put this delicately? You must have surmised from the sign on the door, Captain William is, ah, missing and presumed to have departed this world."

"Presumed?"

"No body has been found, but we have received testimony that he had an accident."

"Who supplied this testimony?"

"A strange fellow with a drooping eyelid, got here before I did to give old Captain William a message from Captain Easton, I think."

"Were there any other papers?"

"None, other than the suicide note supplied to the court by this Helms fellow." Anne and Nathaniel exchanged looks but kept their counsel. "The fellow—Deadlight, I believe he's called by acquaintances, rough sort of chap—found a suicide note here in the house. The place was rather wrecked when I arrived; the old fellow must have been desperate about something. Easy to imagine, this Captain Easton was counting on the old fellow to bail him out—some money the old man had in trust. Anyway, I hear Easton didn't get a penny. But I ramble; please examine the fixtures, what's left of them. I believe the house is sound enough." The clerk waved his hand about, pointing at the structure. "Note the sturdy post and beam construction, and the rather eccentric vaulted ceiling. Not at all impractical in this infernally hot climate, I assure you."

There was an ear-splitting screech from the rafters. "Oh heavens, that damned bird again! It recites rhymes all night from Hades itself—that is, when it isn't snoring like a plank saw. I tell you, that creature's hellish verses have the soldiers so frightened they refuse to stand guard inside the house at night! Please excuse the inconvenience. We have tried everything. It will not come down, and takes cover as soon as a pistol is

277

raised." There was another ear-splitting screech. The white and yellow head of a blue macaw appeared over one of the rafters, turning to the side to focus an eye on the newcomers. The bird picked up a nut from a wooden bowl that balanced on the rafter, and nutshells bounced on the floor planks below. The bird let loose another screech, and the clerk held his hands up to his ears. "Really now, that infernal thing must go!"

"May I have it?" asked Anne.

"Milady, I caution you, the satanic verses that little monster recites at night would unsettle the likes of Henry Morgan himself, let alone its infernal snoring! The laugh it has sounds like an old codger. A most vexing animal!"

"Come Angustine, come to Annie."

"She knows this creature?"

"Aye, she knew the captain." Angustine flew off the rafter and settled on the top of the open front door, where he turned one eye on Anne and bobbed his head up and down, as if scrutinizing her from keelson to masthead.

"Come, sweetie, that's a good bird." Angustine flew off the door and took a perch on her shoulder.

"You may have it, milady, with compliments, please! I confess I would almost pay you to take it! It imitates the irritating laugh of an old man, quite unnerving."

"It's settled then; come, sweetie." Anne's skirts ruffled as she turned and marched out the door, Angustine perched on her shoulder.

"Sir, I hope you don't regret this. Do not take me to task on the morrow after you've been treated to a night with that miserable hellion."

"Aye, sir; I consider myself forewarned."

Captain Harte joined Anne outside. She was sitting sidesaddle on her mount, the blue macaw still perched on her shoulder. Nathaniel put his boot in the stirrup, threw a leg over his horse, and they proceeded down the street.

"It appears poor Captain William is dead," said Nathaniel.

"Aye, and I'll wager Deadlight did him in. Captain William would never kill himself, nor would he fail my father."

"This could not be worse. If anyone knows where Captain William's treasure is, it would be Deadlight. He must have taken all his papers, and with them the words of where the treasure lay. The hoard itself must not have been in Captain William's house, for it looks like Deadlight ransacked the place and could not find it."

"Yes, Deadlight would not have come after me if he had found it. There is hope still. Poor Captain William, that dear old man."

"I hold more hope of finding his treasure than your finding mercy at Spanish Towne or the Government House in Kingston. Your father said they were making an example of him. They will be as harsh as the law allows."

"I must try; I can think of nothing else to do. Perhaps they will listen to reason."

Nathaniel could see tears welling up in her eyes. He did not have the heart to discourage her. What could it hurt, a trip to Spanish Towne or Government House? He was at a loss for a plan of action; it seemed as if the *Jubilant* was forfeit, and Captain Easton was bound to hazard jail fever in the filthy debtor's prison.

He came about and trimmed his sheets on another tack to cheer the poor girl.

"It looks as if you have a new pet."

"I could never leave dear Angustine alone in this world!"

"The bird has a reputation for being difficult."

She laughed, "He imitates Captain William's dry laugh when certain naval practices are mentioned."

"I don't think he's fallen into such ill graces by laughing out loud."

"Aye, Captain, sounds as if Angustine has given up swearing like a drunken bosun, and has taken up verse."

"Verse indeed, if the clerk is to be believed. You cannot take the creature to your lodgings; they'll throw you out."

"Oh dear, you're right, Captain. What shall we do?" Just then they rounded a corner, and the expansive harbor came into view. At the far end of the wharves, given away by her rakish swept-back masts, lay *Jubilant*. Anne followed Nathaniel's gaze and grinned. He looked at her and returned a mischievous smile.

"Dare we?"

"He's familiar with the ship. He sailed in her when Captain William joined our voyages. He'll be all right."

"We'll need a small boat and cover of darkness. I shall make the arrangements, and be at your lodging at sundown."

"Aye, aye, Captain."

"Did you note the bowl of food up on the rafter for Angustine? Curious, wasn't it?"

Chapter 24

GOVERNMENT HOUSE

Riding through town toward the Government House, Anne bought a good supply of fruits and nuts for Angustine along the way. The macaw feasted on these as he waddled back and forth on Anne's empty saddle, bobbing his head as he inspected passersby, and waiting for his mistress to return. The first boat from *Glad Tidings* had come ashore. Angustine spied one of the crew, the one with a drooping eyelid. Suddenly he let out another ear-splitting screech and flew up into an overhanging tamarind tree.

Anne paced the outer hall of the Government House for two hours before a spectacled clerk directed her to a drawing room. The drawing room was furnished with comfortable sofas and chairs and decorated with a life-size painting of King George in his youth. Another hour passed, until she was met by another clerk, who showed her into a tiny office beneath a staircase.

"What may I do for you, milady?"

"I need to see the governor concerning my father."

"And who, perchance, is your father?"

"Captain Jonathan Easton."

"Ah, the continental smuggler."

"Sir?"

"I'm sorry, milady, there is no chance of seeing the governor: He is at sea. Perhaps you could make an appointment to see a deputy."

"Very well then, make it so."

"With regrets, milady, you'll have to visit his office and make arrangements with his clerk."

"I will do so, then; where is it?"

"I'm afraid it would be impossible to just walk right in. You shall have to be introduced. The governor is a very busy man."

"Then please, sir, without delay, make the introduction."

"Certainly. Do you have a letter of introduction?"

"No, I do not."

"I must be frank: Your association with a convicted smuggler lacks authority as a recommendation for the governor's time."

"Don't you understand? I wish to plead for my father. He is jailed in a filthy fever den, and may not survive to pay his debt. Something must be done."

"Quite so, humm, plead for mercy." The bureaucrat looked at Anne for the first time—in fact, he looked her up and down, nodding his head as his eyes fixed briefly on her bosom. "I may be able to get you in, depending on how committed you are."

"I am very committed, sir! It is my father we speak of."

"Quite. Well then, let's see . . ." The little man pulled an appointment book from a desk drawer and began to mumble to himself, "Madam is out of town until the Sabbath, cockfight and cigars at seven, hmmm."

"I thought you said I had to see someone else to get an appointment."

"I am doing my best for you, milady. Do I waste my time?"

"Oh no, sir, please."

"Hmmm, perhaps after his dinner tonight, say ten o'clock."

"Tonight!"

"Quite."

"I shall be here."

"The doorman will show you out. Good day, milady; I only hope you understand the need for commitment in this affair, commitment and discretion."

Anne's puzzlement showed on her face. "Sir, I'm sure if a demonstration of commitment is required, I shall pass any such test, thank you."

"Quite." She turned to leave, and the little man shook his head. These puritanical provincials! She had no idea.

* * *

After sunset, Anne made her apologies to Angustine and covered him with a cloth sack. The parrot began to snore almost immediately. From her bedroom window she saw Captain Harte ride up, and hurried downstairs. The matron of the house gave her a disapproving glare, but Anne was too preoccupied to care.

"How was your audience with the governor?"

"He is away; I am to see his deputy tonight at ten o'clock."

"An odd time to do business. We must hurry, then."

Nathaniel had hired a rowing wherry for the night, but without the oarsman, a necessary detail that cost him extra. He handed Anne, carrying Angustine, into the boat and took the oars. There was little moon as she guided them through a swarm of anchored ships toward the outer wharf where *Jubilant* was berthed. The bird snored under his hood, until suddenly it came forth with a shocking verse, talking in his sleep as the clerk had warned:

"In the cauldron boil and bake;
Eye of newt and toe of frog,
Wool of bat and tongue of dog."

Anne giggled; Nathaniel cocked his head in disbelief. After a few more snores, the dry, singsong voice came again from under the canvas sack:

"For a charm of powerful trouble,
Like a hell-broth boil and bubble!"

Nathaniel stopped rowing. "Devil take me, the bird's bewitched!"

"I think he's taken to *Macbeth*," Anne giggled. "You don't recognize it?"

"Aye," said Nathaniel, and he thought awhile, leaning on the oars. Then all of a sudden he sat up, and with a broad grin on his face said: "Double, double, toil and trouble, Fire burn and cauldron bubble."

"What sort of deviltry goes on there?" The booming voice came from the quarterdeck of a nearby ship.

Nathaniel chuckled and Anne suppressed another giggle. Nathaniel put his back against the oars and the wherry shot away into the cover of darkness.

At length they approached the *Jubilant*. The schooner was tied to the wharf with two customs tide watchers aboard as guards.

"Looks as if the transom windows are open."

"I shall wake our little friend." Angustine let out another screech. "Shush, Angustine, it is I." The old bird cooed and climbed onto Anne's shoulder. Nathaniel looked at *Jubilant* to see if they had alarmed anyone. There was no evidence they'd been seen. Dragging an oar blade now and then to steer, Nathaniel let the boat glide toward the greatcabin transom windows.

Angustine became agitated as they approached the transom of the ship. He left Anne's shoulder to pace back and forth in the bow of the wherry, bobbing his head and turning it to the side. When they were but a fathom from the stern, Angustine flew through the greatcabin windows to assume his accustomed accommodation above a deck beam in the stern quarter. Anne tossed in the open sack of nuts and fruit; they landed with a soft thump on the cushion of the transom settee. Nathaniel backed the boat silently away, then pulled hard in the direction of Kingston.

The stars sparkled on the black water, dancing in the wavelets. Every time Nathaniel gave a pull on the oars, Anne felt a little thrill in the pit of her stomach. Here she was, alone with him at last, gliding through a scene of beauty.

"Aren't the stars wonderful tonight?"

"Aye, and the air uncommonly balmy. Orion's belt makes a fitting crown for your loveliness, milady. I steer by it."

She felt herself blush at the word play. "You exert yourself overmuch, Nathaniel, pray leave off the oars and let us drift about in this fantasy world for awhile."

"A pretty fantasy indeed, to be sharing this vessel with thee." Nathaniel shipped the oars, careful that not a drop fell on Anne.

"Pray relax Nathaniel; I can see the sweat on your brow."

"Aye, milady, permission to untie my neck cloth?"

"Of course…" she almost added, *my love.*

So this is passion, thought Nathaniel, *how much fuller it is. I am a-swim in it!* They lay together on the floorboards of the skiff, until the moon sent a sparkling highway of silver across the dark water. It could have been hours, years; they had no sense of time. And when the dusky shades began to turn lavender with the coming of the sun, the boat swung around to another view of the anchorage. Nathaniel started in shock as he read the name of a rakish Chesapeake schooner.

"By thunder, the *Glad Tidings*! Deadlight Helms was questioning Israel Fowlkes about the destination of that very ship."

"Devil take that black-spirited rogue. I pray he didn't make passage aboard her!"

They giggled as they struggled to dress without capsizing the little craft.

* * *

"Anne Easton, is it?" Stated the Governor, as he turned his back and strode to the sideboard stocked with liquor and cut crystal glasses.

"Yes, sir, may it please you; I have voyaged all the way from Virginia to come to my father's aid."

"And what exactly did you intend to do for your father?"

"To plead for mercy. He is in debtor's prison, and there is no way he can pay his fine while in confinement."

"Ah, the smuggler. Would you care for a drink . . . sherry, claret?"

"Rum and lime juice, if you please."

"A powerful drink for a woman! A bit rugged for such a delicate palate as yours, don't you think?"

"A well-refined drink, I should say; the rum here in the islands is the finest. As for the power of it, you should not underestimate the continental women."

"Ah, the continental women . . . a drink with you then, God save the King." They drained their glasses.

"Would you have another, or do I overestimate you?"

"I shall have another, Your Excellency."

"Please sit." Anne took a seat while Governor Milford Hutchinson poured another two drinks. He turned to her with the drinks in his hands. "About your father then, a dreadful situation; I'm afraid one of his crew turned informer."

"A rogue with a drooping eyelid?"

"Quite so. You know the fellow?"

"More than I care to."

"Quite. Well, your father's was a case without question of guilt. The Admiral has decided it is time to set an example to stop this dreadful smuggling business."

"I plead you make an example of someone else's father. He must be allowed his bond at least, so he can produce the fine."

"*Harumph*, quite, well you see, it's rather more complicated than that. Parliament and Grenville demanding a crackdown on the whole business, you see, *hmmmm*, yes. I'm afraid the Admiral's under a great deal of pressure." As he spoke, he waved the drinks in the air, pointing with his index finger. "Of course a lady of your refinement can see the extreme effort I would have to make in order to influence the admiralty court in the least bit. We must stick together, you know, we refined ones of the world, that is, and make the best of the whole bloody thing."

"You could do that?"

"Oh yes, quite." He sat down on the sofa beside Anne, surprising her as his thigh rubbed against hers.

"To the King!" They drained the glasses. "I suppose I could put in a word, could be quite influential, *harumph*, quite." The governor looked off into the distance, as if pondering the great difficulties of putting in a word for Anne's father. "Yes, something may be done, depending on your level of commitment to the matter."

"I assure you, there is no length I would not go to on behalf of my father."

"Well yes, *hmmmm*, quite." He put a hand on her knee. "You see, I would be putting myself at extreme political risk, yes, not a popular side to take on the issue. No, it isn't, *hmmmm*."

"I appreciate the risk you would be taking."

"Yes, *harumph*, utmost discretion called for." He moved his hand up her thigh, dangerously close to where she'd strapped her dagger. Anne shifted. "Of course a lady of your refinement and commitment would readily appreciate such efforts." He caressed her thigh.

"You are certainly a man of refinement and education, sir. Is that a copy of *Macbeth*?" Anne removed his hand and walked to the bookshelf.

"*Harumph*, quite, yes, hmmmm, another drink?" He was surprised at her capacity, while he himself was verging on tipsy.

"I could only partake of such hospitality in the company of a gentleman of education and refinement, such as yourself. Otherwise, my reputation would be at risk. Another drink, please." He raised himself from the sofa and poured two more drinks, these being mostly rum. "Oh yes, *harumph*, well, the utmost discretion is called for, *hmmmm*, quite."

Anne took the copy of *Macbeth* from the shelf and opened it to Act Four. She read it as the governor stalked over to her. She marveled that Angustine had gotten the verses correct to the letter.

"Bottoms up!" They drained their glasses again. The governor put his hand on Anne's bodice.

"You are an amazing man, Your Excellency."

"Yes, *hmmmm*." He squeezed and looked the other way.

"Intriguing that a man of such impeccable breeding and refinement . . ."

"Intriguing, *hmmmm* quite." He began to untie her stays. "Breeding, *hmmmm*."

" . . . of such high principles and education . . ."

"*Hmmmm*." Her bodice began to fall away. Anne dropped the book in surprise, and the page of verse tore off in her hand.

"High principles, yes, quite."

". . . can think of nothing better to do . . ."

"Yes, *hmmmm.*"

". . . with a woman of the same education and refinement, but to make her into a tuppence whore?" With that, she grabbed his hands, spun around, and twisted one of his wrists painfully. His Excellency backed away and reddened.

"Out—get out this instant! You have no commitment to resolving this affair! Your father can rot in hell, for all I care!"

"You have the manners of a wharf rat, Your Excellency. I am committed to my father, but such commitment doesn't run to fornication with the likes of you. You may go to the Devil." Anne rearranged her clothing.

"Out, out this instant!" His Excellency was beginning to feel the copious rum he had used for his failed seduction. He rushed Anne with violent intent, but he stumbled on a divan and fell headlong on his face. She picked up the page torn out of *Macbeth* and showed herself out of Government House.

* * *

"Allow me to introduce myself, sir; Gideon Helms, better known as Deadlight, at your service."

"You address an officer of the king; state your business or be gone," retorted Lieutenant Lloyd.

"An honest seaman, I am—"

"Ha, a rogue, if ever I laid eyes on one."

"None more loyal than I to the king! You see, it was I who gave information that made a prize of the continental schooner *Jubilant,* which is sitting across the harbor, waiting for the auction to make a parcel of naval officers richer men."

"You informed on *Jubilant?*"

"Aye, it was I who made the capture possible."

"You're not looking for a handout for your services, are you? Not satisfied with your own share of the prize money as informant?"

"Nay, sir! I only wish to pass along a bit of information that could make the two of us wealthier tonight—in the service of the king, of course. If it pleases you, sir."

"You intrigue me. Have a seat."

Deadlight took a seat opposite the lieutenant, next to the ceramic cat that was displayed in the front window for passing naval officers to see. The figurine indicated a whorehouse approved for the custom of king's officers.

"In the harbor are several continental schooners used for smuggling, and I have every intention of boarding each on the morrow. Any fool could have spotted them, so don't think of claiming any informant's money for that work," stated Lieutenant Lloyd.

"Nay, sir, it is not smuggled goods that would make us rich men this night."

"Hush your voice. I sense deviltry here, and I shall be no party to it." Then in a lower tone, "What is it, then?"

Deadlight motioned Lieutenant Lloyd to lean closer across the table. "Nothing but a chest of gold, sir, the black-hearted smuggler's own hoard. Not discovered yet, sir! All that needs be done is take it from under the floorboards of the greatcabin, or thereabouts." Lloyd reeled from the man's foul breath, but his mercenary interest was at its peak, as was his caution.

"Do you propose stealing the strongbox from a prize ship? Away with you!"

"Not discovered yet, sir! It ain't stealing if no one knows the better of it."

"An interesting theory, and one that is sure to soon get you a place on the gallows."

"Would you betray the confidence of an honest seafaring man, who tries to do nothing but better his self, and to do right by you? I say we share and share alike."

"Share and share alike, is it? Use my king's commission to enter a prize ship and rob it? You are outrageous, sir!"

"Nay, not I, hardships as I've seen, and being mindful of the sorry lot of the naval officer's pay—"

"*Harumph!*"

"Begging your pardon, sir, seeing as how it's a hard lot for us fellow seamen—"

"I am not, and never will be, your fellow."

"Aye, that's the rub of it, and me trying me best to provide for us as brothers."

"Brothers? Ha! You chose me because I happen to be the only one in uniform in this place, and my uniform gives me access to the prize ship. I make no mistake of it. Now be off with your mischief, or I shall take you, at the point of my sword, to the constable tonight!"

"Aye, sir, no need for that. I'll be gone. Well, that's the lay of it then, a fortune lost this night; the auctioneers will be about her like flies on a corpse tomorrow."

Lieutenant Lloyd suddenly stood. "Be gone, you foul-breathed dog!" Deadlight retreated. The officer waited and watched the impertinent fool walk down the street and around the corner. He drummed his fingers impatiently and counted down a couple of minutes, then made all haste to the stables.

"I shall require a mount." He roused the sleeping stable boy, "King's officer, now hop to it, boy!" The lad was too amazed to protest. Lloyd took a pry bar from the blacksmith shop next to the stables, placed it in the saddle bag of the horse the lad proffered, and made haste to the deserted outer wharf, where *Jubilant* was berthed.

"King's officer coming aboard!" The sleeping tide watchers were startled. "Sleeping on the king's duty? I could have you both flogged. Get up; walk down the pier yonder and wake yourselves. Another king's officer may not be so lenient as I; go!" The tide watchers dragged themselves off the wharf and began to pace the pier, slapping their arms around their chests and trying to shrug off the rum.

Lieutenant Lloyd descended into the greatcabin and lit a candle. There was little furniture, only a cot and a desk. On the transom settee someone had carelessly left a sack of nuts and fruit. He rifled the contents of the small desk and found nothing. The fool with the drooping eyelid had mentioned the floorboards. Attacking them with his pry bar, he'd managed to pry up enough of the cabin sole to convince himself nothing was there, when he heard the sound of voices and the stamp of feet on deck.

"Lieutenant Shemly! Proud to have you aboard, *hiccup.*"

"Aye, aye, Lieutenant Grant; capital, just capital. Where the hell's the rum?"

There were steps on the companionway ladder. Lloyd put the pry bar in the bilge, blew out his candle, and stood in the shadows. The drunken midshipmen stumbled down the ladder.

"Got to be rum around here somewheres . . ." One of them lit a candle.

"Stand fast at attention! Do you little imbeciles know how to salute a king's officer?" The startled midshipmen saluted the form of an officer that appeared from the shadows. "Very well then, I should have you flogged! A less lenient officer would have you triced up and introduced to the cat. Stealing rum from a prize ship, eh?" Lieutenant Lloyd began to pace the width of the greatcabin, his hands in the pockets of his pale yellow knee breeches, blue uniform coat on his back. The terrified midshipmen stood at attention, following him with their eyes, not daring to turn their heads.

"I remember my days as a midshipman, running amuck with rum, wagering, and other dissolute behavior."

Now, astonished, the younger men saw a miniature of Lloyd's blue and white uniform on a tie rod behind him, near the deck head. A blue macaw parrot paced back and forth in the dim light of the candle, in perfect time with Lloyd.

"This indiscretion could have been the end of your careers in the Navy!" To emphasize his point, Lloyd nodded. "Yes, my lads, an end to all your aspirations."

Angustine bobbed his head in perfect time, and continued to waddle back and forth on the overhead tie-rod.

It was too much for the tipsy midshipmen. Covering their mouths with their hands, they exploded in mirth.

"Of all the impertinence!" Lloyd screamed. "I shall flog you little scoundrels this instant!" The terrified boys scrambled up the companionway like monkeys. In an instant, they were lost in the shadows of deserted warehouses. Starting after them in hot rage, he put a foot into the hole where he'd pried up a deck plank, and went down on his face at the foot of the ladder. "I'll have you flogged!" he bellowed up the companionway.

"Ah ha ha, ah ha ha!" The dry cackling laugh seemed to come from within the greatcabin. Lloyd shook off a moment of fright, peered about in the shadows, and quickly scaled the ladder. Of all impertinences, laughter infuriated him most. The young lads would pay if ever he met up with them again.

"You may return to duty," Lieutenant Lloyd ordered the tide watchers, who had rushed back down the wharf at the sound of his bellowing. "Mind you perform it in a manner befitting the king's service."

On the way to his horse Lloyd strutted by a rotting wooden lean-to. Deadlight sank farther into the shadows, and returned his cutlass to its scabbard. It was evident the lieutenant had not found Captain William's hoard, so he need not murder Winston Lloyd. He would have to search for the hoard elsewhere. Perhaps the gullible lieutenant could be of further service in the future.

As Deadlight Helms slunk along the wharf in the shadows, he heard a sound that made his scalp tickle with fright. From the open transom windows of *Jubilant's* empty greatcabin drifted a dry, raspy voice in the dark stillness: "Like a hell-broth boil and bubble, Ah ha ha, ah ha ha!"

* * *

"Blood and thunder, Mr. Ordineaux! Where did you come from?" *Berbice's* first mate appeared at the small table where Captain Harte sat in the rear of a Kingston tavern. Harte motioned for Ordineaux to sit in the opposite chair.

"From *Berbice*, before dawn this morning, sir. Tiny and I rowed in with the jollyboat."

"*Berbice* ain't under the guns of the harbor, is she?" Harte questioned in a hushed voice.

Ordineaux leaned over the table as he whispered, "Nay, sir, she's standing on and off between Morant Bay and Southeast Point."

"Is the leak repaired?"

"I fear not; a platoon of slave hunters attacked us and Captain Matumbwe's people on the beach before we could finish. They must have thought we were making off with the slaves."

"What of Matumbwe's men?"

"Thirteen were aboard when the raiding party charged the beach. We sent them below. The rest who were left on the beach were massacred or led away in chains. It was a most brutal slaughter. They fired on us as well. We had just finished off-loading cargo and rigging the tackle to careen the ship. We made sail, crawling about on our bellies while bullets whistled overhead, and got out of range."

"Any of our crew hurt?"

"Nay, sir, but there are a great many bullet holes in the starboard bulwarks."

"Our cargo lies on the beach?"

"Aye, but well hidden. That, at least, we accomplished before the attack."

"Do you still pump on the hour?"

"Nay, sir; since she is light, she leaks less. We found the leak near the mainmast chain plates, just above the waterline. Caulking must have worked loose in the storm. The place was hidden behind a hogshead. A simple thing to get at, now she's light. She sails like a witch, too, so long as the wind don't come up."

Captain Harte leaned back in his chair, gathering his thoughts. A smoke ring rose from his clay pipe. He coughed, "Never could get the hang of the sot weed."

"Don't inhale it, sir."

"Aye, why bother with it, then?" He offered the pipe to Ordineaux, who took a couple of puffs and laid it aside.

"I've come for instructions, sir. *Berbice* will stand in to pick me up off Port Royal tonight an hour after sunset. Have you had any success finding Captain William, or with Anne's plea to the governor?"

"Headwinds fouled us on both tacks. Captain Easton still sits in the debtor's prison. *Jubilant* and her cargo will be auctioned on the morrow."

"Speak of *Jubilant*, a queer thing. The tide watchers do not stay aboard her. As Tiny and I rowed past, we observed they keep their distance, near a warehouse on the wharf. And another queer thing, sir: The most ungodly verses came at times from the *Jubilant's* greatcabin. Perhaps one of the tide watchers has taken an evil drunk and the others dare not set foot aboard."

"The customs men do not walk the deck?"

"Nay, except for that monstrous drunk in the greatcabin, who rants verses straight from the Devil's own Psalter."

"Come, then, sir; there is not a moment to lose!" Nathaniel Harte threw several coins on the table and rushed out, followed by an astonished Ordineaux.

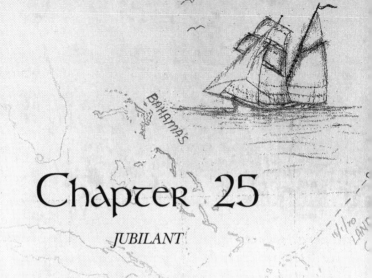

Chapter 25

JUBILANT

"You, sir! Are ye the tide watcher for the royal customs?"

"Aye, Captain; that there is the *Jubilant*, to be auctioned tomorrow morning." *Berbice's* sister ship lay tied to the wharf, similar in appearance except for her name carved in the lower transom.

"May we inspect the vessel?" asked Nathaniel.

"Aye, sir, but," the tide watcher stepped closer as Nathaniel and Ordineaux dismounted, "ye dare not step aboard, sirs, if ye treasure your precious souls!"

"What, man? Speak clearly," Nathaniel feigned surprise.

The two tide watchers walked up close to Harte and Ordineaux, so they could talk in hushed tones. "Possessed by the Devil himself, sir," said one rolling his eyes toward *Jubilant*.

"Aye, we know it is true!" declaimed the other tide watcher, tobacco juice spittle running down the gray stubble on his chin.

"You lads are fanciful. How came you to know of this possession by Beelzebub?" Nathaniel asked casually.

The others flinched at the name. One pointed at *Jubilant's* open transom windows, and his hand shook. "Verses that'd strike fear into an army of saints drift out of the greatcabin at night, sir! A voice straight from hell, I say! When he ain't chanting, the Devil snores."

"That's nothing but an old drunk aboard; come now, fellows."

At this, the tide watchers moved even closer. "There ain't no living soul aboard that ship, sir! Possessed of the Devil, she is; I'll slit me own throat if it ain't true!"

"Very well, gentlemen, I have no desire to do business with the Devil, though in commerce it's hard to say who is who. We shall be back after dusk to hear this demon ourselves."

"May it please you, sir, we shall be here. Our weary watch does not end until the morning of the morrow. Would that it were dawn tomorrow already, sir. We dread another night of the Devil's ranting. We fear for our own mortal souls!"

"We shall bring reinforcements, gentlemen, and perhaps some kill-devil rum, eh? Ha ha!"

"Bless you, sir, that would suit!"

Ordineaux and Harte climbed back on their horses and rode down the wharf. "A queer lot, didn't I tell you? I don't believe a word of it myself. But what shall we do now, Captain? The situation seems grim," said Ordineaux.

"The situation could not be better, Mr. Ordineaux. To start with, we shall need a gallon jug of the foulest kill devil rum in Jamaica."

* * *

Berbice fell off the wind and made for the entrance of the harbor as the sun turned the sky to pink, rimmed the scattered clouds with red, and then sank behind the Blue Mountains. Just after sunset she glided past the wharf at Port Royal, the naval base a good mile off her bullet-pocked starboard beam. The ship rounded up, and a small rowing boat came into her lee. The passengers jumped onto the shroud channels and hopped aboard. *Berbice* made no salute to the fort, nor was there a light to be seen aboard. The men and supplies in the ship's boat rowed in to the wharf where *Jubilant* was moored, but not near enough to be noticed by the tide watchers.

Nathaniel Harte and Simon Livingston climbed from the rowboat and made their way toward *Jubilant* and her superstitious tide watchers. Tiny, Gunny, and Atticus, loaded down with necessary materials for the coming operation, took a route behind the warehouse and waited in the shadows.

"Good evening, gentlemen! We have come to witness the talking spirits of this damned ship."

"Aye, sir; I trust they'll be piping up soon."

"A drink of kill-devil rum with thee, to shore up our courage."

"Aye, Captain, would be a pleasure." Captain Harte passed the jug, and the tide watchers drank deep. Simon and Harte, pretending to imbibe, wiped their mouths on their sleeves. "A pleasant burn in the throat, eh, Mr. Livingston?"

"Aye, Captain, a fine jug this is." They strode towards *Jubilant*, the reluctant tide watchers following.

They stopped at the corner of the warehouse that ran along the wharf.

"A toast to His Majesty's faithful tide watchers! Are we close enough to hear the spirits, gentlemen?"

"Oh yes, sir! Thankee, sir." The tide watchers drank again. Simon took the opportunity to look into the shadows beside the warehouse and saw his messmates at the ready. He turned to look out over the harbor. Just barely visible in the rapidly falling darkness, *Berbice* came about and headed back toward the wharf.

At first all they heard was faint snoring.

"That's it, sir! That's it! Do ye hear it?"

"Take a drink, lads; I hear nothing. Mr Livingston, do you hear anything?"

"No, sir, not a thing. More rum, lads?" The snoring became much louder.

"There, did ye hear that, Captain?"

"Aye, I'd be deaf not to hear it, but it hardly sounds like the Devil. Probably some old drunk ye haven't found, stowed away aft."

"There ain't nobody aboard, sir, of that we're certain." The tide watcher was trembling again. The snoring stopped.

"All a phantom of the mind. There is no sound, probably the wind in the rigging. Pass the jug, have a drink, lads! I've heard many a strange sound when a breeze blows through the shrouds."

"Eye of newt and toe of frog!" The dry crackling voice clearly came from the greatcabin of *Jubilant*.

"Good God! Pass the rum!" The rum jug made the rounds, becoming considerably lighter through the efforts of the tide watchers.

"Wool of bat and tongue of dog!" The verse came from the open greatcabin windows.

"We shall get to the bottom of this!" Nathaniel took a step toward *Jubilant.*

"We shall go no closer, Captain!" declared the tide watchers. "Provoke the Devil and you imperil us all! We beg you, go no farther! You hazard our safety! Come away!"

Nathaniel left the tide watchers and Simon with the jug of rum and edged closer to *Jubilant.* As he did so, the guards backed away, toward the corner of the warehouse. Suddenly, strong arms came from the shadows and struck them from behind with belaying pins. The unconscious sots were dragged into the gloom beside the warehouse, and the remainder of the rum was poured over them.

Captain Harte jumped aboard *Jubilant.* "Simon, cast off forward!"

Captain Harte cast off the stern and spring lines holding her to the wharf. Simon chopped the bowline in two with a stroke of his cutlass. There was no time to spare. *Berbice* was lining up alongside the wharf and bearing down on them, only a few yards away.

"Gunny, Atticus, take those spars and shove us off."

"Let go the foresail tricing lines, Simon!" *Jubilant's* foresail fell from the gaff and foremast where it had been triced up like a stage curtain. It caught the light evening breeze, and she moved away from the wharf and into the gloom of the harbor. A perfect sister ship, *Berbice* slid into her place along the wharf. Barbecue and Anne tossed mooring lines to their shipmates on the wharf, and *Berbice* was made fast in precisely the same spot the other schooner had so recently occupied.

They went to work below. First they piled ballast stones along her port side to bring the leaking plank seam underwater once more. Then they opened the main hatch, and threw in cask lids, empty barrels, barrels half full of bread, and a few loose bread loaves, to float on the rising water. Trickiest of all, they placed buckets of dirt on the 'tweendeck where they would fall off and muddy the rising water in the hold as the ship heeled to port. When all was ready, they rowed off into the night for a rendezvous with *Jubilant*. Only Captain Harte returned, to carry out the rest of his plan.

* * *

"Bloody hell! What's happened here?" The governor flushed beet red. He sat in the open governor's carriage, a massive gilded affair pulled by a team of six and attended by two footmen. They had stopped on the wharf at the warehouse, where a few merchants and shipmasters gathered for the auction of *Jubilant*. Even more shipmasters and merchants were returning to their businesses, shaking their heads and mumbling to each other:

"Worm-eaten hulk they're trying to pass off."

"Aye, rotted so bad she sank at the dock, ain't worth the time to piss on it—ah—good day, Governor!" The gentleman doffed his tricorn as the lieutenant governor walked by.

The smuggler's ship lay scuttled, still tied to the wharf by dock lines tight as iron bars, for they held the weight of the swamped vessel. Debris floated on the murky water in her main hatchway. The cargo was obviously ruined.

"Here they are, milord." The constable held the two dazed tide watchers by their collars in front of the governor. "Found them both passed out beside the warehouse, stinking of rum." As if to punctuate this report, one of the tide watchers bent over and vomited.

"Get that scum out of my sight! There shall be an inquest! Throw them in irons!"

"Shall I call off the auction, milord?" asked a periwigged clerk, still wearing his spectacles.

"No, we shall not. The auction shall go on." The lieutenant governor would receive his due of one-third of the value of the prize ship and cargo. The lieutenant governor fully intended to skim his own share of the proceeds. This could only be done without detection before the governor returned. The auction must go on or the lieutenant governor stood to lose what he could steal of the proceeds. Besides, the ship was a loss. They'd be lucky to get a few pounds for the salvage of her fittings.

The officers of the Navy ship that had made the seizure were in attendance. According to rank, the officers and their crew would share out one-third of the proceeds.

"Bloody bunglers of the customs service, they should never have been given charge."

"Allowed her to sink at the dock, mind you! Outrageous dereliction of duty!"

"Aye, my stupidest cabin boy wouldn't have let a ship sink beneath himself. The lubbers never heard of a bilge pump?"

"The drunken lubbers weren't even aboard."

"The Navy knows what to do with their lot. I hazard the Navy can better tend a prize! Now look at what we've got for our efforts: a wreck!"

"Very well, gentlemen, may I remind you that you are in the presence of His Excellency's deputy," said the clerk. "Mind you do not offend with any impertinence. We shall begin!" The small crowd hushed, and the clerk recited the formalities: the Admiralty Court finding condemned *Jubilant* for smuggling and declared the subsequent forfeiture of the owner's ship and cargo, plus a fine. This now was the auction of the prize vessel and her cargo.

"Do I hear any bids for the cargo?"

"Aye! A half penny for this loaf of sodden bread!" Nathaniel had jumped onto *Berbice's* deck and speared a loaf floating in the main hatchway. He waved it about at the end of his cutlass. The small crowd broke up into laughter.

"Quite. Humm, well then, shall we proceed to bids for the salvage?"

"American schooners—all green wood. Who would pay for a swamped wreck?"

"Looks like she's foul with shipworm and can't stay afloat without the pumps working."

"Bids, if you please, gentlemen."

"Five pounds for the rigging."

"Bids shall be for the entire ship, if you please, gentlemen."

"All right, ten pounds for the lot of it." There were annoyed grumbles from the knot of naval officers.

"Quite; ten pounds, then."

"Fifteen pounds." A portly chandler raised his beefy hand.

"I have fifteen pounds." The naval officers grumbled again. Had the ship been in good enough repair to float, she would have been worth ten times as much.

Nathaniel fingered his prize money from the sword duel in Baltimore. The bids were going too high.

"Sixteen pounds," said Nathaniel, raising the soggy loaf of bread again. Once again the grumbling officers broke into laughter.

"Sixteen pounds, twenty shillings." The portly chandler wanted to stay with the bid.

"He'll be selling us the soggy victuals he can drag out of her," quipped one of the naval officers.

"Seventeen pounds." Nathaniel turned his back and flung the soggy loaf into the harbor.

"Where do you expect to get seventeen pounds worth of blocks and cordage from this wreck?" The chandler grew combative, for he had looked forward to easy profit.

"That would be my own business," replied Nathaniel.

"I have seventeen pounds. Do I hear another bid?"

"Eighteen pounds!" The chandler spat; he saw his profits shrinking. There were the sails he could recut and sell. Then there were the four small iron cannon, probably in the same sad state as the ship itself.

"Twenty pounds." It was all Nathaniel had. If the chandler bid higher, *Berbice* would be lost.

"I have twenty pounds from the gentleman; do I hear another bid?"

The chandler stood with his lips compressed, turning blue. He did not speak.

"Quite. Twenty pounds then, sold to the gentleman with the soggy bread."

The naval officers laughed. It was the most they could make of a very disappointing morning.

"Well, sir," snickered the chandler, "congratulations, you have just purchased a worthless wreck for the princely sum of twenty pounds." He raised his three chins and with a smug grin waddled off.

Nathaniel made arrangements with the clerk for collecting *Jubilant's* papers at Government House. There he handed over the entire sack of prize money won in his sword duel in Baltimore. The rest of his fortune lay in *Berbice*, now swamped at the wharf on the outskirts of Kingston.

* * *

Matumbwe's wife, Anne, Ordineaux, and Barbecue were left aboard *Jubilant* as a skeleton crew. There was little they could do but tack up and down under the loose-footed mizzen from Morant Bay to Southeast Point, for if they were to drop anchor, the four of them could never retrieve it. The thirteen escaped slaves aboard *Berbice* when she was attacked, had gone back to Kingston with Captain Harte and the rest of the crew in the jollyboat and yawl.

"They call me Malika. It is the only name I have known. I was born on the plantation."

"Malika means queen," said Anne.

"Then I have lost my king."

"Do you actually know what happened to Matumbwe? He was with us until the day before the slave catchers attacked. Did he die on the beach?"

"No, I did not see him."

"Then why do you say he is lost?"

"They will hunt him down and surely kill him. They will torture him first." She broke into tears and buried her head in her hands. Anne held her shoulders to give comfort, and noticed the welts from whippings. She did not know what to say, for the despondent woman was right. If Matumbwe were hunted down, and he surely would be someday, he would die a horrible death.

"For a charm of powerful trouble, Like a hell-broth boil and bubble . . ." The crackling dry voice came from the greatcabin. The sun was down and Angustine was asleep.

"That bird belonged to a sorcerer; it has much power," said Malika.

"He belonged to Captain William. I fear I have lost my dear captain. He has been murdered."

"The captain was a friend to you?"

"Yes, in many ways, a friend and a teacher. I will miss him. My father's in debtor's prison. He will die there of jail fever, and I can't get him out. He looked so miserable, and there's nothing I can do for him."

"Waterfall and saman tree, beneath the second rock of three . . ." As if to punctuate the verse, Angustine let out an earsplitting screech.

"The bird has Obeah," whispered Malika.

"He's only reciting part of a play he heard Captain William read," Anne said.

"Oh no, I don't think so Madam. I know of a saman tree and waterfall. Matumbwe and I made love behind the rocks there. Is there a saman tree and waterfall with boulders in this play of yours?"

Anne looked up, startled. "Shakespeare wrote nothing about saman trees. What if Angustine has the 'words' Captain William promised to leave? What if the parrot holds the key to finding the hoard that could be used to get my father out of the squalid debtor's prison? Malika—you found it!"

Anne dropped down the companionway and tore open her ditty bag in the dark. Moving with innate grace, Malika followed silently. Anne found the crumpled page from *Macbeth*, lit an oil lamp, then unfolded the parchment and smoothed it on the chart table. In the dim light she confirmed that the witches of Denmark did not sing of a saman tree, waterfall, or rocks. She turned to Angustine and tickled him under his beak until he ruffled his feathers and stretched his neck. He fixed her with his sideways gaze and began to pace his tie-rod perch.

"Angustine, come boy, what did you say about the rocks?"

Angustine let out a screech.

"The magic bird talks when it pleases him."

"Aye, but it pleases him a lot more when he's had a tot of rum!" Anne uncorked a bottle and poured some into a bowl. Angustine drank a drop and shook his head furiously.

"Gimme grog or you'll be flogged, ah ha ha, ah ha ha." The parrot bobbed his head as he made his dry-throated laugh.

"I think I'll take a tot myself." She poured two glasses and handed one to Malika. The women sat on the transom settee and watched Angustine bow and turn his head to bring them into focus.

"Rocks and saman tree, Angustine, rocks and saman tree—come on, boy."

"Gimme grog or you'll be flogged, ah ha ha, ah ha ha."

"I don't think another tot would kill him." Anne poured a bit more rum into Angustine's bowl. The parrot bent over it and immersed his beak.

"Damn your eyes, damn your eyes!" the bird screeched again.

"That's more like his previous vocabulary."

"Hell-broth boil and bubble."

"The play again?"

"You'll be flogged, you'll be flogged," Angustine ranted in his dry voice.

"That's a new phrase. Maybe he picked it up from Captain William's tormentors. Oh, my God." Anne buried her head in her hands. Malika reached for the rum bottle and poured two more glasses.

"Eye of newt and toe of frog."

"The magic bird has become quite talkative," said Malika as she sipped the rum.

"Aye, it's the rum. He knows not what he says. I think his propensity for the wicked phrases comes from the emphasis his teachers gave them."

"Blood and thunder, strike me blue!" Angustine treated them to a singsong rendition of seagoing oaths and blasphemy. The ladies emptied their glasses and reached for the rum bottle. When their hands closed on one another over the bottleneck, they giggled and laughed until they slid off the settee onto the deck, laughing and slapping each other on the back. Malika stopped suddenly, when she saw the welts on Anne's shoulder.

"You've been flogged, Madam?"

Anne took awhile to regain her composure. "Aye, a villain after the treasure of Captain William."

Malika gave her a long searching look, then she took Anne's face in her hands and peered into those green eyes. Anne regarded Malika's deep brown eyes, and then the the cat-o'-nine-tails welts on her shoulders. Angustine went on bowing and rotating his head.

"There to find bequest of me, waterfall and saman tree, beneath the second rock of three!"

The women suddenly backed away to arms' length, looking alternately at the bird and then each other. "That's it!"

"Do you know such a place? There must be dozens of waterfalls in the Blue Mountains."

"Only one place with a very old saman tree, where the waterfall ends in a pool with three large boulders."

"Where is this place?"

"I will show you." Malika stood and they climbed up the companionway to the deck. "Over there." Malika pointed into Morant Bay. They were so close!

Angustine passed out on his tie-rod perch and began to snore loudly. *Jubilant* rolled on the smooth nighttime swell and awaited the return of her crew, who were now desperately trying to re-float *Berbice*.

* * *

If their work were discovered, all would be lost. The escaped slaves would all be put to death, or worse. Captain Harte made a pact to take them to the north shore of Jamaica, where they could find Granny Nanny's country of the maroons. In turn, they agreed to help salvage *Berbice*.

Jubilant's grossly overloaded boats made fast to the Kingston wharf in the dark. *Berbice* still floated, her main deck less than two feet above water. First the crew and the maroons had to shift the ballast stones back to the middle of the hull. Sputtering and diving into the black water, they groped and struggled to move the stones away from the port side of the bilge. Tiny held Gunny by the legs upside down while he felt for the open plank seam and then stuffed it with oakum caulk.

"Can't swing the iron under water. Got the seam stuffed," gasped Gunny as he dangled upside down.

"Aye, we'll have another try when we've pumped her out enough to reach it," replied Tiny, laying the gunner back on the deck.

They worked the pumps, and began to bale with buckets, a task that seemed endless and hopeless. Yet they toiled on. The escaped slaves too, worked with a will, hoping to be safely gone by daylight. An African work song began, softly at first, then with increasing energy. The quiet but forceful rhythm matched the flow of buckets and the seesawing of the pump handles. All joined enthusiastically in the chorus. This was their song; this was their work. Worried looks and furrowed brows turned to grins. Song was metronomic for the Herculean work. They moved tons of water out of *Berbice's* bilge and into the harbor, a ceaseless stream of buckets dumped over the side, while a constant jet of water issued from the two bilge pumps. Six lines of bucket brigades and both pumps worked on as the eastern night turned into gray. At last, as the orange sun rose above the Caribbean Sea, they finally saw progress. *Berbice* would sail again! It would be none too soon.

Chapter 26

GOVERNMENT HOUSE AND DEBTOR'S PRISON

Lieutenant Governor Milford Hutchinson languished over his midmorning Geneva gin as he sat on the balcony of Government House, looking out over Kingston harbor. Palm leaves rustled in the light breeze. With a desultory wave of his hand, he dismissed the young slave boy who had been pumping an ostrich-feather fan up and down. His periwigged clerk stood patiently by.

"Let him know I am terribly busy," he instructed his clerk. "Important matters of state, you know, humm, can spare but a minute."

"Yes, Your Excellency; I shall show him in." The clerk and governor exited the balcony through a pair of narrow louvered doors that towered eleven feet toward the gilded ceiling of the governor's office. The governor seated himself behind the massive desk that dominated the middle of the room. The visitor was shown in. His Excellency pretended to be engrossed by the paper on his desk, and did not deign to look up.

"Be quick with it, man, I can put off urgent business only so long," he said.

"Aye, Governor."

"I am the lieutenant governor, and you shall address me as Your Excellency, if you please. Another display of ill manners and I shall have you ejected at once."

"Aye, Your Excellency."

"Very well then."

There was an expectant silence on the part of the chastised visitor.

"Out with it, then! What little thing is so important that I must be distracted from matters of state?"

"Aye, well, sir, you may consider this a matter of state."

The governor glanced up. "Oh, you again." The rogue with the drooping eyelid now sported a wiry four-inch beard. "The prize court will distribute the miserable auction proceeds within three months. I believe some of that is yours, as informant to His Majesty. Wait for the proceedings like the rest of us. Now be gone, humm."

"I beg to inform His Excellency, but the prize ship's been stolen."

"What!" His Excellency spun out of his chair and raced to the balcony. "You fool, there it is across the harbor, setting sail as plain as day! Industrious lads, seems they've pumped her out, humm. Now be gone with this, your outrageousness, and waste no more of my time!"

"As an honest seafaring man I just want to do me duty. May it please Your Excellency, but that ain't *Jubilant*."

"How do you know this?"

"Aye, 'tis simple for the seafaring man, Your Excellency, and I can see why it escaped the eyes of all ye landsmen about the harbor here. *Jubilant* had both topmasts. That schooner yonder has but one, the main topmast."

"Where is this topmast, man? Give me my spyglass!" His Excellency shrieked.

"Atop the mizzenmast, but there ain't a topmast there, Your Excellency. *Jubilant* had a topmast. That weren't the *Jubilant* you auctioned off; 'twas the leaky wreck of a sister ship."

"Damn and blast!" At least His Excellency knew which the mizzenmast was, and indeed he spied no topmast there. "Why haven't you come forward before now? Can't you see they sail out of the harbor to the open sea as we speak? Damn it, man! Are you in this plot with them? I shall have you in irons this instant!"

"Begging Your Excellency's pardon, but I been about my duty for a full day, arranging for a meeting with His Excellency's clerk. Seems His Excellency is quite busy."

"Oh, quite. Enough of this drivel, *humm*. If what you say is true—"

"Aye, Your Excellency; I'd swear to it on me own mother's grave."

"Quite, *humm*, there'll be time enough for that. We shall pursue them over the sea! You, sir, shall be my representative and informant."

"Aye, aye, Sir"

"Giles! Fetch Lieutenant, oh, what's-his-name, from the Navy brig that just came in. The fellow who did such dreadful groveling at the reception last night. Fetch him this instant! A matter of utmost importance! Piracy, I say! Piracy!" Deadlight visibly flinched as His Excellency spat these last words.

* * *

"But we cannot go to sea this instant, sir! We must provision and repair some damage to our rudderpost, ah, incurred at the mouth of the Chesapeake Bay," explained Lieutenant Lloyd.

"I'm not looking for excuses for your dalliance, sir!" fumed His Excellency. Lieutenant Lloyd's face turned a shade of crimson. "Master Mariner Helms, here—"

"*Ahem!*" Lloyd gave Deadlight a withering glance.

"Master Helms has seen it his duty to inform me that the condemned prize, so recently auctioned, was a fraud. His claim, though somewhat outrageous on the face of it, is that the speck of sail you see on the horizon was not the prize vessel at all. Of course, Lieutenant, as a master mariner, you would have spotted that yourself, eh?"

"What specific service do you require when *Inflexible* can make sail, sir?"

"Hunt them down, of course, yes, *humm*. Make a full inquiry and get to the bottom of all this. Smacks of piracy to me!" Lieutenant Lloyd skewered Deadlight with another sharp look. "Piracy, I say! May have cheated me out of my just due in prize money! Outrageous, sir! I shall not have it, full inquiry, *humm*, you will pursue them on the high seas, sir, and you shall not fail to bring them back."

"You have my word, Your Excellency, we shall make sail at the very first moment we can, and shall flush out any sharp practice on the part of these Jonathans."

"Quite, *humm*, sharp practice indeed, *humm*," His Excellency pondered the two men fidgeting in front of his massive desk. "Have a seat, gentlemen. This is how we shall proceed." His Excellency had taken pains to have his personal cabinetmaker saw short the legs of the chairs in front of his desk. As Helms and Lieutenant Lloyd sat down, they fell precipitously close to the floor, and found they were looking up at His Excellency over the top of the gilded desk.

"*Humm*, this is how we shall proceed gentlemen; Captain Helms, here—"

"*Ahem!*" Another sharp look from Lieutenant Lloyd.

"I say, Helms shall look after my, er, government house's interest in this affair, as informant." Deadlight gave the lieutenant a sidelong glance from beneath his drooping eyelid. A smug smile broke through his wiry beard.

"Should this affair turn out to be a hoax, Mr. Helms will be held fully and solely accountable. You shall see to this, Lieutenant."

"With pleasure, sir!" It was now Lloyd's opportunity to wear the smug grin.

"I be nothing but an honest and simple seafaring man, Your Excellency, but I fear you use me cruel. An honest complaint is all I offer, complaint against smugglers who do mischief to His Majesty's treasury, and a share in the prize money all I expect."

"Consider yourself hostage to your own venality, sir, and be grateful for your appointment to the task!

If what you say is true, there will be profit for all of us in it. If it is not, Lieutenant Lloyd here will, ah, well, *humm*, quite. I shall look forward to hearing of your success, gentlemen. Bring us back a prize, Lieutenant! *Humm*, that will be all."

* * *

His daily fascination was to watch the spiders crawl along the walls of his cell. At first there were the night sweats, then a lingering lethargy. Captain Easton's cough grew worse by the day. The straw pile on the stone floor that served as his bedding swarmed with fleas. He had no blanket to cling to when the chills came, which was about once every watch. Worse still were the rantings of prisoners who had gone mad, and the moans of the dying. There was no peace morning, noon, or night. Night, the dreaded night, was when the bellows of the insane echoed in the stone hallways, when the rats squealed and scurried in the shadows. How long had it been since he had seen his dear daughter? Was she just an apparition, born of his festering fever? Was he going as mad as the others who raged at the shadows on the walls and talked to the rats as if they were kinsfolk? Where was the better food he had been promised, that Nathaniel had paid for, or was that all part of this hellish dream, as well? The fever began to make him delirious once more, and he saw Anne's mother on her deathbed.

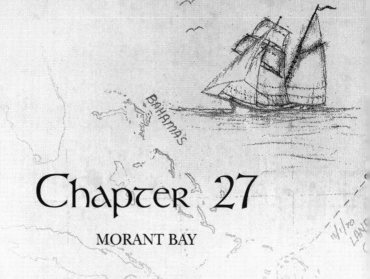

Chapter 27

MORANT BAY

A rainsquall marched down the Blue Mountains toward the bay, an occasional thunderclap resonating between the steep walls of the anchorage. Sunlight below the dark clouds turned the falling rain to shimmering silver threads, dangling below the blackening clouds. As the thunderheads approached overhead, the forest turned from a panoply of bright greens to shades of deep blue-green and dark gray.

Malika was wailing with agony as *Jubilant's* yawl boat approached the beach. She had spied the prostrate body of Matumbwe under the palms. They landed at the spot where just days before *Berbice* had escaped under fire of the slave-catchers. She knew then that the man she adored, her personal savior from slavery and the despicable actions of her master, this man was dead and could protect her no more. Abundant tears bathed her face as she alternately flailed her arms and gripped the gunwale of the small boat. When at last she saw rippled sand through the clear water under the yawl boat, Malika leapt over the side, too anxious to wait for the boat to reach the beach.

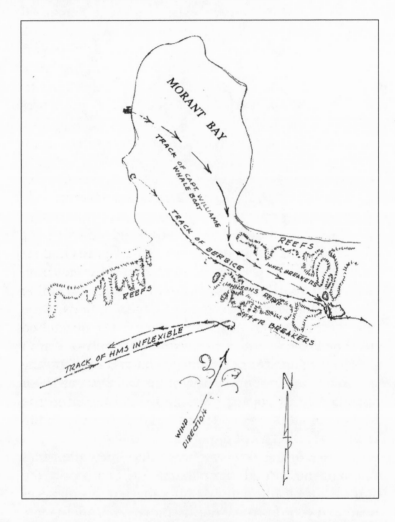

"Matumbwe! Oh, Matumbwe, no! Matumbwe, come back to me! No! No! No!" Malika dragged herself through the shallow water, holding her long dress over her knees, and ran up the beach, screaming to her dead lover all the while. Feeling as if they had lead in their bellies Anne and Barbecue remained silent. What would happen to Malika now? She was but a hapless escaped slave, cursed with beauty that attracted the lascivious attentions of her male owner. Worse still, she was subjected to gratuitous punishments handed down by the jealous white wife of the plantation squire. What could Malika look forward to but rape on one hand and retribution on the other? Now as an escaped slave, she could also look forward to some horrid punishment. Quite possibly death would be her only release from the agony.

Anne could not bear to look at the woman scrambling up the beach. She stared down at the sand and contemplated the arguments of the Quakers of Philadelphia, who contended that all men could reason, and therefore all had equal rights, including the right to liberty. And the Sons of Liberty, what did they say? The Rights of Man they declaimed included liberty and freedom from tyranny. Wasn't slavery the meanest form of tyranny? Using the popular predilection for reasoning out improvements to the established social order, Anne concluded she henceforth could not respect the rights of ownership of any human beings.

Silence fell on the beach so suddenly that Malika's last exclamation of lament still echoed along the steep walls of Morant Bay. Able to avert their eyes no more, Anne and Barbecue looked up the beach. "Malika, no! Malika, don't do it! No!" She began to run toward the despondent woman, but her feet dug into the loose sand, and she felt as if held back in some horrible nightmare where one tries to run, but cannot move. Malika stood above the prone body of Matumbwe, holding a dagger up to the darkened sky. Anne ran with all her strength, but the distance seemed to close imperceptibly. She watched in horror as Malika slowly turned her dagger to point at her sable throat. Thunder rumbled down the Blue Mountains and cold raindrops began to fall, spattering the beach in a rising crescendo. Malika blinked as she stared up at the dagger, cold raindrops falling into her eyes and washing away the salty tears. She swallowed hard and sobbed once more, shut her eyes, and pulled the dagger down to her throat.

"Don' you do dat!" A massive hand enveloped hers and when the point of the dagger was a mere inch from her throat. "Crazy woman, can't a man get some rest?" Matumbwe grinned down at Malika, rain dripping from his muscular features.

Anne dropped to her knees and covered her face. Overcome with emotion, Malika pounded Matumbwe with her fists as he wrestled to embrace her. Barbecue stared in disbelief at the amazing scene a moment, and then kicked the yawl boat with his bare foot. "Well, I'll be buggered!"

* * *

"Set foot abaft the mainmast again, and I'll have you flogged!" shouted Lieutenant Lloyd.

"But His Excellency has appointed me here to oversee," replied Deadlight.

"His Excellency demanded you be aboard, very well. But ye shall not prance about like any sort of gentleman, Mr. Helms. That, sir, would be an intolerable disgrace to a king's ship and her officers."

"Aye, aye, sir, but you use me cruel! Ye still think me to be the meaner sort, after all I done for His Majesty, as well as yourself? And me as deep draft a gentleman as ever there were, only adrift in shoal waters temporarily." Deadlight tugged at his wiry beard and struck an ingratiating wide-eyed look of innocence, head tilting slightly.

"Gentleman! *Pah*! Let me make my feelings on the matter perfectly clear, Mr. Helms. You were born to a whore, a son of a whore ye be, and a son of a whore you'll die."

Deadlight reddened, from his greasy tricorn to his stubbly neck. "You cannot use me so, sir! I demand satisfaction! Pistols—pistols at dawn, sir, in the clearing behind the dyewood warehouse!"

"It will be a pleasure."

"I cannot abide here any longer. Row me ashore at once; I demand it!"

"Very well. Bosun, man the longboat! Take this, this, *gentleman* ashore." There were titters from the ratlines above. "Silence, you dogs!"

* * *

"The rogue has no honor!" declared Lieutenant Lloyd. He and his second were at the appointed spot behind the dyewood warehouse before dawn the following day.

"Not a surprise, sir." The sun was rising rapidly. A steamy fog drifted from the forest into the clearing behind the dyewood warehouse.

"I shall report this to the governor."

"Do you think that wise, sir?"

"Milford Hutchinson should know what kind of knave this fellow Gideon Helms is. He seems to have ingratiated himself with His Excellency."

"And our orders to depart post-haste?"

"I shall brook no misunderstandings in this affair. I desire that His Excellency be perfectly aware that his *representative* has deserted the ship. I want no confusion when it comes time to divide the prize money. Shall we away?"

"To Government House it is, sir!"

* * *

As the two naval officers made their way to Government House, a lookout at Morant Bay braced himself in the notch of a tall tree atop of the steep slope above the bay. From a leather pouch he produced a spyglass and extended it to full length. Putting it to his eye, he surveyed the anchorage, grunting with satisfaction when he found them. An easy row from the beach, *Jubilant* lay at anchor, making ready for sea and rolling to the southerly swell. Close inshore lay *Berbice*, decks awash in men busily stowing casks and bundles of goods fetched out of the boats clinging to her sides. From his vantage point he could see the entrance of Morant Bay and the deep blue ocean beyond. Simon's sharp eye examined every sail on the horizon. There was no Royal Navy warship inbound—yet.

* * *

"Good morning, Nathaniel." Anne kicked her bare foot on the bone-white sand, delighted at the faint ripping sound it made.

"Aye, good morning, Anne."

"Allow me to introduce Malika, Matumbwe's wife."

"I remember." He tipped his tricorn and made a leg.

"We think we know where Captain William's hoard is hidden."

"Aye?"

"His parrot told us."

"The bird has Obeah, the magic." Malika held her hand up and spread her fingers wide.

"Some of the lines he repeats are not from *Macbeth*. I have the page, and some of the verse Angustine cackles is not of Shakespeare's hand."

"I can well believe that! The poet would have been hung for blasphemy. But how could the bird know where Captain William's hoard is? He just repeats what he's heard."

"That's it, Nathaniel, he repeats what he's heard from Captain William."

"Aye, the old captain had such a foul mouth did he? *Ha*! And a snore to raise the dead!"

"Come, Nathaniel, do not make light of me. It is the only chance we have of rescuing my father from debtor's prison."

"Aye, which had best be soon. Simon keeps lookout for the navy from the hilltop as we speak. I am sending Ordineaux off in *Jubilant* to trade with the French or the Spanish, whichever islands he finds favorable wind to reach. He will then return directly to Virginia."

"Malika and I must find the waterfall!"

"I cannot spare the escort for you; I am sending *Jubilant* away undermanned, and we need the rest of the crew here to load and be gone as quickly as possible, before our ruse is discovered."

"We shall need no escort." Anne hiked her skirts to reveal her pistol and dagger, strapped to her thigh. Nathaniel blushed and turned his head, embarrassed at his immediate physical reaction.

"There must be hundreds of waterfalls, and we must be gone from here in due haste or risk losing the ship again," he protested.

"Malika knows the location of the waterfall in the parrot's verse."

"I fear you chase after phantoms. What will happen if you are delayed, and *Berbice* must fly or be captured?"

"Then my father and I will make our way back to Virginia in another ship." She was resolute. She would rescue her father. Nathaniel, however loath he was to lose her company, understood.

"Aye, aye, Godspeed." Anne and Malika walked down the beach toward the far end of Morant Bay.

* * *

Malika left the beach and began to climb the narrow paths up the steep slope into the forest. Anne followed on the track made by feral cattle. Soon daylight dimmed and the buttressed roots of the trees looked like moss-covered walls. Birdsongs of many varieties echoed through the massive boles, and the air became cooler.

"What is the Obeah?" asked Anne.

"You may call it magic, but it is more. A sorceress, a priestess, and a healer can be all one according to my teachers."

"Are you a sorceress then?"

Malika stopped and turned to Anne, to see if she were serious or merely mocking. Anne looked her in the eye. Malika could see there no mocking, so she decided to answer her question, trust her with knowledge. Such knowledge would decide the fate of Anne, her father, and not a few rogues in Kingston.

"I will soon be all three," said Malika. Anne's jaw dropped, it took her a moment to absorb this. It was thrilling – new knowledge – a sorceress!

"Can you teach me some magic? Something I could use to fool the guards at the debtor's prison?"

"I cannot, not the way you think." *Where can I begin with this woman? Is she ready for knowledge? Would it destroy her? It will be on my head if it does.* Malika turned and began walking up the trail again, speaking as she went. "I do not speak of magic tricks the way you think of them. That is play for children. I speak of something far greater, and much more powerful. It is so great, that it is all around you this moment, but you do not see it." Malika stopped once again and turned to look into Anne's eyes. "I can give you something far greater than a child's trick of cards. I can help you to see, and you may receive knowledge if you are able."

Anne was disappointed, "But I can see quite well."

Malika continued up the trail. "You do not see the spirit life in this forest."

"But I see the trees and the ferns, Malika, what do you mean? Do you mean there are spirits around us, like ghosts?" She started to look into the shadows with apprehension, then moved closer to Malika, turning to make sure a monster of some sort wasn't following on the trail, ready to leap over one of the buttressed tree roots and attack.

Malika saw she had frightened her, and continued to walk slowly up the trail. "There are no monsters here, only the birds and the lizards." She held out her arms, pointing to either side, into the ferns and under story.

"No ghosts?"

"I was talking of the spirit *of* the forest, not spirits *in* the forest. And not a ghost, Madam, the spirit is worshipped by my people as a god." Malika saw her powers of explanation were overcome. "I cannot explain it to you. It is something you must see for yourself."

Anne was again intrigued, and a little frightened. "How can I see this forest spirit? And will it tell me how to free my father?"

"It is likely you could have a vision, if you properly prepare. You could have a vision that would help you. Sometimes the visions are clear, and sometimes the visions are difficult to understand, but always there is wisdom in them."

"How do I prepare?"

Malika stopped again, assessing the risk. If Anne were not strong enough, she could lose her mind. But the young woman looked strong, and seemed to be of sound mind. Then Malika remembered the welts on Anne's back from the lash. "I shall show you," and without saying more, turned and continued up the path. Malika started looking at cow droppings, searching for the spirit flesh that grew from corruption. At length she found what she was looking for, and stooped to pick a mushroom. She held it out to Anne.

"We call this the Flesh of the Spirit. It will feed your soul. Eat the flesh of the spirit and the spirit may allow you to see another world. With luck you may have a vision."

"But isn't it poisonous?"

"Many are, but not this one. I have been taught which are which." with that, Malika took a bite out of the cap, and chewed; then passed it to Anne who took a tentative bite. "Eat the rest and I will find another." Farther up the trail, Malika found several more, eating half of each and giving the rest to Anne.

Anne swallowed the raw wad with distaste. It tasted rubbery and bland, a little sour, musty, and gritty from the spores. "Not very appetizing, could use a bit of wine and butter in a pan over the fire." Malika grinned. As they walked up the trail to the waterfall Malika looked back frequently, to see how her charge was doing. Anne was her sacred responsibility now, but as she felt a lightness of being, spring came into her step.

"I feel itchy," said Anne pulling at unseen cobwebs in front of her face. A few more yards up the trail she felt a fluttering about her forehead; but it was impossible to tell if it was within her skull or a fluttering of the leaves in the trees above. "Do you hear all the fluttering?"

"It will pass," Malika knew the Spirit was beginning to visit Anne. Malika picked her way over a fallen log, and noticed the bark seemed to be organized in a beautiful repeating pattern, like the finest embroidery.

Anne was now enthralled with the humming of insects. Their high-pitched songs seemed to ebb and crescendo with her every breath. She giggled, feeling some big joke tickled her fancy. Her giddiness ended when Malika grinned, white teeth like a broad wave crest spilling over her full lips, flowing out between the dimples of her high cheekbones. Anne broke out in a full belly laugh. They stood on the forest trail, dwarfed by buttressed roots of ancient trees, laughing at nothing in particular, except for overwhelming feelings of wellbeing and mirth, until they were breathless.

"We're almost there," said Malika, raising her arm to point.

Anne saw the motion in a sweep of color and exclaimed, "By the powers, you've grown wings!" Sweeping her own hand to and fro, she marveled at her vision of many arms. *Like the several arms of Shiva!*

"The Forest Spirit has come to both of us," observed Malika, serious once more. In a few more steps they entered a vast opening formed by a crystalline pool of water beneath the forest canopy. Arching branches looked like the buttresses of a medieval minster. Bathed in shafts of sunlight, clusters of ferns and rocks glowed with warmth on the edges of the pool, while shadows danced below the water. A huge saman tree supported a vast ceiling of leaves like a fern-covered column, its roots gripping onto massive boulders that formed the edge of the pool. Splattering noisily, a waterfall dashed down ebony rocks in cascades of white.

"Come sit by the pool and rest," said Malika as she sat on a rock. Anne rested on a log carpeted with soft green moss; the energy tingling in her limbs.

Pointing to a butterfly, Anne exclaimed, "Is it one, or a dozen following single file? I can *feel* them fly. Everything glows and breathes; as if alive, the trees look as if they would recoil from my touch – so sensitive!"

"What you see is the Spirit of the forest. Now you can see the life within."

"This is what Saint Francis meant by God in nature."

"Who was Saint Francis?"

"He is said to have spoken with animals."

"Then he knew the Spirit of the forest."

"Even the rocks seem to glow in a way…" said Anne, regarding a pebble at her feet, with new eyes she saw many colors and patterns in the small thing, all beautifully arrayed in a complete form, every bit as beautiful as the finest work of art. Sudden anxiety gripped Anne's gut, "Mustn't we be gone to find the three rocks and waterfall?"

"This is the place. Here is the saman tree, rocks three, and the waterfall."

"But where are the three boulders?"

"Watch me," said Malika. With innate grace, she dropped her tunic and stepped into the pool. Clasping her hands together she dove under, only to burst forth on the opposite side of the pool, sitting on an unseen object, as if supported by the mirror image of palms and sky.

"You see?"

"Aye, there are three below?"

"You shall see!" Disappearing in a splash, this time she did not reappear. Anne grew frantic.

"Malika, where are you?" Whistling tree frogs suddenly felt unbearably loud and confusing.

Searching the pool, in desperation she shucked her dress, unstrapped her dagger and pistol, and dove in, determined to rescue Malika. "Malika, where have you gone?"

"I am here, Anne, ha!"

The voice was Malika's, "Where are you? Behind a tree?" Approaching the waterfall, Anne climbed up the massive saman tree roots.

"Ha ha ha! I am here! I am here!" Her voice was so close. Malika's arm extended through the waterfall. Stumbling down the massive tree roots, Anne plunged into the cool water. Putting her hand tentatively through the waterfall, she was suddenly pulled through. Malika sat in a grotto with bluish light dancing on the ceiling.

"How did you know of this place?"

"It is known by the maroons. I am a disciple of their leader, Granny Nanny, their leader. Did you know she never took a weapon into battle?"

"How did she survive?"

"The Obeah magic from Africa."

"I wish I had the Obeah to get my father out of prison. It seems an impossible task."

"The treasure you seek is here."

Anne peered into the gloom behind the rock on which she sat, and there it was! An ironbound chest secluded on a sandy shelf a little above the water.

"That's it!" They grappled with the heavy box and wrestled it to the top of the rock. There was no lock. Anne's hand trembled as she opened the lid. Her heart sank; it was empty. "Oh no!"

"Look here!" Malika pried at the bottom and a loose board came free. There lay six hundred pounds in Spanish doubloons, the precise amount of Captain Easton's fine.

"We've done it! We've done it! I can find my father and free him!"

"You cannot do that with this gold."

"Why do you say that?" Anne looked into Malika's face and gave a start. In the dancing reflected light of the grotto she saw an older, wiry woman wearing a lose turban. Her face seemed to be superimposed atop Malika's, shimmering in and out of existence as the light danced on the grotto walls.

"You must forgive your father in order to free him. This gold cannot free him. Only you can do that, with the Obeah!"

Anne stared at the vision, her heart pounding. Unable to take her eyes off it for fear it would vanish, the words repeating in her mind over and over, *this gold cannot free him; you must forgive him in order to free him—only you can do that. And the Obeah, the Obeah, the Obeah, the Obeah . . .*

She did not remember exiting the grotto or going to sleep, yet she awoke beneath the saman tree on a bed of palm boughs, her head propped on one of the massive root tendrils. The sounds of the cloud forest began to surround her once more; first the basso continuo of the spattering waterfall, overlain by the woodwind whistles of tree frogs, the falsetto of chirping insects and bird calls, all echoing in the mountain ravine. Malika was building a lean-to, using the saman tree as a wall. Reassured by the sack of doubloons at her fingertips, suddenly she was saddened by the dreamlike prophecy. The gold would do her no good! She couldn't believe it.

"Shall we go to Kingston?"

"Tomorrow I will show you to the end of the mountain trail, where the road to Kingston starts. You must rest now. You have spoken with Granny Nanny. What did she tell you?"

"You do not know?"

"I wasn't under the waterfall; how could I know?"

"But you were there, I saw you!"

"It was the Obeah, not I. What did Granny Nanny tell you? She is wise and led my people, the maroons, to many victories."

"It is a riddle. She said the gold would not free my father, that I must forgive him to find him, that only I could do that, and that I must use the Obeah."

Malika nodded approvingly. "She has told you how to defeat your enemies."

"But how can I use the Obeah? And why won't gold do any good?"

"I can teach you some of the Obeah as we take the trail down the mountain tomorrow. As for the gold, I cannot tell you. You must rest now. You have spoken with Granny Nanny!"

Chapter 28

POWERS AND POTIONS OF THE FOREST

"The Obeah of the whole forest as one is the greatest," said Malika as she searched the forest floor for magical plants. "The powers of roots and leaves alone can never equal an entire grove of old trees. The forest is like a being. To cut a tree is to cut a leg or hand. This is the Obeah Granny Nanny used against the soldiers."

"But the soldiers destroyed Nannytown."

"Because the maroons cut a grove of old trees. Granny Nanny told them not to do it, but her brother Quao insisted. There were many things Quao did not understand."

"I cannot use the Obeah of the forest in Kingston."

"That is true, sure enough, but take this one—" Malika stooped to pull a tuberous plant from the soil. She broke off the tuber and handed it to Anne. "Deadly poison in the juice, but if you squeeze the juice out, you can eat it." Anne put the root into the pocket of her apron. They trotted on down the mountain trail. She was an enthusiastic student of the herbs, and by the time they reached the slope where the trail joined the road to Kingston, her mind reeled with an overload of knowledge. She had a small collection of roots, tubers, fungi and leaves: one could cure the fever, and one could paralyze a person dead in their tracks within moments.

* * *

"I see an appointment is not so difficult to obtain with His Excellency when there is a fine to be paid," stated Anne to the governor.

"I'll brook no impudence from a provincial! I had you thrown out once, and I shall do it again, by the powers! Now let's get about it! Do you come in jest? You may leave immediately!"

"This is no jest." She tossed the sack of Spanish doubloons on the governor's massive gilded desk. "Over six hundred pounds in Spanish gold, precisely my father's fine of treble the value of his ship and cargo. You may bite the coins, if you wish."

"*Harumph!*"

"Very well, then, I demand the immediate release of my father!"

"Quite. Well, you see, that is impossible, quite impossible. This sum is completely inadequate."

"What? You villain! Everyone knows the ruling of the court! Treble the value of the ship and cargo! There it is!" She pointed to the untouched leather bag sitting on the gilded desk.

"*Harumph*, quite. Well, I cannot in truth expect a simple provincial to understand jurisprudence.

Hmmmm, I shall attempt to explain, and then you will do me the favor of ending this presumptuous intrusion. The ruling, you see, was for treble the value of the ship and cargo *as captured*. *Asuni capturo*, as it were."

"That isn't Latin."

"*Harumph*! Quite. Latin scholar, are we? Well then, perhaps you are also aware that the value of your father's vessel was estimated at over a thousand pounds, and treble that—I shall repeat the arithmetic if you cannot follow it—treble that is over three thousand pounds! The court was quite merciful. So if you are not prepared to come forth with a sufficient quantity of this hoard Captain William is reputed to have . . ."

"Who told you any such thing about Captain William?"

"Oh, well, quite. The fellow with the drooping eyelid really is a fount of information about the shady dealings of you colonial merchants. Quite a fount, *harumph*."

She was shocked. She had never imagined the governor would take it upon himself to rob her so blatantly. "You cannot get away with this!"

"*Harumph*, oh, well, I assure you I can, and I will." He dropped her sack of doubloons into a drawer of his desk and shut it. "Now get out."

"Serve me like a highwayman and I shall repay the favor!" She hiked up her skirt and grabbed her dueling pistol; His Excellency looked down the half-inch bore pointed at his nose. When the Royal Marine hit her in the back of her head with the butt of his musket, she collapsed in a heap on the floor.

"Ye shall hang for attempted assassination, impertinent little provincial slut!"

* * *

Anne lay on her belly on a mat of straw. Her head pounded. The first thing she saw when she opened her eyes was a giant cockroach within an inch of her nose. She screamed and pushed herself up.

"Welcome to the dungeon, mum," the guard standing at the door of her cell snickered. She looked around. The cell was eight feet by eight feet; the only furnishings were a slop bucket and a pile of straw. Besides the cockroaches, it was swarming with fleas.

"Oh my God, what have I done?"

"Should have thought of that before ye tried to kill the governor. You'll hang for that one."

She remembered now. She had only intended to scare His Excellency into giving her money back. He had twisted everything, and she was now totally defeated. She would not be able to free her father, but she could be hanged if His Excellency could get the court to believe his side of the story, and why wouldn't they? He would simply put it thus: Her father was being held in prison, she visited His Excellency to plead clemency, and failing that, she attempted his assassination in frustration. No one would believe that he had robbed her. She was doomed to the gallows! Never in her life had she felt such utter helplessness and frustration.

"Oh, Daddy, forgive me. I am such a wretch. I can do nothing for you now!" Tears of remorse flowed down her cheeks. Hour after hour she examined her life, the mistakes, the lost chances, the times she said things she now regretted. Well after midnight she declared to the mute stone wall, "Oh Daddy, I forgive you for the boarding school. I know you only meant to do right by me." Exhausted, she bowed her head and slept where she was. She dreamed of the last voyage of her seafaring life with her father.

They had been warned, "The Barbary Coast is dangerous for European merchantmen; stay under the guns of your English Navy when you pass." Captain Easton resolved it was high time Anne learned the use of firearms, and he began as soon as *Jubilant's* anchor was weighed in Sicily. To his amazement, she was a deadeye shot. The lesson could hardly have been timelier.

"The primer goes like so," he explained. "Hold the butt up against your shoulder; sight down the two notches. Squeeze the trigger gently, and don't close your eyes!" Anne took the polished metal piece with reverence, sighted on some drifting flotsam fifty yards away, and squeezed the trigger.

Boom! The flintlock's primer puffed; the musket bucked into Anne's shoulder. An acrid smell of powder filled her nostrils, but what most amazed Anne was that the flotsam disintegrated in a splash.

"Beginner's luck," mumbled Captain Easton, astonished. "Load and try that one out there." He pointed to a broken barrel about a hundred yards off the beam. "Here, hold the rod thus; that's it, now your powder charge home, good."

Anne took aim at a stave in the wreckage. *Boom!* "It was short, Papa," she pointed where the shot had splashed.

"At a distance you have to aim a bit high," said Captain Easton. So she tried again, and again, and again. Delighting in the new toy, she shot holes in every piece of flotsam adrift off Algiers. She also learned the gross inaccuracy of the pistol and how to aim it at arm's length. She beamed a white-toothed grin from a face blackened by powder smoke.

"This is no way to raise a daughter," reflected Captain Easton aloud. "That'll do, child! Clean yourself up." He was startled at the sight of his own daughter brandishing a pistol and pronouncing an oath. What had he done? It would be the subscription school for young ladies after this cruise, for sure. Time this wild child learned her place in society and how to conduct herself as a proper lady.

Jubilant cleared the coast and was no sooner out of cannon range and sight of the English frigate than a xebec boat rapidly hoisted sail and followed in her wake. At daybreak it was clear the lateen-rigged craft had every intention of overtaking them.

"Load the cannon with round shot first," ordered Captain Easton.

"Aye, aye," replied the bosun. Shot was roused out of lockers, powder casks dug out from the cargo barrels that filled the hold. *Jubilant* was no warship, but she could mount a credible defense.

The pistols and muskets were brought again on deck and loaded, this time in earnest. Capture by Barbary pirates was the worst of fates, and it seemed the term of safe conduct was over. Everyone on board knew two-masted xebec carried one chase cannon and a ruthless crew of cutthroats that would demand total surrender or, if they resisted, would hack to death every soul aboard. Of this the *Jubilant's* company could be sure: They must not allow the xebec to come close enough to grapple and board. For young Anne, even worse would be in store.

"They've fired on us!" cried *Jubilant's* lookout from the masthead. A delicate puff of smoke drifted away from the xebec's bow, and a geyser rose off the stern quarter where the shot had hit the sea. So there it was: no safe conduct. The narrow xebec had both lateen sails set wing and wing, and she flew square sails on her foremast.

"Put out her stun'sls," ordered Captain Easton. *Jubilant's* crew jumped into the rigging to set every square yard of sail she could carry. The captain gripped the taffrail and set his jaw. Staring aft, he tried to keep his raging mind on a course of action, while wild thoughts of the murder of his crew and the enslavement of his daughter sent shivers up his spine. The minutes ground on as he measured and re-measured the distance to the malignant xebec in their wake. With the freshening morning breeze, they were overtaking *Jubilant* at an alarming rate.

"We'll show them we mean business!" cheered Captain Easton, to bolster his crew and give them heart so *Jubilant's* guns would be laid true. The crowd of cutthroats lining the xebec's bows was enough to terrorize the lion-hearted. Sun glinted off the sabers of the Arabs.

"Mister Simpson," Captain Easton addressed himself to the *Jubilant's* first mate, a stout Nantucket man. "We'll put her up into the wind and rake the xebec, then fall off and hope to God we can pull away before they can grapple!"

A stone shot shrieked overhead and put a round hole in *Jubilant's* course. If the pirates managed to dismast her, the game would be over.

"Aye, aye, and I'll be laying the guns true for her rigging, Captain," replied the mate. They waited for the other ship to come into point-blank range, but not close enough to grapple when she turned upwind. The chase gun of the xebec loosed another two shots; one flew wide and the other whistled overhead, much too close.

"Head up now, let's have at them!" shouted Captain Easton. *Jubilant* headed up into the wind, bringing her six small cannon to bear on the approaching xebec, six chances to slow the charge of certain death.

Boom! The first of *Jubilant's* cannon fired, and instantly there was a gap in the crowd at the pursuing ship's bows. The shot had swept her deck.

"Mind lay 'em true, Simpson. Good shot," yelled Captain Easton.

Boom! *Jubilant's* next three shots disappeared into the bows of the charging xebec, causing confusion on her deck. The xebec fired her chase gun again, and the stone shot pounded into *Jubilant's* hull below the deck.

Boom! The next shot from *Jubilant* put an ineffectual hole in the other ship's triangular mainsail. The xebec bore down on *Jubilant*, the white foam of her bow wave strangely broken. A line of musket barrels appeared over her rails.

Boom! *Jubilant's* last shot cut another swath through the xebec's crowded deck.

"Bear off—now!" shouted Captain Easton at the helmsman. "Reload, Simpson, fast as you can."

"Look, she's down by the bow," cried a seaman. The xebec was taking water fast through the shot holes in her bow. "She's trimmed by the head and getting crank," observed Simpson.

"Aye, but the devils are still after us," growled Captain Easton, as he stared aft. A volley of musket fire crackled from the bow of the crippled ship. *Jubilant's* helmsman spun around and fell dead.

"Mind your aim and make 'em pay," shouted Captain Easton. Jubilant's crew returned fire with musket to devastating effect, but the xebec was jammed full with cutthroats.

"Load grape this time, Mr. Simpson," ordered Captain Easton. As *Jubilant* gathered way, again the crippled xebec bore down and swerved to weather as if to grapple, broadside to broadside. Musket fire from the xebec wounded another of *Jubilant's* crew.

"Broadside now, Simpson!" All six of Jubilant's cannon fired grapeshot point blank into the side of the xebec. Half of the rag-wrapped heads above the xebec's bulwark were suddenly gone. But the pirates were desperate. Their ship was sinking from under them; they must grapple and take *Jubilant.* Close enough now for pistol shot, the first grappling hook sailed through the air, but fell short of *Jubilant's* bulwark.

Anne, who'd been restricted below decks, poked her head out of the main hatchway just as three grapples bounced onto *Jubilant's* deck. She knew what this meant. The vastly outnumbered crew of *Jubilant* would be swept from the deck as soon as the pirates could board.

Anne looked at the muskets and pistols strewn about *Jubilant's* deck and grabbed the nearest one. Unnoticed in the desperate mayhem, she slung the musket strap over her shoulder and stuffed two pistols into her belt, then bolted into the shrouds on the lee side. The weapons were heavy, but as she climbed, she felt only fear and excitement.

She could see the deck of the xebec from the mainmast crosstrees, a confused mass of robes and glinting scimitars. She could also see the Arabs heaving the grappling-hook lines, drawing the xebec closer to *Jubilant* in preparation for boarding. The biggest Arab, the pirate captain dressed in brocade vest and red turban, shouted orders at the men manning the grappling hooks. Anne took aim at his turban and squeezed the musket trigger. The xebec captain went down as if swatted. There was a momentary lull aboard the xebec, but another big Arab, naked to the waist, resumed directing the pirates hauling the ships together. Anne took aim at him; her shot landed between his feet. Seeing her in the crosstrees, he screamed at the pirate next to him, gesturing aloft.

The xebec's deck was level with the waves; she would soon go under. Several of the pirates swung aboard *Jubilant* on halyards, as *Jubilant's* crew fought to cut the grappling lines with hatchets. Anne saw an Arab with his cutlass raised in back of Mr. Simpson, ready to hack him down. She aimed a pistol and squeezed the trigger. The saber clattered to the deck as the Arab crumpled.

Then Anne saw a bearded Arab with a curved knife in his mouth climbing the ratlines of the mainmast, coming to kill her. Suddenly terror overtook her. Her hands were sweating so much, she felt as if she could not hold onto the rigging, let alone the pistol that shook uncontrollably as she pointed it at the Arab climbing the ratlines, and she could not take aim. When he saw it pointed at himself, he reached in his belt, and raised his own pistol towards Anne. His wild shot startled her into dropping her own weapon. The Arab continued up the ratlines and Anne, trembling, clung to the shrouds, feeling as if she would fall any minute because her hands would do nothing she wanted them to do.

In the mayhem below, as the xebec sank, no one noticed Anne in the mainmast crosstrees, and the pirate closing in for the kill. The first slash of the Arab's knife cut her arm. Just then the sinking xebec was cut free of *Jubilant* and the ship lurched. In a fog of horror, Anne felt as if cotton were plugging her ears; the mayhem below was forgotten. She groped for her last pistol and held it in front of her with trembling hands. The Arab raised his knife to slash her throat and she pulled the trigger—the bang sounded far away. The Arab fell backward out of sight, into the fog that was closing around her.

It took them two hours to pry Anne from the crosstrees. "There, there, kitten, easy now," coaxed the bosun. He waved his hands in front of her unseeing eyes. "It's over, you can come down now." Over his broad shoulders like a sack of flour, he carried her down the ratlines to the deck.

There was nothing for it but to send Anne to the subscription school, a relieved Captain Easton determined. It had taken them ten agonizing minutes to figure out where she was after the fighting stopped. But first to the Madeira to sell the wine-pipe staves and take on wine, then to the West Indies to discharge their grain and take on sugar and salt!

Chapter 29

KINGSTON PRISON, OBEAH,

AND THE ALLURE OF RUM

Anne was not allowed to sleep long with these dreams of life on the sea with her father. Sent to relieve the sentry at her door, another guard rattled a tin cup on the bars of the cell doors as he stomped down the stone passageway.

"Get up, ye wretches. Judgment Day ain't far off for ye, *hor hor hor*!"

"This one's been making a miserable fuss."

She stood to look through the grating of her cell door into the flickering candlelight of the passageway.

"Always do, the first night in. Best time to have a go at them."

"She's all yours, mate. I'll just be glad to get me some peace and quiet."

"Aye, comely lass this one; have you had a look at her up close?"

The sweat on her brow grew cold, for she guessed what they were about to do.

"Wicked temper, I hear; tried to kill the governor."

"We know just how to handle that, don't we?" The sadistic guard took a length of cordage from his pocket. "Shall we have a bit of fun? I'd like to get the feel of those titties myself."

Anne closed her eyes and thought she saw the bony face of Granny Nanny, speaking to her, "Use the Obeah; only you can free him. Use the Obeah."

"You can look all you want," Anne said, "and the more if you bring me a tot of rum. Why not have a little fun for my last night on earth?"

"Rum she's asking for!"

"They all do." He pulled his comrade closer, whispering, "And the drunker they get, the more you can do to them."

"I like it better when they scream, mate. But fetch us a bottle, will ye?"

The guard left to get the rum. Anne knew what was to come. She stood with her back to the door, wringing her apron in anguish. She felt the moist sap of the manioc root wet the apron, and remembered Malika saying, "The juice can kill you, but grate it and wring it all out, and you can eat it." The apron was now wet with poisonous juice. She knelt and rubbed the root on a rough cobble until she had ground it down to pulp, then replaced the pulp in her apron. Wringing it out, she spread the juice over her hands.

The guard returned with a bottle of rum.

"Aye, mate, now there's a good friend." They drank from the bottle and belched. "What say, lass, care for a tot?" He poured some rum into his tin cup and held it up to the grate on the cell door. She reached for it, but he pulled it back and laughed, "'Here you go, have it then." He threw it in her face. "*Ha ha ha!*"

"Let her have a tot, mate." They poured a brimming cupful of rum and held it up to the grate. She put her fingers through to take it, but could not pull it back through the narrow opening. This sent the two guards into hysterical laughter once more. She held the cup with her right hand and dipped the fingers of her left into the rum. She dropped her left hand to her apron and squeezed more manioc juice on her hand, dipping into the cup again, she mixed the juice on her fingers with the rum in the cup. She repeated this several times before her tormenters tired of such merriment and took the cup away.

She grew bold, for there was nothing that would make the outcome of this nightmare any worse. "If one of you had the keys, we could all have some fun." She backed away from the door and slowly unbuttoned the bodice of her dress.

"Aye, have a look at that now! Go fetch the keys."

She would not have much time. She squeezed the manioc root with all her strength, the juice soaking her apron and running down her fingers. She heard the key rattle in the heavy door, and then it pushed open, squealing on its hinges. The sadistic guard appeared with rope in one hand, the bottle of rum in the other, followed by the other guard holding the ring of keys.

"Give me a tot, will you?"

"Sure, lass," said the guard with the keys, and held out the cup. Anne took it and turned away, dipping her fingers into the rum and managing to squeeze more juice into it before she raised it to her lips and pretended to drink.

The sadistic guard roughly gripped her shoulder and spun her around. "That's enough, then." He grabbed the tin cup and took all he could in one swallow, and then handed it to the other guard. "Let's see what else she's got."

Eyes wide with lust, the other man drained the cup and flung it down on the floor. The sadistic one took another pull of rum and stepped toward Anne, opening his mouth in a snarl. But no sound came. His eyes stared straight ahead as he fell forward. Anne was just able to dodge his limp body as it slapped against the wall and slid onto the stone floor. She looked up to see the other guard pointing to the prone body of his fellow.

"Can't hold his rum, that one. So let's play, my pretty one." He stepped forward but managed only a half step. He seemed to struggle to put his next foot forward a few inches, and then he too fell flat on his face. Half-naked, Anne, stood transfixed in the silent chamber, shaking in terror and trying to gather her wits.

"Thank you, Granny Nanny!" She put her dress back to rights. The inert hand of her jailer gave up the keys, and she hid them in her manioc-soaked apron. Grabbing the rum bottle from the floor, she peeked around the cell door into the passageway. All was still, save for the rustling of the rats. She looked into the next cell. A shadowy figure sat on the floor in a corner. "Where are the debtor's cells?" she asked. There was no answer. She repeated this question at the other cells and gained a series of curses and lewd invitations, but no help.

She fled down the passageway and climbed the stairs. The guard at the top was asleep, snoring loudly. She looked up and down the hallway;

there was something familiar about it. She tried to remember her way, then ran from cell to cell, peering into the shadows, looking for her father. Finally, she recognized him by his boots. He didn't awaken even as she frantically tried key after key. At last the lock turned and she swung the door open.

"You there! What are you doing here?" The voice came from the shadows at the dead end of the window archway, only a few feet away. Anne held up the rum bottle and reached into her apron for the machineel tree leaf with her other hand.

"Villain!" The man took a step forward and suddenly jerked to a stop, his hands held as if to grab her, only inches away. In the gloom she could see an iron collar around his neck where he was chained to the wall. She stepped into her father's cell.

The fetid smell was appalling. Captain Easton lay on a pile of straw. She gently shook his shoulder. "Come now, Papa, we're leaving this place."

He looked up, "I am dead or dreaming. My dear wife, is that you? I took care of our little girl as best I could." He was delirious with the fever. "I did my best with what I had, even though I was at sea. I did not orphan the girl."

"Papa, it is I." Anne stroked his matted beard, but he rambled on, oblivious to her identity.

"The boarding school was hard on her free spirit. It was difficult for me to see her go, wanted her to fit in . . . did my best, as you wished it . . . should have found a suitable husband–"

"Papa, I forgive you, Momma says you did a fine job. It's all right now. I forgive you, Papa, I forgive you for everything. Please, do not die!"

"Aye, its all right now . . . can leave this rotting dungeon in death, finally . . . how pleasant to see thy face once more, my wife . . ."

"No! Papa, you mustn't give up! It is I, Anne; we can leave this place now! Please rouse yourself. We must be gone!" She shook him roughly. "Papa, it is I, Anne. Get up! We must be gone!"

"Aye, gone to join you, my dear wife . . ."

"Get up!" She pushed him up to a sitting position. He looked around as if awakening from sleep.

"Anne?"

"Yes, Papa! Yes, it is I!"

"I am not dead, or dreaming?"

"No, Papa! Get up; we must get out of here quickly! Get up, now!"

"I just want to rest; I am so tired. I must sleep; oh, my sweet wife, it is so good to see you again . . ." He was slipping back into delirium.

"Get up *now*!" Anne pulled his arms, but she could not get him to stand. He slumped onto all fours, and then put his hand on his knee and rose with great difficulty. She steadied him, and with an arm around his waist, guided his uncertain steps from the cell and down the passageway. With her other hand she still clung to the rum bottle.

The toothless guard at the front gate snored loudly, drool puddling where his paunch thrust from his greasy shirt. Anne tried her keys in the lock, but none was as massive as the key required for the gate. She held the rum bottle behind her back and kicked the guard's feet. "You, sir! How dare you sleep on watch! I shall have you flogged! Open the gate at once!" She continued to kick and threaten the fellow while he roused himself and produced his keys from a leather apron that encircled his copious belly. "Damn your eyes, open that gate this instant, you dog!"

"Stand off!" He was awakening. "Who demands this gate be opened? On whose authority? Where are your papers?"

"Papers?" Anne took a step towards him. "Papers, you fool?" The guard stood his ground, fully awake now and no longer intimidated. Anne thrust her angry face up to his whisker-studded cheeks. "I'll show you papers!" She smashed the rum bottle over the fellow's head with both hands. He dropped the keys onto the cobblestones and she stooped to grab them; but he was only dazed for a second by the blow to his head.

"No, you don't!" He grabbed her, encircling her with his arms as she stooped to pick up the keys. She slammed her knee into his crotch as hard as she could. He let go and fell backward, groaning with pain. She rushed to the gate and tried the first of three of the massive keys, her hands trembling almost uncontrollably.

"That'll do, doxie!" The guard came up, and grabbing her with a bear hug from behind, yanked her away from the gate. She kicked but could not free herself from his grip.

"*Umph!*" The guard went limp.

Anne turned and saw her father with a cobblestone in his hand. "I reckon I'm not dead yet, lass, but we shall both hang on the morrow if we do not get far to weather of Kingston!" They opened the gate and walked out into the street, Captain Easton still unsteady in his step.

A muscular black man came out of the shadows. "You be Anne Easton?"

"Aye, who wants to know?"

"A maroon the Obeah woman Malika has sent to fetch you! Quickly now, into the cart!" They climbed into the back of a two-wheeled donkey cart half-loaded with sugar cane, and covered themselves with a tarpaulin.

* * *

The governor paced in front of the terrified guards and began with this preamble: "I came out to this reeking fever den from the comfortable civilization of London to seek opportunity in career and fortune. It has been a grievous mistake on both counts, *harumph*. I have been thwarted on every side by ineptitude. This administration would not be in such a shambles, however, not nearly in such a sorry state of affairs, if were not for the dereliction of duty," the governor paused to fix the two limp guards with a withering stare, "and negligence with which you two have performed your service for the king! How am I to report this affair to the governor on his return? Just *what*, gentlemen, in bloody *hell* went on down there? Well, speak up, speak up!"

"M-may it please Your Excellency—"

"It most certainly does not! Proceed with your pathetic excuses no more! I want to know what happened. I want to know where the prisoners are, and I want to know *now*!"

"I d-don't re-remember, sir."

"You, sir, are a wretched liar!" Turning to the other guard, who wavered in his struggle to stand erect, the governor impaled him with his bony forefinger. "You, sir, what have you to say?"

The guard nearly toppled; it had been quite difficult for him to move since the night before, and he was only now able to stand. "I re-really don't recall, sir."

"And you, sir, are a despicable, beetle-ridden liar! Let me tell you what happened then, since you seem to think the truth can be concealed by your outrageous claim of a lack of memory. Let me tell you what happened. The woman bribed you to set her free, gave you favors, did she? Bribed you to set her free, *harumph*, and then bribed you to let her father go as well. Isn't that so, gentlemen?"

"N-no s-sir, c-couldn't have been."

"You take me for an *idiot*? How else did she get your keys? Did she wrestle you to the ground for them? No! You were dead drunk, and they somehow flew into her cell, or you were dead drunk and gave them to her! Either way, I should have you both hanged! It is clear you both were dead drunk on duty, at a minimum! Look at you, swaying like reeds in the bloody wind. A disgusting display of inebriation! Stand at attention and stand still, man! Have you no discipline?"

The governor began once more to pace. "This will not go unpunished, you can be sure of it, gentlemen, this will not be overlooked, *harumph*, not go unpunished! Now get out and sober up! I give you over to the discipline of your *incompetent* commander!"

They staggered out of the governor's office, trying in vain to regain control of their legs and bowels. In their favor, it was the last time this pair attempted rape of a female prisoner. It took a number of days before either could walk a straight line, which everyone wrongly assessed to be the result of excessive indulgence in rum.

* * *

"Picked him up in the whorehouse near the West India Company wharf, sir." The massive sergeant led Deadlight onto the porch adjoining the governor's office. Deadlight seemed to dangle like a marionette, suspended by his collar in the sergeant's brawny grip. The governor was once again enjoying his midmorning Geneva gin below a potted palm tree.

"Ah, Mr. Helms, *harumph*, sorry for the inconvenience. Please have a seat. You may leave, Sergeant."

"Aye, aye, sir!" The sergeant clicked his heels and spun around, marching out with precision.

"Now, Mr. Helms, I can't say as I'm at all pleased with your behavior to date. Had a bit of a falling out with Lieutenant Lloyd, did we? *Harumph.*"

"He cast aspersions on me reputation, sir. Besides, *Inflexible* ain't outfitted for another voyage yet."

"Quite, *harumph*, reputation indeed, *hmmmm*. Mr. Helms, I have a different little duty for you that does not include *Inflexible* or her lieutenant." The governor gave Deadlight a sidelong glance and was unnerved to find he was being watched from under Deadlight's drooping eyelid. "Nevertheless, this little errand could turn out to be profitable for you as informant—in the service of the king and enforcement of the Navigation Acts, of course. Interested?"

"Aye, always willing to do me duty, Your Excellency."

"Quite. Well then, we've had a bit of a mishap on account of some poor fellows who drank a bit too much while on watch in the jail last night. I would like to reconcile this little mishap with as little trouble as possible prior to the governor's return, you understand?"

"Aye, Your Excellency."

"You will breathe not a word of this special little errand to anyone, you understand?"

"Aye, aye."

"The Easton woman has escaped, and so has her father, I'm afraid—the smuggler."

Deadlight was instantly agitated. "Do ye know where they are?"

"No, I do not know their whereabouts. That is the rub, isn't it? I want the little slut back in jail, but dear me, it would be most inconvenient if she were to go on telling tales about fines paid and not recorded, *harumph*. You see my point?"

"Not quite sure, Your Excellency."

"Well then, *harumph*, I shall give it to you in terms you are more likely to understand. There will be a sum equal to a sixth part of Captain Easton's fine for you."

"Aye, and what be the duty, sir?"

"I shall need to know the whereabouts of Captain Easton and his reprobate daughter. You, Mr. Helms, will provide me and me alone with information on their whereabouts. Slither about the waterfront haunts you seem to be familiar with, and find them out. It would be most convenient if they were to disappear entirely, *harumph*, utmost discretion required. That's two pounds for you; that would be half a year's pay for your sort, I imagine? *Harumph*, payable upon your return with news of a successful outcome to this little errand, *harumph*."

"I be nothing but an honest seaman, Your Excellency, bound to do me duty, as ye know. But a measly two pounds for a risky dance about the gallows ain't enough, sir, ain't enough by far, Your Excellency."

"Not enough, say you? Well then, let me tell you, I've been making some inquiries. Some very interesting information has come to light concerning a certain mutiny on the Virginia coast during the War of Shipmaster Jenkin's Ear. Seems the cabin boy alone escaped the gallows. Interesting description of the rogue, having to do with one of his eyes. Shall I read it to you?" The governor picked up a piece of ancient parchment.

"Nay, sir, that won't be necessary. May it please Your Excellency, those were dark days for old Deadlight, and he done reformed his self. A more honest man than the one standing right here, you'll never find. I'll swear to that on me own mother's grave. It would be a waste of a God-fearing man to send this one to the gallows, Your Excellency."

"Does that drivel mean you're willing to take care of this Easton affair?"

"Aye, aye, sir, ready and willing for duty, sir."

"*Hmmmm*, very well then. You will report any and all information to myself only. When your little errand is accomplished, I shall never see you again. Nor have I ever heard of you from this point forward."

"Aye, aye, Your Excellency."

"One last thing: The two prison guards who botched this whole thing are to be flogged in the square within the hour. You may find it edifying."

"Aye, Your Excellency, which a good public flogging always lifts me spirits, jolly good."

"Sergeant!"

The sergeant clapped his hand onto Deadlight's collar and led him out. Deadlight was in jolly spirits, ready to enjoy the floggings while contemplating how to pursue Anne and Captain Easton. Moreover, he could spend his idle time plotting and savoring the tantalizing opportunity to blackmail the lieutenant governor.

* * *

Captain Easton had been drifting in and out of feverish delirium all the way from Kingston. Malika met them where the trail into the Blue Mountains met the road to Morant Bay. She knelt over the donkey cart and held the captain's feverish head in her hands, feeling the cold sweat.

"Malika, I fear he will die of the fever," said Anne.

"We must get him up the mountain, where the Obeah of the forest lives. The Obeah can save him."

"But he can't even walk." Anne felt tears. Her father was doomed, for there was no way to get him into the mountains in the broken condition to which he'd been reduced.

"Dis de friend of Admiral William?" the muscular maroon man who drove the donkey cart asked.

"Admiral?"

"Yes, it is," answered the canny Malika.

"I carry the friend of Admiral Musket Man anywhere. Let's go." They put Captain Easton on the muscular maroon's back and began to climb the trail. The maroon was nothing but cheerful with his load, although they stopped more frequently to rest as they climbed higher into the forest. Malika searched for a cinchona tree. When she found one, she stripped some bark and stopped near one of the crystalline rivulets that flowed across the trail. She ground the bark on the rocks, carefully collecting the crumbled residue. She put the ground bark and some water together in a large leaf and announced that they would stay there for the evening. Anne and the man gathered palm boughs, then they constructed a rude lean-to against the frequent rain showers. As they worked, Anne questioned him.

"Do the maroons know Captain William?"

"Oh yes, missus, maroons know da Admiral quite well."

"Why do you call Captain William the Admiral?"

"Everybody gotta have a rank; Admiral be his rank."

"Didn't you also call him Musket Man?"

"I most surely did, missus." Malika gave him a sharp look.

"How did he get that name?"

"'Cause he da man wit' da muskets." Malika now stopped her activity; made sure she had the maroon's eye and not Anne's, and gave him a sign to hold his tongue. He evaded the remainder of Anne's questioning until she gave up in frustration.

Malika fed the bitter cinchona extract to Captain Easton all through the evening and night. For fear of detection, they built no fire. In the morning they made their way down the trail towards Morant Bay. Captain Easton was now able to walk with assistance and seemed to grow stronger by the hour. Malika, aided by Anne's insistence, continued to make him drink the bitter cinchona extract on the half-hour.

* * *

It had been four days since Anne left *Berbice*. The crew had the cargo stowed on the third day. Today they rolled idly at anchor, anxious that a navy warship might appear around the headland of Morant Bay. The escaped slaves who had helped re-float *Berbice* and then labored to load her cargo from the beach now sat amidships, speaking infrequently in hushed tones. A lookout watch was kept above on the cliffs and changed as if the ship were at sea.

Captain Harte paced the quarterdeck, looking for any additional little detail to make *Berbice* ready for sea. His anxious eye searched in vain. All was ready and shipshape. He chewed on his lip. He lit his pipe and coughed. The wind took the pipe smoke to the south, toward the entrance to Morant Bay. At least they weren't on a lee shore. Nevertheless, he chewed on his lip and paced, one eye constantly on the headland.

A crewman on watch was also kept at the catheads, ready to axe the anchor cable the moment a navy ship should be sighted. There were anxious moments whenever a sail appeared, but these had thus far turned out to be merchantman headed to and from Kingston. *Berbice's* sails were triced up and ready to let fall at the command.

"Captain's mighty anxious looking."

"Aye, with the Old Man and his daughter still ashore, and not a word from them. Does he abandon them here and save the ship, or does he stay and risk the ship and our necks? A choice I don't envy him. But when the wind clocks to the south, he'll have to reckon what to do."

"What do you think he'll choose?"

"I don't reckon I know, lad." Tiny furrowed his brow. "My guess is he'll stay until the very last moment."

As the shadows grew, Nathaniel declared, "Devil take me, I cannot stand it any longer! Tiny, row me ashore with the change of the lookout watch." It was Simon's turn at the watch when they rowed ashore that evening.

Matumbwe was on the beach. Anxiety showed in his normally jovial face.

"Captain Matumbwe, good evening."

"We all ready to sail, Captain?"

"The ship is ready; we can leave as soon as they return. It only remains for you to go aboard with me and the returning lookout watch. Has there been any word from Anne and Malika?"

"No, sah." Matumbwe's face betrayed the anxiety that his wife, so recently restored to his side, could be stranded here if *Berbice* had to make a hasty withdrawal.

"What if we get attacked?" The slaughter Matumbwe had witnessed on this very beach was only too fresh in his memory.

"Then we will leave with all haste. The safety of the ship is my responsibility, and I cannot abandon it."

"Dat means we leave Anne and Captain William here?" Matumbwe could not bear to mention his own wife.

"I shall not like to, Captain Matumbwe, but what good would we be to them if the ship were captured?"

"Do you need Captain Matumbwe this evening?"

Nathaniel read his meaning. "You have been invaluable to us, but we are loaded and ready for sea, sir."

"Then Captain Matumbwe going to take a look around."

"I envy you your freedom. I fear for them, yet I must stay with the ship."

They walked together up the forest trail to the top of the cliff they used for a lookout.

"The cover of darkness will give us some protection until tomorrow. Please return with good news by dawn, Captain Matumbwe."

As the sun turned the sky over the Blue Mountains shades of pink and lavender Matumbwe disappeared at a fast trot down the forest trail. Nathaniel Harte walked to the lookout and surveyed the Caribbean to the south. The sea was as smooth as an inland pond, reflecting pools of gold and deep blue. Nathaniel's greatest fear was the change in wind direction the calm foretold. The breeze had been from the north, giving them the upwind advantage of escape from the bay. Tomorrow would be different.

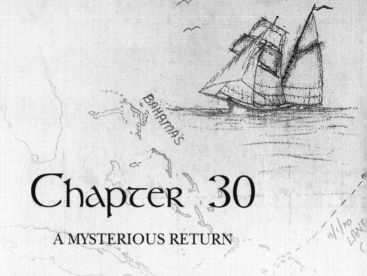

Chapter 30

A MYSTERIOUS RETURN

The sun rose in an orange ball over the Caribbean, at first coloring the water metallic blue and crimson. As the full disk appeared in radiant yellow, the sea began to ruffle in cat's paws. A bank of high cottony clouds hid the sun again as it rose behind them.

"Wind's clocked south, sir," reported Mr. Murty to Lieutenant Lloyd.

"Finally!" They had been tacking back and forth for days, unable to claw back up to the coast of Jamaica since leaving Kingston.

"Very well then, let us take a look into Morant Bay. Mr. Murty, make a course to the northeast." In an hour more, a gentle breeze was pushing *Inflexible* through the water at six knots, on a broad reach. A two-foot chop now marched toward Jamaica's shore, splashing against her weather side and sending spray onto the deck amidships.

Unusually tall white cumulus clouds made a fanciful mountain range as they approached from the south, contrasting with the Blue Mountains of Jamaica to the north.

* * *

Simon was dog-tired as the sun warmed the verdant forest surrounding his lookout camp on the cliff. The birds began to stir and a gentle breeze swayed the tops of the trees. He climbed into the crotch he used as his crow's nest and surveyed the horizon, taking segment by segment in turn, from west to east. A bank of tall, puffy clouds was emerging in the crisp light of dawn. The sea sparkled below them where the sun itself was hidden from view. Then he spied a brig bearing toward Morant Bay about fifteen miles off.

His scalp tingled in instant fear, and he dropped out of the tree to fetch his spyglass. Scrambling back to his lookout, he found the bearing of the brig again, only a speck on the horizon, by sighting down the barrel of the spyglass before putting his eye to it.

"Christ Almighty!" he said, then dropped out of the tree again and fell headlong on his face. On all fours, he raced to his pistol. His hands shook so violently he nearly dumped the priming onto the ground. After he fired a shot in the direction of *Berbice* at anchor, he struggled to reload with trembling hands. Again he fired over the anchorage, and then tore off down the trail to the beach, spent pistol in hand.

* * *

"Blood and thunder! That must have been Simon!" Nathaniel threw on a pair of knee breeches and ran up the companionway.

"Tiny, rouse all hands!"

"Aye, aye!"

"Atticus, cut the cable as soon as the foresail backs on the starboard tack. Barbecue, let go the foresail tricing lines. Tiny, get the foresail trimmed aback." Nathaniel waited anxious seconds while the men carried out his orders.

Simon exploded from the undergrowth at the top of the beach and ran down the dry sand, kicking it up in plumes with each stride. As he drew near *Berbice's* beached yawl boat, a musket barrel appeared beside a palm-tree trunk and steadied aim above the transom of the yawl boat, where he would stop momentarily to push it into the water. Crashing into it, he pushed with his shoulder, his feet digging furrows in the sand. The musket cracked out and Simon fell to the beach.

"Bloody Hell!" Nathaniel had heard the shot on *Berbice*. "Gunny, load grape in the stern quarter swivels, lively now!"

Having followed them at a distance from Kingston, Deadlight chuckled and sat down to reload with his back against the palm tree. He did not use his other muskets to finish off Simon, for he needed them ready and loaded in order to kill Anne and Captain Easton when they appeared.

Simon crawled on his belly around the side of the yawl boat, took a deep breath, and ran into the water, finally diving headlong and swimming toward *Berbice*, anchored close to the beach to facilitate reloading her cargo. She was anchored in the lee of the headland,

and only the faintest breeze wafted down to the anchorage. Nathaniel clenched his fists, anxious for the ship to swing on her anchor through the eye of the wind so they could start off on the starboard tack and get out of the bay. Simon was rapidly closing the distance, swimming as fast as he could, with a wildly thrashing stroke. They threw him a line as he neared, and he scrambled up the main chains.

"Gunny, I marked smoke on the starboard side of that grove of palm trees, next to the tallest one."

"Aye, aye." Gunny sighted down the barrel of the swivel gun, a length of slow match in his right hand.

Anne was the first to run out onto the beach, waving a shirt above her head like a flag of truce and screaming at *Berbice* to wait. Steadying his musket barrel on a fallen palm log, Deadlight took aim for the middle of her body. Anne stopped jumping and stared at the ship, trying to interpret Nathaniel's frantic hand signals. Deadlight waited patiently for Captain Easton to appear from the undergrowth; for he wanted to make sure he had them both. Matumbwe and Malika walked onto the beach, with Captain Easton between them.

So much the better, thought Deadlight. He slowly cocked the lock on his musket, letting them all go down the beach, away from the cover of the forest. Renewing his aim at Anne's midriff, he began to squeeze the trigger.

"*Boom!*" Grapeshot shredded the palm branches above him. Near his head a passing ball cut in half the palm tree he was using to steady his musket. Splinters rained down as he lay prone on the sand, dreading another round of grapeshot. In a moment he rolled over, gathered his muskets, and ran into the forest.

"Anne, get back up here into the woods, now!" Matumbwe turned and thrust Captain Easton to safety in the undergrowth. "Anne—now—run!"

"Good shot, Gunny! Give them another as fast as you can reload; make it halfway down the beach, from the last shot to Captain Easton's group." Gunny was already sponging the swivel and grinning from ear to ear.

Matumbwe looked down the beach where *Berbice* had fired her round of grapeshot. They must have seen something there. Escape across the open beach was now out of the question. It would be suicide to leave the cover of the forest.

"*Boom!*" Another round of grapeshot from the ship ripped through the undergrowth and smashed trunks in the forest beyond. Deadlight hugged the ground once more and cursed.

"This way!" Matumbwe commanded. They ran from the spot where *Berbice* aimed her grapeshot, and struggled through the undergrowth along the beach and onto the forest path. Matumbwe propelled Captain Easton along between himself and Anne or Malika, stopping when one of the women grew winded. He wished he hadn't sent the maroon home to Nanny Town: They desperately needed another strong back.

* * *

Berbice's foresail backed and the ship began to pay off on the starboard tack.

"Cut the cable! Tiny, get the headsails up as fast as ever you can! Barbecue, as soon as the jib trims on the starboard tack, let go the mainsail tricing lines and trim in hard on the wind. We're going to try to weather the lee headland in one tack out to sea. Give it to them, Gunny!"

"*Boom!*" Gunny had an uncanny appreciation for how fast a man in the undergrowth with a load of weapons might travel. The grapeshot ripped a ragged hole in the forest right above Deadlight, raining splinters and coconuts down around him. He dropped on his belly and took a mouthful of sand.

"Huzzah! Huzzah!" The *Berbice* came alive as she gathered way and her crew was again doing what they knew best.

"Eye of newt and toe of frog!" The dry crackling voice came from the forest near the fleeing group on the edge of the beach.

"That must be Angustine, Captain William's parrot. The poor thing has flown away from the *Berbice*," cried Anne.

They stopped for a rest. Captain Easton was panting; streams of sweat poured off his chin. When they let him down, he collapsed against a palm-tree trunk. They could tell from his dry, rasping pant he was desperate for water.

"What shall we do now?"

"We can go to join the maroons in Nanny Town." It would be a hard two-day climb through the Blue Mountains.

"I will stay with my father," Anne said quietly.

"Waterfall and saman tree, beneath the second rock of three." The dry, crackling voice had a ghostly quality as it echoed through the forest, again in front of them, as if to urge them on.

"The Obeah bird reminds me, there is a stream ahead. We can get Captain Easton some water there." Malika took the lead.

They struggled on until they came to a stream that cut through the beach to the bay. Anne brought Captain Easton a coconut shell full of cool water. Malika ground more cinchona bark and let it steep in another half coconut shell, further treatment for the captain's fever.

"Ye better sit here." Matumbwe indicated a ridge of sand behind a massive fallen log, where they would be hidden from their unseen pursuer.

"I wish I had my dueling pistol." The governor's guards had taken Anne's pistol and dagger as evidence of her plot to assassinate His Excellency.

Matumbwe was not a man to sit still and let himself be captured. Crouching beside the log, he peered into the forest in the direction from which they had come. "You stay here," he commanded and disappeared into the undergrowth, staying so low he hardly moved the tops of the ferns.

* * *

Deadlight drove on toward his quarry, careful to keep himself under cover from *Berbice's* swivel guns. As he approached the stream he longed to slake his thirst, but the hillside forest opened up into a ravine, and he grew wary. Meanwhile, Matumbwe crawled from tree to tree. He kept the approach to the log in view, while trying to expand the visible area of forest by climbing higher up the wall of the ravine.

The terror of her situation began to tell on Anne, as she waited for something deadly and unexpected. Her inclination was to run, but she knew she could not leave her father to his fate. He was lapsing into delirium once more.

Malika reached for the coconut shell with the cinchona extract. They heard the crack of the musket and saw the coconut shell explode at the same time. Malika yelped and sat back against the log, trembling.

"Wool of bat and tongue of dog!"

Deadlight lowered the musket and looked around for the source of the dry, crackling voice.

"Ah ha ha, ah ha ha!"

Rolling once, he pointed his musket up the ravine, from whence the cackling laugh had come. Anne looked in the same direction. She had never heard Angustine give an inflection to any of his repeated phrases. The verse she had just heard had a distinct emphasis on the word, dog.

The loud tenor whoop of some sort of bird came from above those on the ravine wall. Deadlight spun and pointed his musket up toward the sound.

"For a charm of powerful trouble, like a hell-broth boil and bubble!"

Now he rolled again, aiming into the ravine. He could see nothing, but the voice was closer. The tenor bird whoop began once more, like the warning calls of Africans. Deadlight had once hunted with slavers. This time the call was closer, still behind him on the wall of the ravine. He crawled in back of a tree trunk and pointed his musket at the wall of the ravine, firing a blind shot. Quickly he grabbed for his other loaded musket, stood, and peered around the tree trunk. A twig snapped in the ravine not a hundred feet from where he stood. Jumping from behind the tree, he saw nothing to fire at.

Deadlight began to panic. He had plenty of courage to hunt down an old man and his unarmed daughter, but now felt he was the quarry. The whooping of the giant bird began again, right behind his exposed back. Diving behind the tree to where his muskets lay he hastily loaded them, intending to flee, but not without loaded weapons. Before he had wrapped a cloth patch around a ball, the haunting laughter came again, this time from no more than fifty feet away.

"Ah ha ha, ah ha ha."

Deadlight grabbed the loaded musket and scurried around the tree, catching sight of movement in a group of giant ferns. He fired into the middle of the ferns, quickly retreating to the cover of the tree to reload. All three of his firearms were now empty. He rammed the ball and patch down the barrel and reached for his powder horn to prime the lock, when he heard another twig snap no more than ten feet in front of his nose.

"Now we see what kind of warrior you are, mistuh."

Looking up he saw the massive figure of Matumbwe in a wrestler's stance. Deadlight was on his feet in an instant, his sheath knife bared. Matumbwe advanced, faking moves to the right and left with lightning speed, making it impossible for Deadlight to keep his balance.

Matumbwe backed away and picked up a fallen branch, breaking off the heavy end to use as a club.

Deadlight charged, knife slashing through the air, side to side. Matumbwe swung his club and caught Deadlight's knife hand, but the club broke in half and Matumbwe lost his footing on some wet leaves. Raising his knife to plunge it into Matumbwe's chest, a coconut held in two bony hands suddenly smashed down on his head. He dropped the knife and fell on his face in the ferns.

Matumbwe looked up at the apparition of a wiry old man dressed in ragged old seaman's clothes, with a wild, white beard and wilder hair stuffed under a salt-stained tricornered hat. There was a bullet hole in the crown of the tricorn. The old man saw Matumbwe's astonished expression and said, "Had to split his bollard; he ruined my hat, he did. *Ah ha ha, ah ha ha!*"

Matumbwe took Deadlight's knife, and seeing that he lacked one earlobe, cut off the other with a flick of the razor-sharp blade. This brought him out of his blackout when he saw Matumbwe with a bloody bit of flesh in his hand, he touched his throbbing ear, and looked in horror at his blood-soiled fingers.

"Da old man say we should cook and eat you, mistah; he look some kinda hungry, don' you t'ink? You wait here; I'll make da fire!" Matumbwe faked eating Deadlight's earlobe and turned as if to go and collect wood for a fire. Deadlight bolted to his feet and raced away through the underbrush, howling like a dog.

"Ah ha ha, ah ha ha!" Captain William slapped his leg, "and that'll pay back for the beating I took at the hands of him and his pirates! Wanted me sea chest, they did!"

Matumbwe gathered up Deadlight's muskets and slung them over his back, and the two walked down to the log by the stream. Anne got to her feet when she spied the old man. "So it was you, Captain William; you're alive!" She ran to the old scarecrow's arms and hugged him.

"Aye, how's my lass?"

Captain William looked at his old friend, Captain Easton, "Got the fever, Jonathan?"

"Aye, Captain, it seems to pass, the more of this infernally bitter drink I take."

"You should try it with rum, aye, the tonic for the tropical damps." Captain William gave Malika a wink.

"Look *Berbice*! She's leaving!" Shouted Anne.

"Look alive then, clear this brush away!" ordered Captain William. At his command, everyone dragged branches and palm boughs away from a pile on the opposite bank of the stream. There they uncovered a gunnel and thole pin, and then the smartly curved side of a whaleboat. Using branches as levers, they pushed the lean twenty-six-foot boat into the stream, then dragged her the rest of the way to the bay. Anne noted an iron-bound oak chest stowed beneath a thwart. It was identical to the one she and Malika found in the waterfall. *Had Captain William known what was happening in Kingston?* She wondered, her anger growing at his apparent manipulation.

They floated the whaleboat at the beach and got aboard. Captain Easton rallied and stepped the mast for the sail, then shipped the forward oar. Malika sat, as instructed by Captain William, in the next seat aft and took up the unfamiliar loom of an oar herself. Matumbwe shipped two oars in the middle thwart, and Captain William took the steering oar, as Anne pushed off the beach.

"You trim the sail," he ordered her. "Mind, she's tender and a wee bit over canvassed, so ease her if need be and don't let her capsize or ship water, or I'll have the hide off—er, I'll be very upset." The two captains exchanged winks.

"Shall we ever catch them?" Anne spoke to no one in particular.

"Aye, just mind your sheet trim, lass!" said Captain William, "Put your backs into it, ye lubbers! Together now, pull!" They put their oars in the sea and leaned back as they pulled, and the smart little whaleboat shot away from the beach toward *Berbice*. "Of course we'll catch them. *Berbice* ain't worth a fart in a gale of wind to weather, compared to this here Nantucket sled."

* * *

"Boat's put off from the beach up the bay!" Simon shouted to *Berbice's* deck from his masthead lookout.

Nathaniel pulled his spyglass from his pocket to look. *Would it be wishful thinking to hope that Anne has somehow escaped?* he asked himself. He could not make out the occupants of the small boat, which looked to be a whaleboat. "Atticus, take this glass aloft to Simon!"

Atticus took Nathaniel's spyglass and climbed the weather ratlines of the mainmast. In a few minutes there was a hail from the main topmast, "It's the Old Man and the rest!"

"Huzzah! Huzzah! Huzzah*!*"

* * *

The whaleboat began to catch the southeast breeze as she came out of the lee of the headland. Anne trimmed the oversize sail, and the slim boat picked up speed.

"That's it, me hearties, put your backs into it!" Captain William urged the efforts on the oars.

Then the sails of *Inflexible* appeared as she cleared the headland.

"Blood and thunder, the bloody navy!" Along *Inflexible's* side were a row of five gun ports. Behind her a sliver of twinkling sunlight on the sea below a sheer wall of billowy white cloud with a dark gray base.

"Oh no! We're ruined!" wailed Anne.

A gust of wind caught the whaleboat, and she heeled her rail down to the sea.

"Ship your oars and get your asses on the windward rail! Lively now! Mind your sheet trim, lass!" They shipped their oars and clambered to sit on the starboard gun'l. When they were on the rail, Anne sweated the sheet in, and the whaleboat took off like a racehorse, a white bone of foam in her teeth.

"*Ah ha ha, ah ah ha!*" Captain William gripped the steering oar with both hands, his white beard framing a broad grin, red cheeks below deep laugh lines, a picture of glee. "This here sailboat race ain't even started, lassie! *Ah ha ha, ah ha ha!*" He glanced to the south, at a towering wall of white cloud approaching and winked again at Captain Easton.

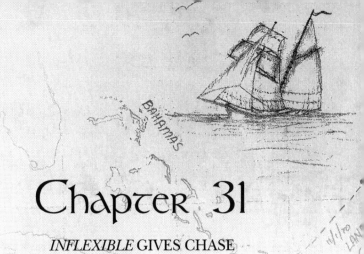

Chapter 31

INFLEXIBLE GIVES CHASE

"Ahoy the deck! Schooner heading out of the bay!"

Lieutenant Lloyd put his spyglass to his eye. It was a Yankee schooner, by the rake of her masts, with yellow and black topsides.

"Take a look, Mr. Murty. I believe our luck has changed with the breeze."

"Aye, sir, I believe it looks ever so much like the Yankee smuggler."

"If what that scum, Gideon Helms, says is true, a look at her papers may be all we need to claim her as a prize. Mind the sail trim; we shall not want to lose them." Lieutenant Lloyd began to pace the windward side of the quarterdeck.

"Mr. Murty, shape your course three points to the northeast of the chase; we shall intercept them as they leave the mouth of the bay." The breeze freshened, driving *Inflexible* along all the faster on her best point of sail.

* * *

The Nantucket whaleboat gave valiant chase after *Berbice*, spray soaking everyone sitting on her windward gun'l as she raced over the waves. They broke out the extra sail Captain William had aboard and put it about their shoulders to shelter from the spray. The wind and the constant wet made them shiver in spite of the warmth of the day. Anne had to play the lugsail sheet to keep the tender boat from capsizing in the gusts, letting out a precious inch or so when the breeze freshened, just enough to bring the boat's leeward rail up a few inches. When the gust blew itself out, she'd sweat the sail back in with both hands, using her back as well as her arms to pull, so as not to lose any precious wind power, in their race to catch the fleeing *Berbice*.

* * *

Aboard *Berbice*, Nathaniel kept anxious watch on both the ten-gun navy brig and the whaleboat, hoping that one would catch up while he evaded the other. There was no question of *Berbice* heaving-to to allow the whaleboat to come up; they could not slow down and risk capture of the ship. The race with the ten-gun brig was much too close. He eyed the approaching cloudbank. There was a drastic change in weather in the offing, and the complications it would introduce in handling the vessels may yield an advantage. He only wished it would come up faster. *Berbice* heeled to the freshening breeze.

"Everyone to the windward rail!" Nathaniel knew the weight of the escaped slaves and his crew counterbalancing the force of the wind on the sails would add some precious speed to *Berbice's* progress.

* * *

As the wind freshened, Anne struggled with the whaleboat's sail. The little craft was now tearing through the water like a wild steed, nearly out of control. The lugsail luffed constantly, losing power and dragging the whaleboat to leeward. The small whaleboat was overpowered; Anne could not trim the sail without risking capsize.

"Reckon it's time to reef, Jonathan," Captain William called to Captain Easton.

"Aye, aye, reckon so." Captain Easton was happy to have a chance to move off the spray-soaked weather rail. He hung on with both hands as he moved, for the whaleboat was bucking up and down on the four-foot chop blown up by the freshening trade wind. Grabbing the unstayed mast with his left hand, he uncleated the snotter and pulled the sprit out of its pocket in the lugsail, allowing half the sail to fold over the lee side.

"Trim it in, Anne, that's a good lass. Now she'll go!"

* * *

Inflexible had the weather gauge, the favored position upwind of *Berbice*. She was on a broad reach with the freshening trade wind abaft her beam, her best point of sail. Lieutenant Lloyd had every sail flying, with stuns'ls rigged port and starboard. *Inflexible* flew along on a course east of the entrance of Morant Bay, the spray flying from her bow and the foam singing along her lee side.

* * *

Nathaniel's heart was in his throat. While *Inflexible* had the wind free, *Berbice* was hard on the wind, bearing southeast. It looked as if they could weather the eastern headland of Morant Bay; but the fast-approaching *Inflexible* might have them under her guns by then. If they could not weather the headland and were forced to come about, they would sail right into the range of *Inflexible's* cannon. *Berbice* was weatherly, but made only indifferent speed close-hauled. It would be a close race, indeed. The whaleboat was being blown off to leeward before they scandalized the lugsail. *Can they catch up now?*

"Breakers ahead!" The call came from *Berbice's* mainmast.

"Devil take me!" Nathaniel jumped down to the main deck and ran forward, as if a closer look at the reef could somehow show him a way out. He was despondent; there was nothing to do but submit to a humiliating capture and ruin. He ran back to the helm. "Nothing for it, Barbecue, we must come about immediately."

"Not necessary, sir," was Barbecue's nonchalant reply. "That just be Johnson's Reef; there's clear passage to leeward sir, right up to the eastern end of the cut."

"And what of the eastern end, Barbecue?"

"Have to luff her dead to windward around a rock there, sir. Weather that and it's clear sailing to Cuba."

"What if the long shore current's against us?"

"Aye, that could do us in, if it runs this hour," answered Barbecue casually. He rolled his eyes and looked off at the breakers approaching to port and to starboard. The decision wasn't his, and he was glad of it.

"Steer her through, Barbecue, but pray keep her to the windward side as much as you dare."

"Aye, aye, sir!"

Barbecue headed straight for the windward line of breakers, the only indication where the reef lay beneath. As he approached he hauled the tiller over to windward, and *Berbice* sailed by close enough to cut through the foam blown to leeward from the seas breaking over the deadly ledge.

Tiny gasped as he saw and the jagged green and yellow rocks racing below their keel through the clear sea. The African landlubbers lining the rail on either side of him looked at him with terror in their eyes. Tiny grinned back and then forced a laugh. His laugh was an unexpected outlet for his pent-up foreboding, and he erupted into a genuine guffaw. Seeing the big white sailor was amused, the Africans laughed with Tiny.

Nathaniel saw the weather rail lined with hearty men in the throes of hysterics. He looked aft at their wake cutting smartly between the lines of breakers and felt overcome with elation himself. They could very well make good their escape, after all.

Tiny shouted, "Cheers, men, for Barbecue's cut, huzzah, huzzah, huzzah!"

* * *

With her shallow keel and the fresh breeze, the whaleboat was struggling to windward. The tradeoff was either going faster a point off the wind, or sailing her as close to the wind as the scandalized lugsail would set, but going slower. *Berbice* was drawing away from them.

"Scandalized lugsail don't set worth a damn," was Captain William's assessment. "We'll fall off to leeward a point. Ease the sheet till she luffs, and then haul in a bit, lass." Anne let the lugsail sheet slip over the tholepin two inches. The taut line groaned as it went out, and water rung from the braids as the sail pulled again. The whaleboat picked up a great deal of speed. Anne looked at *Berbice* charging to windward with the spray flying up from her weather bow and her rail lined with cheering men. Nathaniel was going to escape!

"*Berbice* has weathered the reef; they're getting away!"

"Nay, Lassie," cried Captain William, "they be inside of Johnson's Reef. There'll be some nice ship handling around the rock at the end of the cut, or we'll see the wreck of her by the end of the hour." He looked at the dark gray base of the cloud bank approaching from the south. To the south-southeast he saw *Inflexible*, borne along by her cloud of sail, her bow wave boiling white between the deep blue and her black hull. Anne looked ahead and gasped in horror - they were headed straight for the breakers off the headland.

"We must come about; we're sailing into the breakers!" Anne yelled above the crash and roar of Johnson's Reef.

"Surf's where the whaleboat's at her best, Lassie, and the only way we can catch up to *Berbice* is from the inside of the reef. Come about, and we'll be in the arms of the Navy yonder."

* * *

"Load the chase gun, Mr. Murty; we shall call for their attention." Lieutenant Lloyd strutted along the weather side of *Inflexible's* quarterdeck.

"Aye, aye," Mr. Murty went forward. Inflexible's bow wave surged away to port and starboard, joining the chop blown up by the trade wind and curling into whitecaps. They were flying along!

"Gun crew to the chaser! Haul her in place, lads. On the tackles, together now, heave. Gun captain, inspect the piece."

"Aye, aye."

"Load the piece."

"Aye, aye." A measure of powder was put down the barrel with a wooden ladle. In went the six-pound iron ball. The ball was rammed home.

"Ready, sir."

"Run out your gun!"

"Ready, sir."

"Prime the piece."

"Ready, sir!"

Mr. Murty turned around to face the quarterdeck. "Ready, sir!"

"As soon as they're in range, Mr. Murty, if you please."

Murty's practiced eye told him that would not be too long.

* * *

The size of the breakers seemed to grow as the whaleboat drew closer. Each comber rose up at the outside of the reef into a rapidly moving vertical wall of water eight feet high, charging over the reef until the top curled over and tons of water roared on in boiling foam. Anne was sure they would all die. There was no way to swim out of the boiling maelstrom. They would certainly be picked up and dashed to pieces by the monstrous breakers. Seeming to her a madman, Captain William gleefully guided the whaleboat on into the surf crashing around the reef.

* * *

Nathaniel thought the spout of water was a freak wave dashing on a rock when he heard the thud of the cannon shot. *Inflexible* was closing the range quickly. He looked at the approaching brig, judging the distance and her speed. Sailing through the cut with Barbecue piloting, the reefs boiled on either side. A rock thrust from the sea ahead. The sails of the ten-gun brig now shined in stark contrast to the dark gray of the approaching weather in the background. *If only it would come on to blow and carry away some of her canvas,* he wished.

* * *

Lieutenant Lloyd swaggered forward to the chase gun. "Mr. Murty, do you suppose that whaleboat is attached to the smuggler?"

"Aye, sir, seems to be following them."

"Look's like they're in closer range, wouldn't you say?"

"Aye, sir, by a hundred yards."

"Give them a shot; we can always send in our boats to pick up the pieces on the way back."

"Aye, aye; swivel her around, lads. That's it, a bit to port, that'll do." He put the slow match to the cannon's touchhole.

* * *

Captain William saw the puff of smoke blow away from the bow of the brig. A split second later they heard a *whoosh* and a geyser erupted to leeward of the whaleboat. They were within range! They'd be a wildly dancing target in a few more minutes. He headed the whaleboat into the roiling surf of the reef.

* * *

"Try another ranging shot on the schooner, Mr. Murty."

"Aye, aye; haul her around lads, that's it. Hammer in the quoin a bit; aye, that's enough." Murty sighted the *Berbice* down the gun barrel, lining up the notch at the breech with the notch at the muzzle, the *Berbice* bouncing on the waves dead center in the distance. "We've got them now, sir!"

"Aye, Mr. Murty, take down their rigging. I'd hate to lose the value of the prize, if it can be helped."

"Sponge the piece."

"Aye, aye."

"Inspect the piece."

"Ready, sir."

"Load."

"Ready, sir."

"Prime the piece."

"Ready, sir."

"Run out!" Murty again sighted down the barrel. *Berbice* bobbed and pitched broadside to them. *"Fire!"*

* * *

Nathaniel saw the dreaded puff of smoke waft from the bow of the brig. As if a boulder had hit the foresail, it yanked and nearly tore free, and then fell back. There was a six-inch hole in the stout cloth. By the grace of Providence it did not rip out a seam. *Berbice* sailed on, right through the foam from the breakers to starboard, Barbecue alert at the tiller.

"End of the cut is about a hundred yards ahead, sir," Barbecue informed Nathaniel. Nathaniel ran to the weather foremast ratlines and climbed, looking at the rock and the right-angle passage to the sea beyond. They would turn *Berbice* into the eye of the wind and let her momentum carry her through, but if there were a contrary current, they would be wrecked. There wasn't enough maneuvering room to turn the ship around and sail back out of the cut. He looked inshore for the whaleboat, and his heart sank. It was nowhere to be seen! Then the light craft, looking like a tiny leaf, was tossed on top of a wave, still under sail, heading right into the breakers. In a moment the whaleboat disappeared behind the whitecaps.

* * *

Mr. Murty lined up another shot, aiming for the foremast ratlines. The range was closing rapidly and he was able to aim the chase gun with far more accuracy.

* * *

Nathaniel hung in the ratlines and looked at the approaching rock at the end of the cut. The channel around it was no more than fifty feet wide! There would be one chance and one chance only.

* * *

"*Ah ha ha, ah ha ha!* Ship your oars, boys! Pull like Beelzebub his self were after ye when I give the order. Keep your blade tips high! Don't drag 'em. That's it, me hearties; now pull like bloody demons!" cried Captain William. Each time a wall of whitewater approached, he turned the whaleboat to plunge directly into it, and the boat miraculously lifted each time, rising suddenly and pointing skyward, then belly-flopping into the boiling foam. He guided the whaleboat toward the breaking waves, where they curled into solid walls of racing water.

Perhaps it was the juxtaposition of Anne's father and her father's mentor, but as she stared at the madman clutching the steering oar of the little whaleboat, the sunlight streaming from below the approaching storm gave his visage a preternatural glow. She suddenly saw him, not as an infallible icon of authority, but as a man, struggling in this heroic trial, with resources she now saw as more equal to her own, not those of a demigod sea captain.

"Jonathan, trice up the sail; it will hinder us in the breakers," ordered Captain Wiliam. Captain Easton timed a lull between waves and lunged to pull the spritsail mast out of the thwart. If another wave hit before he had it safely down, he would lose his balance and they would capsize. He tugged at it; it did not budge. With wiggling and tugging it began to pull free, but then he felt the forward surge of an oncoming breaker, and he slammed the spar back home and grabbed for a seat.

"Pull, Matumbwe! Pull for your bloody life, man!"

At first Matumbwe had been terrified, but now he understood the game and was smiling, thoroughly enjoying this contest of brute strength against the sea. Matumbwe's powerful stroke shot the whaleboat forward just in time!

The bow of the boat suddenly shot up, pointing to the sky. On either side they had the awful view of a vertical wall of rushing water. Captain Easton held onto the thwart in the bow with all his strength to keep from being pitched over the stern. The massive muscles of Matumbwe's back flexed as the big man pulled his sweeps with all his might. Then they were airborne, falling, crashing into the foaming sea again. Captain William now held onto the stern thwart, himself nearly airborne as the stern whipped up and then fell out below him. *"Ah ha ha, ah ha ha!"*

The lugsail flogged and dragged them broadside to the next oncoming wave. Captain Easton grabbed the mast once more, this time twisting it round at the base. It came free, and he quickly gathered in the sail. Matumbwe took a stroke at the sweeps and Captain William lined the boat up with the next oncoming breaker.

"Pull, Matumbwe; pull, Malika; pull, lass; pull or meet the Devil!" Captain William shouted. *"Ah ha ha, ah ha ha!"* The old man's white hair stood out around his head, blown back in the trade wind, his eyes squinting as he grinned. He gripped the steering oar with his bony fingers, his wiry arms straining to bring the boat under the precise control required to challenge the surf. Standing up with his whole weight on the oar when required, he grabbed his seat at the last possible moment when they shot up the face of a wave. Facing the oncoming breakers, he was clearly having the time of his life. Anne was sure they would be drowned.

Captain William avoided approaching waves as they curled, for this was when they rushed up in a vertical wall of water.

The backwash now sucked them toward the outer edge of the reef, and Captain William saw a rogue wave approaching from the deep. Much larger than any of the previous breakers, it was rising in a solid wall of water already twenty feet high, coming on at an amazing rate of speed. He knew this larger sea would break in the deeper water. They were not through the surf yet!

"Pull, ye goddamn lubbers, pull with your backs, together now! Pull, like the whoresons ye be! Together now, pull!" They could feel the surge rush them toward the wave in a sickeningly swift acceleration. "Pull, ye sons of the Devil! Pull, damn ye! Damn ye!" The whaleboat flew towards the onrushing wall of water.

* * *

Mr. Murty lined up his shot with *Berbice's* foremast ratlines. There was someone in them, but no matter: These were smugglers. Had they not ignored *Inflexible's* warning shots? Any law-abiding merchantman would have hove-to immediately; the smugglers took their chances. Picking up the slow match from the sand bucket, he brought it to the cannon touchhole, and waited for the rise of the next swell passing under the racing *Inflexible.*

"*Breakers ahead*!"

"Helm, hard to weather! Hard to weather, damn ye!" Lieutenant Lloyd's face rapidly reddened with sudden emotion. Turning a hundred-ton square-rigged ship charging along at twelve knots, and making the maneuver within seconds, is no small task. Seconds is all they had before shipwreck.

Mr. Murty stuffed the slow match back into the sand bucket and spun around to give sail-handling orders. *Inflexible* turned into the wind in a long arc, her headsails finally flogging and her square sails taken aback. As the brig turned, the crew gasped as a massive curling wave rose up and rolled the brig on her beam ends, then plunged into roaring foam right abeam.

Lieutenant Lloyd grew hoarse from screaming nonstop blasphemies as the stuns'ls were lowered and the square sails swung around on the port tack. But then it was high time to shorten sail with all haste; approaching weather was upon them. The gusts blew stronger, heeling *Inflexible* down until her lee rail dragged through green water. As the squall line hit, sails tore apart with the sound of cannon shots, and lines whipped and tangled. *Inflexible* tore away like a wild thing until Morant Bay disappeared over the horizon.

* * *

Nathaniel hung in the ratlines until the last possible moment, memorizing the marks of the narrow cut they would soon luff *Berbice* through. Finally jumping to the deck and running aft, he bolted up the ladder to the quarterdeck, where Barbecue stood gripping the tiller. "Turn on the last streak of foam to weather; the end of the reef lies below." *Berbice is nimble, but can she spin around and shoot through such a tight channel?*

"Wait, wait, steady as she goes." Nathaniel watched the signs on the water, betraying the locations of the rocks below. "Hard to leeward, now!" Barbecue pushed the tiller to the lee side. *Berbice* continued to surge toward the rock thrusting up directly in her path, then her momentum built and she began to turn to starboard into the cut. At first the ship heeled and seemed to pick up speed, but then her sails stalled and luffed as they turned directly into the wind.

"Aye, steady as she goes now, Barbecue. Wait till we clear before ye pay off. Tiny, ready to back the jib! We cannot let her fall onto the port tack." They had to have enough forward motion to have steerage at the end of the cut in order to turn onto the starboard tack again, or they would be blown back on the reef.

Looking for the last rock ledge on the port side, Nathaniel felt *Berbice* was going dangerously slow. She would soon lose steerageway. He stared at the ledge submerged in the clear water, deceptively mild-looking in its green and yellow mantle, but menacing shipwreck, nevertheless.

They crept past, slower and slower. If they turned too soon, they would drag the heel of her keel onto the reef and lose all steerageway, and with the breeze blowing them shoreward, they would be pounded to matchsticks on the rocks.

"Tiny, back the jib! Helm, hard to port!" *Berbice* had nearly stopped.

* * *

Captain William no longer grinned as he looked at the oncoming rogue wave. "Pull, ye sons o' whores, damn ye! Pull together, hard!" Captain Easton fell backward off his seat, the bow shot up so suddenly. Anne gripped her thwart and held on desperately as she found herself looking straight down at Captain William's terrified face. A translucent, vertical wall of water was on both sides of the boat, eerily blocking out the sun. Suddenly tons of water overhead shaded the boat. She heard the bow of the whaleboat punch under, and was hit with a solid mass of falling water. Next came the sickening sensation that they were being swept back with the wave, moving at incredible speed. And then the wave was gone, and they were falling through the air, as the stern of the whaleboat bucked up. She saw Captain William fly up above her now, the steering oar gone; with both hands he was holding onto the thwart on which he sat, to keep from being catapulted over the bow of the boat.

Captain William was amazed to be alive, but the old salt rallied first. "What are ye waiting for? Bail, ye lubbers! Matumbwe, take easy strokes now. and mind your balance—any sudden movement and we'll be swamped." The water in the bottom of the whaleboat sloshed around their calves. They used anything that would hold water to bail. Anne took Captain William's tricorner to use as a bailing bucket and discovered it had holes fore and aft where a bullet had passed through, half an inch from the old man's scalp.

Captain William watched her turning the hat over and putting her finger through the holes in amazement. "We settled Deadlight's account, didn't we? He and his pirate scum beat me and ransacked my house. That's why I had to lay low, lass. I never meant to abandon you or young Jonathan, here. Kept a good lookout from the lee side, I did. You got the doubloons for the governor, all safe and sound, didn't ye?"

"You knew the governor would steal them, didn't you? That's why you put only the exact amount in the sea chest under the waterfall."

"Aye, lass! If there be a mark ye can lay to without doubt of your course, it will be the venality of any official enforcing the Navigation Acts." Captain William looked at the blue-gray squall line approaching from out to sea. He cast a glance to his right. Miles away now, on the port tack, he could see *Inflexible* headed west, heeled down in the powerful gusts of the squall that was upon them, sails flogging madly.

"Well enough, me hearties." Captain William's red cheeks glowed and his grin burst forth again from his white beard. "Step the mast, Jonathan; we've a downwind pleasure sail ahead of us!" The first gusts of the squall line were kicking up whitecaps only two hundred yards to weather.

* * *

Berbice began to wheel on her backed jib. An incoming wave surge sent her back a yard, and Nathaniel caught his breath; the long shore current was going to drag them back on the rocks! The approaching squall would surely drive them up onto the reef to leeward. Dropping a kedge anchor would do no good, for they would swing onto the rocks on either side. They had to clear the channel! There was no time to lower a boat.

"Tiny, ship the sweeps, lively now!" *Berbice* carried eight long oars for maneuvering in calms and anchorages. Tiny plucked them from their racks along the bulwarks and slid them out the scuppers. He put one seaman and several of the Africans on each. "Pull together now, lads! That's it, lean into them; aye, that's it!"

They stood as they rowed, pushing the looms of the long oars forward, then stepping back a couple paces and dipping them again. *Berbice's* momentum was overcome and she began to move forward. Then the squall line hit. The tremendous drag of the rigging and sails as the wind began to howl arrested their progress and then began to push them back toward the reef once more.

"Pull, damn ye! Pull for your lives!" Tiny and Nathaniel threw themselves onto the sweeps, leaving Barbecue alone at the helm. Nathaniel saw they could not overpower the drag of the flogging sails. "Tiny, drop the sails!"

* * *

"They must be in trouble! They've dropped their sails!" exclaimed Anne.

"Aye, it's the turn to windward through the cut that's got them. Ship the spritsail, Jonathan! Sheet in the sail, lass! There's not a moment to lose!" They bailed the remaining water out as the whaleboat took off in the quartering wind like a racehorse. "Mind your sheet, lass; we'll do them no good if we capsize!" The first gusts of the squall line hit the lightweight and over-canvassed whaleboat like a huge fist, pushing her violently over until green water gushed over the lee rail.

"Mind the sheet, Lass, easy now, that's it. Matumbwe, help her sweat it in again; aye, that's it." Captain William urged them on, standing in the stern of the whaleboat, a steering oar under his arm, his white hair flying, framed by the blue-black squall line at his back. "*Ah ha ha, ah ha ha!*" Glee returned to the old salt's face as the whaleboat began to surf down the choppy whitecaps. The whaleboat kicked up a rooster tail as it raced through the darkening water, leaving a line of white froth in her wake.

Anne noticed a swarm of cat's-paws advancing atop the whitecaps. She eased the lugsail sheet in anticipation. As the gust hit, they counterbalanced, sitting up on the weather rail of the narrow boat. The whaleboat accelerated, and then the stern began to rise as a sea came under them. Spray flew from the bows of the whaleboat, and Anne could feel the exhilaration of speed. As the sea reached the middle of the whaleboat, the boat leveled out and the bow rose clear of the water, the spray now flying from amidships. The steering oar vibrated and hummed as they shot through the water, borne by the wave. The wave curled on both sides of the boat and crashed down, roaring along, the whaleboat prancing atop the churning whitewater, a third of her length still flying above the deep blue water in front of the boiling foam.

"Ah ha ha, ah ha ha!" Captain William headed the whaleboat to windward just a bit as every new wave approached; getting a little more speed from the lugsail, then squared the boat with the wave with all his weight on the steering oar for the wild downhill surf ride. *"Ah ha ha, ah ha ha!"*

* * *

The wind was now howling through *Berbice's* rigging, and the men at the sweeps knew they were losing ground, inching toward the reef and destruction. They watched the wild approach of the whaleboat. Even with the whaleboat there would not be enough room for all aboard to escape the wreck of the *Berbice*. A blinding rainsquall now descended, but with it the wind abated. The whaleboat rode a wave crest up to

Berbice's stern, and in one lightning motion rounded up in the lee of the ship, luffing the lugsail.

"Heave us a line, lively now!" Captain William's bellow was barely audible above the roar of the downpour. He made the line from *Berbice* fast to the samson post in the stern of the whaleboat. Captain Easton stowed the lugsail mast, and Matumbwe, Anne, and Malika shipped their oars. "Together now, me hearties, let's show these lubbers how to row!" The whaleboat shot in front of the *Berbice* with the first stroke of her oars. Captain Easton shipped his own oar and put his back into the next stroke. The towline sprang from the water and spray wrung out of the tightening fibers. The whaleboat snapped to a stop and then drifted back towards the ship.

"She's struck!" *Berbice's* rudderpost struck a rock, sending a jolt throughout the ship and shivers up Nathaniel's spine. He had never lost a ship; he determined to fight for this one to the last. They pushed the sweeps with renewed energy, digging against the wet deck with their bare feet for traction.

In the whaleboat, they saw the ship jolt and heard the cry. Captain William urged them on, shouting over the rainsquall, squinting into the stinging droplets as they hit his face and streamed through his beard. "Again, me hearties, put your backs into it. The Devil himself awaits ye on yonder reef! We'll get her off, ye lubbers, if ye can just pull your oars a bit!" Again the whaleboat sprang forward like a sled dog leaping against its leash. "That's it, pull together now!" They toiled for what seemed hours. Matumbwe was tireless, his massive muscles flexing and bending the oar looms like willows every time he took a stroke. The wind died and the rain eased up, only falling now and then in gentle showers. The towline no longer bounced them back like a toy after every stroke on the oars.

Suddenly the men on *Berbice* left the sweeps. "She's hoisting sail!" Captain Easton declared. Nathaniel and Tiny were at the fife rails, orchestrating the simultaneous raising of jib, mainsail, and mizzen.

"Belay, mates," cried Captain William, the grin once more erupting in his white beard. He stooped to untie the towline from the whaleboat's samson post, and then tossed it back onto *Berbice's* foredeck. *Berbice* backed her jib and trimmed hard on the gentle breeze, paying off on the starboard tack.

"Huzzah! Huzzah! Huzzah!"

Nathaniel was disinclined to heave-to after such an ordeal; the forward motion of *Berbice* was such a relief. When the whaleboat danced up alongside, they hauled her up to the mainmast shroud channels and disembarked while under way. It was the first time Nathaniel saw the ironbound oak chests that had been sought after by Deadlight and his associates. They dropped the mainmast backstay tackle down into the whaleboat and tied a cargo net under the oak chest.

"Mind your tackle now; smartly, haul it over, ye lubbers!" Captain William said as they hauled the heavy chests from the whaleboat onto *Berbice's* deck. They dragged the chests into the greatcabin, where Captain Easton and Captain William retired for rum, pipes, and yarns.

* * *

The whaleboat returned from ferrying the last load of escaped slaves to the beach. Dawn would break in an hour. It was time to weigh anchor and be gone, before another encounter with *Inflexible,* for it was certain they would give chase. If they did not sight *Berbice* on her way to Cuba or Hispaniola, it was only a matter of time before they came back to look along Jamaica's northern shore.

"Will you be able to find your way to the Windward maroons?" asked Anne.

"I know the paths," said Malika. "Remember the Obeah; it surrounds you everywhere, if you know how to use it."

"Thank you for the muskets, sah." Matumbwe's perfect teeth shone in the moonlight as he bowed to Captain William.

"You won them in battle, from the villain who ruined my hat! You could not have stronger claim on them, sir." Captain William made a leg, his left toe sticking into the powdery sand of the beach.

"Thank you, Captain Nathaniel, for the safe transport; we all thank you," said Matumbwe.

"Thank you, Matumbwe, for delivering Anne from evil, and you and your fellows, who helped us win our own freedom. We could not possibly have done it alone. Only yesterday we would have been shipwrecked, but for your labors."

Anne and Malika embraced. Malika, Matumbwe, and the other escapees strode confidently up the beach to the forest path. Captain William, Nathaniel, and Anne met Barbecue at the whaleboat, and they shoved it off the beach. They sat for awhile, motionless in the water, watching the new maroons disappear into the forest.

Captain William said, "Five hundred of them, half-starved and naked, fought five thousand of the best-trained and armed soldiers of the British Empire to a standoff back in thirty-nine. Their Queen Granny Nanny was a great warrior, knew how to fight in the forest and fight when outnumbered. Now they've got their own land by formal treaty with the government. Seems almost like magic they could have prevailed against the empire."

"I think it *was* magic, Captain William—the Obeah," said Anne. The full moon made a silver pathway to the east across the bay. The gentle breeze brought down the scents of blossoms and moist soil from the steep hillside.

He turned from gazing at the water and winked at Anne. "I reckon so."

They stroked easily back to the *Berbice*, the svelte whaleboat gliding with ease through the calm water. Anne watched the moonbeam follow them across the water until it silhouetted a lone palm tree on the end of a sand spit. She closed her eyes, squeezing a sudden tear from each, and looked away, the image alive in her mind. She wanted that vision to be her last memory of Jamaica.

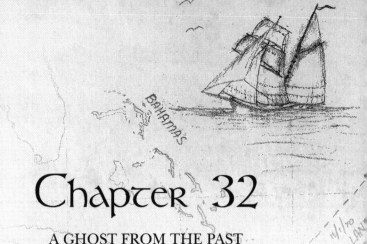

Chapter 32

A GHOST FROM THE PAST

Harborton, New Year's Eve

They feasted on roasted goose with oyster stuffing, country ham and succotash, sweet potato, and apple pie. "May I propose a toast," said Nathaniel, holding his glass aloft, "to a bold and beautiful woman, dearest Anne, my deliverer from highwaymen."

"Here, here!" Captains William and Easton raised their mugs of hot buttered rum.

At this juncture, it would have been appropriate for Anne to flourish the colonial lady's ever-present fan as a semaphore flag of emotion, but she had no use for the foppery of either sex. She emptied her mug instead.

"Another toast," she said, "to the master mariners who made the rescue of my dear father possible."

"Here, here!" Nathaniel winked at Captain William, who responded with his customary, *"Ah ha ha, ah ha ha!"*

Ordineaux stood with his mug raised high. "To the good ship *Berbice* and her captain, for not capsizing when they sailed her out of Kingston with her bilges awash!"

"Here, here!"

"A nearly run thing."

"Could have lost her."

A bit unsteady since on solid ground, Captain William stood and raised his mug of rum. "I have several toasts, so ye best uncork another bottle, Jonathan!"

"Aye, aye!" The merry group drank to that. The rum warmed their innards, and the roaring fire took the chill off their bodies, at least on the side that was facing the fireplace. The parlor of Captain Easton's house in Harborton was warm and snug; outside, a light snow fell, dampening the clatter of wagon wheels and hooves and the jingling of the nosegays on passing draft horses.

"First off," continued Captain William, "to my most profane parrot and loyal messenger. May no one ever read him a catechism aloud."

"Aye, aye! *Hor hor*!"

Angustine snored away under the blanket covering the frame of his perch.

"Second, to a damn nice profit in barrel staves and breadstuffs in Puerto Rico, courtesy of Nathaniel's friend, the sugar mill owner."

"Aye! More rum!"

"Third, ye inebriates all, to an equally fine profit in sugar, molasses, and Spanish wine, courtesy of our old friend, Israel Fowlkes."

"Aye, aye!" They drank more of the hot aromatic brew, seasoned with nutmeg, also from their stop in Puerto Rico.

"And finally," Captain William cast his sharp eye on Nathaniel, and then at Anne, "to the young folks on the lee side of this here table. What a fine-looking married couple they'd make."

"Aye, aye."

Anne felt her face flush; completely mortified, she did not drink to this toast.

Nathaniel rose to the rescue. "I would not say this if we were not all family here, but Captain Easton is Anne's father, and I feel that Captain William is like a grandfather to us all—"

"Split me and sink me, Laddie, I ain't that old!"

"What I mean to say is, I have a personal request to make of Captain Easton."

"Aye, lad; name it, and it's yours," Captain Easton spread his hands in a gesture of good will.

"What I mean to say is, Captain Easton," he paused, "may I marry your daughter?"

Anne suddenly wanted to crawl under the table.

"What, lad, me own daughter? Well now, lad, ye've been around her long enough to know, she ain't mine to give."

"Charts her own course, she does," piped in Captain William.

It was Nathaniel's turn to color the shade of an autumn sunset and wish he could slither out of sight.

"But the answer is yes, son, as long as she's agreeable."

"And if she ain't, ye best lay your course clear of her shoals, 'cause she's a dead-eye with a pistol, *ah ha ha, ah ha ha*!"

Inside his wool blanket tent, Angustine awoke to his master's raucous laugh, then added, "Give me grog or you'll be flogged, give me grog or you'll be flogged!" He punctuated this with a screech.

"Aye, Jonathan, parcel out some more rum from the warming tin. There ye be; here's to the new couple!" Captain Easton raised his mug.

Anne had had more than she could bear. "Silence fore and aft! Would nobody be wanting to know my own mind on this affair?"

"Well—but I—ah, well, I—" Nathaniel had been hulled—aye, struck between the wind and the water— with that broadside.

"I will give my answer when I have had as much time to deliberate on it as you apparently have already. And I will give it in my own way."

"And when will that be, lassie?"

"In my own time."

"And what be your own way, my dear?"

"Nathaniel will know from my words." She winked at Captain William.

"A strange riddle."

"You, of all persons, Captain William, should not chide me for the use of odd words and riddles."

* * *

Nathaniel began to founder. Over the next two months he dared not broach the subject, yet he longed for his answer. In the winter months he sailed cargo between the ports of Baltimore and Norfolk and the plantations that lined the navigable waters of the Chesapeake. The trade was profitable, for the shipping rates between rivers in the Chesapeake were nearly equivalent to the fees for transatlantic shipments. Nathaniel sought out Anne's company in Harborton when ashore, foregoing his former romps in the Fiddler's Green of Baltimore. They kept company almost constantly in the brief periods Nathaniel stayed in Harborton, and he endeavored in various ways to sound her heart, but on the subject of her consent to marriage she remained evasive.

"You will know, Nathaniel, my dear, without a shadow of a doubt in your mind, when you hear the words," she'd say, with a coquettish giggle. This behavior may be what settled Nathaniel's inner struggle with Fiddler's Green versus home and hearth, for he was a man to pursue goals, and now a warm home with Anne became his fondest. In his freezing greatcabin, while the winter stars carpeted the clear cold sky, he would doze off with imaginings of Anne's warm hearth.

* * *

"Papa, Nathaniel and I would like to bundle, if you would permit?" Nathaniel was shocked, and for the first time in his life he turned red.

Trying desperately to suppress a laugh, Captain Easton poured a glass of rum, in hopes of hiding his mirth. *The rake has probably seen the inside of every whorehouse from Egpyt to Belize and back to Baltimore, and he wishes to lie abed with my daughter with a wooden plank between them to ensure chastity! For the love of Christ, but this is droll!*

"Humm, well of course my dear," the last of this speech rose in timbre as he stifled down a guffaw. "I'll send Ellie to stoke the fire." Nathaniel wasn't sure, but he thought he heard belly laughs from the stables a few minutes after Captain Easton hurried from the room.

Later, as Ellie's fire roared in the bedroom, Nathaniel doffed his waistcoat. "Must I take off my boots as well?"

"Of course, you barbarian!" Anne smashed a feather pillow over his head, and dove beneath the coverlet. He soon discovered a wooden plank had indeed been installed in the middle of the bed. *She has planned this humiliation!*

Poor Nathaniel had not yet abandoned his propensity to underestimate womankind, and so he sailed on to leeward and was soon embayed with all canvas flying aloft.

"What do you think of Mr. Paine's article on the Rights of Man?" Anne began.

"A commendable work, which I whole*heart*edly support," said Nathaniel, hoping the pun would be appreciated. *I am invited to bed for a political discussion?*

"I mean rather, to be more specific, what do you think of the rights of woman?"

"Ah, yes, well, to be sure, all equal under the natural laws of course." Nathaniel sensed the room growing uncomfortably warm.

"Would a husband and wife be equals in marriage then?"

"Equal in all things, of course my dear." Sweat now broke on Nathaniel's brow. He realized it was too late to wear ship and run downwind. Here he was, immobilized beneath the covers, with no honorable way out. She had him in irons!

"Such as what? I need to know."

"Is it really that important to you, right now, dear?" He felt sweat running down past his ear and soaking into his neck cloth.

"Yes it is."

"Well then, what specifically do you need to know?" A heaven-sent draft momentarily cooled his exposed cheek.

"What about affairs of the estate, and of business?"

"If man and woman are to have their fortunes entwined, I cannot see the justice in leaving the risk and turmoil entirely to one or the other," He thought he had done tolerably well with that one.

"What about child-rearing?" A stunned silence was his answer. Anne shifted to look at him over the slab of knotty pine between them, and pressed the issue, "I need to know your thoughts on this."

She does presume! He was certain the room had again become hot enough to roast a joint of venison. *Child-rearing indeed! And have I ever in my life had thoughts on that?* "I would imagine the same would hold, if a couple's fortunes are knotted together, they should share the lash for correction of wayward children."

Anne studied the shadows on the uneven plaster of the ceiling. Not to be back winded for long, she resumed, "You make light of this."

"But my dear, you do not afford me the solace of knowing that I have won your hand. Am I to presume by these questions that the matter sealed?"

It was now her turn for stunned silence, as her face became a shade of crimson. She wished Ellie had not stoked the fire so overmuch. Enjoying his respite from the docket, Nathaniel loosened his neck cloth and studied the trowel swirls in the plaster above the bed.

"Nathaniel, what sets you in a mood for pleasure?" Anne broke the silence.

He was startled by the question, but impulsively answered with a private joke, "the Reed Dance."

She sucked in her breath and rolled over to look Nathaniel in the face, "You've seen it?" "Pardon me milady, I did not mean to bring up anything unseemly. I didn't think you knew what it was...er...what do you think it is?"

"It's a dance of virgins in a ceremony for an African king," stated Anne.

Bloody hell, I've blundered now.

"And they are all naked to the waist..."

He began to blubber out an apology as she marched on.

"...and their breasts bounce with the rhythm of the drums."

"Really, I didn't mean to embarrass you..."

"...the rhythm of the hollow log drums is most enchanting." At that she threw back the covers and began to drum her hands on the pine plank that was meant to ensure the couple's chastity. Nathaniel joined in with the counterpoint rhythm, and the Easton household of Harborton, Virginia began to vibrate with a hypnotic primal pulsation. Grinning from ear to ear, Anne got to her knees, facing him and pounding out the rhythm on the plank,. Nathaniel sprung to his knees as well, the two now slapping the erotic drumbeat on the plank.

"Where did you ever hear about the Reed Dance?"

"You are overwhelmed by presumption, Sir, how do you know I haven't seen it?"

Anne slid off the bed and began to undulate, hands holding her hair above her head. Nathaniel saw the curves of her writhing body backlit by the amber light of the fireplace. Then she turned to face Nathaniel, breasts moving beneath her gown. Around and around she turned, her motions becoming more and more sinuous.

He slipped off the bed and came up behind her, encircling her chest as she swayed to the now imaginary drumbeat. When she turned, he raised her chin with the tip of his forefinger and kissed her. Keeping time to the drumbeat in their minds now, they pressed against each other, in an unheard rhythm of passion. Their breath came heavily, catching as some chance touch sent shivers of delight to feed a growing fire within.

* * *

The next morning, Captain Easton thought to check in on the bundlers; but found Ellie had preceded him. There she stood with her ear pressed against Anne's bedroom door.

"Ahem,"

"Oh, sir, I was just…I mean…tea you know."

"Tea indeed, give them a knock and see if our African musician desires some refreshment." But before she could, they heard a knock on the front door of the house. Ellie jumped to descend the stairs, Captain Easton following.

413

"Who would be about this morning?"

"Pray, open the door and see, Ellie."

Blinking in the morning light stood a young woman in ragged dress, tracks of tears clearing the grime from her face below her bloodshot eyes. One of her hands rested on her swollen belly. She looked to be eight months gone.

"What is it you want?" asked Ellie.

"They says to me at Fowlkes Tavern I could find Nathaniel Harte hereabouts."

Captain Easton stepped forward, "Who are you, and what is your business with Nathaniel Harte?" A cold apprehension that it had something to do with her distended belly blew through his mind. When the young woman sobbed, her affected histrionics made Captain Easton suspicious.

"Me name is Maggie, long been a familiar with Master Harte, which is the reason I been searching him out, 'cause of my condition, ye see."

"Aye, your condition is quite visible. Ellie, pray go and fetch Nathaniel, if you please."

Tying his neckcloth, Nathaniel stopped in the doorway.

"Oh Master Harte, God bless ye, I knew you would do right by your dear Maggie. At me wit's end and in desperate straits I is. Oh Master Harte, 'tis good to see ye and present your very own." At this she patted her belly and looked wide-eye at the younger man.

"As I recall Maggie, I was disallowed by your mother from seeing you. I daresay that child in your belly could not possibly be my issue. Now please be gone."

"Oh Master Harte, do not be harsh with me. I knew naught of my mother's prevention of your warmth and comforts, as I've been accustomed to these many years…"

"Maggie, I beg you leave this instant."

"Oh Master Harte ye use me cruel, what with me carrying yer offspring. I is in desperate straights, what with this little one on its way." Again she patted her belly and rolled her wide eyes up to him.

Overhearing this exchange, Anne could no longer keep silent, "Nathaniel, I beg you both leave this house and carry on elsewhere."

He felt her words like a hammer blow, "Anne, surely you do not *believe* her?"

"I know not what to believe, Nathaniel, this is very upsetting."

Taking Maggie by the arm, he led her down the front steps and looked back at Anne, "I shall return my love."

"I think not Nathaniel, not for some time."

This speech struck him like a knife in the chest. His grip tightened on Maggie's arm and his pace quickened.

* * *

At length they arrived at Fowlkes Tavern, where Nathaniel ordered strong drink, then waved Israel Fowlkes away. This was not a conversation he wanted overheard.

"I should box your ears, you slut. What do you mean by this outrage?"

"Oh Nathaniel, don't use me so. You see my desperate condition. Do you not accept your obligation to me?"

"I accept that you have no idea who the father is. You were entertaining a duo on my last visit to Baltimore. When, by the way, your dear mother declared we'd see each other only when the Devil greets us in hell."

"Oh Nathaniel, me dear mother is dead, just this month. More's the pity."

"Why are you here, Maggie?"

"I be in desperate straights, Nathaniel. If ye do not see fit to make an honest woman of me, pray thee, be generous so the little one won't starve." She began to sob again.

"I thought as much. Would a sack of gold and silver coin send ye on your way back to Baltimore?"

"Oh Nathaniel, I knew ye was a generous soul at heart, and all that cruel bluster about ye only the bark of a frightened dog." She had suddenly stopped sobbing.

"Mind your tongue, woman." Nathaniel took his purse from his waistcoat and tossed it on the table.

She grinned when she heard the chink of money. "Ah, dear Nathaniel, I knew you'd show me some pity at least. 'Twas a dream to think ye would take yer bastard as yer own."

"I've not lain with you for over a year, and you know it, you little harlot. Be gone from here, back to your hovel, or I'll toss you off the wharf."

Maggie's cunning told her she had gotten the limit from this exchange, so she emptied her drink in one practiced gulp and swiftly stood to leave, only remembering to slow her pace and look burdened by her belly as she reached the door.

Seeing Nathaniel brooding at his table, Israel Fowlkes took the seat vacated by Maggie. "What confounds ye Nathaniel? Who was the comely lass?"

"Evil past of the sailorman come to haunt me, Israel. Confound indeed, she had the ill manners to seek me out at Captain Easton's house, displaying her belly and proclaiming me the father of the bastard."

"Never to worry, Nathaniel. Ye have begotten no bastard by that one."

"Aye, and I wish dear Anne was so sure. She's sent me packing because of the taint of that little wench."

"Nathaniel, I cannot speak for the jealousy that may devour Anne's love for thee. But I can tell ye this, my dear friend: that belly the trollop from Baltimore wears is goose down to the heart of it."

"What say ye, Israel?"

"Ah, Nathaniel, those of pure heart can never imagine the duplicity of others. Unless you're a Canada goose, ye have no bastards to worry your conscience."

"What? The little bitch made off with my purse for her trouble!"

"And off at a gallop I would wager, sitting astride like a man, in spite of her advanced condition," Israel chuckled.

Nathaniel felt his anger and humiliation rise as he bolted to the door. There in the mud lay a goose down pillow. *Devil take me if that ain't the same size of her bothersome belly!* He could hear hoof beats in the distance, at a gallop indeed. "Damn and blast I've been played the fool, Israel." The innkeeper had himself a belly laugh while Nathaniel finished his drink.

* * *

417

Later, with backing from Isreal, Nathaniel explained Maggie's ruse to Captain Easton. The good Captain forgave him, but Anne's feelings were not as tolerant.

"To think I've as much as shared the same bed with that whore!"

"It's been more than a year since I've even tried to see her Anne, I harbor no tenderness for her. I hope you will allow me to continue our courtship, for you are my heart's desire. I am besotted."

She sighed, "I don't know my own mind anymore Nathaniel, I was so shocked to see that woman – didn't consider that you might have had such a past."

"Aye, well I'll be the first to admit I've made some mistakes, the trollop in question being one; but Anne, that has not come between us in my own heart."

"I'm afraid we can no longer bundle until we – if we marry, for the waging tongues have already made much of that scene with the pregnant woman.

"It was a pillow, she robbed me."

"I know, but I fear we may be indiscrete again," she blushed, "Nathaniel, you carry me beyond my common senses." She looked away. "If we are to meet, it shall be in public, Fowlkes Tavern. We cannot use my father's house as a cover from prying eyes again."

And so, as the winter dragged on, Anne learned all about Nathaniel's formative days on the Rappahannock, from across a table in Fowlkes Tavern. Among their candlelit discussions were Nathaniel's tales of sailing races with the young plantation gentlemen, in his little shallop named *Jack's Favorite*.

* * *

The drilling rains and fog of March came, with many a wind off the ocean so strong that it rattled the windows in the Easton house. Finally, April's daffodils poked up through the mold of the previous autumn's leaves, and spring peepers called out for mates in the ditches and marshy spots surrounding Harborton, shrill heralds of the rebirth of spring. And Anne was ready with her answer.

"We're giving a play tomorrow night, here at the tavern. You must come," said Anne one day at Fowlkes Tavern. The entire British army couldn't have kept Nathaniel away.

"Indeed, milady, I'd be honored to attend," said Nathaniel.

It was the evening of the play when he approached the group seated on the porch of Fowlkes Tavern. Captain William sat on a bench, smoking a long-stemmed church warden pipe of Virginia tobacco.

"Have a puff of sot weed Nathaniel."

"Aye, thank ye Capt'n." Nathaniel broke off the last two inches of the pipe stem and took a draw, tossing the broken stem piece off the porch, where it settled into its place with over a hundred year's worth of two-inch sections of pipe stem that paved the entrance to Fowlkes Tavern. Nathaniel crossed the threshold and saw the tavern had been transformed into a rustic theater, with benches and chairs arranged in rows. A curtain and plank stage had been erected in one end of the room. A group of male pipe smokers lingered at the doorway, as the seats filled with a mixed group of husbands and wives, suitors and sweethearts. Israel Fowlkes caught Nathaniel's eye from one of the front rows and energetically waved him over. The anticipation was palpable. In this vast, undeveloped country of forest, farm, and waterway, it was one of the few entertainments available, and a well-attended event. No one seemed more expectant than Israel.

"I trust your courtship is going well," began Israel, prying.

"Better than ever could be expected," lied Nathaniel.

A hush fell over the well-behaved audience, and the play began. To Captain Harte's delight, the leading actress was none other than Anne Easton. As the drama unfolded, the audience's involvement became total. These were not your jaded sophisticates, but a highly receptive group of men and women willing to sit on wooden benches and chairs for two hours for the experience of being transported out of their immediate world. They suffered with the protagonist, they murmured darkly at the villain, they triumphed and cried, moaned and laughed with the actors as one. Israel Fowlkes was beside himself with delight. The provincials drank in their drama like a thirsty man did cool ale, and Israel loved sitting amongst this sea of emotion as much as he enjoyed the drama itself—and of course the ale.

It was a story of a merchant ship on a voyage to far-off places, with some dangerous episodes and narrow escapes. It couldn't have been played to a more rapt group. Anne Easton, leader of the troupe, sometimes author and director, was recognizable in the first scene and then was lost in a parade of exotica from the corners of the world. There was a slim young man, a slave trader in Jamaica—was that character played by her? A fat Egyptian merchant in Alexandria, a lusty bearded Greek fisherman, an imperious Indian Raja, bedecked with jewels. *Could they all be played by her?* thought Nathaniel. Only the vague trace of her physical form was there, he pondered. *No one could be that good at disguise. I am seeing her everywhere as an illusion from my infatuation and longing.*

At the joyous finale the actors, all dressed as sailors again, joined in an exuberant hornpipe, the traditional dance of the foc'sle. It was all Nathaniel could do to keep himself seated, and he pounded the floor with his foot in time. The audience clapped, the actors leaped and danced - and then all hell broke loose.

Through the door charged a Quaker in a black broad-brimmed hat. He waved a cane over his head as he assaulted the stage, his pasty white face contorted in rage, shouting over the music and gaiety, "Trollops, lewdness, harlots, whores! Women dancing in men's clothing—abomination!" Then he wheeled around at the shocked audience and shrieked at them, "You'll all be damned!" He resumed his assault on the stage, with the apparent intent of beating the actors with his cane.

Solid proprietor Fowlkes, more used to shocking human behavior than most, and used to having to deal directly with it in his own establishment, was the first to lay hands on the black-clad Quaker. Fowlkes easily hoisted him off the floor by his collar and belt and propelled him towards the door, the Quaker's cane flailing and feet kicking. With a mighty toss by Fowlkes off the front porch, the Quaker flew through the night and landed in the mud, still sputtering. Fowlkes filled the frame of the doorway with his form against another attack.

"You've not seen the last of me, profligates and sirens!" shouted the muddy Quaker at Fowlkes' massive back.

Inside the tavern, the actors had frozen in mid-step, and the musicians were silent. An irritated mumble began in the audience as everyone recovered from the shock. It was Israel Fowlkes who shouted, "*Encore—encore, si vous plais—encore!*" The call was taken up by Nathaniel and the rest of the audience in general, who began to forget their rage at the Quaker. "*Encore–encore!*" They clapped their hands in rhythm, and the musicians joined in at the very same pace.

The hornpipe began once more, and the actors set to, weakly, but this time the audience would not keep their seats. The tune of the fiddle and bagpipes and the beat of the Celtic drum were too much to resist. Everyone rose up, the chairs and benches were removed to the walls, and the aged chestnut floor planks of Fowlkes Tavern pounded to a hundred variations of the hornpipe. Such a response from the audience inflamed the actors and musicians, who redoubled their efforts and replayed the tunes again and again. Ordineaux stood on his hands on a bench and danced with his feet in the air, much to the delight of a local maiden he'd been courting since his arrival in *Jubilant* from the Antilles.

Nathaniel joined in with a most professional sailor's version of the hornpipe, with fancy leg and foot movements developed after long practice on a sloping deck. Israel Fowlkes, grinning and laughing in ecstasy, kicked up his legs and bounced his ample frame with surprising lightness, his feet reaching waist level as he turned arm and arm with the barmaid. Nathaniel was surprised to find Anne by his side, mirroring his movements with an equally professional accuracy. Her exhilaration glowed through the moisture on her cheeks and brow. She held Nathaniel's eyes with her own and the room melted away from them, until they were alone together in their jubilation.

"Have you been to all those places?" asked Nathaniel, leaning close to Anne.

"Some of them," she said, and then she grabbed his neck and pulled him down so she could say into his ear, "but not with you!"

The spontaneous dance became a tribal right, an affirmation, celebrating the freedom to express joy, fueled by rejection of the petty righteousness of the Quaker. No one could prohibit *their* hornpipe! The muddy Quaker began to creep away, and then suddenly began to run, for he feared that he'd witnessed nothing less than the victory dance of the Devil.

Chapter 33

LAUNCHING DAY

Work had ended when the first snows came, and the ship's oaken bones seasoned over winter, turning silver-gray. In the early spring the planking was fitted, each plank sawn separately to fit exactly the compound curves of the hull. As the planks went on, the frames were beveled with an adz so the plank would lie flat against them. The riggers and sail makers were busy with spars, rigging, and flax sailcloth. The smell of tar and pitch and the charcoal fire of the smithy's forge now mixed with the aromas of fresh-sawn cedar and fresh-hewn oak.

When the planking and deck were completed, Mathias hired several gangs of caulkers to drive oakum into every seam of planking and deck. The planks of the deck and hull, being wood, would swell when soaked in the sea, so they were fitted with a small crack between to allow them to expand. Into these cracks the caulkers drove strands of oakum, which would form a watertight joint, yet compress when the planking expanded. In this way the living, working form of the ship was made watertight, though flexible. In addition to caulking, the deck seams were payed with hot pine pitch to seal them against leakage.

The caulkers sang shanties special to their work, and their mallets and irons rang out in rhythm. As the structure of the ship tightened with caulk, the music of the blows of the mallets went up in tone. Soon the ship, made of thousands of individually crafted parts, was joined into such a harmonious whole that Mathias often felt the rap of a maul on one end in his fingertips at the other end of the vessel. She was now "tight as a drum" and sounded like one, as the mallets and hammers worked on her.

Mathias never tired of sighting along the curves of the hull, this thing that had once been only his concept on parchment. The compound curves flowed around the ship in smooth contours estimated to cause the least resistance as she sailed. She was much more than a functional wooden machine. She was the state of the art of hundreds of year's worth of development of sailing-ship design, yet she had beauty, a grace of form and function that sang as a whole. She sang to Mathias, from the sharpness of her bows to the flat exit of her buttocks at the waterline aft, and the tumblehome of the greatcabin to her hollow garboards.

The thousands of details of finishing the ship now demanded Mathias's full time. There was the parceling of rigging with tar and hemp, and crafting of ironwood deadeyes, hatches, water barrels, gun carriages, spars, and yardarms. Finally the paint crews began to color the virgin wooden ship, and the yard smelled of turpentine. To Mathias, turpentine smelled like finality and a job well done.

But how to launch this ship standing on the hard ground and weighing one hundred tons? The scaffolding, made of poles lashed together, came down, leaving only a ladder for the finish carpenters to climb into the hull. The timbers that held her upright were reinforced and tied together to make a stout cradle. There was much drag to her keel, deeper at the stern than at the bow. So she sat on the ground with her bow lower than the stern and quarterdeck, like a huge beast with cocked rear haunches, ready to leap from the ground. Below her keel were timber sleepers, extending down to the water. With oxen, capstan, tallow grease, levers, stout hemp rope, and days of much profanity, the ship was slid to the water's edge.

Finally the day came when they levered up one side in order to slide the ship sideways into the water. Mathias, usually a calm and steady individual, was beside himself. So much could go wrong at the last minute! But mostly it was the excitement and expectation of bringing another Virginia flyer into the world, to dance on the clear blue sea, to carry men safely to far-away continents, and then home again.

Only Anne and her father knew the ship was bequeathed to her, soon to be a floating dowry of oak and cedar, iron and canvas. Nathaniel Harte had no idea of any dowry, had never discussed one with Captain Easton, who never broached the matter himself. Nathaniel considered that perhaps he had not attained a social class where he could expect any such thing. It would be privilege enough to marry into the ship-owning Easton family. Yet alas, Anne had not made her mind known to him, and he dispared, reconciling himself to bachelorhood.

Anne was to preside at the christening, using a bottle of French champagne donated by Captain William for the momentous event. Nathaniel was at Anne's side on the rough-hewn platform at the bow of the ship, Captains William and Easton sharing the platform with them. Nathaniel was moody, the joy of the immenant spectacle of the launching conflicting with his depression over the loss of Anne's hand; for certainly she would have given him her ascent by now. Moodiness spiraled into depression, a state of mind Nathaniel seldom indulged in-until now. Anne had again evaded his entreaties for her answer to his hand in marriage.

Captain William made a speech about how proud he was of Captain Easton, whom he persisted in calling "Jonathan," and sometimes, "young Jonathan," to Captain Easton's mortification. Captain Easton made a speech on how proud he was of young Nathaniel, as promising a young seaman as ever was.

Anne thanked everyone for joining the joyous ceremony. She picked up the bottle of French champagne, wrapped in fish netting fitted by the sail maker. The fresh paint of the cutwater let off a subtle aroma. Her heart was in her throat, for she wished fervently for a good outcome, and that she would not be misunderstood. The shipwrights stood with their mauls raised, ready to break out the stops and wedges, and let the new ship slide down the ways to swim for the first time.

Anne summoned her sea voice and spoke at the bow of the ship, "I christen thee, *Jack's Favorite*!"

As the hundred-ton ship slid down the ways, smoke coming from the groaning skids, Nathaniel took her in his arms and kissed her. Now, finally he had his answer; she was his. The crowd nodded in approval, and then Tiny led the cheer, "Huzzah! huzzah! huzzah!"

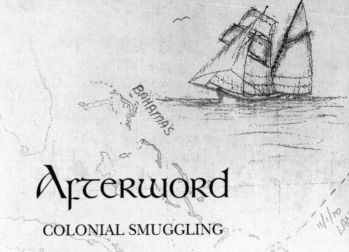

Afterword

COLONIAL SMUGGLING

There are practically no records of the smuggling business carried on by colonial merchants. However, the naïve report of a royal customs inspector of 1770 provides some insight. Upon inspection, he found all papers in order at the customs house in Urbana, on the Rappahannock River in Virginia, but he was irritated that French wines could be had in any shop along the river. The customs-house records had no evidence of duties paid for entry of French wine; in fact, the majority of vessels had registered as arriving "in ballast"—that is, carrying nothing but rocks. He reported to his superiors in London that he suspected a booming smuggling trade was bypassing taxes due the royal treasury.

What the well-meaning customs inspector missed was not to be found in customs-house records. His myopic discovery of the pervasive availability of French wine is humorous in retrospect. He was literally surrounded by the most damning evidence of the prosperous colonial smuggling trade, yet he did not see it. We should forgive him, for after all, he was no doubt an egregious landlubber. His evidence of the colonial lust for carrying out commerce without a fare-thee-well to the customs house lay not in French wines or customs-house records. Perhaps this lubber never saw the most obvious evidence of smuggling because of the pervasive nature of the evidence itself. Many among the hundreds of colonial sailing ships he admired each day were built for one purpose, and that was to evade and out sail the larger vessels of the Royal Navy. This is why the thrifty colonial merchant purchased speed in his vessel, at the expense of cargo-carrying ability. This fact was not lost on his counterparts in the Royal Navy, who had many opportunities to witness the sailing qualities of "Virginia flyers."

The later half of the eighteenth century was one of the most exciting periods in history. The superstitions of the medieval period were falling away before a burgeoning reliance on science and scientific methods of reasoning. With science and an understanding of natural laws, the enlightened individual saw how everything could be improved. The positive attitude that life could be improved with one's own reason, and an understanding of natural laws, was the driving force of young America as an emerging nation. Social systems and governments could be improved. One's lot in life could be improved. Reasoning led to the belief in the rights of man and equality before the law. Humanitarianism was born. Proposals to abolish slavery were discussed nearly a century before the bloody Civil War, and indeed were heard in the Continental Congress.

The Navigation Acts were crafted to suppress the economy of the colonies for the benefit of the mother country. This ran contrary to the positive attitude of the colonials of the Enlightenment, and their belief in the ability, nay, the inalienable right to improve one's life. An indispensable part of the economic growth of the new land was the smuggling trade, in defiance of the Navigation Acts. Demonstrating innate genius that would typify Americans in the years to come, working with primitive tools, the shipbuilders of the virgin forests at water's edge developed sailing vessels that could outperform the larger and more powerful warships of the British Navy. Intrepid colonial mariners used these vessels to run the blockade of warships sent to enforce the Navigation Acts, and commerce that allowed America to become established as a nation flourished.

American shipbuilders were building fast sailing ships early in the 1700's. Light hulls, relatively thin planking, fine lines, and low freeboard with maximum ballast allowed these ships to carry tremendous sail area. Smugglers were typically small and inexpensively built, with little ornamentation, to minimize the capital risk to the owners if caught. The sailing ship type known nowadays as the Baltimore Clipper was born of these necessities on the shores of the Chesapeake Bay. In the early years, these rakish craft were built in the forests that surrounded the bay with prime timber. On the eastern shore of Virginia, in the year 1770, there were one hundred and fifty ocean-going vessels registered. One could scarcely find an equivalent number of individuals to trim a jib sheet there today.

The colonials developed several tactics for evading their more powerful pursuers, illustrated by Captain Harte's run into the Chesapeake in the *Berbice*. The relatively shallow draft of a small ship was of obvious utility for a smuggler with local knowledge, who could make use of the Chesapeake's myriad rivers, creeks, and coves. Many of these creeks and coves were considerably deeper in the eighteenth century. Larger ships are faster simply because of the physics of the waves the hull makes as it goes through the water, for longer waves go faster, and the ship can go only as fast as the wave it makes. How, then, were the Jonathans to evade larger and faster warships?

The answer lay in sailing closer to the direction of the wind, called "sailing upwind" or "beating to windward." The larger square-rigged warships could not sail as close to the wind as the colonial schooners, which were developed over many years with upwind sailing in mind. The ability to sail at a close angle to the direction of the wind is called weatherliness. A smaller but more weatherly colonial could well escape a faster but less weatherly vessel by sailing the shortest distance dead to windward and out of cannon range. This tactic was used with tremendous success by colonial privateers for attacking British convoys during the war of 1812.

A GLOSSARY FOR YE LUBBERS

AND SAILORS ALIKE

Aback: condition where a sail has the wind on the wrong side, and the sail is stalled or pulling in the wrong direction.

Abaft: in back of.

Apprentice seaman: the apprentice system was the common way a lad in colonial times learned seamanship and rose to command merchant vessels.

Articles: A traditional contract drawn up by freebooters and pirates, which outlined the rules of behavior, the sharing of booty, responsibilities, and punishments for crew and captain. Important decisions were made by vote. These Articles or contracts made by the social underclass of outlaw seamen were the first to make use of democratic principles in any society since early Greece and Rome.

Beam reach: sailing with the wind coming over the vessel's side, often a sailing ship's fastest and most comfortable point of sail.

Bloody flux: deadly gastroenteritis.

Bow: front end of a boat, ye lubber!

Bumbo: a mixed drink of rum, grenadine, lemon juice and nutmeg.

Breasthook: horizontal frame at the bow of a vessel.

Capsize: overturn; for a cargo-ballasted sailing ship this was most often the end.

Cathouse: the Royal Navy put a ceramic cat in the front window of whorehouses approved for naval officers, hence the name cathouse.

Cat's-paws: wavelets that reveal the location, strength and direction of a gust of wind - to those who can read them.

Cinchona tree: the bark is used as a source of anti-malarial drugs.

Cocket: ship's manifest.

Clock jack: mechanical device for turning a roast on a spit, with counterweights similar to a grandfather clock.

Counter: the overhang at the aft end of a sailing vessel.

Costa Guarda: derisive term used by colonials for patrolling British Navy.

Crank: a vessel that is hard to control.

Cup of char: cup of tea.

Cutwater: leading edge of a vessel's bow.

Deadeyes: simple blocks, often of ironwood, used to tension standing rigging.

Deadlight: covering for a porthole.

Dead reckoning: method of navigating using time of travel, speed, and heading(s).

Drogue: sea anchor, a cone-shaped canvas bag on a line thrown overboard to drag a boat's head to wind in a gale.

Dyewood: tropical wood from which dye was extracted.

Embayed: caught in the confines of a bay without room to maneuver.

Factor: business correspondent in Europe who imported and sold plantation products; they often loaned money to the plantation owners in the colonies.

Fathering: stopping a leak by passing a sail under the hull.

Fiddler's Green: sailor's heaven; more explicitly, a house of prostitution.

Fife rail: a railing through which tholepins were fitted, onto which running rigging (ropes that control the sails) was belayed (tied down).

Foc'sle: forecastle, the crew quarters in the bow of the ship.

Full and by: steer the ship keeping the sails full and follow the wind direction changes.

Garboard: plank that runs next to the keel of a wooden vessel.

Gaskets: sail ties.

Gimcrack: a colonial term for useless object, also applied to boats used for pleasure sailing.

Goodman: polite form of address for a yeoman.

Gunnel: top edge of a boat's side.

Hanging and lodging knees: massive corner braces used in a wooden hull.

Heading: compass direction or bearing.

Hood-end: the end of a hull plank where it fits into the stem or sternpost of a boat.

In irons: sails are stalled, not catching the wind, and the boat is caught still and unmanueverable.

Jack or Jack tar: slang term for sailor.

Jonathan: derisive term for American colonials used by the British.

Lay line: the (compass) heading to an objective, often the narrowest angle the vessel can sail toward the wind direction.

Leatherjack: leather drinking mug.

Line: rope.

Lobscouse: stew made of hardtack and sometimes meat, milk and vegetables.

Loom of an oar: the upper end of the handle above the blade.

Lowers: the lower sails of a sailing ship rig.

Lugsail: a sail simply rigged to a mast and sprit; the sprit adjusts the sail's curvature by means of a tensioning line called a snotter.

Make a leg: a low bow with one calf extended and toe pointed, to show off one's potential prowess as a horseman.

Maroons: escaped slaves in Jamaica who occasionally raided plantations and fought for their freedom against overwhelming odds. They were finally granted land in the Blue Mountains. Led by the legendary military leader Granny Nanny, who was skilled in guerilla warfare and Obeah magic.

Mephitis: foul smell.

Metheglin: fermented honey and herb drink.

Night soil: excrement.

Noggin: a small mug or cup often made of carved wood.

Nosegay: decoration, often a bouquet of flowers fastened to the harness at the head of a horse.

Nostrum: folk medicine.

Obeah: magic, with a basis in African folklore.

Parceling: protective covering for rigging.

Redemptioners: persons who worked under indentured servitude for an agreed length of time in order to pay their passage to America.

Scandalize the lugsail: disconnect the sprit of the lugsail (or the peak halyard of a gaff-headed sail), thereby instantly reducing the sail area by half.

Scotching: girdling a tree's bark with an ax to kill the tree, saving the labor of cutting it down.

Sheet: controlling line for a sail.

Sot weed: derisive name for tobacco.

Slow match: fuse used to ignite the gunpowder at the touchhole of muzzle-loading cannon, which then ignited the powder in the breech of the cannon barrel, firing the cannon.

Snow: common colonial sailing vessel rig with for-and-aft as well as square sails set on two masts.

Split his bollard: split his head.

Sponging the swivel: after firing muzzle-loading cannon, the barrel was cleaned with a wet sponge fastened to the end of a ramrod in order to extinguish any remaining gunpowder.

Stave: wooden barrel side piece.

Stern: the aft (back) end of a vessel.

Studding sails, or stun'sls: Square sails set on yardarm extensions to increase sail area in light air.

Swivel: small cannon with a stock, the barrel mounted on a gimbals; one gripped the stock to turn or elevate it.

Tarred (hair): tar was a common naval store used for waterproofing almost anything. Sailors of the period often drew their hair back, gathered it in a pony tail and tarred it. Hence the expression "Tar" or "Jack Tar" for sailor.

Tholepin: oarlock made from a hardwood dowel set vertically in the gunnel of a boat.

Tide watcher: customs guard placed on a ship in port that had been condemned for smuggling.

Tierce: medium-sized cask.

Touch hole: the hole for the fuse of a cannon.

Trestletree: horizontal part of the structure that joins lower and upper sections of a mast, making a convenient perch for those inclined to enjoy the view, or keep lookout.

Trimmed by the head: a boat unbalanced by too much weight in the bow; this can cause her to become uncontrollable or crank.

War of Shipmaster Jenkin's Ear, 1739 – 42: Shipmaster Robert Jenkins in the *Rebecca* was stopped by a Spanish privateer and found to be smuggling. England declared war on Spain after Jenkins told the House of Commons how the privateer captain cut off his ear.

Warp: to pull a ship along with a stout rope from shore.

Water butt: water barrel.

Wet the Sails: a tactic for wringing the last bit of speed from a sailing vessel; when the sailcloth was wetted the weave of the cloth would tighten and catch the wind more efficiently.

Wine pipe: a two-hogshead or 126-gallon wine cask.

Xebec: swift type of North African sailing ship used by the Barbary Pirates.

11374827R00283

Made in the USA
Charleston, SC
19 February 2012